21963

Thy Kingdom Come

by
PETER BART

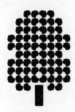

THE LINDEN PRESS ☐ Simon & Schuster
New York, 1981

Copyright © 1981 by Peter Bart
All rights reserved
including the right of reproduction
in whole or in part in any form
Published by The Linden Press/Simon & Schuster
A Simon & Schuster Division of Gulf & Western
Corporation
Simon & Schuster Building
1230 Avenue of the Americas
New York, New York 10020
THE LINDEN PRESS/SIMON & SCHUSTER and colophon are
trademarks of Simon & Schuster
Designed by Irving Perkins and Associates
Manufactured in the United States of America
10 9 8 7 6 5 4 3 2 1
Library of Congress Cataloging in Publication Data
Bart, Peter.
   Thy kingdom come.
   I. Title.
PS3552.A746T5   813′.54   81-4783
                                 AACR2
ISBN 0-671-41912-9

ACKNOWLEDGMENTS

I owe a considerable debt to the many kind people of the Mormon community who were so generous with their knowledge and hospitality during the preparation of this book. There are too many to name—academicians, Church officials, farmers, and fellow writers. Specifically, I would like to express my gratitude to Charles R. Gibbs who, despite his spirited disagreement with some of the book's precepts, was steadfast in his gracious assistance and keen insights; to Marilyn Warenski, whose wise perspectives kept the book on course; to Robert M. Fell for his friendship and sage advice; to Joni Evans, whose astute and ever-cheerful editorial counsel proved an invaluable resource; to Dilys, Colby and Perkins Bart, and to Leslie Cox, whose loving encouragement and enthusiasm kept the words flowing.

Thy
Kingdom
Come

MONDAY, DECEMBER 15

The Call

ALL but one had made it.

Samuel Heber Bryce sighed with relief as he stood unobserved in the great arched doorway, staring out at the ten figures who appeared spectral in their toga-like white robes and pleated round hats. Their chairs were arrayed in a circle around an ornate golden table, sheathed in a tapestry of white lace. Dwarfed by the immensity of the Celestial Room, the circle, to Bryce's eyes, seemed like a distant tableau, the robed figures barely visible in the faint light which filtered down from the three golden chandeliers that hung from the vaulted ceiling high above.

Bryce took a deep breath to steady himself, his hand clutching the banister before him, which was so highly polished its soft woods gleamed like marble. The sheer majesty of this great chamber had always left him awed, especially on momentous occasions such as this. The Celestial Room lay in the innermost precincts of the great Temple and, to Bryce, bespoke the mythic grandeur of the Church—a glorious panorama of soaring archways gleaming of gilt and onyx. The vaulted ceilings were studded with jewel-like ovals of stained glass aglow in blue and gold.

It had been fortuitous that this solemn convocation would be held here, rather than in the more intimate confines of the Council Room, the sanctum sanctorum of the Temple. But that sacred chamber, Bryce knew, was old and fading, like many of the Apostles who regularly inhabited it, and had been closed for renovation. To Bryce, that was just as well; this occasion demanded the Celestial Room's more ethereal ambience.

Descending the thickly carpeted staircase, Bryce knew they had seen him now, felt their eyes fixed upon him. He could sense the hushed expectation. This moment belonged to him—to him and to his Church.

It was a miracle that all but one were here to share it. It was

11

nearly four o'clock in the morning and snowing hard outside. They were old men—all of them. Bryce, at seventy-six, was among the youngest, yet senior to them all in service. Many long years of dedication were required before one was called to honored membership among the Council of the Twelve—the Apostles of the Church of Jesus Christ of Latter-day Saints. The men assembled in the circle, regal in the panoply of Temple robes, had served the Church all over the world. The family names they bore so proudly were themselves a kaleidoscope of the one-hundred-fifty-year history of Mormondom. Their forebears had faced the murderous mobs at Nauvoo with Joseph Smith, had borne the cold and hunger at Salt Lake with Brigham Young, had fled underground before the rabid antipolygamy crusaders with John Taylor.

Bryce lowered himself into one of the French provincial chairs and looked gravely at the gaunt, elderly faces encircling him in the gloom. The hush was broken only by Dalton Evans' hacking cough. Evans' normally ruddy face looked painfully drawn and gray, but at least he had made it here tonight; thank God for that. As the esteemed First Counselor to the First Presidency, Dalton Evans knew more about the inner workings of the Church and commanded wider respect among its myriad functionaries than perhaps anyone else in the room. Isaac Sorenson had made it, too. Second in seniority behind Bryce, Sorenson had rushed back from Latin America where he had just dedicated a new Temple. Next to him slumped the weary, almost skeletal form of Lorenzo Cannon, who, when the summons came, had been reviewing the missionary program in Japan. Only Dayton Smith was absent. That was a pity, Bryce felt; Smith, who was ill and feeble, had been a stalwart ally over the decades.

"Brothers, my heart is heavy with sorrow," Bryce said, his thin, reedy voice echoing softly across the chamber. "The Lord has spoken. President Woodleigh has been called home."

Heads were bowed and there were murmured prayers.

"President Woodleigh was a great inspiration to us all. He was a true Seer and Revelator—a Prophet of the Lord in every sense." It was Ogden Spencer who spoke now in a low rasp that was barely audible. "He suffered so long. . . ." Bald and hollow-cheeked at eighty-nine, Spencer had been closest to Woodleigh over the years, but he fell mute now, his face shrouded in despair.

"Brothers, I know this moment is difficult for us all, but the Lord has spoken and we must heed His dictates," Dalton Evans said, chest heaving as he struggled for breath. Having recently recovered from a bout of pneumonia, Evans, weeks earlier, had expressed his desire to retire from his heavy burden as the Church's chief administrative officer. "As you all know, President Woodleigh was in ill health for nearly two years. Our Church is demanding of leadership. These are times of great challenge."

"Perhaps we could reassemble some weeks after the funeral . . ." Spencer said. "We could organize at that time."

"What were President Woodleigh's wishes?" Lorenzo Cannon asked. "Surely he had devoted prayerful thought to this question?"

"It was his desire that we organize immediately upon his death," Isaac Sorenson said in his commandingly stentorian voice. As was customary in times of decision, all eyes turned toward this stubby, thick-chested man with his mane of flowing white hair. "President Woodleigh and I discussed this question in his final hours before he slipped into a coma and he made his wishes quite clear to me."

". . . But what about precedent?" Spencer protested, turning to Dalton Evans, who was the repository of all such information.

Evans replied, "Brigham Young, of course, administered the Church for three and a half years as President of the Twelve before he was set apart as Prophet. But I would remind you that, after the sudden death of President Lee, the transition was an immediate one."

"Brothers, we must bear in mind that in only seven days we shall be commemorating the one hundred fiftieth anniversary of our Church," Isaac Sorenson intoned. "The brethren will be arriving in Salt Lake City from all over the world. Our new Prophet should preside. We must present a solid rank of leadership. We must organize now."

There were murmurs of assent from around the circle, and then Bryce saw Sorenson turn toward him, his movements slow and ceremonial. "You are in charge now," he stated solemnly, lifting his right hand and placing it upon Bryce's head. Bryce felt the gentle pressure, the sensation racing through his entire body, as though all his nerves and senses were jolted suddenly to a new awareness. He saw the others in the circle rise from their chairs, moving to where he was seated, their bodies looming above him, their hands upon his head and shoulders.

"You are our Prophet." The words came from someone in the circle, and Bryce heard other voices murmur in assent, and he could feel their hands upon him, could hear Sorenson's voice uttering a blessing.

The moment he'd awaited these many long years had come at last. He had been set apart.

□ Bryce stood waist-deep in the water, his body recoiling against the chill. His wrinkled skin glowed ivory in the dim light of the baptistery.

He felt old. He heard the droning voices above him invoking the sacred words of the ceremony but he could not focus on them. He felt removed from it all, distanced by some invisible barrier he was powerless to surmount.

". . . Brother Bryce, having been commissioned of Jesus Christ, I baptize you, for and in behalf of Philastus Oliver Bryce, who is dead, in the name of the Father, and of the Son, and of the Holy Ghost. . . . We lay our hands upon your head and confirm you a member of the Church and say unto you, Receive the Holy Ghost. . . ."

Twenty-six hours had passed since he had received his divine call. Many men had come to pay homage. Many blessings had been said for him, expressions of faith and fealty.

He had been ordained and set apart to lead his people through divine inspiration. Joseph Smith had laid the foundation for a Kingdom of God "living by the word of the Lord that will revolutionize the whole world," and Brigham Young had brought it into being—Deseret, a land of the chosen people, a nation unto itself. Now Samuel Heber Bryce was to rule it, having had the gifts of God bestowed upon him.

Yet, these past hours, through the meetings and phone calls, through all the ceremonial incantations, he had waited to sense that he was somehow in His presence, so that he would know that

God would speak to him as He had to Joseph Smith. The Mormon people were His favored people; He spoke directly only to them.

Though he had waited, he'd felt nothing.

He realized that he was, after all, a frail old man. And he knew that even as he was pronounced Seer and Revelator, cancer was gnawing at his marrow—a secret he had shared with only one brother Apostle. Though his powers and covenants were unfolding before him, his time in this world would not be long.

And so he had made his decision. He had awakened the startled Temple aides and instructed them to prepare the baptismal ceremony. If the spirit would not come to him, then he would go to it.

This would not be an ordinary baptism. It would be, Bryce had told the aides, a vicarious baptism for an ancestor who had lived in the 1830s in a town in New York State not far from that of Joseph Smith, yet who had never known the Prophet nor been confirmed to the faith. In fact, immersed now in the chill water, hearing the aides' somber chant, he knew this was something more. It was not Philastus Bryce whose presence he sought, but rather that of Joseph Smith himself, the father of his Church, the Restorer of the Faith. Through vicarious baptism he would share a moment in the great spirit world where his immortal soul resided through eternity. He would bask in that moment and feel the energies seep into him.

He could not, of course, confide this to the Temple aides. They would be perplexed. They could not perform a vicarious baptism for Joseph Smith. It could not be done!

Yet Bryce knew them wrong. Even now, as he stood in the huge golden font, which rested atop the backs of twelve life-size oxen, symbolizing the tribes of Israel, he felt his spirit soar. He was no longer in the baptistery at Salt Lake, he was free-floating through all eternity. He was in the presence not only of Joseph Smith but of all his brothers through the ages. He was witness to their joys and agonies. He was in Missouri, in the humid confinement of Joseph Haun's flour mill at Shoal Creek in 1838, there with the thirty defenseless Mormon families when the armed mob came crashing in, hungry for Mormon blood; there when they started firing, shooting first the little boy who hid beneath the bellows, blasting his head away in a fine mist of bone and blood. And he was there in Carthage, Illinois, that muggy June morning, when a hundred assassins, faces blackened, wielding knives and guns, stormed the prison cell where Joseph Smith and his brother were interned, saw the mob surge past the guards, heard the thunder of their footsteps moving on the small cell, the crashing of the cell door and then the fatal fusillade of bullets.

He was there through it all. Through all the hatred and the bloody persecution.

And now he heard the voice intone the other words, and he repeated them softly in his own voice: ". . . do solemnly promise and vow and never cease to importune high heaven to avenge the blood of the prophets . . ."

There was silence in the room. The ceremony was complete.

He felt restored. Energized.

Through his tightly shut eyes he saw an ecstasy of light and color. He was part of it all now, the whole heroic cavalcade. They were side by side, confronting an infinity of unrealized possibilities. He could share their ancient exaltation. They would build their Kingdom together—a Kingdom destined to rule the entire world.

He looked up at the dim figures on the platform above where the aides and witnesses awaited him. He saw the tall, resolute man who towered over the others—the man he knew to be Dana Sloat. There were strong hands assisting him up the stairs now, guiding him toward the chamber where he would be washed and anointed, his body cleansed and blessed, his brain made "clear and active, the receptacle of pure and virtuous principles." Passing Sloat on the platform, Bryce paused. Their gaze locked.

"Our time has come," Sloat said softly. "It has begun."

And Samuel Bryce knew he was right. Yes, he was their Prophet after all.

The Prophet

THE snow was falling heavily as Eliza Hastings turned her black Oldsmobile into the parking lot of the Bishops' Storehouse. Though the radio had warned of plummeting temperatures, the flakes were dissolving quickly into slush. Eliza had been pleased when she'd first heard the snow warnings. The Wasatch peaks, which loomed in a great protective crescent around the city, acquired a special majesty when draped in white. It seemed like a formal proclamation that Christmas was just three days away. At the same time she'd felt a pang of concern for the hundreds of women who would be arriving in Salt Lake City for Tuesday's conference. The meeting had enough problems without inclement weather. Yet Utah women were used to coping with snow and sleet, Eliza reassured herself. They were a hearty breed, her sisters!

Fastening a scarf around her wavy brown hair, Eliza opened the car door and walked briskly toward the entrance, feeling the flakes dancing softly against her cheek. Though it was barely nine in the morning, customers were already streaming toward the Storehouse in considerable number, their breath creating plumes of frost that hung in the chill air. Through the big front window, Eliza could see the lines of people standing with their shopping carts, waiting for the clerks to check and pack their purchases, and, behind them, still other shoppers, filing slowly down the long, neon-lit aisles. It looked like a typical supermarket caught up in the holiday frenzy, but Eliza knew that this particular market was not what it seemed to be; it was not selling its goods, but, rather, giving them away. The clerks were diligently matching items in each shopping cart against the yellow "Bishop's Orders" which were handed them by each customer to see that the goods had been properly approved by the local Ward Bishop. The whole transaction would be handled in an amiably routine fashion—no

19

trappings of charity, no hovering welfare workers. It was simply a case of Mormons taking care of their own. Indeed, most of the items had been produced at Mormon farms and factories by volunteer workers and packed under the Deseret brand name. DESERET: THE BRAND MONEY CAN'T BUY, proclaimed a sign that hung above the checkout counter. The slogan had always amused Eliza. It reflected a conceit that was not in keeping with the ideals of Mormon charity, and yet the conceit was deserved. After all, while other communities across the nation thrust their poor upon the welfare rolls, only *her* people demonstrated the true Christian will to supply their needs through their own effort and industry. Eliza herself, as President of the Relief Society, had personally visited many of the eight hundred farms and factories which served the needs of the poor, and most of the fifty-one Bishops' Storehouses. Each month she toiled two days on a welfare farm and two in a cannery, working side by side with lawyers and laborers, the rich and the humble. "Cease to be covetous," she would remind herself, sweat pouring from her brow. "Above all things clothe yourselves with the bond of charity, as with a mantle which is the bond of perfectness and peace." So said Latter-day Saints' *Doctrine and Covenants,* and so she believed.

"Eliza!"

A tiny, white-haired woman in a flowered smock was waving frantically from the corner of the Storehouse. Eliza moved quickly to join her.

"Merry Christmas, Sister Helen," Eliza said, shaking her hand warmly.

"The party for the Bishop is all set up in the cannery," Helen Featherstone said, fairly bursting with excitement. "Bishop Snively will be so surprised! He has no idea you are coming." Helen started leading Eliza toward the large cinder block building which stood adjacent to the Storehouse, clasping her hand as she would a child's, then suddenly releasing it. "I'm so sorry," Helen said, with a look of embarrassment exhibited by a servant who had not been properly respectful toward her mistress.

"There's nothing to be sorry about," Eliza said, trying to hide her impatience with the fluttery little woman who was leading her—an impatience not with her enthusiasm but with her excessive deference. The women in her Relief Society were *all* so infuriatingly deferential: She knew there was something in the very nature of her people, male and female alike, that *needed* to be deferential to authority. She understood that and had tried to live with it.

The cannery loomed ahead through the falling snow, an anonymous hulk of a building that squatted beside a tall white grain elevator—both of them operated by the Church to serve the poor.

As the big steel door leading to the cannery swung open, Eliza all but reeled under the sudden assault of heat and noise. Through the veils of steam, she could make out the clusters of apron-clad women surrounding the big steel vats where the food was being cooked in preparation for canning. Their faces were wet with perspiration, their hair held tightly in nets as they bent over their tasks. Across the room, other women were operating the big packing and sealing machines, seemingly oblivious to the thunderous clanking and hammering that resounded across the room. Hanging in the steamy air was the tart aroma of onions and yams. Two women clad in aprons were busily swabbing the moist floor with big mops.

Watching the women in their "combat clothes," Eliza felt a bit self-conscious in her gray silk blouse and mauve Chanel suit, with its pleated skirt and amethyst buttons. Her brown hair, which had only recently been invaded by a scattering of gray, was swept back in a soft bouffant and turned under slightly at the ends. Given her constant round of public appearances, Eliza, recently turned forty-six, tried to dress with an understated elegance, but today she wished she had come in her work clothes, especially as her gaze met that of her old friend, Amelia Clawson, who was sealing cans with an expert's finesse. The wife of a wealthy realtor, Amelia's photograph often adorned the society pages, her willowy figure impeccably gowned and bejeweled. Eliza could not suppress a smile, seeing her here, her plain cotton dress soaked with sweat and splattered with food. Abandoning her chores, Amelia rushed over to greet Eliza, a warm smile on her face; and others now saw her, too, and joined the growing circle.

Within moments work had come to a halt and Eliza was standing amid a solid knot of women, shaking hands, exchanging Christmas greetings. For many long years, Eliza had known

nearly all of those who now surrounded her: A few were friends
from childhood; others resided in her ward—women with whom
she prayed and planned and worked. Many other faces she could
recall from Church functions or Relief Society meetings. As far as
Eliza was concerned they were all her sisters, but she understood,
too, that in their eyes she represented something more. Eliza was
their representative, their spokeswoman on the loftiest councils
of the Church and community. She was, indeed, the highest ranking woman of the Church of Jesus Christ of Latter-day Saints and,
as such, the embodiment of their ideals and aspirations. That role
set her apart from them and yet, embracing them here, amid the
humid, clangorous confines of the cannery, Eliza could sense
those ties of common heritage and kinship. They were all mothers
and wives, some rich and some poor, with their own private worries and responsibilities. But first and foremost they were women
of the Mormon Kingdom and, as such, they had gathered, three
days before Christmas, turning out goods to be distributed to
those less fortunate. This was a sacrifice that was expected of
them and they honored that commitment unquestioningly.

But now it was time for the party. Eliza was led to a dark corner
of the cannery which, upon signal, suddenly was bathed in Christmas lights, flickering red and green in the steamy air. An enormous cake festooned with candles sat atop a table, and several
women busily set about the task of lighting the myriad candles
and setting out the plates and cutlery.

"All right, Sisters," Helen called, "it is time for someone to
fetch the Bishop. I can't wait to see his surprise."

Moments later the rotund figure of Abijah Erastus Snively filled
the wide doorway, propelled forward by a gaggle of happily chirp-
ing women. When he saw the cake, his round, red face crinkled
with delight. As the women called out their congratulations, the
Bishop clapped his hands in delight like a small boy. Seeing
Eliza, Bishop Snively rushed over, enclosing her entire forearm
in his enormous hands.

"It's so gracious of you to come, Sister Eliza. This whole thing
has left me flabbergasted!"

"I wouldn't have missed it for anything," Eliza responded. "I
love surprise parties, especially for my favorite people."

Amelia Clawson brought out a huge plastic bowl filled with

steaming wassail, which she started ladling out. The Bishop held
a cup under his nostrils, breathing in the rich aroma of cinnamon
and hot apple cider, his face beaming. "Thank God for wassail.
It's the closest thing to spirits the Word of Wisdom permits us,"
he sighed, downing the contents in three swallows.

"How about a toast, Sister Eliza?" a voice called out.

Eliza stepped forward and lifted her cup. "I propose a toast to
our dear Bishop Snively," she said, as voices subsided and the
cannery became quiet. "For fifteen years he has given unspar-
ingly of himself to administer this Storehouse and cannery. It is a
happy irony that Bishop Snively would devote himself to helping
the poor because he himself is a man of great wealth: a wealth of
kindness and generosity. No one deserves his release more than
the good Bishop, but we will all miss him so very much."

"To the Bishop!" all the women cried, as they drank their toast,
and Bishop Snively, flushed with embarrassment and pride, engulfed his second cup.

Eliza drifted outside the circle, observing the animated good
cheer with a mixture of delight and sorrow. The day after Christmas, Eliza knew, the Bishop would undergo bypass heart surgery.
It was his bad heart, not his stated desire to "go fishing," that was
the actual cause of his announced retirement. She had known this
chubby, jovial man for many years. Snively had been a salesman
of farm equipment most of his life, and not a particularly successful one, but he had always been a faithful soldier of the Church, a
hardworking volunteer and resolute contributor of his ten percent
tithe. His stalwart loyalty had been rewarded with a series of
Church appointments, first as Mission President in Norway, and
then as manager of the Bishops' Storehouse. Eliza knew that he
had been a devoted but remarkably ineffectual administrator. Not
that he was alone in his ineptitude. Having observed the functioning of the Church from an intimate perspective for many years,
Eliza had long since concluded that the Saints managed to suc-
ceed despite themselves—despite the plodding procedures and
geriatric administration. Outsiders, she knew, felt that everything
in Mormondom worked with scrupulous efficiency, and perhaps
that was just as well. In reality, so much was accomplished only
because of the sort of zealous unity that was occurring here at the
cannery. There was no obstacle that could withstand the force of

so many people pulling together so ardently for a common objective—so many faithful souls supported by such a wealth of physical resources.

"Sister Eliza."

The voice came from Clara Partridge, a frail, birdlike woman in her late forties, whom Eliza called upon once a week in her capacity as a "visiting teacher" within her ward. Eliza, like most other members of the Church hierarchy, male and female, had continued to perform these humble duties; even President Woodleigh had continued his visitations until his final years.

"It is so nice to see you here, Sister."

Clara Partridge's eyes averted hers. "I just wanted to thank you, Eliza," she said, her voice husky. "I mean, there was no cause for you to do what you did. No cause . . ."

Eliza placed her hand on the woman's arm. "You have nothing to thank me for. . . ."

"I know it was you," Clara said. "You've saved my boy, you know. You've saved his pride, too. . . ." She started to say something else, but just shook her head and darted off into the crowd.

Eliza felt her eyes mist, but caught herself. Her many years as a public figure had long since inculcated the discipline of composure. She could weep inwardly but still retain that easy smile which stared out from a thousand photographs—a smile which even now was firmly implanted upon her gracious features.

It had been only a few days earlier Eliza had learned that Clara's youngest son, Patrick, was about to drop out of Brigham Young University because of the family's financial difficulties. She knew that Clara's husband was a hard-drinking Gentile who had lost one job after another. As a "visiting teacher," Eliza was supposed to deal with problems such as this through the instrumentality of the local ward organization and the Bishopric, but she had decided in this case to take swift action. Through Eldon Knight, the dean of men at BYU, she discovered that it would require fifteen hundred dollars for the boy to complete his education; then she simply mailed a personal check for that amount to the dean with the request that Patrick be told he was receiving scholarship aid. Patrick had swallowed the story but Clara had guessed the truth, and that distressed Eliza. Clara Partridge was a proud woman, the sort of Mormon who would find charity a personal humiliation. Perhaps she could have thought of a better way and not acted so impulsively. She should have asked Turner for his ideas—he would have conceived a better artifice.

"There is a telephone call for you, Sister Eliza."

"For me?"

"The man said it's urgent. There's a phone in the office behind you."

Eliza entered a small, empty office furnished with a gray metal desk and chair. There were three buttons on the phone, one of which was blinking insistently.

"Hello."

"Eliza, is that you?"

"Turner, how bizarre! I was just thinking about you."

"And I was thinking about you." There was a tension in Turner Mead's voice that set off an instinctive alarm. The fact that he would be calling at all was extraordinary. A discreet man, Turner was painstakingly careful never to have her name associated with his in any way. Their relationship was a furtive one and would remain that way.

"I apologize for calling you directly," Turner said in his precise, clipped English accent which Eliza so relished. "I just wanted to be absolutely sure you'd heard the news."

Eliza felt her stomach flutter. "What news?"

"Brace yourself, Eliza. Fifteen minutes ago a press release went out, and President Bryce announced that the Church has a new First Counselor, and that his name is Dana Sloat."

Eliza clasped the phone tighter. She opened her mouth to reply but the words did not come.

"Are you there, Eliza?"

"I'm here." She sank slowly into the metal chair.

"The announcement explained that because of the great growth of the Church and the demands on Church leadership the new Prophet decided to bring in a Counselor from outside the ranks of the General Authorities. I know how you feel about Sloat. I wanted to be absolutely sure you'd heard the news."

"I'm speechless, Turner. I just don't know what to say. . . ."

"Perhaps that is just as well, Eliza. We shouldn't talk about this on an open line. When you reach your office, however, there will be phone calls from the press. . . ."

"You're advising me to watch my step, is that it, Turner?"

There was a hesitation on the other end of the line. "There'll be lots of pointed questions. After all, Dana Sloat is family. . . ."

"Family!"

"Your son married his daughter, Eliza. That's family."

"Of course," Eliza said, the flatness of her voice betraying her bitterness.

"I only wish I could be a bearer of happier news, my darling."

"I just find it hard to believe," Eliza said. "There are so many other qualified men. Sloat is totally unsuited. He is a dangerous man. . . ."

"This is an open line. We have no idea who might be listening. . . ."

That was Turner, always cautious and protective of her. She loved him for those traits, too, among the many others.

"I'll be careful to keep my opinions to myself. I promise."

There was another pause. "I wish it were better news, Eliza. . . ."

"I know, dear. I know."

After hanging up, Eliza sat alone in the small, dark office, trying to piece together the torn fragments of her thoughts. She felt her mind straining like an animal caught in a trap. Dana Sloat! How could it be? How could a gracious and kindly man like Samuel Bryce miscalculate so badly?

Surely it was just that he didn't know? She had heard that Bryce respected Sloat, that Sloat had often been seen in his company. There had even been gossip about financial problems in the vast insurance business which the Bryce family had operated for generations, and that Dana Sloat had helped the old man pull the company together again. She had assumed it was a personal relationship, not one that would spill over to the Church. First Counselor! She had often witnessed the vast authority of that office. Outside the First Counselor's door was always a long line of men courting his favor—political leaders, corporate presidents, Church officials. With a nod of his head or a stroke of his pen he could create a family fortune, merge a company, build a civic center, anoint a political candidate; he could build a career or crush it, as he saw fit. Still, why would Dana Sloat even want such a job? He had his own empire to rule spanning all manner of business activities. Sloat already held enormous wealth and power—more, probably, than any other Mormon businessman had ever possessed.

That was it, of course. He had his own empire to run, but now he had another one as well. A vastly bigger one, involving many billions of dollars in assets and wielding great influence over many economies and governments. The Mormon Church, Eliza knew, was truly one of the greatest and least known repositories of wealth and power in the world—and its reins were now in the hands of Dana Sloat, a secretive man with erratic and reactionary views.

She felt a chill. Pulling her jacket tight around her, she heard a sudden burst of laughter from the crowd outside. She marched off to rejoin the party, a smile firmly implanted upon her face.

THE elevator doors parted and he felt the sudden surge, spilling them all out onto the mall, arms and legs immobilized, a solid clot of humanity being propelled forward by some invisible force. Entrapped, Tad felt a jab in his rib cage—a warning from the elderly matron on his left against further encroachment, however innocent. He glanced at her helplessly. Beyond, the doors of another elevator had parted, spewing forth a new wave of shoppers, arms laden with purses, packages and small children, eyes peering ahead with fervid determination. Though hopelessly entangled, they were all edging onto the main shopping area, the crowd starting to sort itself out among the broad corridors of the indoor mall. Moving easily, Tad took a deep breath, his nostrils detecting a sweet pungence in the air, an exotic intermingling of perfume and Christmas trees and chocolate from the open candy counters lining the corridors. The cavernous mall resounded with the swell of voices, excited, quarrelsome, cheerful, all blending into a clamorous thunder, a great letting loose of holiday zeal. Tad felt caught up in the excitement, adrenaline pumping. He was walking more briskly now, eyes inspecting the brilliantly lit displays of the stores along the mall—toys, maternity clothes, jewelry, stereo components—each window festooned with wreaths and tinsel and bells and artificial snow and the other decorative paraphernalia of the holidays. Strains of Christmas music filtered through the loudspeaker system. Ahead, the corridors were clogged with small children, and Tad could see Santa Claus seated amid them, patiently plopping one child after another in his ample lap, while Mrs. Claus, attired in a billowing red gown, gentle eyes peering from a pudgy red face, herded the jostling children into a semblance of a line. In the background stood a giant Christmas tree, its branches thrusting up three stories to the ceiling high above. The tree, Tad saw, was

28

a fake, a great green impostor of plastic and fiberglass, but the affront was softened by its many lights and by the presence of a small forest of bright red poinsettias surrounding its base.

Tad stood watching the children blurting their wishes to Santa, flashbulbs blinking around them as proud mothers recorded the moment for posterity, and it struck him that he was really delighted by all this—even the noise, the pushing, the panicky last-minute buying. Among his friends and colleagues, who had fathered, according to his calculations, a median 6.7 children, Christmas was clearly a fearsome nuisance. It was good for the family, good for the Church, but otherwise an occasion to be stonily endured. Tad felt differently. Though he was embarrassed to admit it, Christmas caused him to churn with the same excitement he'd felt as a small boy. It wasn't just watching his three children open their presents; he enjoyed opening *his* presents, reveling in the sense of surprise and joy. Everything about the Christmas season pleased him—the inevitable snow, the music, the church services, yes, even the shopping. Especially at the ZCMI—the great white concrete slab that bore the formal name of Zion's Cooperative Mercantile Institution. He felt at home in this store, which occupied one entire wing of the downtown mall. He had been coming here since childhood, recognized many of its saleswomen, trusted its wares and its prices. It was *his* store, he felt, controlled by *his* Church and operated for the benefit of *his* people. Since he'd handled some of the minor legal affairs for the store, Tad knew it was also a vastly profitable enterprise but that did not disturb him. As a schoolboy he'd read of its founding back in 1868—one of Brigham Young's fanciful Socialist schemes designed to pump some life into the sagging frontier economy, but as the Saints discovered that capitalism, not Socialism, provided a more practical basis for growth, the ZCMI had evolved into a chain of modern department stores like Sears or Penney's. Still, it remained substantially Church-owned, and as such, Tad felt he had a proprietary interest in its success.

He found himself sucked into a vortex of customers around the big candy counters, covetously surveying the assortment of chocolates, jelly beans, caramels, taffy, nougats, Fernwood Mint Sandwiches and other sweets. Tad glanced at the avid faces around him, felt the press of their bodies. Gavin loved chiding him about his sugar craze—the "Mormon Mania," his friend called it. Only a people that had masochistically denied itself the delights of coffee and alcohol, Gavin said, could develop such a fierce need for a daily "sugar fix."

Gavin!

It was because of Gavin that he had been incapable of getting anything done in the office this morning. He had arrived at work at eight in the morning as usual and had vainly tried to focus on the mundane details of a sale-leaseback deal, but it was no use. At nine fifteen he decided to give up. Gathering a file of documents to make it seem as though he were going to a business meeting, Tad stalked quickly past the ever-nosy receptionist, climbed into his Pinto and headed downtown. If he couldn't get his work done, at least he would finish his Christmas shopping and still get back to the office by eleven thirty for the call from Los Angeles. Gavin had promised to call the moment the meeting had ended. Just thinking about that phone call made Tad's mind whirl.

On the surface, the deal seemed like a fairly prosaic one. He had tried to explain his excitement that previous night to Nancy, but saw his wife stifle a yawn. Yet Tad understood its implications both for himself and for his friend Gavin. It was their break— their shot at the big time.

Under the deal, which Tad and Gavin had carefully guided and negotiated, Suncorp, a company which already was the West's biggest newspaper and magazine publisher, would achieve its long-term goal of diversifying into the booming field of broadcasting. Through the acquisition of three television and six FM radio stations in an exchange of stock, Gavin Pollard would emerge a hero at Suncorp, a conglomerate which his grandfather had founded and which he aspired to head. And Tad, in turn, would be a hero at his law firm—that in itself would bring a sweeping change in his fortunes. In his three years with his firm, Tad had been relegated to minor real-estate transactions. His colleagues, he sensed, considered him just another sound but stolid young Mormon attorney who would always make a living but never make a mark. When word of the Suncorp negotiations first leaked out to other lawyers in his firm, he could see the surprise on their faces. Even dour old Ellis Marmer, the managing partner, had

dropped by Tad's tiny office to offer his congratulations. It had
been Tad's deal, they all knew, and if his longtime friend, Gavin
Pollard, won the presidency of Suncorp as a result, there would
be many other such deals to follow.

Munching contentedly on a handful of Fernwood Mints, Tad
strolled down the broad aisles of the ZCMI, determined to put all
of this out of his mind. He would quell his excitement by thinking
only of shopping. His big problem was that he had not yet found
anything for Pye. In his heart, he knew why he'd put that off.
Christmas was for family, after all. He had already bought gifts for
his wife Nancy and for the kids. Somehow it seemed oddly sac-
rilegious to buy a Christmas present for one's girlfriend—don't
soften it, Tad chastised himself—one's mistress! The prospect
riddled him with guilt.

Yet, as he moved to the women's jewelry counter, his gaze
settled on the silhouette of a saleswoman across the aisle whose
head was partially turned away, talking to a customer. Watching
the movement of her soft blond hair, the delicate curve of her
breast, the pert, upturned nose, Tad realized suddenly that it was
Pye's hair and Pye's nose he was seeing and he found himself
gaping helplessly. When the girl turned, he saw the foolishness
of his imaginings. Her face was round and her features curiously
bovine; there was none of Pye's small-boned elegance, none of
her innate style. But the brief illusion had been devastating: It
made him ache for her, to hold her, caress her. Only three days
earlier they'd spent the night together, but it seemed like three
weeks.

"Would you like to see something, sir?" asked a thin, elderly
saleswoman with skewered silver hair and a surprisingly deep
voice, and Tad found himself stammering out his desire to buy a
watch. As the woman reached down to unlock the glass case, Tad
knew the reason he stammered was that he was deeply ashamed
—good old Mormon shame, the sort that sent generations of
young men scurrying off to confess their sins to their ever-re-
proachful Bishops. Looking around him, Tad wondered how
many other men in this store were confronting the same dilemma
as he; how many were cheating, either in mind or body, all the
while hiding behind their steely guise of righteousness. And as
the saleswoman set the tray of watches before him, he was aware

of the mist of perspiration on his face and he wondered whether it was the warmth of the store, or, more probably, the urgency of his own discomfort that was causing it.

Guilt! What an absurd ritual, Tad told himself. What a goddamn bore. Those tough old Mormon pioneers didn't have time for guilt. Brigham Young wasn't gripped by guilt when he put his chalk mark upon the door of whichever of his twenty-seven wives he selected to make love to that night. How is it that, from these staunch forebears would emanate such wimpy, guilt-ridden, pussy-whipped offspring? What a cruel twist of history!

The saleswoman was staring at him, impatiently awaiting his decision. "This one's fine," he blurted, pointing at the lowest-priced Cartier.

She plucked it from the tray. "Oh, please gift wrap it," Tad said, gathering his resolve. "It's for my girlfriend." The words sounded good to him. Almost liberating.

The silver-haired woman's glance was unwavering. "Well, honey, I'm sure she worked for it," she said, turning quickly from him.

☐ At eleven forty-five, Tad returned to the office, strode briskly past the receptionist, seated himself at his desk and mumbled a quiet prayer before buzzing his secretary for calls. There had been four calls, she reported, none of them from Gavin. Very well, Tad told himself glumly, as he downed the last of his mint sandwiches which he had carefully squirreled away.

Though still agitated, he felt a lot better than he had three hours earlier. He had bought the watch for Pye, and some perfume for his mother Eliza. On a mischievous impulse, he had also stopped by the Relief Society building and purchased a pair of Mormon underwear as a Christmas present for Gavin. His friend had always needled him about his practice of faithfully wearing his raiment, which admittedly looked like a sawed-off union suit, its long sleeves of cotton fabric stretching over substantial portions of his arms and legs, its Temple markings punctuating each breast and one knee. The underclothing, Tad had explained patiently, was traditional in Mormon society. Indeed it was the practice of conservative men and women never to shed their sacred garments completely; even while bathing or having intercourse at least a hand or a foot would be making contact with the underclothing, thus symbolizing devotion to the precepts of moral purity. In modern times the design had been modified so that the arms and legs were not fully covered and one's private parts could be liberated less laboriously.

"I can't understand why the Mormon birthrate is twice as high as the rest of the country," Gavin once told him, "when it takes them twice as long to get undressed." Well, now Gavin would have his own Mormon underwear and he could learn for himself.

Tad looked up to see his secretary's face peeking through the door. "It's Mr. Pollard," she whispered.

Tad grabbed the phone. "What's the word, Gavin?"

"They bought it! The miserable old sonsabitches approved the deal!" Gavin's voice quavered with excitement.

Tad sprang from his chair, knocking the heavy phone console on its side. "Oh, wow," he effused. "Wow. . . ."

"Wow? Is that the best you can do?" Gavin prodded. "It's absolutely super fucking wonderful!"

Tad grinned. "Okay, super fucking wonderful."

"There—you said it and you haven't been excommunicated yet."

"When will it go to the full board?"

"It doesn't need to go to the board. The executive committee wants to talk it over with a couple of their bankers and then we can just go ahead and lock it up. Let me tell you, Tad, these old boys think you and I negotiated a great deal. As far as they're concerned, you're the Mormon Metternich."

"You're going to be president of Suncorp before the end of the month," Tad said. "I'd bet anything."

"Shit, Tad, I'm gonna go out and get drunk. Wish to hell you were here to celebrate with me."

"Wish I were there, too. I may just go out and get drunk on my own."

"Just don't let any of the senior Saints catch you slobbering in your vodka," Gavin said, clicking off.

For a few moments Tad stood staring at the receiver. Then he placed it gingerly in its cradle and thumped his fist into the palm of his hand several times. Goddamn, he thought to himself, he wished he were in Los Angeles today!

To Tad, Gavin Pollard had seemed like someone from another world. Within a few hours of the time that the big three-master had put into Tonga for repairs, Gavin had totally acclimated himself. He had acquired a working knowledge of the bars, the hotels, the shopkeepers. He knew which girls might avail themselves to a rich young American visitor. He knew the best place for scuba diving, the best place for tennis. He had charted the myriad islets of Port of Refuge Harbor. There wasn't much of a social whirl in Tonga, to say the least, but what little existed in the snug confines of Neiafu, Gavin was instantly the center of. If he was to be stranded in this remote outpost of the Pacific, at least he would make the most of it. His schooner had been ravaged by a major storm two days before, the main mast severely damaged. It would certainly take a few days for repairs, especially given the casual work habits of the local laborers. Nor was Gavin unhappy about the layover. They'd all been at sea for the better part of three months; Vava'u, part of the magical Kingdom of Tonga, beautiful and remote, appealed to his sense of the romantic.

Tad had caught a glimpse of him that first night, coming out of the Stowaway, tall and lean and rakishly handsome, with his tanned skin, and hair bleached by the sun. He was, indeed, the golden boy. Hundreds of private boats had put into Tonga in the seven months Tad had been there, but none of the visitors had quite the flash of Gavin Pollard. It was his first night in port, and on his arm was a lovely girl named Tana, who, since arriving a week earlier aboard a hundred-foot yacht, had been the object of Tad's own erotic fantasies. And now she and Gavin glided past him, slender and sylphlike, in matching white shorts, their slim asses swaying in rhythm as they walked, exuding together a sexual tension that left Tad limp and deflated. After they had passed,

34

he could hear Gavin's husky voice asking, "Who's the freak?" and then her muffled reply; then both were laughing, walking away into the night, her copper-colored hair glinting in the dim moonlight.

He didn't need to hear the jokes they were making at his expense. He'd heard them often enough. He knew how bizarre he must seem to them, clad in his pristine missionary uniform of white shirt and dark blue slacks, his blond hair cropped skinclose, his face pallid as paper. If they thought him an oddity, that was indeed how he'd come to see himself in his seven long months on Tonga.

When he'd left Utah, his missionary zeal had been all but bursting. He was ready to proselytize the world, a soldier in the Armies of Zion. In his imaginings he'd seen himself proudly baptizing converts in Tokyo or Mexico City or Auckland or any of the other cities where the Church was ingesting followers at a breathtaking pace. His heart would be pounding with the sheer excitement of it all.

Seven months later, Tad's zeal had melted amid Tonga's humid lethargy, to be supplanted instead by loneliness and frustration.

As the months wore on, he, too, had begun to think of himself as a freak.

He knew he had no one to blame but himself. He had made his decision at the end of his sophomore year at Brigham Young University. The A− average of his freshman year had dwindled to a dismal chain of Cs. He had set a rigorous pre-med program for himself, but was struggling helplessly with chemistry and biology.

The main problem, he knew, was that he was bored. "The Y" seemed like a tedious extension of his high-school experience. His friends were the same—at least they looked and sounded the same. His social life was a rerun of high school: a chain of pretty blond girls from good LDS homes who loved to neck, but when the going threatened to get more serious, started babbling nonstop about Temple weddings and babies like so many prerecorded announcements. In a sense, Ted realized, they *were* prerecorded. Prerecorded and preordained.

Many of Tad's friends, upon reaching the age of nineteen, were volunteering for missions. Indeed, it was a question of volunteering or being conscripted. President Woodleigh had let it be known from on high that missionary service should be construed as the obligation of all eligible Mormon youths. What had once been a volunteer program had quietly transformed itself into something resembling the military draft. The boys were expected to contribute their two years and their parents were expected to contribute the upkeep. It was as simple as that.

All right, Tad thought, if he had to do it anyway, why not do it now? Besides, it could be exciting: foreign lands, foreign tongues. A chance to contribute something, not just vegetate on the BYU assembly line.

His first shock was the Missionary Training Center. It stood in somber isolation at the edge of the BYU campus, a cluster of coldly modern brown brick buildings which looked like a top secret government lab or perhaps even a mysterious detention facility. Though Tad had learned that a minimum of two thousand would-be missionaries were being "processed" there at any given time, he rarely saw anyone at all around the grounds. When trainees from the Center appeared on campus they would always be walking in pairs and garbed in dark blue suits, their faces harried, their stride brisk, their eyes never making contact with anyone from the "outside." They were strangely automatonlike in their movements, but Tad never gave it much thought. They were not of his world.

But he was soon of theirs.

On his first day at the Center, he was led to his room, a tiny, brick-lined cell most of whose space was consumed by two double-decker bunks. He had no sooner put down his gear when he was summoned to "orientation."

The young man who addressed them was a tall, bony-looking youth with severe blue eyes and curiously knobby hands which he kept rigidly at his sides. With his stiff military bearing, Tad felt he would look more at home in a marine uniform than in his dark blue suit.

The regimen for the next eight weeks, he told them, would be rigorous and unrelenting. They would arise at six every morning and retire at ten thirty. Except for meals, prayer, an hour's recreation and a daily class in "ambassadorship," the rest of their time, day and night, would be spent in nonstop classes in foreign language. The language each would study had already been chosen for them, he said, and so had their ultimate points of destination. Their aptitudes and preferences had not been consulted because they were irrelevant. They would soon be wearing "the armor of God," the young man said, his eyes fiercely upon them, and it was unimportant where that armor was to be planted.

Rules must be followed unbendingly, he warned, waving a knobby hand. During the next eight weeks there would be no outside visitors, no phone calls, no socializing. Each man would buy two blue suits; that was all they would wear. Shoes would be shined daily. Hair would be clipped short every two weeks. There would be no radios or tape recorders, no movies or other diversions. A central computer would know precisely each of their whereabouts and activities at any moment of the day or night, and there would be periodic verifications. Although some women trainees also were assigned to the Center, there must be no "inappropriate encounters" with those of the opposite sex. Shaking hands was appropriate; anything else was inappropriate. No man was ever to be alone with a woman, even if engaged merely in classroom study. All men would be referred to as "Elder" and all women as "Sister." Hence among trainees it would be "Elder Brown" or "Sister Brown." Each man would be assigned a "companion" who would accompany him at all times of the day or night, except while defecating. It would be the companion's absolute obligation to report any instance where the rules of "moral cleanliness" were violated.

"Sex is a sacred power," the young man intoned gravely. "The only righteous use of this sacred power is within the covenant of marriage. I want to counsel you and I want you to remember these words: During your training here and your subsequent work at your mission, you must never let anyone touch or handle your body. Turn away from any who would persuade you to experiment with these life-giving powers. God has declared in unmistakable language that misery and sorrow will follow the violation of the laws of chastity."

The young man paused for dramatic effect, his hands clutched in front of him. There was utter silence in the room. "Remember this," he said at last. "Crowning Glory awaits you if you live worthily. The loss of the crown may be punishment enough."

Listening to these words, Tad found himself trembling. He did not want to lose that crown—he would be strong enough; he would *make* himself strong enough! Fifteen thousand trainees a year had made it through. They'd found the strength and so would he.

Thinking back upon the eight weeks at the center, the memory of that fear and that resolve clung to him with utter clarity, but the rest of the experience had receded into a kaleidoscopic blur of sounds and images: the shock of awakening at 6:00 A.M. to the shrill alarm; colliding with the naked limbs of the three other occupants of the tiny cell; rushing through the fluorescent glare of the orange corridors to class; the small clusters of students and instructors barking at each other in an alien tongue; the relentless repetition of the "lessons" to be imparted to would-be converts. Words and sounds repeated again and again, drilled like bullets into his numbed mind.

And then one morning Tad awoke and found himself in a sweltering little shack in Tonga and there were bugs on the walls and the acrid stench of a nearby septic tank. In the bunk above he could hear the anguished mumblings of his companion talking in his sleep. His name was Lorenzo Bullard. Lorenzo was from Ogden, Utah, and he'd been scared to death from his moment of arrival.

Tad had been greeted that first day by Isaac Hamblin, the Mission President of Tonga, a portly, gnomelike man with a round face and a pasty complexion. He sat Tad and Lorenzo down in his tiny living room and squinted at them through thick, black-framed glasses. The Mission President had taken a leave of absence from his job as assistant manager of a small bank in Brigham City, Utah, so he could supervise the job of proselytizing the heathen.

"A hearty welcome to you both," Hamblin said to them in a high, nasal voice that was anything but hearty. He shook hands with Tad and then with Lorenzo and invited them to sit down. His wife, fluttery and reedlike, with small, suspicious eyes, her gray hair pulled back into a bun, brought them glasses of sugary fruit punch.

Hamblin wasted no time picking up where the Missionary Center had left off. "I want it understood from the start there will be no inappropriate encounters here in Tonga," he said, his voice an

angry whine. "If you have an inappropriate encounter I expect
you to tell me. If you fail to do so, your companion will tell me. If
your companion doesn't, a member of the Church will tell me.
And if a member doesn't, a nonmember will tell me. And if a
nonmember doesn't, then the Lord will tell me."

Hamblin squinted at each of them to see whether he had made
an impression. Tad noticed that Lorenzo Bullard's hands were
shaking.

"If you break the moral code you will be sent home in disgrace.
You know what that means. Your families will be ashamed of you.
You will have trouble finding work. God is not spiteful or venge-
ful; your punishment will flow from your deeds."

Lorenzo Bullard dropped his glass of punch. Pulling his white
handkerchief from his jacket pocket, he scrambled onto the floor
to clean up the spill while Hamblin and his wife looked on dis-
approvingly.

"There is good work being done here," Hamblin started again,
as if to calm his new charges. "The Church has made great strides
here in Tonga. I can proudly say that after only one generation of
proselytizing, one-third of the population of this island have
become Latter-day saints. We've also enjoyed great success
throughout Samoa, Fiji, Tahiti and the other areas of Polynesia.
And these aren't just numbers—these are good, God-fearing, bap-
tized Mormons who attend their sacrament meeting each week
and pay their tithes and help us spread the faith. We have transformed these islands into outposts of Zion. The natives used to be
lazy and dirty and they used to drink and fornicate. Now they are
clean and they follow the Word of Wisdom. They understand the
meaning of hard work. We are changing the whole fabric of this
society."

Tad saw Hamblin's wife hovering behind his chair, her eyes
blazing with righteousness. "Elder Hastings and Elder Bullard,"
she said, "I want to remind you one more time that the Bishop
has the key to the cleansing power. The covenant of baptism itself
represents a washing and a cleansing. Guilt will be gone if you go
to your Bishop."

Armed with their six lessons, and with a determination to stay
cleansed, Tad and Lorenzo set out that next morning to spread
the faith. They arose at six and donned their dark blue missionary

uniforms to embark on their tracting—plodding from door to door in search of converts. By ten in the morning, Tad's clothes were clammy with perspiration, his heavy cotton underwear wadded against his skin like dough. By lunchtime they succumbed to a stupor of drowsiness, lying slumped in the shade, trying to fight off the mosquitoes.

But the next morning they were at it again. And the next one after that. Some of the natives tried to be kind, others taunting. During the first week they talked to one man for twenty minutes before they realized he was asleep. One chubby, coffee-colored matron greeted them warmly and confided that she'd always liked missionaries. To prove her fealty to the Church she started rubbing Lorenzo's crotch. Mortified, Lorenzo burst from the thatched hut and raced down the street as though he'd been assaulted with a lethal weapon. Their third day they found themselves at a family banquet, seated on banana leaves. Their host, who was slicing up a tuna, offered each a freshly cut eyeball. They nodded their gratitude as Lorenzo dropped it inconspicuously down the front of his shirt. But Tad, sensing everyone's attention upon him, swallowed it manfully, trying to ignore its spongy texture and excusing himself moments later to throw up behind a bush.

By the end of their third week they had learned several vital lessons. Confining their tracting to mornings, they concentrated on referrals from the newly converted. In the evenings they returned to the homes of their most promising candidates to resume their "teaching" when the full family was present. Hamblin had already started pressing them for specific reports on how many baptisms they had performed. It was clear to them both that the high-flown ideals enunciated at Missionary Center boiled down to a harsh reality: They were there to produce numbers, just as if they were selling encyclopedias. It was also clear, however, that the numbers were not so easy to come by as Hamblin had suggested. Many of the natives, especially the women, seemed eager to learn about the Church and were especially attracted by the promises of immortality, but their existing mores were totally at odds with Church teachings. It was hard to teach the work ethic to a man who was raised to believe that when you were hungry you fished and when you weren't you slept. It was hard to teach

LDS morality to a people whose language used the same word for marriage as it used for coitus.

Faced with these realizations, Tad decided to sit down with his companion for a serious talk. Elder Bullard, he could see, was not bearing up well under the demands of his new life. His fair skin was marred by big red blotches, and his mournful blue eyes had the glaze of incipient hysteria, yet Lorenzo was still determined to play things by the book. Typically, while Tad had started calling him "Comp," short for companion, Lorenzo still resolutely stuck with "Elder Hastings." Rigidly following instructions, Lorenzo continued to follow Tad wherever he went. When Tad urinated, Lorenzo stood by to check that Tad would not be tempted to fondle himself. When he showered, Lorenzo would stand outside the stall until he had finished. When he undressed, he sensed Lorenzo's eyes upon him.

Tad deliberately avoided subjecting his companion to similar scrutiny in the hope that he would get the message, but it was fruitless. Something had to be done.

"Lorenzo, good buddy," Tad said over lunch, "this is not working out very well. I don't know about you, but I'm going bananas. I hate tracting. I hate Tonga. I hate Hamblin. I hate feeling you breathing down my neck. I hate it when you watch me pee and wipe my ass. I want to go home, but I'm going to stick it out. I'm not going to give up this quickly."

Lorenzo stared at his food balefully, avoiding Tad's glance. He said nothing.

"So I want to make a deal with you, Comp. It's the only way we can make things livable. Here it goes. Ready?"

Lorenzo nodded, his eyes still focused downward.

"Okay. First, we get up at seven, not six. Nobody checks up on us, anyway. The days are too long. They're killing me. Second, between noon and four, you go your way and I go mine. We split. You do whatever you want. I do whatever I want. Frankly, what I want to do is take off my clammy clothes and go lie on the beach. Third, I don't want to have you staring at me all the time. I won't stare at you. You hear me?"

Lorenzo's face was drenched in sweat. Tad could tell he was gravely troubled as he pondered his words. When Lorenzo looked up at him his eyes were watery but there was a look of messianic determination in them. "I can't go along with it. I'm sorry, Elder Hastings. I just can't. I was raised a certain way. I . . . I . . ."

Tad could see him choking back his tears. Lorenzo pulled out a white handkerchief and blew his nose, then got to his feet. "I have to go to the bathroom now." He had taken a few steps when he paused and wheeled around. "Aren't you coming with me?"

"No, I'm not coming with you to the goddamn bathroom."

Lorenzo seemed uncertain what to do, then he reeled off. He was gone several minutes. Tad became worried. He knew he had offended the poor boy. Maybe he was crying. Maybe he was having a nervous breakdown.

Tad froze! He knew where Lorenzo had gone. He'd gone to the Mission President to report him. All right, he would take his medicine. He'd known he was taking that chance when he decided to talk to Lorenzo candidly in the first place. He'd taken the chance and lost!

Tad slammed his fist into his palm and was cursing under his breath when a shadow suddenly crossed the table. He looked up. It was Lorenzo Bullard. His face was flushed, but his eyes were clear.

"Elder Hastings, I have something terrible to confess." Lorenzo's voice was so soft Tad had to strain to hear it. "I went to the bathroom and I masturbated. In fact, I masturbated twice."

Tad stared at Lorenzo, speechless. He ran his hand over his face, as if to clear his senses. "Good for you, Lorenzo."

"You will tell President Hamblin?"

"I will do no such thing."

"But I am unclean."

"That is none of Hamblin's business."

". . . But I have broken my oath. . . ."

Tad rose from the table and put his hand on his companion's moist shoulder. "How do you feel, Lorenzo?"

His companion looked incredulous. "How do I feel?"

"Yes. How do you feel?"

"Better . . . yes, I would say I feel better." Lorenzo was nodding sheepishly, his face aflame with embarrassment.

"Then tell me something, Lorenzo, which way is the bathroom?"

"It is that way," Lorenzo said, pointing to a remote corner of the room. "Why?"

"Because I'm going in there. I'm going to grab my pud and shake it like a sonofabitch."

Lorenzo's mouth dropped open with astonishment. They stood facing each other for a moment, and then Lorenzo smiled. It was the first time he had ever seen Lorenzo Bullard smile.

☐ Life became marginally bearable after that. They began to build their list of reliable referrals, whom they visited with stubborn persistence until eliciting a commitment. At night they often went to the homes of convinced Mormon converts, who would share their dinners and their music. In the afternoon, Tad would go to a remote beach which he had discovered. Since he'd caught President Hamblin's wife inspecting their quarters one day, even going through their closets and drawers, Tad was afraid to own a bathing suit. He swam in the nude, feeling self-conscious about it at first, fearing that his privacy would be compromised.

Nudity was something new and foreign to him. He would swim for hours, knifing through the water, clear and translucent in the bright sun, enclosed in its sensuality like some exotic sea creature. He would see the fronds beckoning from the white strand of beach and, for those brief moments, he would feel totally at peace. By the time he returned to his quarters in the late afternoon, Lorenzo would be lying in bed reading Scripture. He usually had a contented look on his face, so Tad presumed he'd been experiencing his own private diversions.

One day, after a morning of door-to-door visitations, Tad arrived at his beach only to discover a Jeep parked at the edge of one of the low sand dunes. He felt a stab of anger over the discovery: The Jeep represented a violation of his private preserve. Creeping stealthily over the dune, he saw the figures of a boy and girl sprawled on a blanket. Both were naked. The girl was Tana; he could recognize her from her long copper-colored hair. And her companion was the lanky boy in white whom he had seen two nights before. Crawling carefully now to avoid discovery, Tad found he could catch a clear view of them and still remain hidden in the tall grass that fringed the dune. He felt a pang of humiliation for spying on them, yet was powerless to move. The spectacle was too fascinating, the girl's body too lovely.

He relished being the voyeur. Once or twice at BYU he had happened on couples engaged in sexual congress, but in each instance there had been something grotesque about their frenzied movements. There had been a great deal of panting, some muffled cries and then quickly both parties would be zipping themselves up and racing off into the night, like two animals caught in the headlights of an approaching vehicle. Tad himself was a virgin, a condition which only fueled his self-hate. He regarded his virginity as one would a disease, a loathsome affliction that somehow resisted cure. He had tried; one night, ignited by a six-pack of beer, he had searched all of Provo for a prostitute. It was like looking for a Coke in the Sahara. The closest he came was an extraordinarily frowsy waitress at an all-night hamburger joint whose breath smelled of gin and whose pink slacks seemed glued to her sagging cellulitic thighs. When Tad importuned her, she responded cheerfully by producing a battered edition of the Book of Mormon, inviting Tad to join the faith.

Compared with the clumsy sexual contortions he had witnessed in college, the graceful spectacle unfolding on the beach before him seemed like an erotic ballet. The boy, whom Tad later learned to be Gavin Pollard, lay splayed across the blanket, arms and legs spread apart, the girl hovering over him like a lovely pink cloud, her copper hair glinting bright in the sunlight. Tad watched with hypnotic fascination as her lissome body undulated slowly above his, her back arching gently, hips writhing, the small curve of her backside glowing white as the sand around them. So fluid were her movements and so comely her figure that it was several moments before Tad realized with a shock that the two were coitally joined. He knew he should leave now, that it was terribly wrong to violate their privacy, but his body would not respond to his command. He was rooted there, trancelike, a helpless spectator to their private rapture. As she moved above him, the boy's hands were gently stroking her upper thighs, gliding over her slim hips, kneading her buttocks. His own body was writhing now, his head twisting to one side, then to another, eyes closed, surrendering himself to his rising ecstasy. Then, as if on signal, she was suddenly off him, lying at his side, and Tad could hear her melodic laughter as she grasped him, squeezing gently, stroking the length of him, from his root to the pink knob at its tip, both of them laughing like children at some tender game. As she lay beside him, Tad marveled at the delicate contours of her breasts, their nipples tiny and budlike, resting against the boy's jutting ribs, her back a graceful arc against him. They lay that way for several minutes, his arm under her body, hand pressed against her white buttocks, as she continued to play with him as though he were a great toy, placed there for her private amusement and pleasure. Tad had never seen a game quite like this, had never thought of sex as a toy to be mastered. Throughout his boyhood he had thought of sex as seldom as possible. One's sexual parts, he knew, were somehow sacrosanct, placed there to perform a divine purpose. They were for procreation, not for play—a solemn duty, a spiritual act. Yet the girl and boy performing before him now were neither solemn nor spiritual. The act of sex was for them an act of abandon, indeed of laughter, and Tad himself was caught up in their erotic merriment. Watching them now, unconsciously displaying themselves before him, he realized there was indeed something marvelously absurd about the phallus—something curiously ungainly and out of proportion to the rest of the body as it rose once again to its own avid dimensions, the girl teasing, coaxing, prodding it to still greater tumescence until, noticing its quivers of excitement, she was upon it once more, lowering her body slowly, her face serious now, lips parted, eyes closed. Then she was doing her undulating dance as before, rising and falling like the gentle waves a few feet away.

Lying flat against the dune, hands clutching the fine sand, Tad was suddenly aware of his own arousal. He had no idea how long he'd been caught up in this spectacle, hypnotized by it, his senses fully engaged, but he was drenched with perspiration. He struggled to remove his damp shirt, fearful of drawing their attention. His eyes drifted to the water, which was glowing a luminous green in the late afternoon sun. He yearned to immerse himself in the cool ocean, but his eyes were drawn back to the boy and girl, like filings to a magnet. Now he heard a muffled cry, saw the boy bucking under her weight, the girl riding him as she would a pony, and then it was her cry he heard, a terse bursting forth of pleasure-pain as they rolled over on the blanket, then over again onto the beach, their flanks coated with the powdery sand, bodies conjoined in orgasmic embrace. Tad heard another cry now and realized, in his own private horror, that it was his own and that he had vicariously experienced their pleasure and their release.

☐ They had ruined it all, of course. During the preceding weeks, Tad had finally managed to find a modus vivendi, a way of making it all work here on this ridiculous island, doing this ridiculous work, side by side with this ridiculous companion. He had withdrawn into a protective cocoon of sensual obliviousness, and it was working for him.

Now it was shattered. They haunted him. Wherever he went they appeared magically, this golden couple. He and Lorenzo would be walking down the street at night, and suddenly they would appear from around the corner, strolling arm in arm. On the way home from supper at the Mission President's house, they literally collided outside a restaurant. The two of them exuded the sensuality Tad yearned most desperately to erase from his consciousness. Even walking together they seemed the embodiment of an erotic fantasy, arms around each other, touching, rubbing, laughing. Tad would awaken suddenly from a deep sleep and see them before him, her little bottom wiggling in her cutoffs, her surprisingly ample bosom straining against the tiny halter, the boy walking beside her in his white slacks, his protuberance signifying to Tad his arousal.

At least they'd not returned to his beach. Tad was back there the next day, at once hoping to see them, yet praying they would be absent—that there would still be one place that would be inviolate. Each afternoon he would swim for miles, his long arms churning furiously through the clear green water, relishing the sheer animal exertion. He would swim until he was physically exhausted, and then he would feel better.

One day he had just emerged from the water, rubbing the salt from his smarting eyes, when suddenly he saw them there, lying right before him, their bodies intertwined as before. He was shocked and appalled. His instinct was to run. The boy saw him first. They both bolted upright on the blanket, staring at him, surprised by this intrusion yet unembarrassed.

"Where did you come from?" the boy said.

Tad dived forward onto the sand to hide his own nakedness. "I . . . I took a long swim. I always swim here. This is my beach, kind of. . . ."

He felt ridiculous lying there, face down, on the beach, his gaze directed at the sand in front of them, averting eye contact.

"Well, anyway . . . hello," the boy said.

"Hello," Tad said, his chest still heaving from the swim and from the shock of confronting them.

Tana cupped her hand over her mouth and let out a little yelp. "I know you," she said. "You're the missionary, aren't you? The Mormon." Her voice was as high-pitched as a small girl's.

Tad nodded numbly. He forced himself to look up at her now. They both were sitting a few yards away, making no effort to conceal themselves. He gasped as he saw her concave belly moist with sweat, the dark triangle of reddish hair between her legs. She seemed unaffected by his gaze.

"I never knew you guys ever took a swim," the boy said. "I thought you even slept in your blue suits."

"We're not supposed to swim. It's against regulations." Tad felt as if his mouth were full of cotton. He struggled to enunciate his words, like a small boy addressing a room full of adults. "I come here every day to swim. No one ever comes here."

"I'm sorry we invaded your beach, ol' buddy," the boy said cheerfully. "I really apologize. But we won't tell on you."

". . . If you won't tell on us," the girl said.

"I'd better go," Tad said, his senses reeling.

". . . You wouldn't tell on us, would you?" Tana's pert little face was serious now, her eyes troubled. "My mother would really kill me. . . ."

Tad shook his head. "Of course not. . . ."

"He looks like a good guy," the boy said. "My name is Gavin Pollard and this is Tana. I apologize for being bare ass like this. You came by at an awkward moment."

"I'm Tad. Tad Hastings."

"Look, Tad, we've brought a picnic lunch. Some cold sandwiches and stuff. Nothing fancy. You're welcome to join us. . . ."

". . . Oh, I don't really feel I could." Tad realized his own mounting discomfort lying there, the hot sand burning into his scrotum.

Tana was on her feet, slipping into her cutoffs. Gavin tossed a towel to Tad. "Come on," Gavin said, "let's have some lunch."

"I really shouldn't intrude . . ."

Gavin smiled at him. "It's we who apparently intruded."

Tad got to his feet, quickly clasping the towel around him. There was something utterly bizarre about this encounter—coming upon these two people who had been haunting his every thought. Here they were, caught in the midst of lovemaking, and yet, with no awkwardness or embarrassment, inviting their intruder to join them. Tad saw them chattering together now, dividing up the sandwiches, opening the wine, spreading a straw mat atop the blanket.

"You know," Gavin said to him, "I've never actually met a missionary before. Especially a swimming missionary. I'd love to ask you some questions, if you don't mind. I mean, this seems like a weird place for a missionary to be."

There was an openness to Gavin's smile that struck a chord in Tad. Perhaps it was merely that his boyish, friendly manner presented such a contrast to the pinched, pallid faces of the Lorenzo Bullards and Isaac Hamblins. He seemed so at ease with himself.

And it occurred to Tad, why not join these two? Why run off in embarrassment when they are willing to welcome him, to share their food and company? Perhaps, if he sat and talked to them, if he dealt with them as ordinary mortals, he could exorcise them from his fantasies.

They ate and talked. The flow of conversation surprised Tad. They were as guileless and uninhibited in their talk as they were in their lovemaking. They spoke of their parents and friends. They questioned Tad as though he were a Martian, their curiosity directed at everything from sacraments to sex. When their picnic was over, Tad was delighted when they suggested it would be nice to meet again.

And so they gathered on Gavin's boat that next night and then again the next. Lorenzo Bullard didn't protest Tad's prolonged absences; indeed, he seemed to welcome the privacy.

On their third night together, there was someone else with Gavin and Tana when Tad arrived. She was a tall, tanned blonde named Cathy who had just arrived from San Diego. Gavin opened some beers and offered them around, and Tad thought, why not?

Cathy was a vibrantly extroverted girl with a piercing laugh and an animal energy that had an almost narcotic effect on him. After their third beer together, Tad realized it had become quieter in the cabin because Gavin and Tana had quietly slipped away.

After their fourth, he looked up with both surprise and alarm to see Cathy slipping off her T-shirt, exposing a very substantial bosom that was as tan as the rest of her.

"Wait a minute," Tad said, "what's happening here?"

"We're partying," Cathy said cheerfully.

Tad felt a tension building. "Was this whole thing a setup?"

Cathy laughed as she wiggled out of her tight jeans, standing before him now in tiny panties. "Are you scared, honey, is that it?"

"Of course I'm scared." Tad heard himself say it, but those weren't the words he had intended.

"That's fun," Cathy said. "Why don't you just shut up and take off your clothes?"

"I just don't like being set up, is all. Is this everyone's idea of a mission of mercy?"

"I'm not into mercy," Cathy said. "I think you're cute."

"I don't believe you."

Cathy tossed her panties onto the table.

"When's the last time you had a lover, honey?"

Tad sucked in his breath. "Never." He choked on the word.

Her eyes peered at him with a sort of earnest mirthfulness. "Look, honey, it's a lot more fun making love to a scared missionary than being mauled by some macho sailor boy who thinks he knows all the moves. Do you understand?"

"I think I do," Tad said, marveling how four beers could have gone so far in expunging his shame. Here he was, a once-zealous missionary, standing drunkenly before this beautiful naked girl. He stripped quickly, practically ripping off his underclothes so she would not comment on them. When he was finished, he felt her eyes upon him.

He went to her, holding her, feeling the warmth against him. Her skin seemed to pulse with an exotic metabolism all her own. Her hair exuded a clean, heady fragrance that aroused him.

She led him to a bunk. "Now, if you come real quick, hon, don't be embarrassed. There's a lot more where that came from."

"I won't," Tad replied, trying for nonchalance, utterly astonished that she could say something like that. He had never in his wildest dreams imagined a girl speaking about such an intimate act with such benign candor.

Fifteen seconds later he felt a sudden spasm in his loins and heard her giggle. Cathy's smiling face was against his. "As I said, there's a lot more where that came from."

"I hope so," he said prayerfully.

☐ "Do you deny, Elder Hastings, that you were down at the harbor two nights ago at about ten o'clock?"

Mission President Hamblin sat across the room from them, glowering in his old-fashioned wicker chair. His wife hovered, wraithlike, in the shadows, as though poised to swoop down upon them in her pent-up fury. Tad and Lorenzo sat side by side on the sofa in their blue suits, sweat dripping down Lorenzo's petrified face.

"No, sir," Tad replied.

"I am glad of that, at least. A brother saw you."

"I do not deny it, sir."

"What was the purpose of these nocturnal visitations, Elder?"

"A friend, sir."

The Mission President stroked his jowls, his round, fleshy face taking on an inquisitorial mien, head tilted. "You were teaching, Elder Hastings? Teaching sailors aboard a yacht, perhaps?"

Tad drew a deep breath. Every fiber and muscle of his being had been meticulously primed for moments such as this—schooled to react on cue, to spill all that was inside him, to empty out his innermost thoughts and guilts. The button had been pressed and now he was supposed to purge himself of all wrongdoing. He remembered his humiliation, shortly after being ordained a deacon at age twelve, confessing to his Bishop that he had committed unclean acts upon his body, the Bishop chastising him in a voice so loud he knew others could surely overhear, then slinking from the chapel, the tears bursting from him the moment he was outside. For weeks he had bathed three times a day, desperate to wash away the humiliation.

Hamblin was gazing at him through narrowed eyes. Tad studied his fat, oily face, with its thick nose, pouty mouth, curled upper lip.

Tad steeled himself. He was not a callow twelve-year-old any longer. "Our brethren who happen to live aboard their ships require the nourishment of the Gospel just as much as those on land," he said in a voice that was surprisingly composed.

"It was clearly an inappropriate encounter," Mrs. Hamblin snapped, her eyes flashing through her rimless spectacles.

Hamblin's attention was fastened on Lorenzo now. "And you, Elder Bullard? Why were you not at the side of your companion on this spiritual mission?"

Tad heard Lorenzo fart softly. This is it, he told himself. Here's where Lorenzo crumbles. Will he dissolve in tears or simply grovel on the floor and beg forgiveness?

"I was ill," Lorenzo said, his tone tremulous. "I would have been with him but I was throwing up."

"You don't look sick to me," Mrs. Hamblin said sharply.

"I was throwing up, Sister Hamblin," Lorenzo repeated. "I was sick. I am still sick. In fact, I think I'll throw up again."

Lorenzo brought his hand quickly to his mouth and gagged. Tad caught the sudden alarm in Mrs. Hamblin's eyes, fearful now that this odd young man would compromise the tidiness of her sitting room.

"I should get him home to bed," Tad said.

Hamblin gazed at him skeptically. "I want to warn you Elder Hastings, that God is watching your every movement, and I am, too. We are sent here on a sacred mission, whose success is dependent on our moral cleanliness."

"I understand, sir."

Lorenzo gagged again. "May I be excused, please?" he pleaded, talking through his hand still clenched tightly over his mouth.

"You may, Elder Bullard."

Lorenzo bolted from the room. Tad started to rise, but Mrs. Hamblin was upon him. "You should be sent home," she said, her voice fierce. "You have no business mixing with the riffraff that sails in here on these boats. No business at all."

Tad tried to ease himself toward the door but she pursued him, her face so close he could feel her warm breath. "Your mother,

Eliza Hastings, is a great woman, Elder. I deeply admire her work in the Church. If the Mission President and I didn't admire her, we would send you packing. I want you to know that." She sped from the room, like an angry bird scooting back to its nest.

It was Tad who now had the sick feeling in his stomach. All his life he had heard these words, over and over, in one form or another, this paean of praise for Eliza, this hymn of adulation. You are forgiven only because of your mother, they had always told him. You are not living up to her greatness. You are not fulfilling the high expectations which the Church held out for you.

"You may go now, Tad," Hamblin said softly, his face sagging, as though even he regretted his wife's outburst.

Tad moved outside and stood alone. It was a still, hot night, the humid air draping itself upon him in a moist veil. He swatted an insect from his face.

"Fuck." Lorenzo's dark form materialized before him. Tad had never heard him curse before.

"Thanks, Comp," Tad said softly. "You were great."

"What else could I tell them? That you were out whoring while I was home beating my meat?"

Tad flung his arm around the boy's wet shoulder. Suddenly Lorenzo's face was buried in his chest and he was sobbing. "I'm really fucked," he burbled between his heaves. "I've lost my way. I'm falling apart."

Tad put his arms around him and gave him a quick hug. "I know, Comp, I know. Let's just not try to figure it out for now, okay? Let's just go home and go to sleep."

☐ Two nights later Gavin announced he would be sailing out at dawn. They had a last drink together, Tad already feeling a new loneliness.

He had known this boy so briefly, yet they had established a true closeness. Superficially, no two people could seem more dissimilar, but Tad had come to realize that each, in his own way, carried with him an unwanted legacy. Each embodied the lofty expectations of his family, each life weighted down by the burdens of dynasty. Gavin had been nurtured from childhood to be the *next* Nicholas Pollard, heir to a great publishing dynasty. Tad had been groomed to assume high responsibilities in the Church.

Both had already felt the anguish of their own failures.

They talked about none of this their last time together. Instead there was joking and drunken bravado. And when it was time to go they shook hands.

"I'll never forget you—you know that, Gavin." Tad had to grasp the chair to hold his balance against the alcohol.

"I'll never forget you either, Elder Hastings."

"You taught me a lot."

Gavin smiled. "We had some good times."

"I'd say we did."

"You'll be all right, won't you?" I mean, they won't send you home?"

Tad shook his head. "No, they won't send me home. I guess they're scared of my mother. I'll stay here and serve out my sentence."

"All right, then," Gavin said, holding his glass aloft. "To the Good Lord, with gratitude, that He saw fit to create so many pretty girls."

"Yes, I'll drink to that," Tad said, lifting his glass.

They drank their toast, then gave each other a quick, awkward bear hug.

"See ya soon, Elder," Gavin said.

"I sure hope so."

It would be four years before they again were to meet.

HIRAM Cobb had driven several blocks before he realized the pain was there again. He knew that pain well: an ache high in the stomach, right there in ulcer country. His wife Augusta—Gussie as he called her—having observed his occasional flinches and grimaces, had urged him to consult a physician, but in Hiram's view an ulcer, like so much else in the gauntlet of day-to-day living, ultimately came down to a question of mind over matter. Brigham Young, he recalled, had once said, "The mind makes its own place, and can create a heaven of hell or a hell of heaven." Though he disagreed with most of Brigham's pronunciamentos, Hiram admired his knack at mobilizing the appropriate exhortation to deal with locust infestations, crop failures, floods or other catastrophes that were endlessly assailing the Mormon pioneers. The fact that Young occasionally borrowed his aphorisms from other sources, be they Milton, Wordsworth or even Emerson, was irrelevant to his followers, whose energies were consumed with the ordeal of survival.

Grasping the steering wheel, muscles taut, Hiram realized he was driving much too fast, his Toyota fishtailing through the snow, the tires shooting long funnels of slush in his wake. Mind over matter, he repeated to himself, pressing the brake, guiding the car through the easy skid. He had often caught himself like this lately, pushing too hard, nerves flexed, manic. He knew it was ridiculous. This was, after all, Christmastime, the family was together, the children were excited. They had all happily decorated the tree only the night before. Since it was snowing hard, they would drive to the mountains this week and he and Gussie would teach the boys to ski. There was cause to be grateful.

Hiram slowed for a red light, swerving sharply toward the curb as a big red Buick skidded to a stop, its rear fender narrowly missing Hiram's, the elderly woman at its wheel shaking her head in confusion. Thank God for the Salt Lake City's capacious streets, Hiram thought. Old Brigham, again. The great patriarch fancied wide boulevards, so his city was laid out according to his whims in a vast grid of broad corridors. Only in Salt Lake was it possible to own a tiny bungalow fronting on a six-lane street and bearing an address of unique ambiguity such as 825 East South Temple. The whims of the Prophets!

Hiram popped a Maalox tablet into his mouth and lowered the window, taking a deep breath of frosty air. The mountains, already powdered in white, seemed to hover like a great billowy cloudbank over the city. Silhouetted against this awesome backdrop, the jutting structures of downtown—the Temple, the Hotel Utah and even the concrete monolith that served as world Church Headquarters—all acquired a certain dignity and presence which most settings would have denied them. Brigham was lucky about that, too, Hiram thought. Salt Lake was truly an uncommonly drab city, even with its ecclesiastical accoutrements. The revered Mormon Temple, with all its folklore and fanfare, seemed a prosaic structure in comparison to the world's great cathedrals—a fortresslike, multispired edifice of gray granite which looked as though it were designed more to fend off invaders than to invite worshipers.

Little wonder that the Mormon pioneers regarded the Wasatch Mountains, looming high above, with an almost mystical reverence as they stared up from the dry alkaline plain which Brigham had designated as their Kingdom. How utterly confounding it must have been, Hiram often thought, to have been in that advance party with Brigham, to survey for the first time the vast flat void called the Great Basin, to peer into the lifeless, putrescent waters of the Great Salt Lake, and then to hear the Prophet, near delirious with tick fever, solemnly intone that *this* is where he would build Zion.

As he drove, Hiram heard a dull, relentless whine emanating from his right front wheel. Only two days earlier he had taken his Toyota for servicing, but the noise had naturally vanished when the repairman drove it. "Any Toyota that's traveled one hundred thousand miles has a right to whine," he admonished, and he was right, but Hiram was a worrier by nature; he had visions of the

right wheel rolling off some snowy night when Gussie was driving the children home from school.

His stomach was hurting again and Hiram swallowed rapidly to
assuage it, knowing that it wasn't the Toyota that was causing him
distress but rather the cumulative irritants that had long been
building within him. It had been almost a decade! Hiram shook
his head in disbelief: a decade since their quite orderly, simple
lives had been rudely disrupted, their careers devastated. Hiram
still found it incredible, all of it. Especially that it had happened
at BYU, the seat of Mormondom, *their* university, seemingly the
most protective academic cocoon in all America. Yet suddenly,
unexpectedly, he and Gussie had been blown asunder as though
they had trespassed on some treacherous hidden minefield.

It had brought them closer at first; they had braced each other
against the onslaught, one fortifying the other, but now, these
long years later, the cumulative tensions and deprivations had
begun to take their toll. They rarely talked about it, but he could
sense the centrifugal forces at work, even as they continued, side
by side, fending off their adversaries, marshaling their ever-dwin-
dling resources.

Their financial problems were giving Hiram the most concern
of late. They'd been in a tight bind through most of the past
several years, but Hiram, as a trained accountant, knew better
than anyone the distinction between a squeeze and imminent
insolvency. He and Gussie depended for their livelihood on a
bimonthly magazine called *The Kingdom,* which they edited and
published. With its austere layout and rudimentary offset printing, it was more a newsletter than a magazine, but it had found a
niche for itself, establishing a circulation of eighteen thousand,
principally in Utah, Idaho, Nevada and Arizona. There was a nice
irony to its name, an allusion to the Kingdom of God which Joseph
Smith felt it his mission to establish, a mission which, in their
view, had been considerably compromised over the century and
a half of LDS history. The publication sought to provide a running
commentary on life within the precincts of Mormondom, with a
special focus on the functioning of the Church hierarchy—a subject which was scrupulously avoided by the two major dailies in
Salt Lake, whose editors were keenly aware that the guarantees
of a "free press" were interpreted somewhat differently behind

the Zion Curtain than in the rest of the United States. The Utah newspapers were free to publish whatever they wanted with the proviso that any story even peripherally involving the Church or its social and political interests was automatically checked with Church Headquarters, whose functionaries were uninhibited about wielding their tacit right to veto. While the *Tribune* and *Deseret News* (which was Church-owned) avoided any mention of *The Kingdom* in their columns, Hiram knew that his fragile little publication circulated freely if secretly among their staffs, and several of their reporters occasionally phoned him with tips involving the Church which they knew they'd be unable to pursue.

When they had first started *The Kingdom,* the LDS Church maintained a policy of stony obliviousness toward Hiram and Augusta Cobb on the assumption that they were merely ill-advised apostates who would soon pack up and go away. After all, no other voice of dissent had ever sustained itself within the fiercely disciplined confines of the Mormon nation. But the Cobbs had not gone away. With each passing year, as Hiram and Gussie dug ever deeper into the hidden crevices of Mormon history, their attacks had grown ever sharper, their critiques more scathing and their influence more pervasive. Through their writings they had relentlessly picked at all the camouflaged wounds of the past while, at the same time, stressing their own deep-felt commitment to the humane values and traditions of the Church and its people. Marshaling a formidable arsenal of long-suppressed personal testimony and archaeological data, they had committed the ultimate heresy of challenging the key events on which the whole belief system of Mormonism resides—the visitations by an angel named Moroni to a rural youth named Joseph Smith in the early 1830s. They had challenged, too, the legitimacy of the Book of Mormon —effectively, the Mormon bible. The story told by the Book of Mormon suggests that a tribe of Jews migrated to America about 600 B.C.; that these so-called Nephites built a great civilization which was vanquished by the evil Lamanites (whose descendants were the Indians); that only through the efforts of a man named Mormon and his son, Moroni, were the records of this historic interlude recorded on golden plates and ultimately presented to Joseph Smith some one thousand, four hundred years later, along with magical spectacles which enabled young Smith to translate the hieroglyphics in which the plates had been mysteriously inscribed. All this, argued Hiram and Gussie, seemed more the fanciful outgrowth of a reckless and unschooled adolescent imagination rather than the basis for a modern religion—indeed, the only great world religion of U.S. origin.

They had argued insistently that much of Mormon ritual was effectively plagiarized from the rites of Freemasonry, describing in their magazine the long-secret details of LDS ceremonies of initiation, marriage and vicarious baptism. They had even cast doubt upon the revered institution of divine revelation, presenting evidence that the Prophet's revelations legitimizing polygamy were more self-serving than spiritual. Summoning long-suppressed documents, they depicted the thirty-year reign of Brigham Young as clumsy and autocratic, reflecting the Prophet's total disdain for democratic institutions. They unearthed, as well, long-hidden deliberations of the surreptitious body called the Council of Fifty which had functioned as the "secret government" of Mormondom. The Cobbs, too, had published agonizing accounts of the unspoken violence that had lurked just beneath the surface of Mormon life: the terrorist activities of the Danites who once wreaked revenge and Blood Atonement upon the enemies of the Church; the terrible massacre at Mountain Meadows where Mormon frontiersmen wiped out a band of non-Mormon settlers; and the modern-day violence of the ever-growing polygamous cults.

The Cobbs's investigations did not confine themselves to the past. They opened for public scrutiny detailed accountings of contemporary Church business holdings, citing vast tax-free ownership over large corporations and agricultural fiefdoms. They delved into the deployment of Mormon power and money to influence the election of political candidates favored by the Church.

In presenting their findings and conclusions, Hiram and Gussie had sought to couch them in temperate terms. In each issue they tried to stress their love for the Mormon people and their support for the many good deeds of the Church. Their people had much to be proud of, yet much to question, they reiterated.

But their articles still sent repeated shock waves through sectors of the community. The Church, after all, was not accustomed to criticism from within. Throughout its history, it had hermetically sealed itself from the probing curiosity of the outside world, exercising a unique control over its own history and releasing to scholars only those documents which it felt reflected favorably upon its leadership. When Hiram and Gussie, through their growing circle of closet allies inside the Church, repeatedly penetrated this repressive veil, the repercussions could often be alarming. They had been awakened in the middle of the night by menacing phone calls. Rocks were tossed through their windows. Their two boys had been taunted at school and scolded by their teachers. Long-term friends avoided their glances.

Excommunication, they had always known, would be inevitable. They had steeled themselves for it. Yet the terse finality of the notification, when it finally arrived three years after *The Kingdom* had started publication, left them stunned and devastated: "You are hereby notified of your excommunication from the Church of Jesus Christ of Latter-day Saints. . . . The reason for your Excommunication is Apostasy and engaging in activities contrary to the best interests of the Church. Your name has been removed from the records."

Removed from the records! Generations of dedication erased with that one sepulchral sentence from the Bishopric. The door had been closed on them. Not just the door to the great protective womb which the Church embodied, but to the Celestial Kingdom and to all the mystical bonds that lay beyond. Membership in the Church meant belonging to an extended family. There would always be a helping hand, a brother or a sister there in times of ill health, a quick handout, no questions asked, in times of financial distress. Now the door had been slammed. They were outside.

After the excommunication came other sure signs that the screws were being tightened. They were little signals, at first sporadic, but in recent months, Hiram noted, they had begun to form a clear pattern. Their printer suddenly notified them of a major increase in prices. Another competitive printer declined to accept their business. Their paper supplier also decided that he would have to charge a higher price. Booksellers and owners of magazine stands, who for years had sold their magazine across the counter, suddenly were phoning to say they wouldn't be able to handle it anymore. They declined to state their reasons. They didn't need to.

The trusted sources they had cultivated, that small coterie of informants within the Church administration, also seemed to be growing increasingly skittish. Most of them were low-level employees—clerks and librarians and administrative assistants—people with access to key documents and with the dogged determination to smuggle them to the Cobbs. But now that determination seemed to be wilting beneath some unspoken fear.

Hiram had not confessed his growing alarm to Gussie, nor had he told her they were two months behind on their rent and lagging on other payments as well. Gussie, he knew, was a stalwart, level-headed woman. Behind those marvelous, soft-brown eyes, that gracious smile, lay a stubborn will, but there were limits to anyone's perseverance. He had managed to protect her over the years from some of these harassments, since their arrangement called for Gussie to focus on writing, while Hiram attended to the historic research and to running their personal financial affairs. There was no reason, after all, for his wife to be troubled with the nagging bill collectors. As it was, Gussie blamed herself totally for their "fall from grace." Her problems at the university, her defiance of her accusers, had destroyed her own teaching career, and inadvertently and tragically, it had ruined his career as well. Gussie's knowledge of that fact, Hiram knew, caused her great torment. In the early years he heard her soft sobs at night, long after she thought him asleep. He knew she wept for them both. So often, in those days, Hiram had tried to ease her pain. He had cradled her head in his arms, and told her that his love was as strong as ever. The decisions they had made had been shared, he had reminded her. They had followed an arduous path but they had followed it together.

But now the Church was tightening the screws on him once more; that had become clear, and he had to do something about it. Yes, the Church of Jesus Christ of Latter-day Saints had awesome resources when the brethren decided to get tough.

This morning's escapade was yet another example, however trivial, of the little pressures and inconveniences. In order to receive a simple phone call it was necessary for him to drive ten minutes from his home to a pay phone located at the back of a Laundromat. It seemed like a scene from a spy novel, but the man he needed to talk to, Turner Mead, had been quite insistent. He and Mead had often talked in times past, but a month ago Mead had calmly informed him in that clipped English accent of his that, in the future, they would have to use a prearranged public telephone away from Hiram's residence. Hiram had demanded to know the reason for these arrangements, but Mead had simply changed the subject and Hiram knew that he had, of course, supplied the answer. Mead felt Hiram's phone was tapped and, if that's what he believed, it was surely true. As the head of the Church's Department of Public Communications, Turner Mead was hardly an ally of Hiram's, but at the same time there was a candor, a directness, to this tall, rather diffident Englishman which Hiram found appealing. If there was a story to be checked or a fact to be verified, Turner Mead would respond immediately or else reply, in that crisply cheerful way of his, "Hiram, I don't want to answer that question, and if you force me to answer, I'll have to tell you a lie." That had been the reply he had given, for example, when Hiram had asked him to confirm the present-day existence of the fabled Council of Fifty—once the Church's secret ruling body. Hiram, of course, had understood Turner's evasive reply. Upon occasion, Turner would also have a question to ask of Hiram—always a discreet question, one that would compromise neither of them. Most recently, Turner had advised Hiram to contact a reporter for *Time* magazine who was trying to research an article about the far-flung but secretive media holdings of the Church. Turner had been instructed by his superiors to stonewall the reporter and that he had done. At the same time, however, by putting Hiram in touch with *Time*, Turner had seen to it that the facts got out. Turner Mead was a decent chap, after all; someday, if he kept reading *The Kingdom*, he might even open his eyes to the realities around him and learn to love the Church for the true verities it embodied.

At exactly 11:00 A.M. the pay telephone behind Moakley's Laundromat started ringing and Hiram, huddled against the cold in his car, scrambled into the booth to answer it.

"Hello?"

"Good morning, Hiram. I gather you wanted to get in touch with me. What can I do for you?"

As usual, Mead was brisk and to the point. "I wanted to see if we could strike a bargain," Hiram said, his tone tentative. "I guess that's the best way to put it."

"What sort of bargain?"

"I heard the news of Dana Sloat's appointment this morning. I imagine that has raised a few eyebrows around your shop."

There was a pause on the other end of the line. "Some of us at Church Headquarters were rather surprised, Hiram. Let's leave it at that."

"I would think so. Sloat has always been an outsider—a very secretive man."

"At the risk of sounding rude, Hiram, this is a busy morning for me. I take it you had something else in mind besides Sloat's appointment."

"I have some information about Sloat—information that might have eluded the General Authorities."

"I see. And that, I assume, is where the 'bargain' comes in. You did say you wanted to 'strike a bargain.' "

"That's correct, Mr. Mead."

"This is really quite unlike you, Hiram. You and I have talked many times. You never struck me as a negotiator."

"I feel awkward about all this, very awkward, indeed. But times are very hard for my wife and me. My suppliers are suddenly raising their prices, sales outlets are drying up. The Church is bringing a great deal of pressure to bear."

"I'm sorry to hear that," Turner Mead said. "I certainly do not agree with what you write, Hiram, but you are perfectly within your rights in publishing it."

"I need your help, Mr. Mead. I know you have some staunch friends and allies in the hierarchy. If you really believe I have a right to stay in business I need you to call off the wolves."

There was another pause. "I see."

"I don't expect any miracles. I just want some of the pressure taken off me. You understand?"

"I will look into it, Hiram. These things must be handled delicately and patiently."

"I appreciate that. And I also appreciate your help."

"I can't promise anything. . . ."

"I appreciate it nonetheless."

"Very well, Hiram. It was good talking to you."

"Don't be so hasty, Mr. Mead. I said I was prepared to offer a bargain. I haven't lived up to my end as yet."

"You don't need to make deals with me, Hiram. What you asked of me is reasonable enough."

"No, I still owe you the information. I think it will provide some insight into the problems you'll be facing with your new First Counselor."

"Exactly what are you getting at?"

"I've been working on a special piece about the Fundamentalist Mormon cults in Utah and Arizona, Mr. Mead. In doing my research I came upon a young man who recently terminated his stay at a place called New Nauvoo. Perhaps you know it. It's a very secretive polygamous colony just over the Arizona border."

"I've heard of it. That's all."

"They have quite a thriving commune down there. Quite affluent for one of those sects."

"What about it, Hiram?"

"This young man I mentioned—he told me that the principal leader of New Nauvoo—the local guru, you might say—is a young man named Dawson Sloat. Name ring a bell?"

Turner Mead was silent. "It does, indeed," he replied at last.

Hiram could detect the tinge of excitement in that always cool facade. He continued: "All the newspaper pieces about Dana Sloat, all the official biographies, say that he has one son and one daughter—and that the son is a businessman in Australia. That's always been the story."

"So it has." Yes, the excitement was still there, along with a mounting impatience.

"Well, I wanted you to know the real facts, Mr. Mead. I don't want it to sound like I'm trying to blackmail anybody. Sloat has a right to his privacy just like anyone else. But the fact that he would have such a close family tie to one of these polygamous cults—that tells something about the man, Mr. Mead. So does the fact that he would so carefully conceal it."

There was silence at the other end of the line. "Hello . . . are you still there? . . ."

"I'm here."

"You had me worried."

"Hiram, are you aware of the other . . . well, shall we say discrepancies that have turned up in Brother Sloat's background? His file at Little Cottonwood has been tampered with."

Now it was Hiram who felt a sudden agitation. "His genealogical records? . . ."

"That's correct. I am told certain 'adjustments' have been made."

"But I would assume there's another file on Sloat. The one in the Confidential Section, as you people like to call it. The room of Saintly Secrets."

"Yes, the Confidential Section. Since he's not a General Authority, I doubt if Sloat even knows of the existence of that file."

"I could do some investigating, Mr. Mead. I have access."

"I was hoping you'd say that, Hiram. You do have the most remarkable sources."

"I'm just a humble accountant. I'm not a spook."

"Of course," Mead said, his voice heavy with irony.

"Have you had a look at his file?"

"No, I haven't. Sloat would surely learn of it."

"So perhaps I should arrange for it."

"That would be greatly appreciated, Hiram. As you said before, it would be helpful to gain some further insight into this man."

"He's a strange one, Mr. Mead. A real throwback to the days of Joseph Smith. The kind who thinks the millenium is at hand— the Kingdom can simply be established with the wave of a wand."

"No political speeches, please, Hiram."

"Sorry. But we do have a bargain, then, do we not?"

"Yes, we have a bargain."

"Then I'll be signing off."

"One further thing, Hiram. You said you were working on a story about the polygamous cults. When were you planning to publish it?"

"Next issue."

"I wish you'd wait, Hiram. Hold off for a while."

Hiram realized he was shuddering. It was freezing in the booth. He stomped his feet on the cement floor to regain circulation.

"Anything wrong, Hiram?"

"I am freezing to death in this phone booth."

"Terribly sorry for the discomfort. I won't keep you any longer."

"Look, Mr. Mead. My piece on the cults—it's a very good story.

It will sell a lot of copies. People always love to read about polygamists."

"Hold it for a while, Hiram. These are peculiar times."

"Is that a warning?"

"No, just a word of advice from an old fellow newsman. You asked me to help you, right? Well, I think this is a time for prudence. For caution, if you will. Emotions run very high on the issue of polygamy. You and I both know these colonies are proliferating faster than anyone wants to admit. There's much more alarm about these defections, Hiram, than about the so-called liberals who leave the Church. The liberals weren't tithe-paying Church members to begin with. But the new Fundamentalists—these are the loyalists, Hiram. They are the proselytizing Saints who are out there doing the Lord's work."

"That's why I've been working on the story."

"That's also why you should save it, Hiram. Save it for tranquil times."

Hiram considered his response. "I think what you're telling me is that you sense, as I do, that this Sloat is a rough customer. Is that it?"

"I think we've said all we need to say. Good luck, Hiram. Go and get warm."

As he made his way to his car, exercising his arms to restore circulation, Hiram continued to ponder Mead's warnings. Words like these seemed out of character coming from someone of his stature; they ought not to be dismissed too quickly. He was poised to open the door to his Toyota when he noticed the pickup truck parked nearby, its driver, a big hulking man in overalls, dozing at the wheel. Hiram peered at the truck warily. There was something peculiar about it, something that seemed too anonymous, too ordinary. Could it be, he wondered, that a tail had been put on him? Had it really come to that?

His paranoia was getting out of hand, Hiram told himself as he unlocked his car and climbed behind the wheel. He just couldn't let himself think these things.

Yet as he started up the street, darting between two cars, Hiram thought for one fleeting moment that he caught a glimpse of the anonymous pickup in his rearview mirror. At least it looked like the same truck—there were so many in a city as big as Salt Lake.

TURNER Mead stood before the big clock, his eyes tracing the second hand as it edged slowly, ineluctably around the dial. One last turn, he told himself, rubbing his hands together and feeling the perspiration on his palms. Standing in the corridor outside the television control booth, he could see the taut faces of the director and his three aides, their eyes flicking nervously from the red and green lights on the big control panel to the figures below on the floor of the Tabernacle, who were poised tensely to receive their signal. Seconds from now the ceremony would begin.

A hush had fallen over the Tabernacle, whose vast recesses only moments earlier had resonated with the sound of ten thousand nervous, expectant voices. They were all out there, the faithful, seated sentrylike, row upon row on the stiff wooden pews, stretching so far back across the enormous, domed building that they merged into a distant tapestry of somber hues. In their minds, Turner knew, this was an occasion of great historic import, the climactic moment in the Sesquicentennial Celebration of their Church. The stalwart institution which had been established one hundred and fifty years earlier had set the pattern for an entire society, with unique values, customs and beliefs. A people had been "set apart." And many seated below, possibly most of them, Turner realized, could trace their antecedents directly to those who were there in those early years of ferment. Few would have believed, back then, that the Mormon people could have survived—indeed prospered; that among all religions in the twentieth century, only Mormonism and Islam would continue to grow and flourish. And yet here they all were, awaiting the voices of their great choir to proclaim the start of the festivities. The three hundred fifty members of the Mormon Tabernacle Choir sat facing them from their own raised pews at the front of the audito-

66

rium, the men clad in their dark blue suits, the women in dresses of pale blue, their eyes riveted on their conductor who stood before them, baton raised expectantly as he awaited his signal from the control booth. Behind the choir loomed the huge gold-hued organ pipes which soared from floor to ceiling, enclosed at their summit in intricately carved mahogany encasements.

How often in the past had this precise moment been reenacted, Turner thought—the choir prepared to sing, the faithful arrayed before them, the august leaders of the Church seated between them in the rose-upholstered front pews. He could picture Brigham Young roaring his exhortations from the pulpit, fierce eyes staring reproachfully at his followers. Yes, old Brigham, with his flair for theatrics, would have delighted in today's spectacle —this seemingly tradition-bent observance transformed into an international media event. The surface clues of an electronic presence had been carefully kept to a minimum. Two screens had been hung from the ceiling to carry the image of Samuel Bryce, the Prophet, who would broadcast live from the farmhouse in Fayette, New York. Three television cameras were unobtrusively situated in the Tabernacle to capture the choir and the introductory messages and to pan across the imposing vastness of the assemblage. Yet deftly concealed beneath and behind the simple, century-old wooden facades of this venerable building were all the complex support systems. Technicians stood by in the mixing and switching rooms to interconnect the big, eerie-looking silver dish outside, which looked as though it had just fallen from the heavens, with the Westar satellite hovering over the Pacific and the Satcom I at the eastern edge of the continent. Huddled in the ancient catacombs beneath the Tabernacle were teams of translators who were instantaneously transmitting the Prophet's words into Navaho, Cantonese and fourteen other languages.

There was something metaphorically appropriate about all this, Turner thought: a frail, elderly man standing in a primitive one-room farmhouse in New York State and a choir poised to sing in a splendid old Tabernacle in Utah, whose ancient domed roof had been put together with wooden tholepins and leather thongs, all conjoined and interconnected by hundreds of millions of dollars in electronic magic. These odd juxtapositions, Turner sensed, were fitting symbols of the modern Church as he knew it, clinging

tenaciously to its ideas and customs of old, a theology held together by thongs and tholepins, yet selling salvation with space-
age zeal.

Suddenly the Great Hall was throbbing with sound as the Tabernacle organ announced its triumphant opening chord, and the
choir began to sing, heads raised, faces radiant, and Turner felt
that tingle he always felt whenever he heard this awesome confluence of sound. Looking to the rows of Church leaders clustered at
the front of the Tabernacle, he could sense they, too, were stirred,
their lined, aged faces flushed with excitement. At the front sat
the Council of the Twelve, the ruling Apostles of the Church,
clad in blue suits, white shirts and dark ties, most of them white-
maned and elderly, squinting through black-rimmed spectacles,
some wearing hearing aids. Those who were scheduled to speak
also wore tiny portable amplifiers to carry their thin voices over
the microphones. At the center of the Council sat Isaac Sorenson,
newly designated President of the Twelve as the result of Bryce's
ascension, and Dana Sloat, First Counselor to the President of the
Church. Facing them in the front pews were the dozens and dozens of "good soldiers," the men who ran the vast mechanisms of
the Church, spiritual and temporal, who devoted their lives to its
service. In the first rows were the senior functionaries comprising
the Quorum of the Seventy, many of whose members had specific
responsibilities governing finance, missionary work, Church publications or welfare. Scattered among them were others representing the esteemed rank of General Authority, such as the Church
Patriarch and the Presiding Bishopric. And behind all these sat
still others of the Church elite—the Stake Presidents, Regional
Representatives and Bishops, and officials of the women's organizations such as the Relief Society and the Primary Association,
which runs religious training for young LDS children. Across
these ranks of officialdom, row upon row, most of these faces, too,
were elderly, hair white, bodies bent with age, reflecting the traditions of seniority to which the Church had always clung. But
here and there Turner could spot the younger ones, whom the
Church was grooming for higher office, many of them executives
in insurance or banking: somber young men with earnest faces,
determined jaws, close-cropped hair, and attired in the dark suits
of their elders. In keeping with tradition, Turner knew, the

Church would see to it that their business careers would prosper as their service to Zion continued to expand. They were the favored few; over a period of a lifetime, they would take care of the Church and the Church would take care of them, as it had their forebears.

The opening hymn had concluded and Ogden Spencer, oldest of the Twelve Apostles, uttered an opening prayer for President Woodleigh, who had passed on seven days before. Heads were bowed in the Tabernacle. When they all looked up again, it was Isaac Sorenson who was standing at the rostrum. Though now in his late seventies and slowed by arthritis, the feisty, bantam-sized Sorenson, with his flowing white hair, still retained the same imperious presence he had exercised during his younger years when he ruled over Utah's largest utility company. Though Sorenson represented the most conservative—indeed some felt reactionary —forces within the hierarchy, Church leaders, Turner observed, instinctively turned to him for guidance in decisive moments.

Now Sorenson surveyed the throng before him and the television cameras on either side. His severe blue eyes resided under bushy white eyebrows and his face had a vibrant glow.

"The eyes of the entire Christian world are upon us today," Sorenson began, his deep voice rumbling across the vast hall like distant thunder. "My heart is filled with gratitude for the opportunity to be here on this, the birthday of our Church. The Church of Jesus Christ of Latter-day Saints is, as Daniel prophesied, not just another human institution. It is a spiritual Kingdom, begun through the intervention of God and flourishing today, in a troubled world of secularism, because of the intervention of God.

"The Church has survived exile from four states, an extermination order from a governor, the execution of its Prophet, disenfranchisement and confiscation by the federal government and continuous persecution of its leadership and members. And yet it continues to gain strength, a refuge of spirituality, spreading the Gospel, doing the work of salvation, serving the Savior. Our victory comes in accomplishing the work of God, as His chosen instrumentality. . . ."

I hope the old man doesn't get carried away, Turner Mead told himself, as he looked down upon the scene now from the top of the balcony. He had heard these rhetorical flourishes from Sorenson many times before. Sorenson was a man who enjoyed sermonizing; he could hold forth for hours at a time, and had done so at many Church conferences. But this was not the time—not with millions of Mormons and non-Mormons alike watching around the world on television, not with Samuel Bryce, the new Prophet standing by in the little restored farmhouse in Fayette to issue his "Proclamation to the Nations." It was in this one-room log cabin where, on April 6, 1830, Joseph Smith, first President of the Church, had gathered with five followers to formally establish his new religious crusade. Though the Mormons, driven by persecution, soon fled New York for Ohio, Missouri, Illinois and ultimately Salt Lake City, they continued to regard Fayette and its surrounding towns as their birthplace, and had spent tens of millions to restore the log cabin, a chapel and other buildings in the area.

And now, mercifully, Sorenson had concluded his remarks and the image of President Bryce materialized on the two broad screens at the front of the Tabernacle. He stood at a rostrum mounted on a rough wooden table in the middle of the room. As the camera pulled back, one could see the crude walls of the restored log cabin and its simple, primitive furnishings. Though he knew Bryce to be a frail, even fragile man, Turner Mead marveled at how splendid he looked now, chin high, his eyes clear and determined, peering out from behind his rimless spectacles with a commanding dignity. He looked, indeed, like their Prophet; the leader of the faithful. During the previous week Turner had seen him briefly on two occasions, and had thought him uncertain in his new role, his manner tentative. Now that had changed.

"My dear Brothers and Sisters," the President said, "I cannot describe to you how deeply moved I am to be standing here today where the Prophet Joseph Smith stood one hundred and fifty years ago. Last night I flew here from Salt Lake City, covering in a matter of half a dozen hours a journey which our forebears painfully traveled over many months as they searched for a place where they could worship God according to the dictates of their conscience. . . ."

Yes, Turner thought, he is coming across excellently. The whole spectacle is working as he hoped it would. He could see the newsmen in the first row of the balcony, scribbling intently on their pads. After all his years with the media as a reporter, editor and finally as the Director of Public Communications for the Church, Turner knew how to read the newsmen, knew when they were listless and when their attention was caught. Today he could tell from their glances and gestures that they were intrigued by the new leader of the Church, and fascinated, as well, by the new First Counselor who sat impassively in the first pew, his uncommonly long legs folded before him.

Studying Sloat now, Turner wondered whether the newsmen, with their ever-alert instincts, shared his uneasiness about this rod of a man, so tall as to be almost ungainly, with his taut, lean face and spare frame, not an ounce of extra flesh anywhere, not a jowl or sag, eyes narrow, lips thin, dark hair impeccably groomed. Sloat had what the military liked to call a "command presence," cultivating it carefully, projecting it deftly, every word and motion guarded, every gesture calculated for maximum effect. Turner wondered whether he was even listening to the President's speech, or whether, more probably, his mind was focused on his own plans for the Church, his own grand design. Surely Sloat had to be coveting the surprise that the formal announcement of his appointment, only that morning, had generated, the break with precedent that it represented. Samuel Bryce had reached outside the inner circle for his closest aide. He had selected his chief administrator on the basis of ability, not seniority. And looking at Sloat now, Turner Mead sensed how deeply he must be reveling in that unique tribute. Sloat had always prided himself in being a "Mormon Maverick." He had built his business empire without help and nurture from the LDS establishment. And now the very establishment that had always been so unresponsive was beckoning him into its very vortex of power.

Turner saw Isaac Sorenson listening attentively, his face impassive, like a tough little bulldog heeling for its master. Sorenson craved power more than anyone, Turner knew, yet now his ascendancy must await the death of the man addressing them all. What a paradox that it was Samuel Bryce, the benign moderate, not Sorenson who had tapped Dana Sloat for power. Even Sorenson would have been wary about that bold a step. Was that, indeed, one hidden reason for Bryce's move? Was Bryce, Turner wondered, seeking to neutralize Sorenson's ever-encroaching authority? The inner politics of the hierarchy were always murky, even to someone as informed and insightful as Turner Mead.

Samuel Bryce was reading his "Proclamation to the Nations" now, elaborating the enormous gains of the Church, the thirty percent increase in U.S. membership over the last five years, the ninety-three percent increase in South America, the ninety-eight percent increase in Mexico, the two hundred thousand new converts worldwide this year alone. Turner knew the facts well; he had helped prepare the speech. The expansion Bryce was enunciating was awesome by any standards. The Church would build seven grandiose new Temples this year, bringing the total to thirty-one around the world, and would also start construction of seven hundred new chapels. By the year 2030, the Church, at its current rate of growth, would encompass some fifty million members and would be the predominant religion in many countries of the world.

Bryce was calmly announcing these gains, not in the accents of a megalomaniacal evangelist, but as a benign ecclesiastic, his manner one of innocence, like an elderly bishop enunciating doctrine at Sunday school. As he talked, he clasped the Bible one moment, the Book of Mormon moments later, stressing the all-encompassing breadth of the Church and the universality of its aspirations.

"We solemnly affirm that our Church is in fact a restoration of the Church established by the Son of God when, in mortality, He organized His work upon the earth. We declare that the Book of Mormon was brought forth by the gift and power of God and that it stands beside the Bible as another witness of Jesus the Savior. It is His Kingdom we are building. . . ."

Turner's gaze was surveying the crowd, searching for the slight figure of Dalton Evans, and he found him now, seated inconspicuously in the fourth row among the General Authorities. It was typical of this man to consign himself so quickly to a relatively anonymous position. Had he wanted, Dalton Evans could have sat with the Apostles. They would gladly have honored him with that status. With all his benevolent modesty, Turner wondered what his feelings were, seeing Dana Sloat seated in the honored place which, for so many years, had belonged to him. If there was anyone in this vast hall whose mind could encompass this period of great change and who could grasp the curious interdependency that existed between Bryce and Sloat, it was Evans. And if there was anyone who had the power to save them all from the dangers that lay ahead, that power, too, resided with this slight, gray-faced man, if only he still had the will and the strength to utilize it.

Turner drew a deep breath and rubbed his hands together once more. It was all going so splendidly today—all of it. Yes, it was going just as the brethren had prayed it would.

☐ The hall was emptying quickly, the elders of the Church filing out through the stage exits, exchanging words of satisfaction and approval about the morning's convocation. The television cameras had blinked off, the control booths were deserted. Turner had talked briefly with several of the newsmen, who were rushing off to write their stories. Strolling across the floor of the Tabernacle, he spotted Dalton Evans talking with a young reporter from the Church-owned *Deseret News.* Evans' gaze caught Turner now, and the older man gave him a signal to join them. Turner recognized the reporter as Ray Cutler, an ambitious young man whom Turner distrusted.

"Here's the man you should be directing those questions to," Dalton Evans told Cutler, as Turner joined them.

Cutler gave Turner a frustrated glance, then turned his attention back to Dalton Evans. "It's just, sir, that the news of the Sloat appointment came as a real surprise. We wanted a comment . . ."

"The formal release will be at your office by the time you get there," Turner said. "It shoud cover all your questions."

"I just wanted Mr. Evans' reaction to the Sloat appointment. Especially since the First Counselor has always been drawn from among the General Authorities. . . ."

"There is nothing in Church doctrine that suggests the First Counselor has to be selected from among the General Authorities," Evans said quietly.

"I don't really think this is the time for an interview, Ray," Turner said, seeing the discomfort on Evans' face. "Perhaps at some later date we can set up a formal interview."

". . . But the story's breaking today," Cutler protested.

Dalton Evans put his hand on the young man's shoulder. "I know you've got a job to do," he said, in the tone of an understanding parent, "but please respect my position as well. This is just one of those days I should keep my old mouth securely fastened."

"Ray understands," Turner said, as the young reporter, his face flushed, backed away, his notebook still clutched in his right hand.

Dalton Evans guided Turner toward the front of the Tabernacle, greeting, as he walked, a variety of friends and associates, shaking an occasional outstretched hand, nodding to one person, waving to another. They had entered a network of corridors reserved for the choir and dignitaries, as Evans, leading the way, ducked into a small empty room and eased himself into a metal chair. Seated across from him, Turner saw the patterns of weariness etched on the old man's face.

"I'm sorry I let Cutler corner you," Turner said. "I should have noticed earlier and warded him off."

"You can't be everywhere, Turner," Evans said, placing a hand over his mouth as he coughed.

"There will be other reporters looking for you about the Sloat thing," Turner said. "They'll all have questions."

The old man nodded with resignation. "I really don't want to say anything. Any quote at all would seem suspect. You understand."

"Of course I do." Turner's eyes met the old man's and he could feel the depth of his concern. There was so much he yearned to ask, and yet he hated to impose his own apprehensions on him at this time.

"Sam Bryce is really something, isn't he, Turner? There are times he seems right on top of things, like he was today. And then you talk to him a few hours later and his mind is cloudy; one sentence doesn't follow another. He's full of surprises. Like this Sloat thing. . . ."

"Did you have any advance warning of the appointment?"

"We had a talk some weeks ago, after President Woodleigh started fading. I told Bryce it was my desire to retire and I could see an ambiguity in his reaction. He tried to persuade me to change my mind, but I knew something was going on in his mind. Then my staff informed me he was ordering a great deal of material copied and sent to Sloat. Something was in the wind."

Turner started to say something, then hesitated.

"Say it, Turner. You don't have to hold back with me," Evans prodded.

"Dana Sloat can't do your job—not in a million years. He doesn't have the temperament or the judgment or the knowledge. The Church isn't just another corporate conglomerate; it can't be run like one."

Dalton Evans nodded his head ruefully and coughed again. "There are times, my boy, when I regret ever having left the practice of medicine. I'm only seventy-two years old, Turner. If I hadn't given up my practice for the Church twenty-two years ago, I would still be your friendly old family doctor whom you'd call if you couldn't reach a younger man. At least I wouldn't have to worry about the Dana Sloats of the world. I wouldn't find myself waking up in the middle of the night and thinking about our brothers out there, all those millions of good souls who believe in their Church and in its leaders."

Evans coughed again. "You know the real problem as well as I, Turner. The Mormon people do as they're told to do. They think as they're told to think. We've all been brought up that way. Heber Kimball laid it on the line right here in this Tabernacle. 'Brigham Young is our governor and our dictator as well. We do as he tells us to do.' Well, that's all fine and good, Turner—it explains why we've always accomplished so much. But it also explains why we're so vulnerable."

Turner said nothing. He did not know what to say. Dalton Evans was a very reserved man—that he well knew. It was rare that he would unburden himself, as he was now doing. Turner was among his few confidants, perhaps his only one. Given their age difference of thirty-three years, there was a father-son aspect to their relationship. Turner had first met Dalton Evans when he was seventeen years old and had just arrived in the United States from London to attend Brigham Young University. Turner's father, Kendall Mead, had, like Dalton Evans, been a doctor and a Mormon; Kendall Mead had met Evans at an LDS conference and they had become lifelong friends. Though Turner lived in a dorm

at BYU, Dalton Evans' house was a second home for him. He
spent many weekends and vacations there and learned to love
this gentle, thoughtful man, and to respect the scope of his intellect. That year Evans interrupted his medical career to accept a
calling to the Quorum of the Seventy, and was immediately
placed on key policy committees. Shortly after being called to the
Council of the Twelve, Evans had phoned Turner and asked him
to come by for a chat. Turner had been working as city editor of
the *Deseret News* at the time, but Evans soon changed all that.
The position of Director of Public Communications was about to
become vacant, he told him. Perhaps Turner would like to fill it.
It was an opportunity to serve the Church. It also was an opportunity to work with Evans, whose responsibilities included this
area. Besides, Evans said with a smile, the pay was better than
that from his newspaper job. But there was another reason he'd
offered him the job, Turner knew. Turner's wife had developed
cancer, a disease which, two years later, was to take her life.
Evans could see the depth of the shock in Turner; perhaps a new
job, with all its incumbent distractions, would help. The change
had helped him—had saved him, perhaps.

"I know the question you really want to ask me," Dalton Evans
said, his gaze on Turner now, "but I do not know the answer.
Dana Sloat has developed a game plan, presumably with Sam
Bryce's advice and consent. For the past two months Sloat's been
working on it. But as you know, we are dealing with an obsessively secretive man. I know some of the ideas he has in mind,
but only some of them."

"Dalton, there are certain things I have learned about Sloat—
disquieting things. By tomorrow night I hope I will be able to fill
you in."

Evans listened intently but said nothing.

"Some things that Sloat has told us do not square with the
facts," Turner continued. "Certain things about his family, his
background."

"That would fit the pattern, wouldn't it?"

"Suppose we learn the worst?" Turner asked, as they started
walking back toward the Tabernacle stairway. "Suppose Sloat's
policies and beliefs are totally inimical to everything we believe
in, to everything the Church stands for? What then? What can be

done? The LDS Church is not like the government of the United States. There are no checks and balances."

Evans took several steps as he pondered the question, then halted and turned to Turner. "The Church is a complex mechanism, Turner, my boy," he said softly. "There are many subtleties to its functioning which may elude the casual observer."

"What are you telling me, Dalton?"

"My father used to say, 'It takes time to ruin the world. It's too big a job for one man.' He had a point there, Turner."

Turner nodded grimly.

"Cheer up, Turner," Dalton Evans said. "After all, we've survived one hundred fifty years, haven't we?"

THE meeting was about twenty minutes old when Eliza Hastings realized she had made a tactical mistake. She had called the women together to deliberate what she considered to be a simple, straightforward point: whether to postpone tomorrow night's conference out of respect for the late President Woodleigh. Eliza had invited the four women who were the principal organizers of the conference to come to her house at 6:00 P.M. to consider the question, but when fourteen appeared, Eliza realized the issue was more complex than she had anticipated. And when discussion about possible postponement began to spill over into an emotional debate, it briefly occurred to Eliza that perhaps she should have been more arbitrary and simply canceled the conference on her own.

Her instincts told her it was the right thing to do. The late Prophet deserved his period of respect. Though the women's conference had been planned three months earlier, it was only that morning that Bill Chadwick, assistant to President Bryce, as he had been to President Woodleigh before him, had phoned to "suggest" that a postponement might be a good idea. Chadwick was not ordering Eliza to cancel the conference; that was not his style. A hearty, convivial man, Chadwick exchanged gossip with Eliza for a few moments and then said nonchalantly, "By the way, Eliza, I get the feeling the brethren might be more comfortable if this conference tomorrow could be moved back awhile. It's barely been a week since we lost our dear Prophet, and our new President is just settling in. Besides, so many of our distinguished brethren from around the country are in Salt Lake for the anniversary. It's just an awkard time, don't you agree, Sister?"

And indeed Eliza *did* understand. She understood that the prospect of two hundred and fifty Mormon women assembling under one roof to discuss their mutual concerns was distressing to some

78

individuals in the hierarchy, possibly to Samuel Bryce or even more probably to Dana Sloat, so trusty old Bill Chadwick was passing the word. It didn't surprise Eliza at all. When word of the meeting had first been dropped, her sophisticated antennae had picked up a distinct uneasiness among the brethren. To those who inquired, she had carefully explained the benign purposes of the convocation—it was to be an informal coming-together, not an Equal Rights Amendment rally—but the uneasiness remained nonetheless. And so, spurred by the Chadwick call, she decided to summon the conference leaders to weigh the alternatives. There would still be time to call off most of the women before they arrived in Salt Lake, and tell them of the postponement. They would be sympathetic.

But Eliza had miscalculated the mood of the conference organizers. It was Grace Turley who lit the spark tonight, and that surprised Eliza as well. A stout, round-faced woman, her steel-gray hair combed in a semibouffant, Grace was the wife of an extremely wealthy building contractor, and until recently had focused her attention on raising her seven children rather than on Church causes. Tonight she spoke in a high, almost girlish voice, her tone unsteady but her words emotional. "We were all planning to meet tomorrow to talk about our mutual problems and needs, but now we are told it would be wise to cancel that meeting, that in doing so we would be showing our respect for the brethren. That may very well be true, but how about our respect for our sisters? Our discussion has already been postponed too long—one hundred and fifty years too long. As a result many of our sisters are lost and confused. We whisper about their secret dependence on tranquilizers and alcohol, and yet we do nothing. We pretend we have a perfect society, that we, as Mormon women, share none of the problems of our Gentile friends. And yet privately we know the truth! Eliza, with all respect, I personally believe we should go forward with our conference. Those we offend would be our enemies anyway."

Eliza watched as Grace Turley flushed, clearly surprised by the intensity of her own feelings, and then seated herself on the sofa, folding her hands to stop them from shaking. There was silence, and Eliza could sense the palpable tension settle over her living room which already was becoming warm from the fourteen visitors crammed together on the sofas and chairs. Grace Turley's remarks had a decidedly feminist ring to them, yet Eliza, having known this shy, soft-spoken woman for many years, knew she'd been at best indifferent to the feminist cause and remained totally aloof from the earlier battles over the ERA. Yet here she was, outraged that the problems of her sisters might be shunted aside as a result of the processes of hierarchical succession.

Eliza looked around at the women seated in her living room. They were an oddly diverse group in terms of age and appearance, she thought, yet there was an undefinable congruence of style, a distinct racial bond. Most of the women were blond, with sharp Nordic features. Most were on the heavy side. All were well groomed and attractively dressed, though Eliza knew that, by the standards of New York or Los Angeles, they would be considered dowdy. Their tastes reflected Penney's, not Halston, and their hair was styled in the bouffant or bangs look of an earlier era. Yet with all their foibles, Eliza sensed a compassion in these women, a concern and loyalty, that she did not find among those she encountered in her travels. Their faces reflected the character and sacrifice of the frontier—the look of women capable of building a new Kingdom.

"I am very moved by Grace's words," Eliza said, breaking the silence that had fallen over the room. "And I share her feeling that our problems have been shunted aside too long." There was a murmur of approval in the room.

"I must also say it is always easier to issue a call to arms than a call for restraint, yet I feel it is restraint that is required at this moment. I am not talking about canceling our conference, but simply postponing. It basically comes down to a question of timing. Mormons have learned the hard way to be realists—Mormon women especially. And whenever more than five Mormon women get together in a room to discuss their common concerns, there is an aura of suspicion. This is particularly true at this moment. We have a new President, who is only now assuming the duties of his office. Some of you may not even be aware that we also have a new First Counselor, Dana Sloat. Brother Sloat is a conservative, if not a Fundamentalist, on Church affairs and also on women's rights. I would also remind you that some of our General Authorities still carry within them a deep anger from the debates on the

Equal Rights Amendment two years ago. They are old men and their wounds heal slowly.

"What I am saying is that in this interim period my instincts tell me that the prudent course would be to avoid holding a conference where inevitably some things may be said that could be taken out of context, things that could cause unnecessary alarm during this sensitive period. I know these words may strike you as excessively cautious, even cowardly perhaps, but I feel impelled to speak them nonetheless."

Eliza stopped to sip from a glass of fruit juice, and she saw the eyes of Grace Turley peering at her intently, boring into her. And she saw the expressions of the other women, restless and distressed. And for the first time she understood the magnitude of their impatience.

"Eliza." Eliza recognized the distinctively sonorous voice of Helen Taylor, a tall, articulate woman whose husband taught economics at the University of Utah. Helen Taylor was the only one among the conference organizers who had been a proponent of the ERA, though had done so in a quiet, tactful way so as not to incur excommunication. "Eliza dear, I respect your candor and sense of reality," Helen Taylor said, smiling warmly in Eliza's direction. "Many women like to give speeches and listen to the sound of their own voices, but our dear Eliza knows how to get things done, and I have always admired her for it. In this case, however, I think our caution will work against us. In my judgment, we must go ahead with the conference at this time for the very reasons you suggest we delay it. We have new leadership in the Church; very well, let's inform the new leadership about our expectations and our concern. You may think I've blown my cork, Eliza, but I think we should seize this opportunity and expand the agenda of the conference. Our objective was to have informal dialogue about the problems confronting our sisters and to establish a chain of 'sisterhoods' to provide guidance and counseling. I think our agenda should go further. Why shouldn't we be able to discuss the question of electing our own officers in the Relief Society? Why should we be the only women's church auxiliary in the world whose leaders are appointed by men? Or the question of women achieving the priesthood—another of the great silent issues no one can mention in public." Two of the women in the room started to clap, then placed their hands in their laps again, embarrassed by their outburst.

Undistracted, Helen Taylor forged ahead, her right hand jabbing the air for emphasis. "I think it's time to ask the big questions we have always been afraid to ask. The unmentionables. Since the lay priesthood of our Church effectively includes every single Mormon man, why does it exclude every single Mormon woman? Why is divine revelation the exclusive province of men, not women? If a woman does not marry, why is she denied full status in the Celestial Kingdom? If a woman divorces, why does she forfeit her place in the Celestial Kingdom while the children of that union remain sealed to their father? If a man remarries, why does he regain his place in the eternal world, but not his wife? Why is there still a stigma if a woman pursues a career and hires a housekeeper to help with the chores? Why must we all have one child after another, irrespective of our emotional needs, simply because our beloved Prophet believes there are spirits waiting for a human shell—they have waited through the ages, why can't they wait a little longer? I still vividly remember when my family moved to a new neighborhood eight years ago, our new Bishop came to see us and he asked me very critically, 'Why is it you have only three children, Sister Taylor?' and I felt like saying, 'Because I only feel capable of dealing with three children—why is it any business of yours?' But fortunately, my husband broke in and said, 'Bishop, we want to have many more children—we keep trying all the time, night and day.' And the Bishop became very embarrassed and changed the subject."

There were smiles and nods of assent around the room.

"May I interrupt you, Helen?" The voice belonged to Amelia Stubbs, a tiny, ruddy-faced woman with chubby cheeks, whose light brown hair was held back in a tight bun. Surprised by the intrusion, Helen Taylor continued to stand as Amelia started talking, blurting out her words in a sudden stream. "I really agree with what you are saying, Helen. I really do. One of the things I wanted to raise at the conference ties into what you are saying."

Amelia, who had recently returned from New Zealand where her husband had served as Mission President, dug into her bulging purse to bring forth a blue-covered report. "Six months ago a research team consisting of a psychiatrist and a sociologist concluded a study of our LDS women. The study had been financed with federal grants, but after seeing the findings the brethren have deliberately suppressed it." Amelia started to thumb through the pages of the report, then gave up in confusion. "Let me tell you some of the things they found. They found that LDS women have a higher incidence of depression, chronic headaches and other psychosomatic illnesses than women in other faiths. Our suicide rate is rising sharply. Child abuse is rising sharply. Drug abuse is rising sharply. We have one of the highest rates of teenage pregnancies in the country. Our teenage suicide rate is far higher than in the rest of the United States. These are important findings, Sisters, and yet material like this is suppressed—it just disappears from the face of the earth. . . ."

"May I ask how you obtained the report?" Grace Turley interjected.

Amelia Stubbs's face flinched with discomfort. "It was given to me by a man named Hiram Cobb. Now I know Hiram Cobb is not a popular figure with many of you. I don't agree with most of what he writes, either, but his forebears came to Utah with Brigham Young and so did mine, and our families have known each other for six generations.

"The important thing is not where the report came from. The important thing is that it confirms what Helen has been saying, and Grace, too. I mean, we are told we must talk only about lollipops and rose gardens. Brother Brigham brought us all out here, and then he suddenly told us that women do not possess the 'light and the knowledge' that our husbands possess. He said we don't have 'power over our own passions' as men do. Those were his words. Well, I think we should start showing our light and our power, and I think tomorrow's conference should be the starting point." Amelia fell silent, remaining on her feet, fumbling with the blue-covered report still in her hands. Then she sat down quickly, dabbing the perspiration from her face with a white handkerchief.

"Bless you, Amelia. Bless you." Eyes turned toward the painfully thin woman who sat tensely at the edge of the circle. Her name was Reo Cross, and she was well known to the other women, and to Eliza especially. For four generations Reo's family had held positions in the hierarchy and Reo herself had headed the Primary Association before dropping out suddenly from Church work. There had been gossip that she'd been ill, and indeed her attractive angular face seemed drawn and there were dark circles under her eyes. "I have been listening to what you all have been saying and my mouth keeps popping open with surprise. I am surprised by what you say and surprised that you're saying things I myself feel so deeply.

"Let me tell you, when Amelia gives you those statistics they are not just abstract numbers. I was hooked on Valium and Nembutal and Tuinal. I suffered severe depression. I had a terrible nervous breakdown from which I am only now recovering. I have been living apart from my husband. I am one of those numbers Amelia's been telling you about.

"You know, one of the great ironies of our upbringing is that we were always told we would never feel alone. What a terrible falsehood. As a young woman I felt very much alone staying home with five small children while my husband was off at his Church meetings two nights a week and all day Sunday. I felt alone worrying whether I could ever become the perfect Mother of Zion I was brought up to be, whether I could make it into the Celestial Kingdom even though I didn't quilt very well and hated grinding my own flour and always felt foolish at Relief Society meetings when I had to give demonstrations on how to do one hundred practical things with a Clorox bottle. But I kept on worrying and doing all that was expected of me and trying to pretend I loved my husband even though I resented him and telling myself I would be all right if I lived the Gospel and suddenly I woke up in a hospital one morning and all the pretending was over. And I was very sad for a long time. Now I am also very angry."

Reo Cross took a deep breath and kept going: "So I just want to say 'thank you' to Amelia and Helen and Grace, and Eliza, too, because she was gracious enough to invite us all here and let us talk when she could easily have simply canceled the meeting all by herself. And I just want to tell you I sense we're all going to be okay now, all of us, provided we can help each other and be honest with each other and not keep marching along like automatons without figuring out what's best for *us*. I guess that's all I have to say."

It was Helen Taylor who started applauding, and the other

women immediately picked it up, clapping their hands excitedly. And Eliza suddenly found herself applauding as well, the sound reverberating through the quiet, sedate rooms and hallways of her home. No one had ever applauded in her home before. It was a foreign but welcome sound. The faces of her guests were glowing with enthusiasm, and that was new and welcome, too. Eliza felt a rush of pride for her sisters. The words they were saying were coming from down deep: emotions too long ignored, anger too long suppressed. How she yearned to embrace them and to join in their exuberance. Another woman was on her feet now, her face flushed, talking with animation. Eliza struggled to retain her composure, determined now, as always, to present a front of certitude and stability, but she knew, more than ever, that the old certitudes were becoming unraveled in her mind. It was fine to maintain a front, but the front was meaningless. She wondered how the other women regarded her. Remote from their concerns, perhaps; someone caught up in the hierarchy, consumed with retaining her own power rather than reaching out a hand of compassion to her sisters. Yes, that is the way they must see her. If only they knew the turmoil she had endured this week, the swelling excitement over the approaching conference, and also the gnawing fear. They were in dangerous territory, all of them. That she knew. All her instincts were alerted to it. But there was another fear as well, a fear that was different from what the others could imagine. All her life she had known where she was going, what she was doing. Her goals and ideas arrayed themselves neatly in her mind. She understood what she wanted and what she stood for. Yet lately all of it seemed to be whirling in her head —a tangle of unresolved emotions and ideas. Suddenly she was not sure anymore.

This week she had been reading, as she often did when she was troubled, from the diaries of the proud and resourceful Mormon pioneer women. Those accounts, however primitive and crudely written, had always provided her with a wellspring of strength and reassurance. Sitting now in her living room, with the others speaking animatedly around her, she found herself thinking of those diaries, voices from the past invading her mind. She heard once again the anguished cries of the young wife, generations earlier, as she lay in her bed, cuddling her infant child, listening to the footsteps of her husband treading down the hallway to the arms of his newest "plural wife." "My heart is breaking . . . why yet another?" And she saw in her mind the men and women on the trail, sliding and sloshing amid the mud caused by forty straight days of rain, wagons stuck in mudholes, the moldy smell of damp cloth and wet flesh, all of them coughing with illness, the earth smelling foul and rancid from the relentless downpour, yet everyone dancing with a frenzied desperation because while they danced they could not think of death. Eliza saw the grim suppers of squaw cabbage, cornmeal mush and pigweed greens, the men eating hungrily, the women waiting until they finished to eat the scours because there was not enough to go around. And the women, standing together and singing quietly amid the suffocating heat, the wheat crop parched by drought, the children's bellies puffed out with malnutrition. The loud, insistent voice of Brigham Young, imploring the women on to greater deeds, "to sew, spin, weave, cultivate vegetables, provide the sustenance. . . ." The women, in return, spelling their men in the fields and creameries, operating the telegraph, tending the needy. And when the edict came down to start a silk industry, start it they did, gathering leaves for the voracious worms, cleaning their foul trays, the families dining and sleeping in their woodsheds to escape the awful smell which the worms exuded. And always the women struggled, eager to do what was expected of them, to measure up to the Prophet's expectations. "Learn to labor," Brigham Young intoned, and labor they did. "Do as you are instructed," Brigham's closest adviser, Heber Kimball, commanded, and obey him they did.

And suddenly Eliza realized that it all repelled her. The faceless subservience. The suffering. The unstinting dedication.

They were not Saints at all. They were fools. All of them.

And Eliza especially.

They were looking at her now. They had stopped talking, her fourteen guests gathered in her living room, and their eyes were on her, awaiting her answer. Their stares shocked her back to the realities of the moment.

"My Sisters," Eliza heard herself say, her voice soft, almost muffled. Then she fell silent again. "Dear Sisters," Eliza started once more, "I confess that I have been sitting here, these last few moments, listening to myself and not to you. I have been watching you and sensing your feelings, but I have not been hearing your words. And now I am struggling with my own."

She could see the surprise on the faces around her. They were troubled by her own uncertainty, apprehensive, too, over her reactions to their outburst.

"Sitting here, it has occurred to me that we have all been moving backward for a very long time. Moving the way good Mormon women move—with dignity and loyalty—but moving backward nonetheless.

"It occurred to me that we started in a different place.

"In the Bible, women as well as men were involved in 'spreading the Good News.' Women were 'fellow workers in the Christ Jesus,' the Good Book said, Romans 16:3. And when our first Prophet, Joseph Smith, embarked on the task of reconstructing the Church, the Mormon sisters, too, received 'gifts of the spirit' and performed priestly duties. When we were needed to help build the Kingdom we were accepted as equals. If Mormon women were lesser creatures, no one informed Ellis Shipp in 1875, when she left her four small children and went off to medical school in Pennsylvania. No one told Patty Sessions who delivered four thousand babies on the frontier or Eliza Snow when she set up the Relief Society in every ward in the territory. And no one told the six thousand sisters who assembled at a great mass meeting in 1870, to defend their menfolk's beloved institution of polygamy when it was threatened by the federal authorities. When times were bad, no one told Emmaline Wells when she started her Save the Grain campaign to ward off starvation. And no one told Louise Felt and Elmina Taylor when they organized the Retrenchment Society to encourage everyone to buy less because there was not enough to go around.

"No, when Zion needed to be saved, women were the equal of men. And now that the Mormon Kingdom is wealthy beyond the wildest dreams of our forebears, we find our roles diminished. Our two million sisters in the Relief Society must accept the officers appointed by the male General Authorities. They cannot choose their own leaders as they did in 1842 when they elected Emma Smith as the first President. Nor can we even control our own budget, as we did until a generation ago. Nor publish our own magazine, as we did until only a decade ago.

"When you tell me you want to talk about the acceptance of

women into the priesthood, I find myself wincing over the futility. What is the point of talking about pushing forward, when in fact we have allowed ourselves to slide backward?"

Eliza was aware that her voice was shaking—that calm, steady voice that had served her so faithfully for so many years and so many speeches. Yet now it was betraying her. Eliza sipped some juice and cleared her throat.

"When you first heard my opening remarks this evening, I felt the impatience and restlessness in your eyes. I want you to know I share your impatience."

Again she had to stop to clear the lump that seemed lodged stubbornly in the middle of her throat. "Well, I will say this to you. If you want to go ahead and hold this conference, I will support your decision. If you want to expand the agenda, I will support you on that, as well. All I can say is, God bless you and protect you. Protect us all."

Eliza closed her eyes and lowered her head for a moment, and when she opened them there was a blur of moving bodies, and she was aware that her guests were on their feet, were embracing her, patting her exuberantly. Two or three kissed her on the cheek. Eliza was aware, as well, that tears were coursing down her face. She hadn't cried in public for so many years she couldn't even remember. Others were crying as well, and Eliza suddenly felt a great release, as if some terrible pressure within her had instantly dissolved.

EMMALINE, of course, was perfect. At age seven, she did everything that was expected of her, and did it perfectly. Watching her now with paternal admiration, Tad Hastings acknowledged to himself that she was an absolute jewel of a child, with her glowing blue eyes and pert nose and flaxen hair. Why was it, then, that she could be such a terrible pain in the ass? That's exactly what she was being now, as he watched her standing in front of the whole group, carefully reciting her lesson on the spiritual values of family closeness. As usual, Emmaline had prepared herself thoroughly. She had read her Mormon lesson book, and was throwing it all in—the appropriate quote from Scripture (Matthew 7:7-11), as well as the Edgar Guest poem. Tad had always hated Edgar Guest, and he resented the unctuous earnestness with which his daughter recited the poem. Yet he saw his wife, Nancy, seated across the room, eyes fixed on her daughter, her face radiating that almost bovine contentment it assumed in moments like this. Next to her sat her closest friend, Zina Hubbard, her own two children huddled nearby in respectful silence. Even Dana, Tad's four-year-old son, was sitting mutely, repressing his usual hyperkinetic twists and twitches.

Perhaps it was the hamburgers, and not Emmaline, that were the source of Tad's own discomfort. He had wolfed three of them at supper, laced with raw onion and catsup, and now he could feel them protesting their fate from the depths of his digestive system. But then he'd always eaten too much, too quickly, on Family Home evenings, and the reason, Tad knew, was that there was a part of his nature that dreaded these Monday-night observances. While the rest of the nation greedily embraced its beery bouts with Monday Night Football, only the Mormons, Tad thought, would cling all the more fervently to their own Monday custom of family togetherness. It had always been thus, and so it would remain. Three weeks earlier, when an especially important game was being televised, Tad had gently broached to Nancy that they skip that week, but she had reacted as though he'd just suggested bombing the Tabernacle. Tad remembered with fleeting gratitude how his mother Eliza had reduced Home Evenings to once a month after Tad had reached fourteen; he'd rarely found himself feeling grateful to his mother, but for that concession, at least, he owed her.

Not only did Nancy insist on weekly rituals but she performed them by the book. Friends and relatives were summoned to join them, along with their offspring, and the agenda was followed meticulously. First came the Pledge of Allegiance, which tonight was slurringly recited by young Dana, who glumly clenched the flag as he spoke, like a mountaineer clasping his piton. Then it was Emmaline's turn to say a prayer, as adults and children alike bowed their heads. Next, tradition dictated that time be set aside for what the Mormon handbooks called "family business." Tad could imagine the fierce old Mormon pioneers sitting around with their numerous wives, settling their polygamous domestic quarrels, trading tales of Indian raids and locust infestations. By God, in those days "family business" must really have meant something! But tonight, as usual, the interplay was numbingly bland. A volunteer was needed to cut Grandma's lawn. Nancy's friend Zina, whose husband was away on a prolonged business trip, shyly inquired if anyone knew of a baby-sitter, since her regular had come down with the mumps. And then Nancy explained that her Bishop had informed her that an elderly couple had just moved onto the block—all the neighbors should be alerted to include them in the Monday-night gatherings.

Tad shifted his position uneasily and suppressed a belch. Oh, for a good Indian raid or even passing locusts to give them something to talk about! But now the evening was plunging inexorably onward, as Zina prodded her older girl, a gangly ten-year-old named Clorinda, to try a solo. "I want to grow up and have many little babies," Clorinda sang obediently, "three little, four little, five little babies. . . ." And Tad squirmed in his chair, picturing an endless chain of Mormon babies, sliding, like link sausages, from this child's slender loins. Mercifully, Clorinda's solo was blotted out when little Heber, Tad's thirteen-month-old, who had been sleeping on Nancy's shoulder, awoke with a scream, and efforts to calm him proved unsuccessful. Despite her little brother's cries, the ever stalwart Emmaline rose to her feet and launched into "The First Noel." Suddenly Heber stopped crying and Dana's small, high-pitched voice joined his sister's, as did those of Zina's two children. Tad looked at the children, their eyes mirroring the distended glow of the Christmas tree, and he realized that it was really quite beautiful and also quite comforting, being in the living room, listening to the young voices. He had to admit to himself that there was, after all, something terribly touching and sweet about all of them sitting here, sharing these moments, adults and children together. Tad felt annoyed with himself, for resisting it, indeed deprecating it. Gavin would surely make fun of him if he were here, and so would Pye, lovely Pye. They would needle him about his vulnerability to ritual. But how could they possibly understand? They hadn't been brought up with it, nurtured by it. They were not raised as Mormons; only a Mormon could understand.

His glance caught Nancy's eyes, looking at him with impatience, and he wondered why until he realized that the doorbell had been ringing insistently. Nancy, he knew, would regard this as a violation. It was always understood in Mormon households that Monday night was not the time to go calling. The ringing would surely represent the intrusion of a Gentile salesman—let it ring, Nancy's eyes were telling him. But Tad was on his feet now, driven as much by heartburn as by hospitality, moving quickly to the door, flinging it open. He started to take a deep breath of the crisp night air but the breath caught in his throat.

Oh, shit. It was Dana Sloat.

☐ Within moments Zina and her gangly girls had been sent on their way, the Family Home Evening abruptly terminated. Tad, Nancy and their unexpected visitor were arrayed around the dining-room table. Emmaline and Dana stared, bugeyed, at the tall man they knew to be their grandfather but who was in fact a shadowy figure in their lives. Nancy, who had yelped with surprise when she first saw her father, had brought out some fruit punch and now sat, peering intently at him, cradling little

Heber in her arms. Tad's lethargy had quickly dissolved as he sat across the table from this trim, dour man in his dark blue suit, white shirt and black tie.

"I still can't believe it," Nancy blurted, fumbling with her glass. "It's such a wonderful surprise having you here."

"I would have called," Sloat said. "I was in a long meeting. I thought it would probably go on till late."

"You don't ever need to call," Nancy said. "You're always welcome here."

"Anytime at all," Tad heard himself saying, as if the man seated in their midst was an intimate friend or relative who had been a frequent visitor to their house. In fact, his father-in-law had visited their home once in eight years of marriage, and that was a brief appearance at a reception welcoming Nancy home from the hospital following the birth of Dana, his namesake. Except for that one visit and for their wedding, Tad had seen him less than ten times in his entire life. There'd been a rather chilling meeting in Sloat's office a month before their wedding which lasted fifteen minutes in all. Tad had entered the office timorously, expecting to be grilled relentlessly by his future father-in-law, but instead Sloat had shaken his hand, sat him down and informed him briskly that he wanted Nancy to have a large family, and that Nancy agreed. To this end, he would establish a trust fund of one million dollars for each child at the time of his birth, which he could draw upon after reaching the age of twenty-one. He would not contribute to Tad's or Nancy's day-to-day living expenses, he added, because he believed that struggle builds character. Surely Tad would appreciate the wisdom of this decision. With all this still spinning in his mind, Tad found himself being ushered to the door, the meeting having been terminated with the same brisk efficiency.

Sloat was patting little Dana on the head now. "I feel bad that I missed the Family Home Evening," Sloat said.

Nancy plunked Heber onto Tad's lap and was on her feet, marshaling Dana and Emmaline "Children, sing your grandfather a Christmas carol," she said excitedly. The children whined their reluctance, but Nancy shepherded them before Sloat. "And then I want Emmaline to recite her lesson. She did it so well this evening."

Tad watched Sloat sternly nod his approval, as the children

embarked on a reprise of "The First Noel." He was trying, God knows, he was trying. His eyes focused on them with keen interest, and he even managed a smile when they stumbled. Yet there was a stilted formality about this man, an impersonality which was also apparent in his dealings with his daughter. Nancy loved her father deeply, yet was careful not to embarrass him with untoward displays. She addressed him as Father, and he called her Nancy, and when they met she would give him a perfunctory kiss on the cheek—that was the extent of it. With Tad, it was strictly a matter of formal handshakes. He sensed Sloat's acknowledgment of the chasm that existed between them—a chasm too wide to bridge with casual chatter. Sloat, after all, dwelled in a rarefied world of presidents and potentates, hurtling from one crisis to the next in his Lears and limousines. Tad was just another anonymous young Mormon lawyer, slogging along with his routine law practice, far removed from Sloat's cosmic concerns.

Looking at him now, Tad noticed the tension about Sloat's face and posture even as he listened to the singing of his grandchildren, body erect, expression taut. Nancy had once said she considered her father the handsomest man she had ever seen, and he *was* handsome in a way. At fifty, his hair was still jet black, styled in a close-cropped, almost military fashion. There was an austere quality to his features, with his thin, slightly aquiline nose and firm jaw. Yes, Tad thought, he *is* an imposing man, especially with his great height which measured, Tad guessed, six feet four inches. His legs were so long and thin that Sloat must surely have gone through a gawky stage in his early teens when he probably looked like a great web of arms and legs. Tad would have liked to have known him then, when he was tall and clumsy and had not yet developed that steely control. Perhaps his remote, inaccessible qualities emerged as a defense mechanism against this gawkiness, Tad thought. However they originated, they were indelible now—there in his eyes, those strange, remote eyes. Even at that first meeting, Tad noticed that Sloat would look at him and yet past him at the same time, as if his inner gaze were directed to some distant reality, far beyond Tad's ken. His skin seemed unnaturally pale, yet his cheeks had a strange, pinkish glow. His voice, too, was absolutely flawless: deep, rich, at times vaguely ominous. Sloat did not speak, but rather intoned.

The suggestion of a smile traced across Sloat's features now as

Emmaline concluded her recitation. He clapped his hands several times, and the children looked pleased and embarrassed. Sloat patted each on the head before Nancy hurried them off to bed, returning to collect a squirming Heber from Tad's arms. Tad found himself suddenly alone with this man, seated across the table, and he was keenly aware of the fact that they had nothing to say to each other, feeling an edge of panic as silence descended.

"I shall be spending more time in Salt Lake," Sloat said at last, crossing his legs and picking some lint off the otherwise immaculate sleeve of his blue suit. "There will be an announcement in tomorrow's newspapers that I have been appointed First Counselor by President Bryce."

Tad felt himself fumbling for the right words. "That's wonderful. I mean, it's a very big responsibility. An awesome one." Even as these words escaped, Tad felt appalled by their inadequacy, their foolishness. The news Sloat had disclosed could have great impact upon his own life, not to mention that of his mother, who occupied the highest position in the hierarchy that any woman could hold.

Sloat's face creased into a smile, but Tad felt the smile reflected the older man's amusement over his own awkwardness. Sloat reached for the pitcher, refilling Tad's glass with fruit punch and then his own.

"As you know, Tad, the First Counselor traditionally is the principal administrator of the LDS Church. It is, as you correctly say, a big responsibility."

"I know Nancy will be absolutely thrilled. . . ."

"These are demanding times for the Church. The rate of expansion has been so great. Do you have any idea, Tad, what the Church's gross income amounts to?"

Tad shrugged absently. "I would guess hundreds of millions. . . ."

"It's approaching two billion a year," Sloat said, "far bigger than the budget of the State of Utah. The problem is we don't have the proper structure to manage this sort of operation. We weren't prepared for our own growth. It's like trying to run General Motors as you would a candy store."

"But your own companies, sir—how are you going to manage them at the same time as you're taking on this new job?" Some

months earlier Tad had decided to do some homework on Dana
Sloat and had assembled articles and Wall Street reports detailing
the scope of Sloat's empire. He had known, of course, that his
farther-in-law's holdings were far flung, but the full scope of his
enterprises, as detailed in the material, left him in awe: a mini
conglomerate of automotive and electronic parts companies, two
Midwest commuter airlines, a major oil and natural-gas explora-
tion company, some ninety-two shopping centers and malls, a
company supplying key missile components for the defense industry—a maze of interlocking corporations. Tad had not realized
that Sloat's companies also had been buying up hundreds of thousands of acres of farmland in recent years and was becoming a
major "agripower," as *Forbes* magazine put it. Nor that it was
bidding for control of several AM and FM radio stations. It was
typical of Sloat's furtive nature, Tad felt, that there would be no
omnibus company to shelter these ventures—no Sloat Enterprises. Instead, he operated them under a multiplicity of names
and identities, shielding his own persona from public scrutiny.

Sloat cleared his throat and stared at Tad thoughtfully. "My
candid response to your question is, 'I don't really know.' The
Church, as you are aware, Tad, comes first in my life. It always
has. I'll give this new position whatever time and energy it re-
quires. That is what He would want me to do, or else He wouldn't
have given me the call." Tad pondered momentarily whether the
"He" referred to President Bryce or to God, and decided on the
latter.

"Well, I wish I could say something like 'Let me know if I can
be of help,' but of course that would be foolish."

"On the contrary, you and Nancy can indeed help," Sloat said
quickly. "As First Counselor, there will be many Church functions I will have to attend, observances that will require my presence. As you know, since the death of my wife Bethel seven years
ago, I have been a very private person. I have devoted myself to
my work and avoided social involvements. But our good people
have a great sense of family, Tad. I think it would be appropriate
if you and Nancy would accompany me to these affairs—present
a sense of unity in our family. It would be very helpful to me, and
I think it could also be helpful, quite frankly, to your law practice,
Tad, to be seen at functions of this sort."

Tad nodded his head agreeably, but he had the feeling that

some sort of corporate lien had just been placed on his body, and he was as yet unable to interpret what that lien entailed. "We would be delighted to help in any way," he heard himself saying.

Nancy had rejoined them now, seating herself next to her father, carrying with her the faint smell of baby talcum. Tad told her the news of her father's position and her face positively glowed with delight—indeed she impulsively planted a kiss on his cheek. Tad saw Sloat stiffen but he managed a quick smile.

"I'm so thrilled for you!" Nancy effused.

"As I explained to Tad, all of us will be affected. . . ."

"Well, I think it's wonderful."

"There will be times I'll need you at my side."

"Tad and I will be proud to be there," she said. "First Counselor! My goodness, Father. It just takes my breath away."

"I feel very humble before these responsibilities," Sloat said. "I only wish dear Bethel were still here at my side."

It was unusual for Sloat to invoke her mother's name. Nancy paused reflexively, then plunged ahead in her own exuberance. "The Church needs you so badly, Father. Everyone loved President Woodleigh but he was ill for such a long time. There must be so many things that need to be done."

"Very many things."

"Well, as I said, I'm so very proud." Nancy glanced quickly at Tad now. "I'm proud of both the men in my life. I'll bet Tad has been too modest to tell you *his* news, Father." Sloat's gaze met hers.

Tad felt his cheeks redden with embarrassment. "Come on, Nancy. This stuff is so trivial compared to what . . ."

"Nonsense," Nancy snapped. "Tell Father about it."

Sloat's eyes were upon him now. Tad squirmed in his chair. "Nancy is talking about an acquisition I put together this week. It's something I fell into, really. I found myself representing one client that wanted to sell something that a friend of mine wanted to buy. Simple as that."

"Tad's being so modest, Father. He engineered this big multi-million dollar deal. . . ."

"Don't you want to give me the details, Tad?" Sloat asked.

Tad took a breath. "Well, it's pretty simple really. A colleague of mine at the firm got sidetracked on a long-drawn-out litigation, so I was assigned one of his clients. A company called Pacific. At first I thought it was another one of those moribund holding companies—you know, a couple of shopping centers and some real estate. Anyway, I was called to Los Angeles to meet with an old man named Curry who has been running the company for the Gaunt family—that's an old Southern California Mormon family —and it turns out their company also owns several television and FM stations which it wants to unload."

"And I take it you found a buyer very quickly?" Sloat said.

"I knew Suncorp was looking . . ."

"And of course you've been a friend of Gavin Pollard for some years now."

"Yes, that's true." Tad looked at Sloat quizzically. He couldn't recall offhand having told Sloat of his friendship for Gavin, but perhaps he had forgotten or perhaps Nancy had told him. "Gavin was very interested. It was just a matter of constructing the right deal. And today I got the call telling me that the executive committee of the Suncorp board had approved the acquisition."

"Good going, Tad," Sloat said. "Very alert work. That's what a good young lawyer should be doing—keeping his eyes open, putting his clients into good situations."

Nancy was beaming. "I knew you'd want to hear about it, Father. Tad's been working night and day on this deal for weeks now."

As the conversation continued, Tad could see Sloat becoming listless, as if some inner alarm had sounded, warning him that the time allotted for social visitations had ended.

Moments later they were all on their feet, walking Sloat to the door. Tad shook hands with him, and Nancy kissed him on his cheek.

"The children were so thrilled to see you," she said. "Emmaline included you in her prayers."

Sloat looked at her gravely. "That's very good of her."

Tad could see the sleek black limousine waiting at the curb now, the chauffeur standing at the ready.

"Promise we'll see more of you now," Nancy reiterated, and Sloat smiled wanly and nodded. Standing by the open door, Tad felt himself shuddering in the subfreezing chill, but Sloat, coatless, seemed not to notice. The white glow of the outside lights caught Sloat's face now, and in the fleeting moment before he turned to his limousine Tad saw again the curious pink tint to his cheeks and it occurred to him that Dana Sloat looked embalmed.

□ Tad sat alone in the darkened den, cradling his glass, the vodka taking on a blue-gray tint in the opaque light deflected from the television set. Dana Sloat had left an hour earlier, and Nancy was already fast asleep. He had gotten into bed with her but she was dozing the moment her eyes were shut. The ease with which women could simply erase their thoughts and succumb to sleep had always amazed him. Yet who was he to generalize about women? At twenty-eight, he had literally slept with only one other woman besides Nancy, and that was Pye. He wondered what Pye was doing at this moment. He could picture her, standing in her panties at her makeup mirror, carefully removing her mascara, her flesh alabaster white in the dim light, her lovely nipples standing erect on her perfect breasts. Pye! He'd never really slept that much with Pye, either. They weren't able to keep their hands off each other long enough.

Of course there were the girls on Tonga—the girls Gavin had introduced him to. Lord knows, he never really slept with any of them. No, Gavin's girls in Tonga were not the sort you went to sleep next to. They were girls for play, and Tad was the innocent Mormon missionary lad who learned to play.

Tad took another sip of the vodka and smiled to himself. If only Dana Sloat, the Church's new First Counselor, could see his son-in-law drinking spirits only an hour after his departure! Dana Sloat doubtless pictured him as a good Mormon lad. His romance with Nancy was the model Mormon romance. In love in June. In bed in July. In the Temple in August. Emmaline in April. A true Latter-day Saint love story!

He took another gulp and felt the spirits warm its way down to his stomach. Tad kept the vodka behind the ice trays in the freezer, hidden away in two little canisters labeled POISON— FREEZONE." As far as Nancy or the kids were concerned, the cylinders were for use in picnic baskets to chill the soft drinks. Tad wondered where the other solid citizens of the Church kept their secret stashes of vodka or beer or tobacco or coffee or tea or all the other goodies that were officially banned according to the Word of Wisdom.

Tad had nothing against the Word of Wisdom. He had nothing against the Church, either. Down deep he knew he loved the Church. It was embedded in the depths of his psyche, and he understood that as well.

Tad swirled the vodka in the glass. What was bothering him about Sloat? What was it? One thing he'd noticed—even as he was telling him about the Pacific deal, he felt Sloat wasn't really listening. No, that wasn't precisely right—he was listening, but Tad felt he already knew what he was hearing. There was something in the glances he exchanged with Nancy, as though they both knew but were letting him tell it anyway. Humoring him. He shook his head in self-reproach. No, that didn't make any sense at all. Dana Sloat was not the sort of person who would go through the motions. It was too late in the day for paranoia.

And yet why did Sloat really come by tonight? It wasn't just that he happened to be in Salt Lake. Hell, Sloat had been in town many times without dropping in on them suddenly, dramatically, as he had tonight. Perhaps he wanted to tell them about his appointment, to alert them that he would need them at social events and Church functions: his family props. Sloat had always been so secretive about his personal life that Tad relished the fact that he was being recruited as a makeshift intimate. Rent-a-Relative!

No, there was something else, something typically inscrutable about his visit. It was as though Sloat were on an inspection mission.

He was checking him out. That was it!

Tad poured the rest of the vodka down his throat and flicked off the television set.

Checking him out! But why?

THE notion of lighting ten candles had been an impromptu one, but now, standing in the yellow glow which suffused the room, Eliza was delighted she had thought of it. This was, after all, the tenth anniversary of their first meeting, an occasion to be commemorated. She checked her watch; it was nine o'clock. Turner would be arriving momentarily and she hoped he would be as amused as she at the motley array of candle holders she had assembled in her sudden dash about the house. There was a heavily ornate wrought-iron piece from Mexico, and next to it, a childlike representation of an elephant given her by Tad at age eleven; then a graceful sprig of sterling silver, a wedding present from her grandmother, which was itself dwarfed by a bulbous bronze candelabrum from Peru presented only a week earlier by visiting Latin missionaries. Adjacent to that was Angel Moroni, trumpet in hand, a piece carved in Nauvoo, Illinois, handed down five generations through the family of Draper Hastings, her late husband. Standing back and viewing this strange assemblage, Eliza realized what a wry commentary they posed on her life: diverse, unpredictable and not quite fitting together. Yet, if that's what they all suggested there was some truth to it.

Two hours had passed since Eliza had ushered the last of the ladies from her living room and, though the shock of the meeting remained, she had composed herself once again. She was determined to have herself together, knowing that Turner, too, must have weathered a day of considerable stress.

Besides, she'd always prided herself on her resiliency, and tonight she had gone about it with her usual methodical resolve. First, she went to her small study off her bedroom, unplugged the telephone, closed her eyes and meditated for twenty minutes. She then treated herself to a leisurely bubble bath, using a preparation she had appropriated from a hotel in Zurich two weeks before. Lying in bed in her robe, she'd called her older sister, Rebecca Best, in Ogden, and chatted easily with her for several minutes. Of her two brothers and three sisters, Becky, who was principal of a school for retarded children, had always been the closest. She was also the family maverick, having left the Church and divorced her husband while still only twenty-seven, supporting herself and her two children since that time. After talking to Becky, Eliza then threw herself into her favorite release—cooking. The dinner she had concocted, like the candlesticks, was designed to delight and amuse Turner: potato soup, quiche, macaroni au gratin, baked potato and, finally, chocolate cake. It was the ultimate starch-and-sugar orgy, but Turner, despite his slender build, shared the Mormon predilection for sugar and starch.

She hoped, by the time he'd worked his way through the macaroni and saw the potato beckoning, that he would laugh—that wonderful, hearty, booming laugh that would shake the chandelier. How she wished she could laugh that uninhibitedly; when she was a child, it was considered undecorous to laugh aloud, so Eliza had gone through life with a tiny, repressed titter. Yet laughter was the single quality she and Turner most lovingly shared. Despite his serious, even brooding appearance, she had long since discovered that Turner was really a wondrously silly man who had taught her how to be silly as well. They both loved games, and together would invent bizarre modifications of Monopoly and Scrabble, which they would play for hours. A gifted wordsmith, he would read her Ogden Nash jingles when they took long, lingering baths together, and would invent appendages to Nash's poems that dealt gently but irreverently with Brigham Young and Joseph Smith. During secret trips away together—stolen weekends in Monterey or Aspen or Tucson—they would go to old movies and listen to jazz and take long walks. Most of all, they would simply play—mindless, delicious play. Eliza never knew that sex could turn into pure play, and she found herself relishing it as she never had before. Draper had approached lovemaking as he had all other tasks: a duty to be accomplished with maximum efficiency in minimum time. Turner dawdled over lovemaking for hours; during their weekends together they would order room service and slowly make love between courses. He was outrageous, this bizarre Englishman, and he made her abandon all the rules of modesty and decorum with which she had been inculcated. And she knew, of course, she loved him, loved his lean, patrician face with his proud upturned nose, dark brown hair, deep-set gray eyes which could at once be moody and mischievous; loved listening to his fastidiously enunciated accent and to his whimsical stories; admired the warmth and yet reserve with which he dealt with people. Though a deeply religious man and a committed Mormon, Turner was so utterly different from the other denizens of Church Headquarters, with their somber, mortician-like demeanors. Yet she never saw him patronize them or show impatience during their dry-as-dust recitations of Church business. His patience was limitless, as was his compassion.

They had met at a Christmas party ten years earlier. Turner was then the dashing young city editor of the *Deseret News*. They were casual acquaintances at first, and, later, colleagues when Turner became Director of Public Communications for the LDS Church. After Turner's wife had died of cancer, their friendship began to deepen. Eliza at the time was still maintaining the facade of her marriage to Draper. Her husband had been promoted to executive vice-president of his insurance company and had been transferred to the main corporate office in Chicago. The transfer had been a relief to them both. After more than two decades together, they had grown totally out of step with each other's needs, and yet divorce was out of the question. It would be harmful both to his corporate career and to her Church position and, more importantly, inimical to their mutual belief in the eternal exaltation which marriage provided. Now they could live apart physically as they had emotionally. Eighteen months after the transfer, Draper's corporate jet crashed while trying to land in a snowstorm. And only two months later, much to her subsequent guilt and discomfort, Eliza had begun her surreptitious love affair with Turner Mead.

The affair left her shocked at first, shocked that her own needs and appetites had been so long denied that she could surrender so quickly. Shocked, too, that she could have such a blatantly erotic relationship with a man seven years her junior; shocked that she could find herself totally reorganizing her disciplined life to allow for their furtive trysts and secret weekends together, the logistics of which had to be meticulously planned to elude the ubiquitous gossips of Salt Lake. Yet, oddly, the secrecy seemed to work in their favor. They were loath to admit it to each other, but there was something exciting about living a shadow life which was inaccessible to everyone around them, even their closest intimates. They were now the secret outcasts. They had always thought of themselves as serious, responsible people whose lives were open to public scrutiny, but there was something in each of them that now rebelled against the Puritan rigidities they had so long endorsed. From time to time, they discussed the possibility of "going public," but in the end were reluctant to disturb the status quo that had worked so well for them.

And yet, they both sensed that it had to change. Two years had elapsed since Draper's death, a suitable period to permit her to remarry. But Turner had never broached marriage, and that distressed her as well. Increasingly she realized that she was haunted by the fear of losing him. She would awaken in the middle of the night, having dreamt that Turner was with someone else, someone younger and more attractive. She would arise sometimes and peer at herself in the mirror, critically assessing her face, her figure. At forty-six, her face was still youthful and unlined, she told herself reassuringly. As a young woman, she had often heard herself described as beautiful, though recent newspaper and magazine accounts described her now with words like "stately" and "handsome"—words that made her cringe. Her figure was still firm, her stomach flat, hips slim. Her breasts, she felt, had become gracelessly large, almost pendulous, yet Turner seemed to like them. Since becoming his lover, she had faithfully gone to exercise class four days a week and jogged every morning and had lost twelve pounds. Indeed, friends kept telling her she looked lovelier than ever—"How do you do it?" they would demand—and she smiled inwardly because she knew the reason and they did not.

She desperately fought her bouts of jealousy. Once, some weeks earlier, she had seen Turner lunching with an attractive young woman, and she could hardly restrain herself until two o'clock to call him and discover the identity of her rival. When Turner told her with obvious amusement that she was a correspondent from a New York magazine who was already on a plane back home, her jealousy was only partially assuaged.

The problem, of course, was that it had gone too far. Though she hadn't had much experience with these sorts of things, there comes a point between lovers, Eliza deduced, when mutual needs, once blissfully casual, and mutual passions, once blithely innocent, suddenly converge with forces deeper and more profound. Something subtle and disturbing had happened between her and Turner: They had somehow grown into each other, become part of each other's lives. Their two solitudes, having long bordered and protected each other, had now congealed into a whole.

Yes, it had all gotten out of hand. That she now understood and would have to deal with. And yet it panicked her. Despite her high responsibilities and extensive travels, she had always dwelled within the tightly protective cocoon of LDS society. She was not a woman of the world, schooled in the subtle techniques of manipulation. Her first lover had been Draper Hastings, and she had married him and borne his children. And now there was Turner!

But where *was* Turner? It was nine twenty-five—almost half an hour beyond the time he had promised to arrive. Turner was never late.

Could he have forgotten? It was possible, she thought, as she fussed in the kitchen, adjusting oven temperatures and checking consistencies. The quiche would be all right, she decided, but would *she* be? She needed him now; she longed for him.

He might still be stuck at the office, dealing with the myriad details of the one-hundred-fiftieth convocation, the speeches, the announcements, the out-of-town press. This was, she knew all too well, an incredibly difficult day for him. The announcement of Dana Sloat's new position had gone out that morning as well, she recalled with a deep sigh. Yes, it had all piled up on Turner today.

Fretfully, Eliza walked through the living room and opened the front door, peering outside into the night. The street was empty, random flakes still falling laconically. Returning to the living room, which only hours before had been filled with women, arguing passionately, emotions running high, Eliza realized that she felt very much alone. She had lived by herself effectively for a long time now but had rarely felt lonely. After Draper's death she had decided to, remain in the big two-story house of white

brick, graceless but solid, which had been in her family for three
generations. The house, oddly, reminded Eliza of her father—
heavy-shouldered, powerful, lumbering. Its interior was also intensely masculine, with its dark-paneled living room, heavy sofas,
big, brick fireplace. Eliza had tried to add a touch of style here
and there. She'd bought some lamps of fine china, had ordered
the sofas recovered with a delicately flowered fabric and had
freshly wallpapered her bedroom. But she admitted to herself
early on that she really didn't have much of a flair for interior
design. There were always more urgent things to do.

Eliza strolled into her study and sat down at her rolltop desk,
stacked high with reports and correspondence. Her eyes turned
briefly to the photograph of Tad, taken when he was a grinning
little boy of thirteen dressed in bathing trunks, water dripping
from his skinny body, face gleaming with delight. She loved that
photograph and kept it close by. She also had photos of him taken
in more recent years, but when he was thirteen she and Tad still
had that wonderful closeness which somehow dissolved as he slid
into his teens, to be replaced with the distanced, resentful attitude she now felt from him—an attitude which saddened her, but
which she felt powerless to counteract.

The doorbell sounded. She sprang from her desk. Turner had
not forgotten after all. How could she think he would ever forget?

□ They kissed and he was effusive in his apologies.
Turner had bought her a lovely necklace with a delicate gold
pendant shaped in a heart, to denote their tenth "anniversary."
And she in turn presented him with an Italian-made navy velour
jogging suit, to reinforce his resolve to run every morning. They
kissed again and sat down to dinner and had made it all the way
to dessert, chatting easily about trivia, carefully avoiding the concerns that weighed on them both, each waiting for the other to
shift the mood. But when Turner asked for a second piece of
chocolate cake, complaining blandly, "These low-calorie dinners
of yours never fill me up," they both started laughing, Turner
grasping her around the waist, pulling her toward him and kissing
her still again. He'd caught on to her culinary joke the moment
she brought out the quiche, he said, but was determined not to

give her the satisfaction of acknowledging her "cruel jest" until dessert.

They retired to the living room with their herbal tea, as was their custom, and Turner took off his shoes and rested his feet on the coffee table. Eliza, unable to wait any longer to unburden herself, began to relate the details of Bill Chadwick's telephone call and the subsequent emotional meeting. Turner sat back and listened solemnly, hearing the anguish in her voice, watching her lovely face as she spoke, her expression animated, her hair like finespun amber in the lamplight.

When she was done he sighed, and said simply, "I suspect your hunch is right, Eliza. I think it was probably Sloat who asked Chadwick to call you."

"Well, I don't want to let him get away with it," Eliza replied sharply. "He's been in office one day. Let him find out he doesn't own us."

"There are risks," Turner said, his face grave.

"He's not the Prophet. He shouldn't try to interfere in areas where he's totally ignorant."

"Aren't you letting your personal dislike for him color your judgment?"

Eliza's eyes blazed. "Are you suggesting I should accede?"

Turner shook his head calmly. "I am only suggesting, my darling, that you do what you think best. But, as you said, this is his first day in office. We should give him time to show his hand."

"He's shown his hand already in trying to postpone this totally harmless meeting."

Turner sipped his tea, his brow furrowed. "Look, Eliza, I share your apprehensions—you know I do. So does Dalton Evans. So do many thoughtful people among the General Authorities. We're going to learn a great deal about Dana Sloat in the coming days and weeks. I just don't want to see you do anything that could bring you harm. You've worked so long and have built so much."

Eliza reached out and clasped his hand. "My darling Turner. Always the patient one." She felt his hand enclose hers tightly.

"I do believe in patience, Eliza. I believe the Church is doing God's work. I believe He will protect us as He has in the past."

"I'm going to hold the meeting," Eliza said resolutely. "If Dana

Sloat is afraid of two hundred and fifty Mormon women, he's going to have to go there himself and tell them to go home."

She felt Turner's eyes upon her, studying her.

"You said I was a patient man, Eliza. I am not patient about all things."

"I see," she said, arising from her chair. As they walked toward the stairway he put his arm around her waist and hers around his. And Eliza realized, much to her astonishment, that her anger had dissipated, like mist before the warming sun.

SHE had distrusted Dana Sloat from the moment of their first meeting. The strength of her adverse reaction had astonished her. She had rarely responded to people that way. She believed in trust, not antipathy.

It had all started with an excited phone call from her son. Then twenty, Tad was newly returned from Tonga and he had been going with a girl named Nancy Sloat. And now, to her chagrin, Eliza was hearing his voice on the other other end of the line, informing her breathlessly that he had proposed to Nancy, that she had accepted and they would be married in six weeks.

Six weeks! Eliza had met Nancy on two occasions. She seemed like an attractive, if bland, young woman. She had tried gently to persuade Tad to wait. After all, this was the most vulnerable period for a young man, she reminded him. He had just returned to college after two years of celibate service to the Church. Why not wait a year or so and meet other girls?

The easy course, Eliza knew, would have been to feign enthusiasm for the marriage. On the surface it was indeed a felicitous union. Dana Sloat was an enormously wealthy man who doubtless could help Tad in his future career, but he was also said to be intensely reactionary and obsessively secretive—a Morman Howard Hughes, some said jokingly. The only thing he was open about was his wealth, which he flaunted with an aggressiveness which Eliza found truly vulgar.

Listening to his mother's protestations, Tad reacted with typical defensiveness. Eliza was trying to meddle, he said. No girl he selected could meet her stringent standards. It was Nancy he would marry. His mind was made up.

The next day she received her first call from Dana Sloat. He had just been informed of the engagement, he said, his tone cool and businesslike. He was gratified that his daughter was marrying into a fine old LDS family, and would look forward to meeting with Eliza and her husband as soon as their schedules would permit. It was all very formal and proper, like an ambassador making a courtesy call.

A week later Eliza was phoned by a woman named Miss Cosgrove, who identified herself as an assistant to Mr. Sloat. Sloat was presently in Amsterdam on business, she said, but had asked her to advise Eliza that she was, on his behalf, arranging a reception for the young couple to announce their forthcoming marriage. If she had anyone she wished to add to the guest list the names would be more than welcome.

A reception? Eliza asked. That seemed hardly necessary. It would be sufficient to have a reception after the wedding.

No, that was not Mr. Sloat's wish, reported Miss Cosgrove. After all, two of the most prominent families in the community were merging. Mr. Sloat felt that called for a special occasion.

The week before "the occasion," the newspapers were full of stories on Dana Sloat. One story said he was donating four million dollars to Brigham Young University to construct new dormitories. Another said he was acquiring a major commuter airline in the Midwest. Dana Sloat, it was clear, was making his mark and was determined to let the community know of it.

The reception itself was held amid the rococo elegance of the old Hotel Utah, adjoining Temple Square. There was an awesome abundance of food, an orchestra was playing and hundreds of guests crowded the room. They included the mayor, the state attorney general, a United States senator and other political figures and members of the press, none of whom Eliza had invited. Also present were a generous sampling of General Authorities and other Church officials. When Eliza entered, Dana Sloat was already holding court, towering over the circle of admirers that surrounded him, playing, to the full, the role of the business tycoon, the generous benefactor, the Mormon Medici. When an aide whispered of Eliza's arrival, Sloat moved quickly to greet her and Draper, marshaling at his side a shy, rather pale little woman whom he introduced as his wife Bethel. They all made a determined effort at conversation. Sloat praised Eliza's career in the Church, and said how much he admired her work. Draper, in turn, expressed his admiration for Sloat's fast climb. Much to

Eliza's interest, at no point did Sloat's wife say anything; nor did either of the Sloats, in the course of their conversation, refer at any time to Nancy or Tad, who were hovering uncomfortably at the side of the room, not knowing quite what was expected of them.

But Eliza knew what was expected of them all. This was to be an elaborately ostentatious show, designed to further the fortunes and reputation of Dana Sloat. They were all being paraded out before the community leaders, like prize poodles at a dog show, and she disliked it. They were not there to honor the young engaged couple, they were honoring Dana Sloat.

And he was drinking it all in, looming tall and darkly handsome in his blue suit, his manner gracious but stilted, his face curiously monochromatic, his presence bordering on the imperious. There was something in his style, Eliza sensed, that surpassed the boundaries of normal ambition. There was a hunger lurking in his dark eyes, and it was a hunger for more than money, more, even, than power. And it haunted her.

It haunted her still.

SUPPER had been a difficult time. The boys, Eric and Ethan, who had been scrapping all day, continued to prod each other all through the meal. Augusta Cobb knew that two young brothers inevitably would have bouts of sibling rivalry from time to time, but the clashes between her boys, in both constancy and cacophony, surpassed all expectations. Her husband Hiram also seemed remote and troubled during supper. Part of the problem was that the dish he'd fussed over for forty-five listless minutes had not turned out well.

"I think your daddy is an absolute magician with leftovers," Gussie had said encouragingly, but to no avail. Eric was picking at his food disdainfully and Ethan had already pushed his plate away, turning his attention instead to the bread.

"Don't waste your breath," Hiram advised his wife glumly. "It's too tough a clientele we've got here."

Because they both worked at home, Hiram had been cooking their main course for the past several years, with Gussie preparing the salads and vegetables. Hiram seemed to derive genuine pleasure from his kitchen forays and, after an awkward start, had become a proficient chef. Gussie found his specialties, with their subtle reminders of his Southern upbringing, a pleasant relief from her own bland, meat-and-potatoes cookery.

But tonight, standing over a sink full of greasy pots and dishes, she was glad the meal was over. It had been a difficult dinner to get through, and also a difficult day. Having put off her final round of Christmas shopping until that morning, she had set forth to the ZCMI to confront the thankless task of purchasing two gifts on a budget of under ten dollars. The surging crowds and lofty price tags had demolished what little enthusiasm she'd been able to muster. She'd brought the required presents—a ski cap for Ethan, some bright red socks for Hiram—but their meagerness left her

111

depleted and embarrassed. Poverty itself was a uniquely unrelenting humiliation, she'd long ago decided, especially to those who had once known the pleasures of modest affluence. That was especially true in a place like Salt Lake City where poverty was so rare and where those few needy were so discreetly taken care of. On her way home, she'd driven by one of the Bishops' Storehouses and saw the people toting their bulging bags of food and clothing, feeling a twinge of anger that the vast resources of this great and wealthy Church had been denied to her children, whose ancestors on both sides of the family accounted for a cumulative ten generations of loyalty to the Latter-day Saints.

There was a blatant symbolism to the Bishops' Storehouses, Gussie reflected. Obedience equals reward. It was as simple as that.

Must faith be reduced to such a squalid equation? Gussie wondered. As a child, she had thought faith meant love, not surrender. It made Gussie sad, and more than a little angry.

Her anger had remained with her through the long afternoon as she locked herself in her tiny office to finish an article for the next issue of *The Kingdom*. It was to be a frivolous piece, reporting the modest efforts of some of the undergraduates of Brigham Young University to expand the rigid dress code. Four of the boys had decided to wear long-forbidden blue jeans and to grow mustaches, and their female compatriots turned up in slacks rather than the required dresses. Their protest lasted a single morning before they were summarily suspended.

Gussie had tried to write the story in a facetious vein, but she realized, after two hours at her typewriter, that its tone was shrill. Even after all these years the very mention of BYU left her with a sick, hollow feeling.

How strange, she thought, that those brief two years at BYU would color the rest of her life. Lord knows, she'd never planned it that way. BYU had been an accident, really. As a youngster, Gussie had resisted the urgings of her father to attend that great Mormon educational sanctuary, sensing some undefinable oppressiveness about the place. She'd been a straight-A student through high school and thought of herself as bookish and hopelessly sedate. She longed to find a college that could help her break out of her mold. BYU was clearly not such a place.

Nor was the University of Utah, which she ultimately selected. The student body was more varied, the curriculum more eclectic, but it was not enough. In her junior year, over the adamant protests of her parents, she transferred to Barnard College in New York City, where a whole new world opened up to her. Compared to her antiseptic environs in Salt Lake, and her scrubbed-clean friends, the sheer unruliness of New York, its seedy fecundity, wove a hypnotic spell. Gussie blossomed. She studied American history, not just Mormon history. She learned there was a Carl Jung, not just a Brigham Young. She discovered the glories of the Museum of Modern Art, Greenwich Village and the theater. For the first time in her life she drank coffee, sipped wine and even tried smoking grass. She loved the coffee, but the wine and the weed put her to sleep. She lost twenty-five pounds, shed her glasses in favor of contact lenses and discovered, to her astonishment, that boys were enormously attracted to her pretty face and lissome figure—attributes of which she had no prior awareness.

She decided to stay. Having earned her B.A., she moved the two blocks from Barnard to Columbia University where she began work toward her doctorate in political science. During this period, she had never returned to Utah, not even for a weekend, and had steadfastly avoided dating Utah boys, especially Mormons. Toward the end of her second year at Columbia, however, she met a young business administration student named Hiram Cobb, whose blond, handsome charm and lilting Southern accent she found utterly beguiling. It was not until their third date that she learned he was a Mormon. His great-great-grandfather, he explained, had been conscripted into the fabled Mormon Battalion, but when he learned that Brigham Young had dispatched the battalion to march all the way from Kansas to California, he defected and instead took a wagon train to New Orleans, and there he and his descendants had remained.

But he was still a Mormon! Why would she find herself, after all this time, dating a Mormon? It was not just a question of his charm and good looks, she reluctantly concluded. There was also that subconscious sense of kinship, that subliminal bond, she had struggled so hard to deny. They were both children of Zion— slightly deviant and faintly rebellious perhaps—but Mormons nonetheless. They were also in love.

They were married in the Temple at Mesa, near Phoenix, with a proper LDS wedding, and had a glorious honeymoon in Mexico. Hiram concluded his studies in accounting and dutifully dispatched his job applications. He received one excellent offer— from an accounting firm in Salt Lake City. Not back to Utah again! Gussie almost fainted when she heard the news. She started to cry and then took a long walk alone in the rainswept streets. When she returned she said she was sorry, she was acting selfishly. Determined to play the role of the faithfully supportive young wife, Gussie applied for instructorships at several Utah institutions. None was interested—none except BYU. Very well, she told herself, if all roads led to BYU, she would go to BYU.

She started in September 1970. Her initial assignment called for her to teach three courses in introductory political science. Her head of department, Ethan Rice, was a kindly, rumpled old man who said Gussie reminded him of his daughter and who encouraged her through her initial seizures of classroom panic. The students themselves were amiable and respectful; indeed, compared with the abrasive personalities at Columbia, they were positively benign.

At the end of her first year, Professor Rice enthusiastically renewed her contract, and she started work on her Ph.D. dissertation as well. Hiram's practice was growing so fast he quit the firm and started out on his own. And now and then he reminded her impishly of her reluctance to return to Utah. Here they were, happy, making good friends, earning an excellent living; it was all working out so very well after all. And indeed, Gussie was enjoying herself enormously. She loved teaching. She enjoyed the delicious irresponsibility of being childless. Most of all, she enjoyed Hiram.

Her happiness was such that, when the storm clouds first began to loom during her second year at BYU, she remained utterly oblivious. There had been gossip among the faculty that BYU's new president, an aggressive corporate lawyer named Earl Wardlow, was an archconservative with a past record of fervent opposition to left-wing encroachments on Mormondom. Gussie paid little attention to the talk, however. Even at Columbia, the faculty was always complaining about the conservatism of its administration.

In one of her classes, however, there was one youth whose appearance and behavior were giving her qualms.

He was named Brian Wood, a big, blond youth whose face, with its flat nose and rounded, receding forehead, reminded her of a seal. There was something vaguely malevolent about his hooded eyes, as there was in his persistent questioning on certain specific topics. Wood would take every possible opportunity to question her views about the New Deal, the ideology of Franklin D. Roosevelt, the political beliefs of Socialists such as Eugene Debs or Norman Thomas. Was this young man oddly fixated on these subjects, she wondered, or were his motives more complex? One day, while passing out exam papers, she made a sudden deliberate move toward his chair, only to see him grasp a small, black instrument that had been perched on his knee and shove it into the concealment of his briefcase. How odd, she thought, that this singularly unscholarly young man would not only be asking her provocative questions, but also recording her responses for posterity.

She mentioned the incident at a faculty lunch two days later, embarrassed by its seeming triviality, but Edwin Colfax, a young economics professor seated down the table, seized on it immediately. There was a student in his class as well, Colfax said, who was taping his lectures, and also asking spurious questions. Conversation around the table quieted ominously.

"There is nothing to be alarmed about," Ethan Rice assured them good-naturedly. "BYU students have always carried on a lively business in selling class notes. Think nothing of it."

But Gussie had trouble putting it out of her mind. Suddenly all the rigidities and regimentation of BYU began to get to her again: the coldly modern sameness of the yellow brick buildings, the military briskness with which the entire student body came to attention when the National Anthem was played each morning over the campus's vast network of loudspeakers, the clonelike similarities in appearance among the thousands of undergraduates, their obsessive tidiness, the steely absence of any overt signs of affection among boys and girls, as mandated by the administration. The system worked—of that there was no doubt. Some twenty-five thousand undergraduates each morning filed into their classrooms to receive their daily rations of learning from their clean-cut, close-cropped professors. But were they really being educated, Gussie wondered, or were they merely passing down the assembly line with numb obedience?

A week later, in the middle of her class, Gussie was summoned to Professor Rice's office. The old man's face was haggard, his eyes troubled. "Two more instructors have reported finding tape recorders," Rice told her. "Gussie, I want you to return to your classroom. I want you to go up to the student who's taping your lectures and tell him to be at my office this afternoon at four. I'm getting them all together. I'm going to lock the door and I'll keep hammering away at them until I get to the bottom of this."

Stunned and frightened, Gussie returned to her lecture hall, stalking immediately to the row where Brian Wood customarily sat. His chair was empty. "Brian's sick today," explained the student who sat next to him. He was a slight blond youth, almost effeminate in his prettiness.

"What is your name?" Gussie asked.

"Tad Hastings." And she noticed it then—the small black tape recorder which Tad was desperately attempting to wedge under his crotch.

"I want you to be at Professor Rice's office at four o'clock this afternoon, Tad. Is that clear?"

Tad's face was crimson. "Why?"

"Be there," Gussie said sharply.

☐ The inquisition went on for almost an hour before Professor Rice, his face reddened with exertion, began to make some headway. At first the four students gathered in his office blandly professed their innocence. It was all a coincidence, they insisted. There was a studied calm about them that seemed almost rehearsed, Gussie sensed from her perch in the back of the office. Of the four, only Tad Hastings showed distress, squirming constantly in his seat, eyes shifting from one person to the next, face moist with sweat. When Brian Wood finally joined the meeting, sniffling from his cold, Tad's eyes bore into him with a fierce resentment.

"I suspect you're the leader of this sorry group," Professor Rice told Brian, pointing his finger sternly. "I'm waiting for an explanation."

Brian Wood's face was expressionless. "There is nothing in the rules against taping lectures," he said.

"Tell him the truth!" Tad Hastings blurted suddenly. "You got us all into this mess. You told us it was perfectly all right, that you had it all set up with the administration."

There was panic now in Brian's hooded blue eyes.

"Shut up," he hissed.

"I'm not even part of this caper," Tad continued, directing his words at Professor Rice. "I told him I didn't want any part of it. The only reason I was holding the tape recorder today was that Brian was sick."

There was a pall of silence in the room now; Gussie could feel the tension building. She saw Brian Wood remove another tissue from his pocket and blow his nose furiously.

And then he started to talk.

As he spoke in his muffled, nasal voice, Gussie, seated there, could hear most of his words but could not bring herself to believe the things he said. Even weeks later, during the Administrative Hearings, she could still not quite accept the facts that Brian Wood laid before them that afternoon.

All of them, Brian Wood explained, had been recruited by Rolf Bangston, a zealous young vice-president in the BYU administration. Bangston had started with Wood, whose record as an activist in the John Birch Society was well known, and through Wood had lined up eight recruits—five others in addition to the three in Rice's office. None of the recruits had ever met with President Wardlow or with any other member of the administration, but Bangston, in giving them their instructions, repeatedly emphasized that he was speaking for the administration of BYU.

The university, Bangston told them, had always been steadfast in resisting the incursions of outside radical forces, but now there was fresh cause for concern. More and more left-wing professors were infiltrating the faculty, he said. Other undesirables—homosexuals and feminists—were appearing in the student body. The time for renewed vigilance was at hand.

The task of Wood and the others, Bangston said, was to monitor classes taught by suspected radicals and to help document the charges of radical expression that would ultimately be brought against them. At the same time, they were to start surveillance of those fellow students whose activities were suspicious, reporting all evidence to the campus security officers.

Professor Rice listened silently to this appalling recitation, his face an ashen mask. When Brian Wood had finished, he continued staring at the boy for several minutes, then lifted up the telephone and told his secretary, "Get me President Wardlow."

Revelation of the existence of the "spy ring" produced an embittered barrage of charges and countercharges on campus. Professor Rice, together with several other senior faculty members, demanded an official university investigation. President Wardlow, pleading ignorance of the entire scheme, promised to take it "under advisement." The local chapter of the American Association of University Professors warned that BYU's official accreditation could be jeopardized, and fired off a formal complaint to the Council of the Twelve Apostles, who exercised ultimate responsibility over university affairs. The campus paper was ablaze with letters and editorials attacking and defending the various students and professors involved in the "spy ring."

For her part, Gussie found her thought processes all but immobilized by the imbroglio. Despite Professor Rice's continued encouragement, she had lost her zest for teaching. Her students, she felt, looked upon her as a curiosity—a cultural freak. She was guarded in her remarks to them. Most of the kids, she knew, came from highly protected environments. Politically, they were hothouse plants. They had never before been subjected to controversy nor had they ever pondered the nature of dissent. They had been taught one set of religious beliefs, Mormon beliefs, and one set of moral values which flowed from them. Living in totally Mormon communities, they'd spent their childhoods being shuttled between their public schools and their adjoining seminaries, where Mormon doctrine was inculcated during school hours. To these students the events unfolding before them seemed more like science fiction than reality.

Paradoxically, Gussie had come from an identical background. Though she had come of age in the radical sixties, her own moral and political beliefs were traditionalist. She had experimented with alcohol and marijuana in her New York days to be sure, but they no longer held any fascination for her. And yet suddenly she was being looked upon as a radical!

It would all soon blow over, Professor Rice still assured her. Administrative hearings had been set up. The student members of the "spy ring" had signed their official confessions. The faculty was solidly behind them. An apology would be made by the administration, Rice said, and all would go back to normal.

Two days before the hearing, however, Gussie got a call to appear before Rolf Bangston. The moment she entered his small, antiseptic office, with its gray desk and spartan furniture, she knew that Professor Rice had been tragically mistaken. Bangston was a bone-thin, almost ascetic-looking young man with a tense, predacious face, his blond hair clipped in a military crew cut. He did not rise to greet her.

"I have listened to some of the tapes recorded in your classroom by Brian Wood," Bangston said, his light blue eyes focused intently on her. "I know all you people are very confident about these hearings. You all think this will simply blow away. But I have listened to your remarks, Miss Cobb, and I want to assure you it won't simply blow away."

Gussie felt a chill. "To begin with, it is Mrs. Cobb," she replied, surprised by the edge of indignation in her voice. "Secondly, I resent your veiled threat. I have never used my classroom as a platform to express any radical or subversive beliefs. I hold no such beliefs."

"I can cite examples," Bangston said, leaning across his desk. "I have the tapes. I can cite chapter and verse."

"You can do no such thing."

"You said Roosevelt's New Deal got the country out of the Depression," Bangston persisted. "You said that. You said this Communist, Norman Thomas, had some useful ideas that ultimately"—Bangston paused to scan some typed pages on his desk—"that ultimately found their way into the mainstream. Do you deny saying that?"

"You're out of your mind," Gussie said, "if you think those are seditious beliefs."

But Bangston continued scanning his papers. "You said, Miss Cobb, that the United States should have initiated ties with Red China as early as 1960. Do you deny saying that?"

Sitting there before this oddly boyish zealot, watching his eyes glisten like a hunter stalking his prey, Gussie felt a surge of rage such as she had never known before. She wanted to rise from her seat and grasp this young man by the lapels of his dark blue suit and shake him until his head bobbed uncontrollably. She wanted to tear up his notes and bury him in their fragments.

"Mr. Bangston, I do not intend to sit here and debate my political beliefs. I do not think you have the intellectual capacity to make the debate very interesting. Nor do I understand the purpose of this meeting."

"I have called you here just to remind you that we know where you stand, Miss Cobb. Two days from now at the public hearings you will hear official denials and explanations. All sorts of things will be said to placate the press. But I want you to know, whatever is said in public, that we're not going to let this die. We will continue to protect the integrity of this great university."

"Are you firing me?"

"I do not have the authority to hire or fire. That power resides with the faculty."

"In that case, I'll be on my way," Gussie said, rising to her feet. "Oh, by the way. Why don't you play those tapes one more time? Brigham Young said, 'Education can wield a potent influence for good among the people of the earth.' Take Brigham's advice and educate yourself. It may do you some good."

At the public hearings, Gussie sat through the procession of speakers. A letter from President Wardlow was read, reiterating his ignorance of the whole scheme but pledging his support for the faculty. The dean enunciated the confessions of the "spy ring" students once again, and emphasized that they had acted improperly. Everything, Gussie realized, was being deftly swept under the carpet.

When she rose to speak she could sense a nervousness in the room. Her remarks were terse and to the point. "I realize that, in the short term, it would be best for all parties to pretend the whole thing had never happened, but I cannot bring myself to accept that resolution." She described her meeting with Bangston, explaining that Bangston's attitudes seemed to be truly those of the administration and of President Wardlow, not the bland assurances that had been read to them today. Given this atmosphere of hypocrisy, she could not continue teaching at BYU. She would always feel the constraints. She would always know that someone, somewhere, was monitoring her remarks to be certain that they had been properly sanitized for the tender ears of the LDS student body.

When she had finished there was a sudden, passionate burst of applause. Then it quickly subsided and an uneasy silence settled over the room, a kind of hushed embarrassment. The dean rose to adjourn the hearing and everyone hurried from the room.

The following morning Gussie submitted her resignation. Four other professors followed suit that week, but all of their resignations were ignored by the BYU student newspaper, as were her remarks. Despite the curtain of silence, an Associated Press reporter picked up the story and sent it out on the wire, and it appeared in hundreds of newspapers around the country the next day, two short paragraphs even surfacing in the *Salt Lake City Tribune*.

A week after her resignation, several of her colleagues held a little farewell party for Gussie off campus. Everyone struggled to be cheerful and upbeat, trying to ignore the fact that most of those invited had failed to attend. Toward the end of the evening Professor Rice took her aside and gave her a good-bye kiss and Gussie could see the tears streaming down his face. "We'll miss you, dear Gussie," he said tearfully. "Try and put all this behind you. . . ."

And when she returned to their apartment that night, Hiram asked her to sit down and quietly informed her that six of his eight clients had withdrawn their accounts from his frail young firm as a result of the publicity. He would have to close his office, Hiram said, and now it was Gussie who was crying, too.

☐ Gussie had just about concluded her chores in the kitchen when she heard the knock at the front door. She felt an edge of alarm. The boys were both home, as was Hiram. It had been many weeks since their latest "incidents," as she and Hiram euphemistically described them—in that case, a large rock being hurled through an upstairs window—but Gussie instinctively regarded uninvited nighttime guests with caution. Peering through the tiny peephole, she recognized the enormous man who stood on her doorstep wearing, as usual, his black suit and funereal frown.

"Good evening," she said cheerfully, opening the door for Hosea Cloor.

"Good evening, madam," Hosea said, nodding stiffly. On the several occasions she had previously met Hosea, Gussie had never seen him smile.

"I have been asked to deliver this note to you, madam," Hosea said, as he retrieved a small white envelope from inside his jacket.

"Thank you, Hosea."

"Merry Christmas, madam," Hosea said, turning quickly and retreating to the long black limousine whose engine was still running at the curb.

"And Merry Christmas to you," Gussie called after him.

Shutting and bolting the door, Gussie returned to the living room, tearing open the small envelope. A single piece of paper was inside. It was a check. Gussie sighed deeply when she read the amount, and let herself tumble onto the sofa, her eyes misting with tears of exhilaration and relief.

Five thousand dollars! That wonderful gracious woman! Gussie opened her eyes and stared once again at the check, as though to confirm it was not an illusion.

It was real! Gussie felt overwhelmed with gratitude. She must have sensed how desperate they were. Gussie had never said a word to her about their financial straits, but she was a shrewd, insightful woman. She knew. And now Cora Snow had come to their rescue yet again.

TUESDAY, DECEMBER 23

The Prophecy

PULLING his Pinto into the parking lot at seven minutes before nine, Tad Hastings noted with satisfaction that he'd made the drive from Salt Lake to Snow City in only forty minutes, averaging a frenetic seventy-five miles per hour, all the while fighting grogginess and a nagging headache, and thoroughly regretting the vodka he'd consumed the night before. He had endured a troubled, half-drunken sleep, steeped in erotic fantasies which he chose not to remember, awakening at seven thirty with both an erection and a hangover, helpless to allay either. The last thing he felt like doing was fighting the traffic out to Snow City.

At least the snow had abated—that much had helped him—but this was one of those chill, drab mornings when the gloom seemed to press down from the mountains. He had driven much of the way through whorls of gray mist, like giant clots of steel wool, obscuring the sun and dulling the senses. Looking up, he could barely see the snow stacked high along the shoulders of the Wasatch. How nice it would have been, Tad thought, to have stayed home this morning, savoring a second glass of juice and dawdling over the morning newspaper instead of making the long drive. Tad was well aware, however, that his appearance today was a mandatory one—Ellis Marmer, his boss, had made that quite clear. The Snow family was probably his firm's biggest client, second only to the LDS Church, and, in many ways, also the most demanding.

Their legal affairs were handled personally by Marmer himself and his senior partners; indeed Tad had never even met the Snows, and the only reason he'd been "invited" to attend this morning's meeting, it was made clear, was that Ellis Marmer needed bodies. Cora Snow, the iron-willed Mormon matriarch who ran the affairs of the family, reputedly felt slighted unless at

125

least four attorneys from the law firm responded to her every summons. With two partners off on ski vacations and another down with the flu, Marmer was quick to recruit Tad to complete his quorum.

And Tad was glad he had done so, now that he was here, trudging across the broad parking lot, the shock of the damp, frosty air stinging him awake, his adrenal glands pumping away the grogginess. He looked forward to meeting Cora Snow—or "Snowballs," as his colleagues termed her with something less than affection. He might even catch sight of her fabled progeny and that would give him something to tell his own children when he got home. At the center of the gilt-edged brood was eighteen-year-old Jebediah "Jeb" Snow, and his twin sister, Charity, both of them milk-fed, God-fearing Mormon kids who had made it big on alien soil—the sordid world of entertainment—where they had established themselves as the stars of a long-running TV sitcom series. Each week Nancy and the two oldest kids gaped avidly at the Snow's television show, though Tad himself found the kids toothily irritating as they worked their way through their familiar "family-oriented" situation comedy routines. Yet there was no quarreling with success, and the huge gold letters spelling out SNOW CITY which towered above him now were a bold embodiment of that success. SNOW CITY represented the family's most extravagant venture, a newly completed complex of sound stages, recording studios, dressing rooms and offices, which had been opened six months earlier amid a fusillade of publicity. Tad remembered the newspaper accounts of the dedication, the extraordinary intermingling of Mormon patriarchs with show business celebrities, Cora Snow proclaiming to them all that SNOW CITY represented the family's ultimate dream. No longer would her children have to descend into the moral squalor of Hollywood to tape their shows. Now they, and others like them, could stay home in God's country. The local newspapers each published editorials applauding this as yet another example of Mormon self-sufficiency.

Though the hour was still early, the sprawling semicircular lobby Tad now entered already was teeming with activity. Some thirty or so wide-eyed teenagers were being herded together by a pretty, blond-haired tour guide, who was garbed in a bright red uniform. A cluster of men in dark suits waited sedately on the mauve sofas in the reception area. Standing in line at the receptionist's desk, Tad inspected the photographic blowups of the Snows which were emblazoned across the bright yellow walls of the lobby—photos of Jeb and Charity, blond-haired and apple-cheeked, smilingly accepting awards, of Cora and Vernon Snow standing beside the late President Woodleigh and other elders of the Church and of their three younger children as well, none of whom had ventured into show business. Prominently positioned near the lobby entrance were several ornately framed oil portraits of sturdy-looking Mormon pioneers whom Tad took to be the Snows' forebears, their faces severe and bewhiskered, their expressions doggedly righteous.

Directed down a brilliantly lighted yellow corridor, Tad entered a large, circular conference room to find his three colleagues already locked in intense discussion. Ellis Marmer, gaunt and owlish in his tortoiseshell glasses, greeted him, hand extended, as did the two others, their sudden conviviality a reflection, Tad reminded himself, of the successful outcome of the Pacific negotiation. In times past, their greetings had been at best perfunctory. It is amazing, Tad thought, how one successful deal can transmogrify an anonymous employee into an honored colleague. "Have a look at these, Tad," Ellis Marmer said, as he pushed over a stack of documents. Thumbing through them hastily, Tad saw they consisted of an agenda for the meeting, financial records covering the company's past fiscal quarter and updates on pending litigation. Glancing at his colleagues, Tad saw the tension on their faces as they sat in their dark gray suits, white shirts and dark ties, awaiting the arrival of their clients. How different from the conference table at Suncorp headquarters in Los Angeles, where everyone worked in shirt-sleeves, ties uncinched, drinking coffee and smoking cigarettes. While he disdained coffee and loathed cigarette smoke, Tad wished, nonetheless, that something of the ease and informality of the outside world could rub off on the Mormon business establishment.

The hands on the large wall clock had just hit nine when the door opened and Cora Snow and her husband Vernon strode into the room, followed, to Tad's surprise, by their son Jeb, as well as a retinue of four lawyers and business advisers. Tad and his colleagues were on their feet now, arrayed at attention, as the three family members made their way around the table, moving from one to the other, shaking hands, exchanging salutations. ". . . Good morning, Brother Marmer . . . trust you are well? . . ." There was something almost ceremonial about their courtliness, like royalty greeting their faithful retainers. Cora Snow herself looked smaller in person than Tad had imagined. In her photographs and public appearances, she took on the demeanor of a formidable, yet self-effacing matron, standing faithfully at her husband's side, her clothing conservative, hair tied in a chignon. The wispy woman who stood before him now seemed almost sparrowlike, as though a strong wind might blow her away, but there was nonetheless a presence about her, even an authority, that belied her diminutive stature. A sharp intellect, Tad suspected, lurked behind those riveting blue eyes which peered out from her thin, seamed face. Tad had been told that Cora Snow, in her younger years, had flourished on her own as a singer, but had immediately abandoned her career when she'd married, expunging all mention of it from official biographies.

"Good to meet you, Brother Hastings," she said in a strong buoyant voice which was in turn matched by a vigorous, viselike handshake. As she moved on to a colleague, Tad flexed his fingers in preparation for Vernon Snow, who now stood before him, hand extended. Vernon looked considerably older than his wife, pudgy and slightly bent, his craggy face that of a farmer, all knobs and bone, lacking the clean, smooth planes of his son, who moved forward to present himself, his handshake slack, his glance askew. "Howareya," murmured Jeb, as he moved absently toward a chair next to that of his mother.

"Shall we begin, gentlemen?" Vernon Snow said, seating himself, his eyes glancing at the papers before him. "I see we have our quarterly P & L right here, so mebbe we should talk about that first." Vernon, who spoke in a dry Midwestern twang, looked quickly at his wife, seated silently at his side, and then continued:

"Now these figgers are disappointing. They really are." He licked his fingers as he sorted the pages in front of him. "We have a net deficit of four hundred sixty-eight thousand, nine hundred twenty-two dollars for the fourth quarter. Now, we were also in the red in the third quarter but it wasn't this bad. So, we find ourselves going downhill here, which is all the more vexing when you consider that last year at this time, before we opened this studio, we were ahead of the game, weren't we, Purvis? . . ."

The chubby, red-cheeked man on his right nodded vigorously. "We had a net profit of four hundred eighty-two thousand in the fourth quarter last year, sir."

"Yes, so what I'm gettin' at here is that we are all a little concerned at these figgers. I mean, we knew we would be in the red for a spell while we got this spread on its feet and all . . ."

"Start-up costs have been higher than anticipated, sir," Purvis put in.

". . . Yes, start-up costs," Vernon Snow said, "but what we're looking ahead to is another year in the red and mebbe bigger losses and we'll be chawin' away at our basic assets. . . ."

As he listened to Vernon Snow's rueful recitation, it occurred to Tad that this was a curious spectacle, the head of one of Mormondom's most famous families and architect of its most prominent success story sadly wallowing amid a sea of red ink. What a yawning chasm exists between reality and what the public perceives to be reality. Glancing around the table, Tad saw Ellis Marmer listening intently, a look of studied concern implanted upon his sallow features. Cora Snow sat upright in her chair, listening respectfully to her husband's remarks, eyes straight ahead, her expression noncommittal.

". . . Now when we built this studio we knew we'd be taking on a burden," Vernon Snow continued, his tongue flicking over his lips. "We all knew we might have tough sledding at first, but I think we all figgered that within six months there would be lots of folks clamoring to rent space. Folks from Hollywood who would like to shoot their movies up here in the clean air and beautiful country. That's what I was told would be happening. Isn't that correct?"

"That is correct, sir," an aide responded. He was a corpulent, balding man whose face resembled that of a baleful hound dog. "According to projections, our own Snow family projects will utilize only a maximum twenty percent of our capacity. If I may put in, sir, we've just added another man to our staff in Los Angeles to help bring in some more business. He's a really good man . . ."

"I'm certain he's a real good man," Cora Snow interjected, her voice casting a sudden pall over the room, "but I don't expect the addition of one man will turn things around overnight."

"Quite right, quite right," the hound dog said in full retreat.

"How many companies outside the family have booked space here at the studio over the next three months?" Cora Snow asked.

The man named Purvis was shuffling through some papers. "Three companies," he responded, his voice thin with panic. "Three so far, but things are slow around Christmas. . . ."

"That's not too bad," Vernon Snow said softly.

"Isn't it true that two of those bookings are one-day shoots for commercials?" Cora Snow shot back. "And the third booking you mentioned is for some recording artist I never heard of—we don't even know if he can pay his bills."

Purvis flushed and the room was silent once again. Yes, Snowballs is definitely getting down to business, Tad thought.

"If I may make a suggestion," Ellis Marmer said, "surely our brothers in the Church could help on this matter. There are hundreds of LDS people in positions of corporate leadership around the country. They could influence their companies to film their commercials here at the studio. Has there been a systematic campaign to approach these people?"

"Not systematic," Vernon Snow replied. "We've talked to people out there who we happen to know . . ."

"There is a list," Ellis Marmer continued. "The Church has a very comprehensive list of LDS company presidents and the like. Perhaps you could send each of them a brochure . . ."

"I appreciate that suggestion," Cora Snow cut in. "But I think that you can help us with something more important than a list." Cora Snow paused as though for dramatic effect. She didn't need to, Tad noted. Whenever she spoke, all eyes were upon her, including those of her husband. "We have a good, solid cash-intensive company here, Mr. Marmer," she continued, her right hand making an expansive gesture. "Our basic capitalization is sound. Our ratio of debt to equity is sound. So is our history of pretax profits. Our product is selling better than ever and our audience is loyal. The bottom line is that we need additional short-term financing to compensate for our high start-up costs and tide us over until we can generate more business here at the studio. Isn't that what you were getting at, Vernon?"

Vernon Snow nodded. "Yes, Cora, that's exactly what I was trying to tell these folks."

"I understand fully," Ellis Marmer said. "Given the soundness of this company and the family's exemplary reputation in the community, I am confident additional short-term financing would be readily available to you."

"The prime rate jumped two points last month," Vernon Snow said plaintively.

"The Snow family is not just a family—it's a national resource," Ellis Marmer persisted. "I am sure the local banks would bend over backward to make the best deal possible."

"Ma has something else in mind," Jeb put in.

"We think you might be able to give us a hand," Vernon Snow said.

"Of course, I'd be delighted to help in any way I can," Ellis Marmer said. "But I'm sure your contacts at the banks are easily as good as mine. . . ."

"Your law firm does a great deal of business for the Church of Jesus Christ of Latter-day Saints," Cora Snow said, her eyes focused sternly on Marmer once again. "My understanding is that you handle as much of their business as any other law firm."

Marmer looked perplexed. "That is true, of course," he replied.

"Over the last five years alone this family has contributed over two million dollars in tithes to the Church," Vernon Snow said.

"That is remarkable," Marmer said. "Surely the Church has been enormously grateful."

"Well, maybe it's time we got some of it back," Vernon Snow said mildly. "Just for a spell, mind you."

For the first time since he'd known him, Tad saw Ellis Marmer's normally impassive features take on a look of total bewilderment. His heavy-framed glasses dropped a notch down his nose. "I don't think I really understand, . . ." Marmer started to protest.

"What Vernon means," Cora Snow said, "is that we would like to arrange a loan from the Church. A short-term loan reflecting its confidence and appreciation for everything the family has done for the Church."

Ellis Marmer ran his veined hand through his thinning gray hair and took a deep breath. "Well, I suppose that's something that could be discussed at the appropriate level," he said fretfully. "As you surely know, it's rare for the Church to make loans to commercial enterprises, other than institutions."

"We have a new administration in the Church," Cora Snow said. "President Bryce attended the dedication of this studio when he was still an Apostle. I don't know this Sloat fellow, but I am told he is a smart businessman."

"Dana Sloat is one of the nation's leading business figures," Ellis Marmer said. "I have had some dealings with him and find him to be enormously bright and responsive."

"I'm glad you think well of him," Vernon Snow said.

"I am, too," Cora Snow said, leaning forward across the table. "Because here's what I want from him. My husband and I want a three-million-dollar five-year loan. Interest free. Isn't that right, Vernon?"

Vernon nodded his head.

"Are there any questions?" Cora Snow said.

Tad saw Ellis Marmer remove his glasses, his rheumy blue eyes staring at Cora Snow with a mixture of fear and alarm. All right, Snowballs, Tad told himself, you have him on the ropes. Stick it to him!

"I must remind you that I am not a General Authority of the Church," Ellis Marmer said, measuring his words carefully. "I cannot enunciate Church policy. I can state, however, that I have never heard of an interest-free loan being approved. Our brethren are wily businessman, after all, . . ." Marmer said, struggling for a note of levity.

Cora Snow did not smile. "I thought I heard you say the Snow family was not just a family—it was a national resource. Well, then, surely a man of your tact and ability can convince them that exceptions must be made to guard national resources."

Tad had all he could to keep from cheering. Nothing pleased his lawyer-like mind more than to see someone turn one's opponent's words to his own advantage. Snowballs was truly a first-rate tactician—relentlessly moving in for the kill, yet, at the same time, appearing to defer to her husband, making him feel that these were *his* tactics, that she was acting under *his* direction. Tad recalled the last time he'd tried to hit Ellis Marmer for a raise, remembered how coldly dismissive he was. How he wished he'd had Snowballs at his side.

He was startled out of his reverie by a persistent tapping on his shoulder, and looked up to see a young secretary leaning over him.

"Aren't you Mr. Hastings?" she whispered.

"Yes."

"You have a phone call."

Tad looked toward Marmer. "Whoever it is, tell them I'll call back."

"The man said it's urgent. He told me to interrupt."

"I don't care—I'll have to call him back."

Tad saw the secretary flush, then lean closer to him so that her lips brushed against his ear. "It's a man named Gavin Pollard," she whispered, her words barely audible. "He insisted that I tell you . . . well . . . he said to get your ass out of the fucking meeting. . . ."

Tad saw the young secretary's face redden with embarrassment. Without saying a word, he sprang to his feet and moved as quickly as possible toward the door.

□ "What is it, Gavin?" Tad was standing over a secretarial desk in a cramped office across from the conference room. "You just took me out of one of the most amazing meetings —I wish I owned the television syndication rights to this meeting. . . ."

"The Pacific people are playing games with us. They're changing the goddamn deal." There was a tightness in Gavin's voice that sent off alarm bells in Tad's head.

"What do you mean, changing the deal?"

"They agreed to sell us their radio and television stations. Now all of a sudden they insist we buy the whole goddamn company."

"Who told you this?"

"The old man—Curry—called me ten minutes ago."

"He can't change the deal. . . ."

"He's the chief executive officer of Pacific. He can do whatever the fuck he wants."

The secretary started hammering away on her big gray IBM electric, and Tad, straining to catch Gavin's words, touched her shoulder to signal her to stop. She looked at him, irritated.

"Did Curry give any reason?"

"He mumbled something about estate problems and that sort of bullshit. The bottom line is that we got problems. Big problems."

Tad felt his throat grow dry. "Look, Gavin, let's take a good look at the whole picture before we get hysterical and blow the deal. Maybe this is a lucky break. The stations were undervalued —maybe the company's other assets are also a bargain."

"Have you done an analysis of the parent company?"

"Yes, I've done—well, not complete in the sense that it's a privately held company. There are certain financial documents I asked for, but Curry said he couldn't find them or they weren't ready yet—stuff like that."

"There's something peculiar—something that doesn't add up."

"What do you mean, peculiar? It's an old-fashiond kind of operation. We've been through all this."

"Look, kid, get your ass on a plane to Los Angeles right away. You hear me?"

"Yeah, I hear you."

"What time can you be here?"

Tad glanced at his watch. "I can be in L.A. by midafternoon. It's a bit awkward getting out of this meeting, is all."

"Well, it will be more than a bit awkward if your ass isn't here this afternoon."

Tad noticed the secretary staring at him with a puzzled expression. "All right, Gavin. I'll be there." He handed the phone to the secretary.

"You all right, Mr. Hastings?"

The secretary's gum showed through her teeth as she smiled.

Unhearing, Tad started absently toward the door, then turned. "Look, when the meeting breaks could you give a message to Mr. Marmer?"

"Sure."

"Tell him I'm on a plane to Los Angeles, okay?"

She was scribbling on a pad. "I hope this doesn't ruin your Christmas," the secretary said.

But Tad had already darted down the hall.

IT was ten o'clock when Turner Mead received the summons he had nervously anticipated. Mr. Sloat, the secretary advised, would like to see Mr. Mead in one hour. Would that be convenient? Yes, of course it would be convenient. But at eleven thirty, having waited half an hour for his audience, Turner had grown fidgety. A dank chill permeated the granite expanses of the old Church Administration Building which sat, in all its stolid grandeur, directly across the street from the modern headquarters skyscraper. A dark-haired woman Turner had never seen before had ushered him into the presidential board room where he had been told to wait, and now, thirty minutes later, his feet had grown numb with cold. Turner had been in this building many times, yet was puzzled this morning to see so many new faces. A few of the plump, matronly secretaries who had long served the Prophet and his Counselors had already apparently been supplanted by younger women with cool, efficient demeanors. Even Bill Chadwick, the presidential assistant and gadfly who normally chatted with Turner while he awaited his presidential meetings, was nowhere to be seen. Yes, Turner told himself as he got to his feet to pace across the room, there are definitely changes in the air. That much was abundantly clear; indeed, it had been clear all morning.

He had arrived at his office at 8:00 A.M., as was his custom, feeling rested and alert, harboring a deep gratitude toward his body for requiring so little sleep. He had left Eliza's house at three o'clock in the morning, was asleep in his own bed by three thirty and awake by six, reaching instinctively for her, wishing she was at his side. Riding up the fourteen floors to his office, smiling at the others on the crowded elevator—faces he had smiled at every morning these many years—Turner had the sudden impulse to announce aloud exactly how he felt, the words

135

running through his mind: "Good morning, dear anonymous Brothers and Sisters, would you believe that this austere-looking Englishman with whom you share this elevator has the miraculous good fortune to be in love? That after many long years of living alone in arid righteousness, he finds himself consumed with passionately libidinous urges he thought had long since deserted him? There is hope for us all, dear Brethren." No, Turner quickly decided, he would not make any such speech, but it was, indeed, a delicious temptation.

Turner's afterglow from the previous evening had dimmed badly, however, within several minutes of his arrival. The telephone calls had started early and by 10:00 A.M. had reached their crescendo, his secretary struggling desperately to cope with the insistent overseas operators, the anguished voices, the panicky demands to be put through immediately. "Mr. Mead will call back as soon as he gets off the phone. . . . Mr. Mead cannot accept the call at this time. . . . Mr. Mead is talking to Australia but when he gets off. . . ." He had taken as many of them as he could, issuing calm reassurances, promising to put their questions to the appropriate authorities as soon as possible. His callers were diverse but determined. A columnist from Washington, a Mission President from London, a newspaper publisher from New Zealand, the head of a Wall Street brokerage house, even Burt Hoagland, his old friend who had succeeded him as city editor of the *Deseret News*.

It was not long before a clear pattern had begun to emerge. The LDS Church was like a great pulsing organism that sprawled, in all its power and influence, around the globe. Whenever change was imminent, even its most remote nerve endings would begin to twitch nervously. And so it was with the calls this morning, all of them responsive to the subtle oscillations, concerned, even alarmed, demanding information and reassurance. Was it true the Church was selling its controlling interest in one of its great insurance companies to acquire a major bloc of stock in a prominent U.S. corporation? Was it true that vast funds sequestered in Switzerland and Liechtenstein were being converted to other currencies? Was it true that the Church was bidding for a substantial U.S. broadcasting company? Was it true the Church was locking up control of a major television station in Christchurch, New Zealand, and a publishing house in Tokyo?

Turner, to be sure, had no idea whether these things were true. But he did know that Dalton Evans' suspicions were correct, that Dana Sloat had indeed been hard at work for some time developing his game plan, and the time for implementing this plan was now at hand.

But what *was* the plan? Clearly the rumors of corporate maneuverings and currency conversions, if true, were merely surface manifestations. The Church's holdings were already so vast that the actual details were kept from LDS members, partly for fear that the information would discourage the ten percent tithe contributions. Included among these holdings were four insurance companies, a publishing company, a broadcasting empire consisting of fourteen radio and television stations in key cities such as New York, Dallas and Chicago, a newspaper, vast ranches and agricultural lands, a village in Hawaii, shopping malls, thousands of acres of priceless urban real estate and, of course, Brigham Young University, plus substantial minority investments in countless diverse companies around the world. Representatives of the Church hierarchy sat on the boards of companies like Anaconda, Phillips Petroleum, Bankers Trust and Union Pacific Railroad. Church income, Turner knew, approached some two billion dollars a year, most of it tax-exempt, ranking the LDS Church high on the list of the nation's fifty biggest corporations and among the wealthiest churches in the entire world. Certainly the hierarchy in Salt Lake City exercised direct control over a domain more extensive than that controlled from the headquarters of any other religious group in the United States—the big Roman Catholic portfolios and land holdings were generally controlled by their local diocese. But the Mormon empire continued to expand relentlessly, as tens of thousands of loyal, tithe-paying converts were persuaded to join the Church year after year, especially in such distant but prosperous places as Japan, New Zealand and Western Europe.

Dana Sloat, Turner assumed, would inevitably have his own ideas about how this great wealth should be invested and deployed, but these stratagems were trivial in the grand scheme of things. No, a man like Sloat would not be content simply with juggling an investment portfolio, however grandiose. His obsessions dealt with power, not money—that much Turner knew. That much, and nothing more.

And then came the phone call. Dana Sloat wanted to see him. Very well, Turner told himself, he would go over and see Mr. Sloat and hear what he had to say. He was looking forward to it.

But now, pacing back and forth across the board room, shoulders hunched against the chill, Turner found himself struggling once again with his forebodings. The prospect of confronting this man, of hearing him hold forth on Church policy, made him flinch with distaste. Sloat no doubt would already be lining up his own new staff people and advisers—corporate hotshots with business school pedigrees. They, too, would have *their* prescriptions for modernizing the conduct of Church affairs.

His basic problem, Turner realized, was that he didn't *want* the Church to be "modernized." The Church was fine the way it was, with all its crotchets and contradictions and charming anachronisms. The hierarchy, no doubt, was old-fashioned in its approach to many things, but, indeed, religion itself was old-fashioned. Piety and faith were old-fashioned!

Turner slumped into a leather chair at the head of the long conference table and ran his hand through his sleek dark brown hair, his eyes surveying the long, high-ceilinged room to which he'd been relegated. Yes, even the presidential board room, in all its elegant quaintness, reflected the Church as he knew and loved it—the Church of the Brigham Youngs and the Woodleighs, not the Sloats. It was in this room that the various Prophets of the Church down through the decades had received the American presidents, all of whom, from Teddy Roosevelt to Jimmy Carter, had come, either publicly or secretly, to pay their formal respects to the leader of the Mormon nation. And leaders of foreign nations had come as well. Indeed, the room itself, in its stately elegance, reflected the international breadth of the Church: Its huge chandeliers, which seemed like a sunburst of crystal, had been brought from Austria; its vast mahogany conference table from the Philippines; the handsome dark paneling that covered the walls was of Circassian walnut from the Soviet Union. At the front of the room stood a seven-foot-high marble fireplace, big enough to spit-roast an entire steer. Adorning the walls were only two paintings—one of Joseph Smith as a young man, a second depicting the rustic serenity of the Sacred Grove.

"How are ya, Brother Turner."

Recognizing the smiling face of Bill Chadwick, Turner rose to shake his hand. "It's good to see you," he said. "There are fewer and fewer familiar faces around here."

Chadwick nodded with a dolorous smile. "I prefer to look at it this way—at least there's a new audience for my old jokes."

Bill Chadwick is definitely a survivor, Turner told himself. Whatever the twists and turns in the administration, he will make it through.

"I'd have come out earlier, but no one told me you had an appointment," Chadwick said.

"I got a call from Sloat's office," Turner said.

Chadwick nodded gravely. "I see. I'd hoped the meeting could wait until the old man got back. The President's flight from New York is not due in until midafternoon."

The remark puzzled Turner. Clearly, Chadwick had some inkling about the purpose of "the meeting." Why would Chadwick want Bryce there?

The tall woman who had greeted Turner twenty minutes earlier was standing in the doorway. 'The First Counselor is ready to see you now," she said.

Turner looked toward Chadwick, who gave him his familiar wink. "Good luck, kid," he said.

To Turner's surprise, the woman was leading the way to the Prophet's office, not to the office traditionally reserved for the First Counselor. As he walked through the familiar reception and secretarial areas, he noticed that the rooms were cramped with the addition of new desks to accommodate the additional secretaries who already seemed to be typing feverishly, as though they had been there for months. Stacks of papers were in evidence in the normally orderly offices and phones were ringing.

Entering the presidential office, Turner saw Sloat seated on the sofa at the far end of the room, engaged in intense conversation with a visitor across from him. As Turner approached, Sloat made a perfunctory gesture to rise, his hand extended, in the manner of a man who wished to convey to his subordinates that, while he understood the rules of civility, he considered himself aloof to them.

"Glad you could join us, Mr. Mead," Sloat said briskly. "I

would like you to meet Todd Slocum. Brother Slocum is going to be working with us here at Church Headquarters."

Turner shook the smooth, perspiring hand that had been extended to him, wondering to himself what the words "working with us" connoted. Was Slocum to be his new superior, perhaps even his replacement? He was a cherubic, fleshy-faced man who wore oversized black-rimmed spectacles. Turner guessed he was in his mid-thirties.

"Happy to meet you," Turner said.

Sloat motioned Turner toward the dark green leather rocking chair which President Woodleigh had always favored. "There are some important things I thought we should get into today, Mr. Mead," Sloat said, plunging ahead without further amenities. "Our Prophet, as you know, will be back at his desk tomorrow morning. By the time he returns, I would like to resolve certain administrative and structural issues so that he can get off to a smooth start."

"Of course, sir."

"By the way, I have borrowed President Bryce's office today while the workmen complete the remodeling of the First Counselor's."

Turner nodded his understanding. At least he wants to be cautious about usurping presidential privilege.

"We've never had a chance to talk, Mr. Mead," Sloat continued, fixing his stern gaze upon him, "but I've heard excellent things. You have many admirers at Church Headquarters. You've shown an excellent gift at handling your job with discretion."

"That's good to hear, sir," Turner said.

"I would imagine there will be considerable pressure on you these next few weeks, Mr. Mead. The press will doubtless have many questions."

"The questions have already started, sir. They are pouring in from all over the world."

"I see. And what sort of questions are they?"

"Questions of all sorts. The Church is supposedly buying companies, selling companies. There are rumors of currency movements, purchases of television stations, even banks."

Sloat sat back on the sofa, folding one long leg over the other. Turner heard the sound of knuckles cracking, and saw Sloat manipulating his long fingers nervously.

"And how have you responded to these rumors?"

"I told my callers I would convey the questions to the appropriate officials."

"And that you have now done, Mr. Mead."

"Would you like me to prepare a list of specific questions?"

"That won't be necessary. We are all doing the Lord's work here. Our responsibility is to the Prophet, not to the press."

"I take it, sir, that you do not feel we should make any response at all to the reporters."

"Not until the appropriate time."

"Very well, sir."

"Now I would like to turn to our administrative matters." Sloat glanced quickly toward Todd Slocum, who sat at the front of his chair, like a schoolboy eager to please his teacher. "As I mentioned, Mr. Slocum will be joining us, effective today. We are establishing a new Office of the First Counselor, and Mr. Slocum will be a key part of that new office. His responsibilities will include overall supervision of the Church's public image—the face we present to the world."

Turner felt a chill. His instincts were correct, after all. This fleshy-faced man was, indeed, the first of Sloat's new hotshots. "Am I to assume, then, that I will be reporting to Mr. Slocum?"

"That is true, Mr. Mead, but you will continue to be responsible for running your department, and for administering its programs —press relations, films, your television specials, your advertising campaigns. We'll be sharply increasing the scope of these programs, so your job will expand, not shrink. Mr. Slocum's responsibilities are conceptual. His role is to rethink the overall posture of the Church—to redesign the message we are trying to get over and also the technology to deliver it."

These were, Turner sensed, the cadences of Madison Avenue, not those he was accustomed to hearing within these hallowed presidential walls.

"All of us admire the print ads your office has being doing," Slocum put in, rubbing his palms together. "Especially the *Reader's Digest* inserts. Your television spots, too. The trouble is, they've been too circumspect. They've talked about the ideal of the family and the value of prayer. That's all fine and good, but we feel we need to sharpen their thrust. We want to sell the Mormon faith, not the family, you understand me?"

Turner turned from Slocum to Sloat and back to Slocum again. "And how do you propose we go about that?"

"I have discussed this question at some length with the Prophet," Sloat said. "He has devoted prayerful thought to this issue and has spent long hours in the Temple seeking divine guidance."

"I see," Turner said, mindful of the fact that Sloat had just endowed his remarks with a spiritual sanctity which Turner was powerless to challenge.

"Our Church has reached a historical stage in its development," Sloat continued, his hands sliding across his knuckles once again. "The Church is wealthy, it is powerful and secure. No longer should we be inhibited by our old fears of persecution. Nobody's got the muscle to take anything away from us anymore—not even the federal government."

Slocum was chafing to be heard. "The best way to sell the LDS faith is to show that it *works*. And the best way to do that is to reveal the Mormon nation as it stands today—a tower of morality and strength." Slocum's small dark eyes were glowing with fervor. "We are the standard-bearers of the American dream. We are the super Americans."

Turner was staring at Slocum incredulously, trying to absorb his message, but it was Sloat who was talking once again, his voice calm and modulated compared with Slocum's fervid drawl. "All you have to do is travel around the country, Mr. Mead, to see that the American dream is dead or dying. Americans have become a downbeat people, obsessed with recession and energy shortages and crime and immorality. This has always been a nation of high ideals and high expectations. Parents always knew their children would have *more* than they had—more jobs, more opportunity, more money. Yet today people expect less for their children, rather than more. Consider that—it's a revolutionary change, Mr. Mead. Make no bones about it, it's a change that will undermine the fabric of American society. America is fueled by its expectations."

"I do not fully understand how the Church hopes to turn these trends to our advantage. . . ."

"Look around you, Mr. Mead," Slocum said, with an expansive gesture. "In the Mormon nation our dreams are growing, not diminishing. Our economy is expanding, not shrinking. In Utah alone we have one hundred percent employment. We have the fastest-rising income in the nation, the highest percentage of our children in schools and colleges. Our people believe in themselves and in their futures—that's why we have a birthrate twice as high as the rest of the country. Our citizens obey the laws and do as they're told to do. We have clean, prosperous cities where people are not afraid to walk at night. Freaks are not lurking around every corner. The Mormon nation is the last embodiment of the America we all wanted for our children."

"Mr. Mead looks worried," Sloat said crisply.

Never at a loss for words, Turner found himself groping. "It's just that I think there are dangers. There are dangers in holding ourselves up as models. It could work against us. . . ."

"Not if we do it right," Sloat said abruptly. "You are an Englishman, Mr. Mead; you should not forget that of all the world's great religions only Mormonism has American roots. It is the only truly American religion in world history—Americans must be made to feel a unique pride in their Church."

"We're going to package our message aggressively, yet subtly," Slocum effused, "through carefully planned media buys—advertising, television specials, magazines, all the media at our disposal. We will present the Mormon nation as it stands today. The facts are on our side, Mr. Mead. We will show our clean streets, our happy children, our hardworking teenagers who are spreading the Gospel, not smoking pot. And then we will tell them why. We will tell them about our faith, about our political and economic beliefs, about our emphasis on education, our insistence on caring for our own. We will tell them about our hatred of pornography and alcohol and abortion and the ERA and drugs and all the other things that are dragging this nation into the doldrums."

"Please understand," Sloat cut in, "we are not talking here about some sort of quickie media blitz. We are talking about a program involving many years and hundreds of millions of dollars. A program that will involve our political institutions as well as the media, that will be ideological as well as spiritual. We are selling a way of life, Mr. Mead. A way of life that can only be achieved by embracing certain social and political and economic doctrine. We intend to sell that doctrine as aggressively as we know how. And we expect our friends in Congress and in other branches of government to give us the legislative support to achieve our objectives."

Turner Mead found himself hearing the words, understanding them, and yet, somehow, not absorbing them, sensing them whirling in his mind like foreign objects that had invaded an alien universe. He found it hard to believe that he was sitting here, in this office, amid the memorabilia of Prophets past and present, listening to high-powered talk about "repackaging" and "blitzing." So often, in years past, he had sat here for hours as President Woodleigh held forth in his leisurely, discursive way, reciting anecdotes of his rural childhood, or of his experiences as a young missionary amid the poverty of Mexico, or spinning tales about previous Church Presidents. President Woodleigh could be a tough administrator and a shrewd businessman, but his concerns were humane and ecclesiastic, not political. He had loved to travel and talk to the people and hear their concerns. Indeed, his office, which President Bryce had not as yet touched, reflected his humility and wide-eyed view of the world. Spread around the room were exotic headdresses from Africa, the golden mask of a Japanese warrior, the jewel-encrusted likeness of an elephant complete with ivory tusks. The room itself was furnished with stark simplicity in contrast to the great halls that surrounded it— simple green leather chairs with orange cushions, a utilitarian brass chandelier, a broad mahogany desk, dark green wall-to-wall carpeting. A legend carved in wood which hung above his desk expressed his basic view of life: DO IT! the sign stated.

Do it! Turner thought. That's exactly what these two men now expected of him. He had received his marching orders and now he was expected to carry them out. He felt their eyes upon him now, assessing him, testing for a response. He understood full well that if they sensed his skepticism or reluctance, they would find someone else to do the job.

"I like the idea of presenting our story to the public more assertively," Turner said. "I would like more time to think it all through, however. We have a complex story to tell. I am concerned whether we can effectively tell our story through the normal media. It's a tall order."

To his surprise, Turner saw Sloat nod approvingly. "I think you are correct, Mr. Mead. And that is why we have Slocum in our midst. We can spend millions of dollars on advertising but that alone will not do the job. We must do more. We need to make our beliefs, indeed our presence, felt in the day-to-day lives of the people of America. We must be all-pervasive. We have been all-pervasive in Utah and that is why our society works. The same conditions must prevail elsewhere. There are ways of accomplishing this. I am not prepared to discuss all of them, as yet. Let me just assure you that the Mormon presence will be felt more explicitly in the future. There will be developments shortly . . ."

"The whole communications universe is changing," Slocum interjected. "The days when the liberal Eastern press can maintain a stranglehold on national thinking are over. That goes for magazines, newspapers—the television networks. Their days are over." Slocum shot a nervous glance at Dana Sloat. It was the glance of a subordinate who was worried that he had gone too far, but Sloat seemed unconcerned. Indeed, his normally impassive face seemed flushed with excitement.

"Mr. Slocum is alluding to satellite communication," Sloat said. "The LDS Church will shortly be making some major moves in this area."

"We are going to construct a system whose technology will bypass the traditional broadcasting infrastructures," Slocum said, his forehead moist with perspiration. "It will be a direct-to-home system of satellite communication. We won't need cable—we will go right to the home. The consumer will be his own television programmer, and we will beam our messages directly to him—we won't need to beg New York network liberals for help or support."

"Are you aware there are eighty-four million people in the United States who consider themselves born-again Christians, Mr. Mead?" Sloat asked. "That's not speculation—our studies show that fifty-three percent of all Americans eighteen and older claim they have made a personal commitment to Jesus Christ. There are many of our brethren among these numbers, of course, but most of them are scattered among these evangelical sects and television preachers . . ."

"They're splintered," Slocum interrupted. "They're in the hands of these electronic yahoos. . . ."

There was a fleeting distaste in Sloat's glance at his ebullient aide. "What Slocum means is that there is a high degree of disorganization. Some of these television ministries pull in tens of millions of dollars in donations, yet they don't even know who their supporters are. In contrast, our Church will be putting a computer on stream next month which will tell us, at any given time, exactly where each of our members resides, whether they have paid their tithes, what their income is, how often they attend sacrament meeting—all of it. We will have our hand on every Saint throughout the Kingdom, Mr. Mead. We will know everything there is to know about him, and we will know it instantaneously.

"That is why I say that the Christian movement in this country is crying out for a point of focus, and we will supply that focus. The whole nation is drifting to the right. We are going to see that the drift turns into a fast-moving and well-directed current."

Sloat leaned forward, his long, thin fingers poised in the air. "We are God's chosen people, Brother. Our Church has been given the call because we alone have the discipline and the resources. No other priority ranks with this one. It can change everything. It can change the world."

There was a moment's silence in the room. Turner heard Sloat's knuckles crack once again. Slocum sat in reverent silence.

"By the way, Slocum," Sloat said suddenly, turning to his subordinate, "I read the study on the two-dish system. I think our initial judgment was correct. We can't let ourselves get bogged down in a transponder traffic jam on Satcom One. There's going to be a whole crop of earth stations aimed at Comstar, Westar and any future satellite. . . ."

Turner saw Slocum nod thoughtfully and deliver his response to his superior, and suddenly the two of them, who a moment earlier had been caught up in lofty stratagems and epochal ideologies, were talking shop, their argot sprinkled with such arcane words as "downlinks" and "torus prototypes" and "transponders," which Turner found utterly bewildering. Yet he could see that these had become routine expressions to these men, part of their regular vocabularies. Listening to them talking earnestly now, Turner sensed that they were truly of another world. While he had been busying himself with the mundane problems of his department, the present and the future had somehow converged in a vast blur of technological change. A whole new era had dawned and Dana Sloat was prepared to plunge into that era with all the money and power that his Church had so carefully and cautiously harbored. Where Turner's Church had once humbly dispatched its callow missionaries into the world to convert the masses, now it would also be marshaling its Comstars and Westars and beaming its transponders. Turner found it all terrifying.

Dana Sloat was on his feet now, thanking him for coming, dispatching him on his way. Slocum walked him to the door of the presidential office, assuring him that they would be spending more time together in the near future, that they would explore these ideas and plans in greater detail. And suddenly Turner Mead found himself back in the chill marble hallways, standing alone once again, relieved that he was no longer in the scrutiny of these two men, that he would no longer have to feign enthusiasm and support. He felt a sudden pervasive weariness.

He had to get back to the quiet of his office—that much he knew. He had to shut off his phones and pull it all together. He had to sit by himself and think.

And then he would go and see Eliza, and he would hold her quietly for a very long time. Hold her and feel her quiet strength.

WHEN Eliza Hastings rounded the corner on her way to the Beehive House shortly after eleven, she saw the line of tourists already snaking through the gates and onto the street, most swathed in parkas, scarves and ski caps against the penetrating cold. It was not uncommon to see the faithful lined up outside the squat, yellow, stucco-and-brick structure where Brigham Young once had lived and ran his Church, but the swarm of visitors was especially great this week, Eliza knew, because of the one-hundred-fiftieth convocation. Eliza had promised to greet a group of Church leaders from the Pacific islands, but now, strolling quickly down the street from her own Relief Society building, she'd regretted having made the commitment. From the moment of her arrival at the office at seven forty-five this morning, she'd been enmeshed in one meeting after another, and when she'd finally returned to her office after her ten-thirty budget session, she was astonished to see that her phone list spanned almost two pages—more than a hundred calls had come in and the morning wasn't even complete! Eliza was perplexed about the heavy volume of calls, and frustrated, too, that she'd not had time to return any of them. Some of the calls, she assumed, related to the women's conference scheduled for eight that evening, but that would hardly account for such frantic activity.

Eliza caught herself walking too briskly, as was often the case. Slow down! she instructed herself. Breathe deeply. Clear your mind. Enjoy the walk. It was, after all, a short but extraordinary walk. The brief stretch between her Relief Society headquarters and the Beehive House provided a microcosmic glimpse of Church history, its proud structures brightly illumined in a sudden shaft of sunlight that shone through a cleft in the pale clouds that looked like great flakes of marble as they glided swiftly past. Only here and in the Vatican, Eliza presumed, could virtually the

148

entire history of a church array itself along a single corridor of power.

Eliza recalled her mother taking her down this street as a child, and being awed not only by the weight of tradition but also by the fact that her mother had taken her alone, without her other brothers and sisters. Her mother, Abigail Wakefield, had always tended to favor her: It was Eliza who worked the hardest at school, who helped the most at home. Sometimes, when she remembered how *perfect* she aspired to be as a child, how squeaky-clean in appearance and manners, Eliza positively winced with exasperation. But then that was the way she felt her mother had wanted her to be, and pleasing her was the most important thing in her life, second only to her Church. Her mother was a hems-at-the-ankle, back-to-homespun sort of matriarch, the prototypical Mother of Zion, Eliza realized years later. A devout, hardworking woman, Abigail died at the age of forty-six, having conscientiously reared her six children, kept house for her husband and labored many long hours for the Relief Society. Though Eliza's father was a prosperous businessman, a vice-president of Beehive Clothing Mills, which manufactured Temple garments, Abigail had refused to allow domestic help in her household, embracing the Church-endorsed notion that a woman should perform her own chores with the assistance of her offspring. And perform them she did, although it made for a rigorously joyless atmosphere in the home; everyone seemed always to be working or running off to Church meetings but seldom laughing or playing. Their life was a maze of preparation for Sunday school or seminary or Mutual or firesides or Bishop's interviews. Her father, Oliver Wakefield, was a stern, portly man, a descendant of an early Church Apostle who himself rose to high office in the Church, serving first as a Bishop and later as a Stake President. Though basically a kindly man, there was a rigidity to his character which Eliza often found appalling. Father's mind, her mother once told her, was a bit like a Mormon dugway, and Eliza knew exactly what she meant. The Mormon pioneers, much to the scorn of Gentile travelers, utilized dugways when traversing steep hills, digging ruts so deep that a wagon wheel could not bounce out—ruts that were helpful when going uphill but occasionally treacherous on the descent. Oliver Wakefield's narrow, rutlike mind was often in dread evidence during family crises. To this day, she could recall his cosmic rage in learning that her youngest brother, Parnell, had refused to go to the chapel for a vicarious baptism. Talking to the boy, Eliza discovered that the eight-year-old was frightened of being held underwater during the baptismal ceremony. To Parnell, complete immersion was a terrifying prospect. Eliza pleaded with her father to be patient; it was simply a passing phase. But Oliver Wakefield would hear none of it. He was determined that all of his sons should march steadfastly through the various notches of Church ritual, rising from deacon to teacher to priest to elder to seventy to high priest in their inexorable ascent through the Aaronic and Melchizedek Orders, ultimately achieving leadership, as had their father, in the Mormon community. In keeping with these expectations, the screaming little boy was carted off to meet his fate.

Disturbed by these rigidities, Eliza had tried to be more compassionate with her own children, excusing them occasionally from Sunday school and even canceling a Family Home Evening. Leniency, she told her women in the Relief Society, need not diminish virtue. Let's be zealous about our responsibilities, but let's also try to have fun with our children. Yet, while voicing this advice, Eliza was acutely aware that she herself was often guilty of these same failings in satisfying her own urgent striving for perfection. There was much of her mother's obsessiveness in her, Eliza knew, and much of her father's as well.

Making her way up the front walk of Beehive House, she squeezed past a hefty Polynesian woman who blocked the narrow doorway, the woman shrinking to one side, wide-eyed, when she recognized Eliza. "I'm so proud to meet you," the big matron said. "I've dreamed twenty years to see this place—all people in my ward wait to see my photographs."

"I'm so pleased to meet you," Eliza replied, shaking hands with her and with the others who clustered around them, faces smiling, brown skin glistening. Eliza harbored a special fondness for these formidable Polynesian women, not only for their openness and loyalty, but also because of the special debt which she felt her Church owed them. The Church's proselytizing efforts had been incredibly successful throughout the Pacific; on some islands the LDS religion had become the predominant faith, with Mormon

customs intruding themselves deeply into existing cultural patterns. The results of these wholesale conversions were not totally
beneficial, Eliza knew. Through her Relief Society, she had tried
to give assistance to the hidden pockets of poverty-stricken Ton-
gans and Samoans who had migrated to Salt Lake City, as though
to Mecca.

As she threaded her way through the visitors, Eliza climbed to
the top of the polished staircase where still other eager Polynesians clustered around their guides, hanging on each word of de-
scription and doctrine. Eliza herself had served as a guide here
when she was young, and though she loved the house, she'd been
impatient with the brethren who had worked so hard to restore it.
In their zealousness, they had replaced all the original furniture,
polishing and manicuring everything down to the smallest key-
hole. There was something too elaborate and mannered about the
place as it now stood, its plush velvet French provincial furnishings too "prettified" for Brigham Young's rugged pioneer image.
And yet, Eliza knew, Brigham himself might have approved. It
was Brigham who had explicitly designed the ostentatious Gardo
Room where he entertained important visitors—a room in which
virtually every object, from the curtains to the upholstery, was
bathed in gold. Throughout the house Brigham had insisted that
the walls, though of humble pine, be specially polished and finished so as to resemble the rich, caramel-colored Tennessee marble which he admired. Clearly, the Prophet felt a degree of
showmanship was demanded of him in building his Kingdom.

As she chatted with the visitors, Eliza recognized the familiar
face of Grace Turley, signaling her, struggling through the crowd,
her expression agitated. Eliza sighed in resignation. It had been
Grace, who, that previous evening, had triggered the emotional
debate in her living room, and while she had appreciated her
remarks, she had no desire to hear more of them now. In only
nine hours the meeting would begin; Eliza felt the apprehension
gnawing at her even now.

Grace had reached her, standing so close she could smell her
sour breath. "I'm sorry to intrude like this, Eliza, I know you must
have a lot to do. . . ."

"Yes, I do."

"I wanted to tell you something," Grace said.

"Well, here I am."

". . . I don't really know how to put it. . . ."

"Surely you were remarkably articulate last night, dear Grace," Eliza said. "I'm sure you can summon up the appropriate words this morning."

". . . It's just that I want you to understand something, Eliza," Grace continued, her voice pinched and tremulous. "Everyone thinks we are very well off, my husband and I. I am aware of that. My husband's construction business has always been very successful, but he got in bad financial trouble last year. Real bad trouble."

Eliza looked into Grace's fearful eyes, totally puzzled by this outpouring. Why was this woman choosing such an awkward moment to recite her financial problems? What business were they of hers?

Grace Turley peered around to see if anyone familiar could overhear them. "My husband got deeper and deeper over his head until he finally went for help. He had to."

"I'm glad for him," Eliza said, trying as best she could to contain her annoyance.

"Mr. Sloat really saved him. He saved the business."

"I see. And why are you telling me this?"

"Just don't judge me too harshly, Sister. That's all I ask. I beg you not to judge me too harshly. You don't know Mr. Sloat, Eliza. If I didn't do what he asked . . ." She started backing away, her eyes panicky, her body moving slowly toward the top of the stairwell.

Eliza stood rooted where she was, Grace's curious pleadings running through her mind. She was warning her—that was it, of course. In her own clumsy, cowardly way, she was warning her. Grace Turley had started down the stairs but turned one last time, her eyes connecting with Eliza's. She hesitated briefly, as though there was more she wanted to say, but Eliza did not need to listen to further explanations. Even as new strangers pressed themselves upon her, Eliza knew now what it was Grace Turley was explaining to her. She should have realized last night, of course, that Grace was a plant. Yes, she should have known it was all a trap.

ΑT exactly three forty-five, Lillian Thompson, cursing under her breath, rose from her desk and started walking slowly down the corridor. She was furious with herself for having agreed to do this thing. She respected Hiram Cobb and admired his courage, yet he frightened her. Several times last year she had copied some microfilm records and smuggled the material to him, but that was before she realized how notorious he had become. As far as she was concerned, Hiram Cobb was a handsome, rather benign man, an obscure dissenter who wrote articles saying things about the Church she felt needed saying. But in the last few months, Hiram had clearly gone too far. The *Deseret News* had carried two editorial assaults on him, and even her Bishop had warned the people in her ward not to subscribe to Hiram Cobb's magazine.

Walking down the narrow corridor which smelled of pine oil, Lillian zipped up her cardigan against the chill. The temperature in the vaults was kept in the low-to-mid sixties to protect the microfilm—she was used to that—but somehow this afternoon the cold seemed especially pervasive. Maybe it was just that she was scared. She always got cold when she was scared.

Lillian looked up to see the tiny red light of a television surveillance camera staring at her, an ominous, ever-vigilant mechanical sentinel. They were all over, these cameras. She'd gotten used to them, too. Security had always been rigorous here under the mountain, but it had been tightened still further recently. Badges were being carefully checked and clerks confined to certain restricted areas. As chief of clerical personnel, Lillian was among the few employees who had access to all areas, but even *her* access to the so-called Confidential Section had been limited. Elvin Pearson, who was in charge of this section, had warned her not to enter his files without prior clearance, but Lillian obviously could not consult with him about this assignment. She could imagine the reaction of this shrunken, gray-faced man if she were blandly to inform him that she was checking the file of the First Counselor, Dana Sloat, because Hiram Cobb happened to be curious about its contents. Elvin would surely have cardiac arrest. Fortunately, at precisely three forty-five every afternoon Elvin Pearson always took a half-hour break from his work in the Confidential Section to sip on some bouillon in the employees' commissary. Hence Lillian had decided to make her foray into his sanctum sanctorum at this hour. The whole thing should take only twenty minutes. She would glance at the material, commit as much as possible to memory and then get the hell out of there before the old man returned.

Moving down the long corridor, she heard her own footsteps reverberating through the underground stillness like the metallic clicking of a metronome. She had worked here for four years now but, in all that time, had never been able to erase from her mind the fact that she was six hundred feet down, working in an underground city blasted out of a mountain of solid granite. Every morning as she passed through the fourteen-ton steel door at the entrance to the tunnel, she felt that grim claustrophobic twinge, that sense of being entombed. Only the Mormon Church, she told herself, would lavish millions and millions of dollars to build an underground city here in the granite substrata of Little Cottonwood Canyon, a city capable of withstanding any disaster—even thermonuclear attack. And all simply to store records!

They were, of course, special records—special, at least, to a Church whose faith was based on the promise of immortality, on the eternal links among all its members, living and dead, indeed, even to the point of conducting vicarious baptisms to bestow its ordinances on those who died without having received them. Baptism was deemed essential to salvation in the Celestial Kingdom, and hence an obligation of the "living Saints" under the laws and ordinances of the Gospel. In order to perform these baptisms for those long gone, it became necessary to hire a veritable army of genealogical detectives who would fan out around the world, checking through parish halls, archives, registries and ancient newspapers, dispatching their records back to Salt Lake City to be sanctified in the secret caves under the mountain at Little Cottonwood.

Lillian remembered driving by the concealed entrance to the caves time and again on her way to ski, without even dreaming of the empire that lay within. No sign marked the caves, only a small, anonymous service road which led to the sheer face of the granite cliffs. Yet within, as Lillian ultimately learned, lay catacombs of vaults and corridors and secret rooms, an entire underground network of concrete and steel, all tidy and clean and secure.

As a librarian at the University of Utah, Lillian had grown accustomed to processing and codifying large amounts of information, but the sheer vastness of the genealogical vaults at Little Cottonwood at first took her breath away. There were, she discovered, six vaulted rooms, each containing well over one thousand cabinets. On every roll of microfilm in those cabinets was implanted the equivalent of twelve hundred pages of genealogical data. A century of the London *Times* was stored in two file drawers. And with each passing month some four thousand new rolls of microfilm would pour in from around the world, thus fulfilling the insatiable desire of the faithful to trace their family histories and forge their link with eternity.

A fifth-generation Mormon, Lillian Thompson had carefully traced her own forebears and had dutifully recorded all the ancestral names and pedigree charts, pasting the available photographs in the Book of Remembrance which every good Saint is called upon to keep. All this was supposed to give her a sense of contact with her celestial family, but, having completed her tasks, she still did not sense that mystical link to her relatives, living or dead. She did not bask in her newfound immortality. Instead, she felt all the more resentful that her husband had died in an absurd automobile accident and that her only son was a drifter who had shifted constantly from one place to the next, succeeding only in getting himself in trouble.

She resented her job, as well. The pay was good, to be sure, but spending her days in these frigid, empty corridors, her skin glowing yellow in the eerie fluorescence, left her depressed and lonely. Sixty other souls labored with her down in the catacombs, but, having been set apart from the outside world by that great fourteen-ton door, they seemed to identify more with the rolls of microfilm, and with those in the great beyond, than with their colleagues with whom they labored.

Reaching the end of the corridor, Lillian confronted the steel door that marked the entrance to Elvin Pearson's secret domain. There had always been a certain mystery to this section of Little Cottonwood. When she had first come to work here, Pearson had informed her matter-of-factly that the room was reserved for rare records and special memorabilia. She soon learned otherwise. Though her access had been limited, she was able to discern that the room contained files which the Church wanted to protect from the scrutiny of all but a favored few. These included minutes of early sessions of the Council of Fifty, and other historical documents which the hierarchy, for reasons of its own, wanted to sequester. They also included genealogical records of certain Church leaders, dead or alive: In some cases, Lillian observed, there were two versions of these files—one in the outside room and one surreptitious file in the Confidential Section. Few visitors went back to Elvin Pearson's secret chamber, but once, in a rare moment of loquacity, old Pearson had told her that he was occasionally visited by teams of CIA men. "I've got material in there that even Washington can't get its hands on," he boasted.

Well, whatever it was Elvin Pearson was hiding in there, Lillian knew she needed to have a quick squint at it. Standing in the corridor, she sneezed loudly, the sound startling her as it echoed down the long empty corridor. She felt as though she were trapped in a giant anthill, an anonymous creature without a will of its own, doing as it was told, far underground, removed from the sunlight and from the attention of any human being.

She shuddered with the cold, and tugged her sweater more tightly around her. On the other side of that door, she knew, sat a young file clerk named Andrea, a small, chubby girl who was new at the job. She would have to think of an explanation for Andrea. No she wouldn't! Andrea was the sort of girl who was intimidated by authority. She could simply give her a stern nod and walk past.

And she thought again, How did I let Hiram get me into this? I don't owe him anything! Why am I jeopardizing my job for a virtual stranger—a man who had become a pariah to the Church and an outcast in his community?

That, in itself, was the reason, of course. She knew it was. She was helping Hiram Cobb because no one else would. He was an outcast, a stray, and she, more than anyone, understood how that felt. When her son Richard was sent home from his mission, a young man banished in disgrace, she saw the way her neighbors shied away from them both as though they were lepers. Only Hiram and Gussie took the trouble to extend their sympathies. Only they had tried to help. They'd even managed through a friend at Church Headquarters to get Richard a few assignments as a free-lance photographer. The only sin her son had committed of course, was to take a Japanese girl to a movie; he was a lonely American kid, thousands of miles from home, taking a girl on a harmless date. And they'd simply packed him off and sent him home!

Pulsing with the old anger, Lillian twisted the handle and shoved the door open. Andrea looked up from her desk in surprise. Lillian nodded curtly to her and continued walking. She saw Andrea's lips move, as though to form some words, but none emerged. Lillian's instincts were correct—if she only managed to look officious enough, the girl wouldn't have the courage to say a thing.

The vaulted room housing the Confidential Section was smaller than the others, and also considerably colder. Lillian found herself shuddering as she made her way down the long rows of steel cabinets. There was a chemical smell to the room, like that of a lab. That, plus the brilliance of the overhead lights, was giving her a headache.

All right, she would get on with it. The appropriate cabinet should be right around here. She would find Sloat's file and would glean as much information as she could, as quickly as she could.

"Can I help you, Sister?"

The voice was an unfamiliar one and Lillian whirled around, her heart pounding.

He was a man she had never seen before, heavyset with black hair and thick eyebrows that met in the middle. They stared at each other for an awkward moment.

"Do you have clearance for this room?"

Off guard, Lillian groped for an appropriate reply. She was not good at this spy game. Damn Hiram Cobb!

"I beg your pardon!" Lillian was surprised to hear her voice sounding indignant.

The heavyset man's expression seemed to melt. "I'm sorry if

I'm disturbing you, Sister. My name is Barker. Wilson Barker. Elvin Pearson came down with the flu last night and Church Headquarters asked me to fill in. I'm not with the genealogical section; I'm in security."

He mustered a weak smile and extended his hand. She shook it, almost faint with relief.

"I'm Lillian Thompson. Administrative head of clerical personnel."

"Of course," Barker said, looking perplexed. "I was told no one had clearance to come back here this week. . . ."

"Oh, I only come back here when there's a special assignment from the First Presidency."

Barker turned ashen. "The First Presidency? . . ."

Lillian smiled to herself. She wasn't a bad spy after all. This Barker fellow was so scared he could hardly move. "Yes," she said. "It's just a routine matter, but something they asked me to look into right away."

"Of course . . ." Barker said, backing away slowly, in full retreat. ". . . If there's anything I can assist with . . ." Barker said meekly.

"I appreciate that very much," Lillian replied, as she guided open the metal drawer, her eyes darting quickly over the rows of microfilm. "But it's all very confidential. You understand." Barker vanished obediently.

Yes, this would be her last job for Hiram Cobb. Absolutely her last.

T

THE sudden thump jolted him awake.

On instinct, Penrose grasped the steering wheel and held it tightly, struggling to get his bearings. He heard the ominous crunch of gravel and swerved to get back on the asphalt, feeling the pickup tipping precipitously with the sudden turn. All right, he was on the road again. He heard the welcome hum of the tires and saw the highway stretching ahead, arrow-straight, across the flat plain. Everything seemed okay.

Except his head was hurting. It felt as though someone had struck him with a hammer. He must have hit a pothole and the sudden impact had sent his head against the hard metal roof of the truck. God, it hurt!

Penrose steered to the shoulder of the road, guiding the truck to a stop and turning off the engine. He climbed out, rubbing his head with his huge, hamlike hand. He peered at his palm nervously. At least he wasn't bleeding; Christ, he hated the sight of his own blood. The freezing wind stunned his senses into clarity now. The grogginess evaporated.

He glanced at his watch, and realized he'd been driving for six straight hours without a break. That was dumb, Penrose scolded himself. No wonder he'd dozed off. If Dawson ever found out . . . Oh, God!

At least the cold felt good. He'd always liked freezing weather —the colder, the better. The wind was so cold it made his eyes tear. Maybe if he walked for a few minutes his head would stop pounding. That would help—that, and a good pee.

He glanced around him. The late afternoon light was dying fast now, the plains fading to mauve between the broad patches of snow. Only the sagebrush and the dry gullies scarred the naked landscape. Far to the east he could see the mountains glowing a chaotic red against the sky, their peaks crowned in white. There were no structures in sight, only the blacktop stretching out over the little hills like an undulating ribbon.

He wondered where he was. He checked his watch again. He should be reaching Route 15 soon. The idea of seeing Salt Lake again had thrilled him. Not that he would ever want to live there —he loved living in New Nauvoo. People there were nice to him. At New Nauvoo, Penrose knew what was expected of him. He had a role to play, and people understood and respected his role. For the first time, these last three years, Penrose had not felt embarrassed about himself.

While growing up, embarrassment had been a constant companion. Some of it had to do with his size. He'd passed six feet by the time he was in the fifth grade and was six feet six by junior high school. He was always knocking things down—even classmates. He was clumsy as hell. He was also dumb—Penrose had long since accepted that. He would sit in class, cramped by those tight little desks, and never understand a thing that was going on.

He pretended never to hear the giggles of his classmates, but he'd heard them all; they had followed him around for as long as he could remember. Now and then he would cry, and that would only make him seem more ridiculous—this great tower of a boy sobbing his eyes out. His mother would stare at him blankly and say, "You're bigger than they are—hit 'em." But that only made him cry harder. He was afraid to hit anybody. He knew he could hurt them bad and that would only get him sent away.

Mr. Wright, the guidance counselor, was the only one who really tried to help. The two of them would spend long hours together, Mr. Wright coaching him with his lessons, easing him over the hurdles. He talked straight to him, too—to this day he could clearly remember his words. He had really tried to put it nicely. You come from a long and honorable family, Penrose, he had said, clearing his throat. You have much to be proud of. Your ancestors pulled their handcarts all the way to Zion because they *believed.* They were good Saints. Mr. Wright cleared his throat some more. You just have to understand, Penrose, that some of the early settlers lived in isolated communities. They practiced polygamy. Over a period of time there was some intermarriage. That meant certain traits were handed down. They couldn't know what we know today about genes. But you have nothing to be ashamed of, Penrose—nothing at all.

But Penrose knew what he was telling him, and he *was* ashamed. His ancestors had kept marrying each other and somehow it ended up that Penrose was too dumb to learn, too dumb to stay in school with his classmates. There was no nice way of explaining *that.*

He remembered staring at himself in the mirror, standing there, enormous in his nakedness, his flesh pink and hairless, and thinking—I don't look *that* strange! He had two ears like everyone else, and two eyes and a nose and mouth. His hair was so blond it was almost white and his eyes were a faint blue. His jaw was long and solid like the prow of a vessel. One of his teachers had once said he looked like a Viking and he liked that notion—he had looked up the Vikings in his history book and tried to read about them. Maybe if he were very careful and quiet in class, they would let him stay in school. Maybe they would overlook the things Mr. Wright had so gently explained.

But it didn't work out that way. After finishing eighth grade, he had been sent to summer school. Penrose had stayed there two weeks before running away. Thinking of that school still made him shudder. It was full of boys who drooled or cried or mumbled to themselves all day. They were all boys from backgrounds like his, Penrose knew—good Mormon boys whose family trees had gotten messed around—but Penrose knew he was not like them. He would never be smart, but he was not a drooler or a mumbler. He could make his own way in the world. He found odd jobs to do. His size was an advantage now. Farmers would give him chores. People still made fun of him because he was slow, but at least they paid him. He always felt that if he ever found someone who treated him right, he would be very loyal for a long, long time.

Dawson Sloat had seemed to understand that from the start. He realized that though Penrose couldn't cope with books, he could cope with many other things, and when he asked him to come live in New Nauvoo, he assigned him specific jobs to do—jobs he could do very capably. He felt happy there from the start.

Dawson had even given him a title. He was the Sentinel. Penrose liked the way it sounded: responsible, official, a man to be respected. Yes, Penrose was the Sentinel of New Nauvoo and he intended to stay that way. Even if it meant taking on an occasional job that scared him a little. Like the job he was on today.

Penrose realized his need to pee had grown urgent now. He also realized that only one vehicle had passed by since he'd pulled over. He could just take his chances and pee on the side of the road. He looked around once more in the hopes of finding some shelter, even if it meant kneeling behind a rock, but there was nothing, and he was getting very cold. To hell with it, Penrose told himself as he unzipped his jeans, then zipped up quickly. Wasn't that the sound of a distant car?

Silence. Penrose cursed and unzipped again, heaving a deep sigh at the sheer pleasure of relieving himself. By the time he heard the roar of the motorcycles, there was no way of stopping. It seemed they came from nowhere, the growl of their little engines bearing down upon him.

There were two of them, and each carried two people, a man and a woman. Penrose turned away from them as they roared down upon him, but he heard them slowing down and shouting at him, and there was a woman's voice calling out to him and laughing. The bikes were whirling around him in a circle now, the voices laughing, dust and exhaust rising in a cloud and the deafening sound of the engines like angry hornets. Penrose kept spinning, in total humiliation, trying to shield himself from their gaze. They kept circling and laughing.

Then suddenly they were gone again. Penrose found himself standing in the settling dust, alone once again. He stared down at himself. His penis hung like an unwatered, discouraged flower. He remembered standing in the shower at school, and the boys calling out, "How can anyone that big have a pecker that small?"

He felt embarrassed, and that made him angry. He had promised himself he would never be embarrassed again. He ran to the pickup truck. He would race after them and drive them off the road! He would give them a lesson.

As he pulled back onto the asphalt, he realized he couldn't do that. He was on an important mission. He had promised Dawson he would get the job done. He could not let him down. He would forget the bikers, forget his humiliation. He would also try to forget his anger.

The truck was picking up speed now. He decided to keep driving until he reached the main highway. Then he would find a place to get some soup and that would keep him awake till he reached the city.

He wished he were on his way home, his mission completed. There was something about this trip that really bothered him. He didn't feel right about what he was doing—even though he was the Sentinel.

He had confessed his fear to Dawson, but Dawson had made him see it differently. Dawson had always been able to do that, Penrose knew, but that did not bother him. Dawson was his leader. He ran his town just as Brigham Young had run the Kingdom in frontier days. Dawson and Brigham probably had much in common, Penrose sensed. Both were men of God, forceful leaders who knew where they stood and could persuade others to follow them. Dawson, like Brigham, had a role to play in the history of the Mormon people, and Penrose, too, had his role. Dawson had explained all that to him. There had always been an Erastus Penrose among the Mormon people; God had seen to that. The first had been Orrin Porter Rockwell. He was a giant of a man with a long black beard who dressed in skins. He was Joseph Smith's protector. When the angry mob came after Joseph Smith at Nauvoo, it was Porter Rockwell who rowed him across the Mississippi at midnight. There was Sampson Avard, too, who organized the Danites, the Sons of Dan, the Destroying Angels. When the enemies of God tried to destroy the Church, Avard and the Danites took their vengeance.

Vengeance! Blood Atonement! The Saints could not shrink from these truths. The apostates were always at hand, ready to exploit any weakness. It had to be made clear to them that while the Saints wanted to live in peace, they could also live by the sword. "There are sins that must be atoned for by the blood of the man," Brigham Young had preached. "If men turn traitors, their blood will be shed."

Yes, Penrose understood the role he had to play. Each servant of God had to contribute to the cause in his own unique way, and Penrose knew what his contribution would be. He was the Avenger, the Danite. He understood the Danites' mission and had taken their oath. Instructed by Dawson, he had put on the white robe and knelt in the darkness, lit only by a single torch, and pledged "in the name of Jesus Christ, Son of God, I do solemnly obligate myself ever to conceal the secrets of this society, and should I ever do same I hold my life in forfeiture and be laid in the dust."

When he thought of that oath Penrose felt a swell of pride. He was not a man alone. He was part of them, and they were part of him. Their blood was intermingled.

And someday soon the world would be theirs—a Kingdom of God, united under their divine guidance. A Mormon Kingdom! Dawson would see to that. If there were things Penrose had to do which displeased him, they must be done nonetheless. It was all part of the broader scheme of things.

This man whose name had been given to him was an enemy of his people. He would have to be dealt with as Rockwell and Avard would have dealt with him.

Penrose reached into his pocket for the paper on which Dawson had written the name. He found it now. The name and the address.

He checked his watch again. In a few hours he would meet Hiram Cobb, the apostate.

HIRAM Cobb recoiled before the clouds of acrid smoke billowing toward him and the shriek of the canned disco music. Why do I always let Lillian Thompson choose our meeting places? he asked himself in total exasperation, his nostrils rejecting the stale smell of beer and cigarettes. Why did it always have to be The Ute?

In his mind, Hiram Cobb understood why private clubs like The Ute existed. Dry states like Utah would inevitably foster these shabby oases where, for a token annual fee, customers could avail themselves of a drink and the accompanying camaraderie. But why did these establishments always have to be so seedy?

Part of his problem, Hiram realized, was that he shared the Church's official disdain for alcohol and tobacco—a fact that made him profoundly uncomfortable. The origins of Mormon scorn for alcohol were shrouded in mythology, but one popular theory held that Joseph Smith's first wife, Emma, resented her husband's friends who sat around all night, drinking, smoking and chewing tobacco. The booze was bad enough, but cleaning out the spittoons was the final indignity. She prevailed upon her husband to declare these habits as official evils—a notion which Smith, with typical modesty, ultimately enshrined as a "revelation." In due course this revelation was codified into the Word of Wisdom, which wrapped abstinence along with chastity and fidelity under the overall banner of "moral cleanliness." To Hiram, who held all of Joseph Smith's motives as suspect, the "cleanliness" package seemed absurdly all-encompassing; certainly Smith himself had been unwilling to live within its constraints, a reluctance he shared with his followers. The diaries of Zion's early settlers contained many reports of flourishing distilleries and breweries. Tithes from the town of St. George in the early years actually were paid in bottles of wine. And as for chastity and fidelity,

165

Hiram felt that Joseph Smith and his compatriots soon hedged their bet by embracing the doctrine of "plural marriage," as it was deftly called. In Hiram's view, it was easier to preach fidelity when one had four wives and easier to advocate abstinence when one's neighbor operated a distillery.

Entering a place like The Ute, however, his eyes probing the bleary air in search of Lillian, Hiram felt an instinctual sympathy for the Word of Wisdom, with all its accompanying hypocrisies. Only dear Lillian could lure him to a place like this. One reason she favored it, Hiram knew, was that she didn't care to be seen with Hiram in any place where someone in authority might recognize them. Surely The Ute, located on the remote outskirts of town, with its blue-collar clientele and bawdy atmosphere, offered a safe haven from the ever-watchful eyes of the General Authorities. Besides, Lillian clearly coveted the excuse to have a drink or two. It was a vice she savored.

He saw her now, looking dowdy in her gray woolen dress, her hair cut in bangs across her forehead. Huddled at a table in the far corner of the room, Hiram thought she looked rather like a school librarian isolated here among the boisterous, denim-clad men. The first time he'd met her, Hiram had been put off by her schoolmarmish appearance. She just didn't look like the type who would become a prospective subscriber, no less a key source of information.

Lillian had called his house out of the blue, sounding timorous and uncertain. She had read one or two of Hiram's magazines at a friend's house, and found them stimulating. Could she come by for a visit? She wouldn't take up too much time.

Hiram and Gussie had grown accustomed to calls such as this. Readers of their magazine so often would telephone, their voices quavering, as though fearing immediate retribution. These calls had surprised Hiram at first. After all, no one called the editors of *Time* or *Newsweek* asking to meet them, but then he knew that *The Kingdom* was different. It upset people. It spoke to their consciences. It was inevitable that readers would want to come face-to-face with the source of these troublous discourses.

Lillian had appeared at their house for their first meeting, looking, Hiram thought, rather frumpy and ill at ease, but as they talked, Hiram began to sense a resoluteness in her seemingly passive face and, even more importantly, a deep inner anger. She had explained how her son had been sent home from his missionary work in Japan, how the banishment had crushed his spirit. He had loved Japan, Lillian said, and felt a keen satisfaction from his missionary work there—the first time in his life he had really found pleasure in a task. Because of his "disgrace," he'd had trouble finding a job back in Utah. It seemed so cruel, so arbitrary, and it had started her wondering about the Church. It was then she happened upon their magazine.

Hiram and Gussie felt a deep fondness and compassion for this stricken woman. They invited her for dinner. They exchanged phone calls. Hiram had even tried to help Lillian's son Richard find a new job. And when Hiram discovered that Lillian worked at Little Cottonwood, he was especially surprised and pleased. Little Cottonwood was a veritable treasure trove of information. If only there was a way Hiram could gain access to some of it. If only Lillian were angry enough to help!

He had been reluctant to ask her. Hiram had read his share of spy novels in which agents were always bullying the misfits and the outcasts to elicit secret data. It all seemed so squalid. Yet he needed information, and he needed allies.

When he finally broached the subject, she'd agreed to it quickly and matter-of-factly, as though he were asking her to mail a letter. Sure she would help, Lillian declared. She would help any way she could.

And help him she did. With her assistance, he had pieced together many a historical mystery. Members of the Church hierarchy, he knew, were constantly confounded as to where and how he came up with information to which they themselves had been oblivious. If only they knew that much of it came from folk like Lillian Thompson—their kind of people, the sort they would never suspect.

Hiram seated himself at Lillian's table now and she smiled at him. "I trust you are well," Hiram said.

"Getting better by the moment," she replied, draining the liquid from her glass.

Hiram winced at another blast of music from the jukebox. "Somehow I feel this is not your type of place, Hiram," Lillian said, smiling mischievously.

"Not exactly."

She pushed her empty glass across the table. "Why don't you try one of these—it would help you get acclimated. And while you're at it, order me a second?"

Hiram took the glass reluctantly. "You sure you want another?"

"Hiram, don't lay the Word of Wisdom on *me!* Remember, I work down in the vaults. They keep the temperature way down because it's good for the microfilm. By the end of the day, I need my antifreeze."

Hiram rose again and made his way warily to the bar. There were two or three men ahead of him, waiting to place their orders. The bartender was a barrel-chested man with thinning red hair who went about his chores with a studied leisureliness.

Hiram falteringly ordered two Scotches, then made his way back to Lillian's table.

She was pleased that he had chosen to drink with her, rather than settling for his usual tomato juice. "Here's to our unique association," she said, taking a sip. Hiram grimaced against the bite of the alcohol.

"You should try to have a drink every day," Lillian advised. "It would keep you from being so jittery."

"I've tried. I just can't cultivate a taste for it."

She clicked her tongue mockingly. "You're a real case, Hiram. You keep attacking the teachings of the Church, but they're inscribed on your brain."

Hiram tried another sip, disguising his reaction this time. "Did you know, Lillian, that the first plant ever cultivated by man was the grapevine? Whenever the Bible mentions wine, it is usually with approval."

"Now you're talking, Hiram."

"Furthermore, did you know that our livers secrete an enzyme called dehydrogenase which has no use other than to metabolize alcohol? It's man's adjustment to the fact that alcohol has been in his diet since the beginning of time."

"Your scholarship always awes me, Hiram."

"But you're right . . ."

Lillian looked up from her drink. "About what?"

"The Word of Wisdom is indeed inscribed on my brain. Whatever my intellect may tell me, I still can't smoke and I can't drink.

Call it conditioning or brainwashing or whatever you want. I'm a lost cause. Old Joe Smith could drink like a fish, yet he talked the rest of us into total abstinence."

Hiram tried another sip, almost gagging this time, and Lillian laughed softly at his stalwart efforts. Hiram smiled, amused at his own awkwardness.

"Do you realize, Hiram, that was one of the few times I've ever seen you smile?"

"I'm afraid that's a skill I've lost from my repertoire."

She put her hand on his arm. "You're too serious, dear Hiram. You can't think about laughter as a skill. We're talking about a feeling, not a skill."

Hiram gave a helpless little shrug. "I guess feelings are a skill I haven't mastered."

They exchanged knowing glances. "There you go again, Hiram!"

What a curious sense of closeness one develops with one's co-conspirators, Hiram thought. He knew remarkably little about Lillian, really, had no real notion whether she was happy or unhappy, whether she had many friends or was lonely, whether she had a lover or lacked male company. Nor, he imagined, did she have any real insight into him. They were strangers, and yet also the warmest and most trusting of friends, their emotions intertwined by one key strand of their existence—their Church, and the whole chain of values which the Church embodied. The Mormon ethic touched every facet of their being. It was their antipathy toward that ethic which locked them together, comrades-in-arms.

"Let me tell you about our friend," Lillian Thompson said, drawing herself up in her chair. "I know you're aching to get down to business, Hiram."

"I hope there were no problems. . . ."

"A few awkward moments," Lillian said. "I'm getting used to those. There are always the little surprises where you suddenly find your heart in your throat and you swear, never again will Hiram Cobb persuade me to go spying for him in the Confidential Section."

"Is that the way you feel now, Lillian?"

Lillian shrugged. "I know I'm doing it because it's what I want to do. It's as simple as that. Still, you should have seen me a few hours ago. I was in a state."

Hiram instinctively glanced at the tables adjoining theirs, checking for eavesdroppers. The men around them were engrossed in their own conversations.

"I read the material in the file—as much as I had time for. I was very jittery. I couldn't copy any of it. The circumstances weren't right today."

"I understand," Hiram said.

"The man you are interested in has two sets of genealogical records, just as you guessed. The first file sits in the regular vaults, and the second one is back in you-know-where. On the surface they seem identical, but if you read them carefully there are some interesting discrepancies."

"Such as what, Lillian?"

"According to the first file, Dana Sloat has a pedigree chart that would grace any family Book of Remembrance. It's a long and distinguished family. The first Mormon convert in his family was Ephraim Sloat who was a lawyer back in Missouri—Dana Sloat's great-great-grandfather. He was a second cousin to Heber Kimball and came out to Utah ten years after Brigham Young. The file makes no reference to his practicing law in Utah, though he apparently was quite prosperous—again, the historical record is fuzzy here. Anyway, Ephraim took three wives and was a pillar in his community."

Hiram listened to this recitation with growing impatience. The facts Lillian laid out for him were identical to those which appeared in numerous newspaper stories about Sloat. Sloat had always made much of his distant familial tie to Heber Kimball, who was one of Joseph Smith's principal disciples. Though Sloat himself had always been outside the inner circle of Mormon leadership, Hiram felt he had tried to use his remote tie to Heber Kimball as a means of gaining acceptance among the brethren. It was his badge of dynastic respectability; at least, that's what he wanted it to be.

"Tell me about the other file, Lillian."

She gave him a conspiratorial wink and sipped her Scotch. "The confidential file had things a little different. To begin with, Ephraim Sloat was not a second cousin to Heber Kimball, but rather a third cousin at best. The link is vague."

"Interesting."

"Ephraim was a lawyer in Missouri all right, but he seemed like a lively old coot. His first wife died on the trek to Utah. When he was thirty years of age, he took himself a second wife. She was a girl who'd just turned sixteen. Reading between the lines, I would say it was not exactly a marriage made in heaven."

"What makes you say that?"

"Best I can reconstruct it, Ephraim went off hunting about six months after their marriage and his bride marched right over to the judge and got a civil divorce on the grounds that Ephraim drank and beat her frequently."

"How did he keep the divorce out of the Church records?"

"When Ephraim returned to town, it seems he took the girl to federal court in St. George where he probably knew the judge. He got her to promise never to mention the divorce in public. It wasn't until twenty years later that the divorce was made final in the LDS Temple. By that time, the girl had remarried and Ephraim Sloat had taken himself three new wives."

"So he retained both his pride and his respectability," Hiram said.

"His respectability was important to him. He had some influential clients and developed ties to people close to Brigham Young. He was one of the people who could get things done around Beehive House. He was a fixer. That's why it seemed strange, Hiram, that all references to Ephraim's legal career in Utah were absent from the material in the regular file. Anyway, I kept plodding through the microfilm until I found an item which shed some light on that question. It shed some light on a lot of questions."

Lillian paused for dramatic effect. It was a trait that drove Hiram to distraction. He stared at her impatiently.

"One of Ephraim Sloat's clients, it seems, was a gentleman by the name of John D. Lee. Name ring a bell?"

Hiram's eyes narrowed. He opened his mouth but nothing came out.

Lillian smiled. "My goodness, Hiram, I do believe you're speechless. That's another first for you—speechless and smiling on the same day."

"You *are* serious, Lillian? This isn't a joke."

"I knew that little item would perk your interest. The moment I saw it, I thought, Hiram is going to sizzle over that one!"

But Hiram did not hear her. John D. Lee! The sheer mention of his name had sent Hiram's mind racing down new and unexpected channels. That Dana Sloat's ancestor would be involved in defending that man— What a tight, inbred little community they all dwelled in, these denizens of Zion! And thus it was with Dana Sloat. Never did Hiram think, in his wildest moments of speculation, that this path would lead back to Mountain Meadows!

"Are you still there, Hiram?" Lillian titled her head coyly as though she were awakening a small child.

"I'm sorry, Lillian. I was just thinking, Ephraim Sloat probably was brought in to represent Lee and his friends during the 1859 grand jury investigation. If Ephraim was 'a fixer,' as you described him, some very clever fixing was done during that first trial."

"So it seems, but I'd have to go back to the files and spend hours poring through them in order to figure out what happened. . . ."

"That won't be necessary, Lillian."

"I was hoping you would say that." She saw that he was still lost in his thoughts.

"May I ask you a question, Hiram?"

Hiram looked up. "Of course."

"I never ask you this, but, well . . . this time."

"What is it?"

"Are you going to use this information in your magazine?"

Hiram shook his head. "No," he said softly. "I don't think so. Not for a while, at least."

"I'm glad," Lillian said. "I don't even know this man, Sloat, but I hate to see anyone embarrassed by old family secrets. It makes me cringe. Especially someone like Sloat who has pulled himself up."

"Pulled himself up? . . ."

"Well, Sloat's family really went downhill after Ephraim. I mean, other families with ties to Brigham Young tended to prosper. Brigham saw to it that his friends received timberland or farms or manufacturing deals—you know the pattern, Hiram."

"I do, indeed."

"But the Sloats went back to being farmers or drifters. It was a strange family. Dana Sloat seems to have been the first member of his family since Ephraim to make something of himself."

"Well, don't worry yourself about it, Lillian," Hiram said. "There's only one man I promised to tell, and he's a very prudent person. You're not going to get anyone in trouble. I'll call him the minute I leave here tonight and that's the last I'll breathe about it."

"That makes me feel better," Lillian said, clutching her coat around her shoulders as she got to her feet. "I'd better be going. Take care of yourself, Hiram."

Hiram was standing before her, smiling ruefully. "Lillian, if I wanted to take care of myself, I've been doing it all wrong these last ten years."

She squeezed his arm and then, as had always been their procedure, she left the club first. After she had gone through the door, Hiram walked into the hallway leading to the rest rooms. The hallway was dark and smelled of urine. The pay phone was dimly visible on the wall. He lifted the receiver, deposited his dime and dialed Turner Mead.

☐ After leaving The Ute, Hiram knew he needed to walk. The unaccustomed drink and smoky air had left his head throbbing. The last glimpses of daylight had faded in the forty-five minutes he was inside. The starless night seemed to press down with a dank relentlessness, and Hiram walked quickly, zipping his parka tightly against the frosty air. The streets lay empty before him. Most people were home at their dinner tables, Hiram knew. Only foolish renegades and apostates such as he were left skulking the streets at times like this. But he knew he had to sort out his thoughts.

John D. Lee! Lillian knew she had hit a responsive chord. No wonder Dana Sloat, or perhaps someone looking out for him, had seen to it that his file had been doctored and that his real genealogical records were stashed away for safekeeping. The brethren had always been very careful to see that all traces of Mountain Meadows were hidden from public scrutiny. No wonder, too, that Dana Sloat would go to such lengths to conceal his son's connection with a polygamous cult. A man like Sloat would have to be very careful. Given his sensitive position, he could not afford to have information like this reach the public eye. If anyone found out about his son, Dawson, well, the Mormon people could forgive him that—indeed, it might even arouse public sympathy. His connection to Dawson was less dangerous than his connection to his ancestor Ephraim and to Mountain Meadows.

The saga of Mountain Meadows had been a source of special fascination to Hiram for a long time. Like so much in the Mormon past, for generations Mountain Meadows had simply disappeared from the community conscience as well as from historic records. It had been officially erased—a non-event. When Hiram first began his research into the episode, poring over old diaries and court transcripts, he could only feel a morbid fascination as it all unfolded before him.

The Mormons of Utah, by the mid-1850s, had established a semblance of order in the Great Basin but found themselves increasingly at odds with the great nation that was burgeoning around them. Brigham Young, mindful of his economic and military vulnerability, had sought admission to the United States for his self-styled "State of Deseret," but he demanded admission on his own terms—terms unacceptable to the skeptical authorities in Washington. The Easterners scorned the Mormons' well-publicized institution of polygamy, questioned the autocratic processes by which Brigham Young ruled and criticized the Church's iron control over the schools and political institutions. Deseret seemed like a foreign country, ill-suited to membership in the Union.

The Saints, in turn, made no bones about their own contempt for those few symbols of federal authority that had penetrated their Kingdom. They openly defied Indian agents, federal judges, land surveyors and other Gentiles who strayed into Zion. When one federal judge demanded that U.S. marshals, rather than territorial lawmen, be empowered to serve writs, a band of Mormons broke into his courtroom and tossed all the court records into a giant bonfire. Theirs was a fierce determination to show the world that Saints alone would rule their domain.

The victims at Mountain Meadows had no comprehension of the political caldron into which they were heading, and seemed unlikely candidates for the tragedy that befell them. The Fancher

Party comprised 137 prosperous farmers, their wives and children, who, in the late summer of 1857, were passing through southern Utah on their way from Arkansas to California. Unlike the usual ragged, badly organized bands that traversed Mormon country, the Fancher family and their friends were well-armed and well-rehearsed to confront the inevitable outlaws or Indians who lay in their path. They could have no advance knowledge, however, of the adversaries who now awaited them.

As their wagons snaked down into the Meadows near Cedar City, John D. Lee and other members of the Mormon militia were knelt in a prayer circle, invoking the spirit of God to inspire them in their deeds. It was the notion of Lee, and his superiors in the militia, to perform an act that would dramatize to the Gentiles the sacrosanct status of Zion. After all, even Brigham Young, in a moment of hyperbole, had invoked the threat of Blood Atonement and had warned: ". . . if any miserable scoundrels come here, cut their throats."

Lee left his prayer circle with a plan that was indeed inspired in its deviousness. He would perform an act of Blood Atonement, one that could not be traced to a Saint, but would instead be blamed on the hapless Indians. Accordingly, he and his militia colleagues shed their uniforms, daubed their bodies with red paint and decorated themselves with feathers. They then descended on a small band of surprised but passive Indians, promising them some easy prey. The rewards would be considerable, they advised, and the risks minimal.

The curious band of disguised militiamen and their newfound Indian allies surrounded the Fancher camp that night and opened fire, killing seven members of the party. The well-mobilized Fanchers responded with such an awesome barrage, however, that the Indians scattered in disarray.

Stunned and frustrated, John D. Lee retreated to his camp and conceived a backup scheme. Attired in his regular militia regalia, he rode into the Fancher encampment to present an official apology for the Indian attack. This apology, he explained, was being rendered on behalf of the Mormon nation. The militia, he continued, had now negotiated a truce. The Indians had turned over their weapons to him; if the Fanchers would follow suit and surrender theirs, the militia would escort them to safe territory.

Warily, the travelers conferred among themselves, finally

agreeing to the proposal. Handing over their weapons to Lee and his aides, they climbed into their wagons to resume their westward trek. It was a brilliantly clear summer's day. Perhaps with the help of the friendly Mormons, their luck would turn.

According to Lee's suggestion, the women and children were to be loaded into the first wagons and the sick and wounded into the following. Then, led by John D. Lee himself, the men of the Fancher party were to form a procession heading north up the hill. Two hundred yards from camp, the militia had formed a file on each side of the narrow trail, and beyond, the Indians lay concealed among the cedars and scrub oak.

The first wagons rolled by uneventfully. As the procession of men reached the double file of militia riflemen, they called out their thanks for arranging the truce and fending off the Indians. The Mormons stood in silence until a militia officer suddenly called out the words, "Do your duty!"

The slaughter began. As the militia fired their deadly barrage into the column of defenseless men, the Indians ahead descended, screaming, onto the terrified women and children. Within minutes the massacre was complete. Some one hundred nineteen people lay dead. Lee took eighteen of the youngest children, whose lives had been spared, and escorted them to a nearby farm, as the Indians stripped the bodies of their fallen parents.

When word of the massacre first reached Salt Lake City, the response was official silence. The well-oiled mechanism of a cover-up went into operation. A tragedy had apparently taken place. It was the deed of the Indians. Surely the Mormons could not take responsibility for the actions of the savages throughout their vast territory.

The federal busybodies had to take some symbolic action, of course. That was expected, but they would be as impotent as usual. Brigham Young and his friends would see to that.

A federal judge named John M. Cradlebaugh was dispatched from Salt Lake City to Provo and a nervous jury impaneled. Scores of witnesses would testify, he promised, not only about Mountain Meadows but also other violent crimes against Gentiles, as well as the murders of Mormons who had been declared apostates. The witnesses began to appear, including one who presented a list of all the militiamen who had participated in the Mountain

Meadows Massacre. But the fixers had been at work on the jury. Two weeks into the trial, the judge realized his all-Mormon jury had been instructed to listen patiently but to return no indictments.

Judge Cradlebaugh was incensed. He told the jurors: "Until I commenced the examination of the testimony in this case, I always supposed that I lived in a land of civil and religious liberty. But I regret to say that, as far as Utah is concerned, I have been mistaken in such a supposition. Men are murdered here. Coolly, deliberately, premeditatedly murdered—their murder is determined and deliberated upon by Church council meetings . . . You are the tools, the dupes, the instruments of a tyrannical Church despotism. The heads of your Church order and direct you. You are taught to obey their orders and commit these horrid murders."

The speech was an impressively courageous one, but it didn't affect anything. The jury was dismissed, the charges dropped and everyone went on his way.

The business at Mountain Meadows was not laid to rest, however. Throughout the next decade, the issue kept flaring like an errant brush fire, only to be stomped out each time. During this period, not only was Lee a free man, but he was even in touch with Brigham Young himself, and was a guest in the Prophet's official residence.

In 1874, seventeen years after the massacre, the pressure had built once more and finally John D. Lee was arrested. The cover-up had finally crumbled. The Prophet, it was said, had decreed that the wounds at Mountain Meadows could not be allowed to fester, even if one Saint had to be sacrificed as the price for stilling the strident voices of the federal interlopers. That sacrifice would be the now aged and enfeebled John D. Lee.

It took two trials to convict him, but finally Lee came forward with the appropriate apologia. The deeds he performed at Mountain Meadows, he explained, did not embody his own free will. He was only "an instrument" of his Church, he said, "just as much of an instrument as the knife that was used to cut the throat of the victim." Like all good Mormons, Lee declared, he had been brought up with the stricture that orders were to be "blindly obeyed." If he had done wrong, he was sorry.

The jury of twelve took an hour to return a verdict of murder in the first degree. Lee was given a choice of being shot, hanged or beheaded. He opted for shooting.

He smoldered silently in jail for some weeks, until, finally, venting his anger in a short statement: "I have been treacherously betrayed and sacrificed in the most cowardly manner," he wrote, "by those who should have been my friends . . . In return for my faithfulness and fidelity to him and his cause, he has sacrificed me in a most shameful and cruel way."

He never specified who the "he" was, but he didn't need to. On the morning of March 23, 1877, twenty years after the massacre, John D. Lee was returned to Mountain Meadows, which had long since been laid barren by overgrazing and torrential flooding. He stood at the place where a small monument had once stood, only to be destroyed by Mormon soldiers. At the signal, five shots rang out and Lee fell without a sound. He was buried, as he'd requested, in his Temple robes.

Brigham Young, his Prophet, was to die only six months later of a painful illness.

EVEN under ideal circumstances, Turner Mead abhorred Christmas parties, and, standing now in a hot, crowded room amid the press of bodies and the clangor of forced joviality, Turner was keenly aware that the circumstances were anything but ideal. His nerves had been pulled taut by the day's unrelenting pressures—the phone calls, the rumors, most of all the jarring session with Sloat. Turner was a man who needed things to be focused and orderly. When he felt events slipping away from him, his instinct was to seek refuge until he could restore some sense of perspective. Turner believed in perspective. It was his abiding suspicion that the chain of human experience was in fact a chain of trivial worries which we magnify to give us a sense of exalted purpose. Mindful of that, Turner longed now to bolt from the room and take a solitary walk in the clear night air until he could align his thoughts into some sort of focus. If only he could get some time alone.

Yet these were all his friends and working associates—these bodies which now pressed in around him, noisily exchanging holiday greetings and banter. As members of the Utah Press Club, they faithfully assembled during Christmas week each year to renew friendships. They were a disparate group: most were Mormons, a few had drifted from the faith. Some smoked and drank, others abstained. Some affected beards and sweaters, others wore the dark suits and the close-cropped hair that marked their association with the Church.

Turner had known most of the men during the years he had spent on the *Deseret News*, first as a reporter, ultimately as city editor. Only a minority had stayed in the newspaper business, either with the Church-owned *News* or with the independently owned *Tribune*, while others, like Turner, had gone to allied jobs in the media or in public relations. Though he had now spent

179

eight years working directly for the Church, Turner still felt a strong kinship for these men, a part of him still yearning for the simpler days when a good story was all it took to get his youthful adrenaline pumping, when guiding an important article through the maze of bureaucratic intrigue ranked supreme on the list of life's satisfactions.

The annual Press Club parties were always held in the back room at Lamb's, a busy, somewhat disheveled restaurant on Main Street which served as a rendezvous for the press and politicians. It was a pleasant room with paneled walls and brass railings, rather like a men's club, but the low ceiling and cramped quarters only served to heighten Turner's discomfort. He was determined to circulate the room as expeditiously as possible, to shake the hands extended to him and return the greetings, and then to disappear inconspicuously.

But even the jests, which he had always taken good-naturedly, somehow pained him now. His lofty position in Church councils, and his access to useful information, caused some reporters to treat him with a certain cautious deference. But others—especially his former colleagues on the *News*—enjoyed applying the needle. "You look more like an Apostle with each passing year," Ned Simmons told him, pumping his hand. Simmons had worked at the desk next to his for four years, but Turner found himself hard-pressed to respond with the grin that was expected of him. And when a bearded young television reporter greeted him facetiously as "Bishop Mead," Turner simply turned away. It was all supposed to be good-natured kidding, he told himself, annoyed with his own impatience.

He was about to abandon his resolve and head for the exit when he confronted the somber presence of Burt Hoagland, who occupied his old post as city editor.

"Turner, my friend, I hope I won't hurt your feelings by telling you that you're looking rather piqued," he said, a sly grin tracing across his lined face. Hoagland was the sort of newsman who would never leave the paper, Turner knew, no matter how great his dissatisfactions. Indeed, his face looked as though it had been washed empty by disappointment.

"If the truth be told, I *am* feeling piqued," Turner replied, shaking his hand warmly, grateful to be in the company of an old ally.

"Your phone must be ringing off the wall," Hoagland said. "A generation ago no one outside the State of Utah would even notice if a new First President and First Counselor took office in the Mormon Church. Perhaps the wire services would move two hundred words—that would be it."

Turner gave him a pained smile. "I'm afraid we're a little more in the public eye these days."

Hoagland nodded understandingly. "The price of success, my British friend. The world press has finally come to realize that there's a big story hiding within the Mormon pantheon."

Turner felt his tension subsiding as he talked to this slight, almost fragile man with his mournful eyes and fringe of white hair and skin the color of parchment. Hoagland had been a friend for a long time. More than anyone else in the room, he could comprehend the crosscurrents which were buffeting him. Over the years the two of them had agonized over many dilemmas involving the newspaper and the Church—situations which, in the hands of a less understanding man, could have gotten out of hand. Hoagland had always been a professional. He wanted to print the truth. Yet he was pragmatic enough to understand what could and what could not be published by a newspaper that was not only owned by the Church but that served a community whose principal industries and leaders were beholden to the Church. Some of the situations had been painful to them both, and some merely laughable. When one of the Apostles called to protest a reference in the News to the "Kremlin's aging leadership," they both had laughed about it and decreed thereafter that, in deference to the similarly aging leadership of the Mormon Church, no invidious mentions would be made about aging Russians. Similarly, when an eager young Deseret News police reporter got hold of the information two years earlier that President Woodleigh, then seventy-eight, had accumulated five speeding tickets in the course of one year, Burt Hoagland spiked the story without a word, sending a photocopy to Turner "for your files." Both Turner and Hoagland had long known about the problem, of course. President Woodleigh, in his waning years, fantasized himself to be a race-car driver. While his chauffeur cowered in the backseat, he often hit seventy or eighty miles an hour on the way home. Forewarned when the Prophet was leaving his office, the local police would clear the streets along his homeward course.

Other incidents had been less amusing. A year earlier, a local reporter for The Associated Press had put together a story about the fast-expanding financial holdings of the Mormon Church. The story had been well-researched. Hoagland, like other editors around the country, received his first glimpse of the story when it arrived on the wire. He dispatched it by messenger to Turner, who in turn showed it to President Woodleigh and his First Counselor, Dalton Evans. Despite Turner's resistance, they both said, "Kill it." Turner passed the word. The story did not run in any newspaper in the State of Utah, and received amazingly little attention elsewhere. Even more distressing to Turner was the suppression that summer of a series dealing with the problems of single women in Mormon society—with their feelings of neglect and failure in not living up to the Mother of Zion image. One of the most conservative of the General Authorities, Isaac Sorenson, got wind of the series a week before it was scheduled to run and demanded it be killed. Turner and Hoagland both read it and agreed it was a fair story which did not cast the Church in a bad light. Sorenson was adamant, and one night the president of the Deseret News called Hoagland instructing him tersely to destroy all copies of the story and forget it. Brigit Magill, the bright young reporter who wrote the series, resigned in anger, and her resignation was dutifully covered on the local television news. Hoagland, a good Mormon with seven children, flew to Las Vegas and stayed drunk for two days. Turner almost joined him.

Chatting together in the middle of the crowd, pausing occasionally to greet a passing friend, Turner and Hoagland steered away from these troublous recollections, channeling their conversation instead to more comfortable subjects. Turner was in midsentence when he realized Hoagland was not listening to a word he was saying, that his mind had drifted far away.

"Is it my dazzling dialogue? . . ." Turner chided him.

Hoagland's eyes locked on his. "I apologize. My mind drifted."

"That was fairly obvious."

"Look, Turner, I think we should have a private chat. . . ."

Turner studied his friend's baleful face. "Is it a personal problem, Burt? I'd be glad to . . ."

"I think you would call it a business problem. Look, you know the little coffee shop on the corner? Meet me there in ten minutes."

"That pressing, is it?"

"You've known me a long time, Turner. Do I send off false alarms?"

Turner shook his head gravely. He felt the tension gnawing at him again.

☐ "This afternoon I found out something I really didn't want to know."

Burt Hoagland was sitting across from him, an elbow perched on the shiny Formica table. The puffy patches beneath his eyes looked blue-gray in the overhead glare. Hoagland had ordered black coffee. Turner had tried a spoonful of vegetable soup, but found it to be inordinately greasy, like beef stock that hadn't been skimmed.

"You remember Jamie Wight?" Hoagland asked.

"Isn't he your new hotshot kid in Washington?"

Hoagland nodded. "Turns out he's slipping stuff to another newspaper. Stuff he figures we won't publish."

"I would say he needs a slap on the wrist, Burt. And a reminder that it's your job to decide what's publishable." Turner felt relieved that the indiscretion of a kid reporter was all that apparently was worrying his friend.

Hoagland sipped his black coffee, his expression still grim. "I'm afraid it's gone beyond that, Turner. For the past few months, Alvin Boroff of the Pollard papers in California has been trying to put together a series about the Church's influence in politics."

"I heard about that one. They'll never get enough hard stuff to make the story float."

"With Jamie Wight's help, they will. He's been feeding them hard news."

Turner pushed the greasy soup aside. "What have they got— the usual quotes from Isaac Sorenson saying the Commies are going to take over the country?"

Turner had been through all this before. Reporters, especially from out of state, always enjoyed interviewing Isaac Sorenson and quoting his declarations that the nation was succumbing to Socialists, pornographers and abortionists. The real story the Eastern press was after, Turner knew, was more complex: That state and local elections in the Mormon nation still were controlled by the hierarchy. Turner believed this to be untrue, but he could understand the reasons for the Easterners' suspicions. In the era before statehood, the politics of Mormondom were at best eccentric. The Church did not exactly tell its followers how to vote, but it decided who could run for office and barred all parties except its own. When Utah finally achieved statehood, the two-party system was implemented in the most cavalier manner: Bishops simply assigned the left half of their chapels to be Democrats and the right half to be Republicans.

But all this, in Turner's observation, was in the past.

"Yes, they have the usual Sorenson quotes," Hoagland said, staring into his coffee. "They also have affidavits—loads of them. Affidavits from brethren in Idaho claiming they received an Approved Candidate List for the board of education from their Stake President. From brethren in Nevada that the Fast and Testimony service was used to rally support for an LDS congressional candidate. From brethren in Arizona claiming their Bishop instructed them how to vote in the gubernatorial election."

"Burt, my good brother, that's all old news. You know it as well as I. That's not to condone it, but I would remind you that it's not illegal to distribute political material in church. It's not even illegal for a church to endorse candidates, although it may get hairy from the standpoint of tax exemption."

But Burt Hoagland didn't even seem to hear him. He kept peering into his steaming cup, as if expecting a genie to present itself. "Jamie also gave them the whole layout on the Church's anti-ERA campaign. How the Church levied thousands of dollars in assessments on local stakes to finance the drive, how anti-ERA material was handed out at sacrament meetings, how Regional Representatives were told that they had 'priesthood callings' to lobby against equal rights in their local legislatures."

Turner exhaled between his clenched teeth. "I hate to see that stuff dredged up. The wounds of ERA are just starting to heal."

"The boys exceeded their authority on that one," Hoagland said. "You know it as well as I, Turner. They were forcing the brethren to take sides on a purely political issue."

"Let's not fight that one again, Burt. You know my private opinions, my friend. But I can't believe any major newspaper would run a story on any of this—it's history; it's just a glorified sidebar."

Hoagland lifted his gaze. His pupils seemed shrunken, like those of a man who was accustomed to regarding life's foibles from a safe distance.

"All right then, tell me if you consider this a sidebar: Did you know that Dana Sloat quietly flew to Washington to address a prayer breakfast last Friday morning?"

"No, I never heard a word about it."

"Our distinguished junior senator, Ezra Hurlbut, ramrodded the meeting. He got a really good turnout—all the top-ranking brethren in the CIA, FBI, National Security Council, Justice Department . . ."

Turner held up his hand. ". . . What did Sloat have to say to them?"

"He laid down the law, Turner. He said the time had come for the Church to take a more aggressive leadership role. Brethren in government positions must work harder to support Church objectives, as well as help other brothers climb the leadership ladder so that there will be more of us in authority. . . ."

Dana Sloat again! Wherever he seemed to turn, that name confronted him. "Are you telling me your kid reporter leaked this speech to the press? . . ."

"Damned right he did."

Turner whistled softly, slumping back against the banquette. "We got problems, Burt."

"That's what I've been trying to tell you."

"Sloat's playing right into the hands of the Mormon haters and he doesn't even realize it. The worst thing that could happen now would be for a major newspaper to publish a list of our LDS brethren holding high positions in the government—especially the security establishment. It would start all the paranoid rumors going again—the Mormons run the CIA, the Mormons are a secret government, Mormon missionaries are all CIA plants. I can hear them all playing back to us."

Hoagland pursed his lips. "You know as well as I that those 'rumors' aren't all that paranoid. I never cease to be amazed at the quiet power our brethren exert, the positions they've attained."

Turner was nervously spooning his soup once again, his face flinching with the aftertaste. "How did you find out about this incident, Burt? Where did you learn all this?"

"Believe it or not I have my own spy with the Pollard papers. He's just a copyreader, but he's loyal. Jamie Wight leaks them our secrets and this brother leaks me theirs."

The two men caught each other's glance and they both smiled. They were sad, bemused smiles. They had known each other too long and trusted each other too deeply not to share the absurdity of it all. Here they were, sitting in a deserted coffee shop two days before Christmas, discussing events which defied credible explanation. Events which, they knew, could shake the very foundation of the Church which, with all their fleeting reservations, they both loved and revered.

Burt Hoagland shoved his coffee cup to the end of the table and leaned forward toward Turner, his expression intent now. "I want you to tell me something, Turner. I want you to give me a straight answer."

"What is it?"

"This man, Sloat. You must know him. You must have met with him."

"I have."

"What is it he wants? I mean, I've sifted through the news clips on him. I've read his bio, his speeches. I still haven't a clue what makes the man tick."

"I can't answer your question, Burt. I'm sorry."

"Is it that you don't know or won't tell?"

Turner's eyes averted his friend's. "A little of both. Yes, I've met with him. Even today I saw him. And I've learned some things from my meeting, some other things from other sources. I have my suspicions, Burt, but they're just suspicions. All I can tell you is that Dana Sloat sees a different kind of Church than you and I grew up with. You might say he's a kind of visionary."

"But what the hell's his vision?"

"Look, I know what you're trying to get me to say. He scares the shit out of me, too, Burt. Is that enough for you? Do you get the picture?" Turner's face was bristling.

Hoagland shrugged in frustration. "Yup, I guess I get the picture all right."

"I'm sorry," Turner said quickly. "I didn't mean to snap at you like some sort of goddamn bureaucrat. Forgive me."

Hoagland nodded his head. "It's okay. I shouldn't press you."

"No, you have a right to press me. You're sitting on a powder keg, and so am I."

They were silent again, Hoagland fidgeting with his spoon, Turner staring at the wall.

"You know the thing that scares me most, Turner? If a man like Dana Sloat goes to Washington and tells our brothers what to do and what to say, most of them will do it. They'll do it for the Church. They would do Sloat's bidding just like I dutifully spiked stories whenever I was instructed to. It pained me to kill a good story, but I did it anyway. Every time I spiked one, I got a pain in my gut. And with each passing year the pain got worse—what do you think of that, Turner?"

"I think it's a sign of old age, my friend," Turner said softly.

"No, you don't."

"We both did what we thought was right at the time. We both believe in the Church. We undertook an obligation to defend it."

Hoagland reached across the table and clasped Turner's forearm in a viselike grip. "But do we believe in the same Church Dana Sloat believes in? Ten years from now are we going to be filled with remorse for allowing ourselves to be manipulated like puppets by a megalomaniac we don't even know or understand? Are we acting like damn fools, Turner?"

Hoagland could see Turner Mead's face color with anger, his mouth open, poised to say something, then snap shut again, lapsing into silence.

"It's a simple yes or no answer I need from you," Hoagland persisted. "Are we acting like damn fools?"

Turner stared thoughtfully across at him for several moments, then nodded his head slowly. "Sure," he said finally, "I suspect we're a couple of damned fools." He said it so softly his voice was barely audible, but the words hit Hoagland like a blow to the stomach.

TAD tilted his head to let the hot water pound against his shoulders and upper neck. He felt his muscles slacken as the comforting sheath of steam slid over his body.

He knew a hot shower would provide solace. When he'd returned to his hotel room at the Century Plaza fifteen minutes earlier, he'd felt the depression envelop him, as though he were a ship sailing into a thick fog. He sensed himself sagging under its weight.

Part of it, of course, was merely a reaction to the pressure. He'd been on the run since early that morning, rushing to the Snow meeting, rushing to the airport, rushing to the hotel, rushing to the meeting with Curry. And now, standing in the shower, feeling the steam seep into him, the whole thing seemed like some sort of comedy pastiche. He had been wound up like a little robot and sent scurrying off in different directions. He felt used—and just a little bit foolish.

After checking into the hotel, Tad had immediately phoned Curry. He wanted urgently to meet the old man who managed Pacific's affairs and find out why his company had suddenly changed the terms of the deal. He had to have that information before confronting Gavin Pollard.

Yet Curry was reluctant even to see him. There was nothing more to discuss, the old man said. Pressing him hard, Tad finally got him to agree to meet at his club—after he had finished his regular round of golf.

When Tad found him in the bar, attired in a bright red shirt and yellow polyester trousers that looked as though they'd stretched to fit him, Curry was already well into his afternoon quota of Scotch. The old man greeted him with the studied gruffness of a patriarch, and led him to a corner table. Though removed from the barroom hubbub, Tad still had to strain to hear his low rumble

188

of a voice amid the noisy banter of bets being paid off and golf scores being exchanged. Through their conversation, Curry seemed disinterested, even bored. The changes in the Pacific situation were trivial, he said. Alonzo Gaunt had the final word on anything relating to the company, since he owned seventy-five percent of the stock. Gaunt was a man in his mid-seventies who spent most of his time in Hawaii. He had approved the original terms under which his radio and television stations were to be sold to Suncorp, then called a few days later and changed his mind. If he was going to sell the stations, he might as well sell the whole company. What difference does it make, anyway? Curry asked. It's still a damn good deal. If Suncorp wants to back away from it, he'll set it up elsewhere.

Feeling a sudden edge of panic, Tad tried to summon up reassurances: The deal could still be made. It was just that the sudden shift had unsettled his clients. It was a much bigger deal now.

"Hell, it's just paper," Curry growled, his pink little globe of a face reddening even further. "They're just exchanging stock, my boy. What does another hundred million dollars in paper mean when you're up there in the bracket with people like the Pollard family?"

"Or people like Alonzo Gaunt. Why would another hundred million dollars in paper mean so much to him that he would risk blowing the deal?" Tad persisted.

Curry looked exasperated and ordered another Scotch. "You sure you don't want a drink, kid?" Curry asked. "Old man Gaunt would never even have a Pepsi. An old California Mormon family, you know. Never figured out why he put up with a crusty old Irish Catholic like me."

Then Curry was off on one of his interminable anecdotes about how he had met Gaunt in the early days of broadcasting, how they had owned and operated a number of stations over the years, how Gaunt had never interfered with his operation. "He had three rules," Curry said. "No rock and roll. That was the spirit of Satan. No beer commercials either. And on Sundays I had to have at least one hour of the Mormon Tabernacle Choir. That's all he ever asked of me." Curry chortled to himself. "That, and a hefty profit each year. Old Alonzo loved his profits. But he didn't even care about these the last few years, after his wife died."

Draining his glass, Curry leaned across the table and confided: "You know, kid, you and your friends in Utah are the last people who should worry about this deal." He gave Tad a wink, as if he had just imparted some remarkable piece of intelligence.

Tad sat there, feeling foolish once again. "I'm afraid I don't understand."

"What do you mean, you don't understand?"

". . . Don't understand what you were referring to. . . ."

"Jesus, kid, it was your own law firm that drew up the new will. They didn't tell you, huh?" Curry shook his head. "Hell, you Mormons are so fucking secretive, you don't even talk to each other. Six months ago the old man changed his will, leaving his entire interest in Pacific to the LDS Church."

Tad felt his palms growing moist. ". . . The Church would inherit it upon his death?"

"Christ, no. He wanted to duck any estate problems. The Church will effectively own Pacific three months from now."

Three months from now! The words shocked Tad when he first heard them, and now, an hour later, replaying the conversation in his mind, their impact had not lessened. Gavin Pollard thought, and so had he, that they were making a deal with an old man in Hawaii. Instead, they were making a deal with the Mormon Church!

And Tad had not even been told. That realization left him seething with anger. Why in hell hadn't Ellis Marmer informed him of the will? He was, after all, the attorney assigned to Pacific. If the deal went through, the Mormon Church would end up owning a big hunk of Suncorp—a fact that would surely be of interest to his friend Gavin Pollard. Is that why Marmer hadn't told him? Had Marmer assumed Tad would promptly tell Gavin and that Gavin would react negatively? But why? Hell, Gavin had no love for the LDS Church, but surely he'd have no trepidations about the Church joining the list of Suncorp's minority stockholders. The Church had holdings in hundreds of companies and had always proven a passive, undemanding business partner.

No, something didn't add up, Tad told himself. A key fact somewhere was being withheld from him, whether by Curry or Marmer or even by Gavin. He was being left in the dark, treated like the "kid attorney," the new boy who couldn't be trusted all the way.

All right, if everyone was going to be so goddamned secretive with him, Tad would return the favor. He would keep his mouth firmly shut until he learned the real answers. He would keep his ears open but his mouth shut.

Stepping now from the shower, Tad realized all the soothing effect of the steam had worn off; he was just as agitated as before.

Reaching for a towel, he started scrubbing his skin furiously. Damn them all! Tad told himself. All his life he'd been treated like a kid and he was fed up.

Glimpsing himself in the full-length mirror, Tad noticed that his white skin shone pink from the fierce toweling, giving him the appearance of a cooked lobster.

He'd always resented his chalky skin and nondescript sandy hair, just as he was impatient with his boyish features. He remembered taking showers at school, noticing his classmates with *their* pale chalky skins and blond hair and hairless bodies, all of them looking as though they'd come off some sort of ethnic assembly line. Once in junior high he recalled his embarrassment when he'd been caught staring avidly at the swarthy body of a handsome youngster of Hispanic ancestry, yearning ardently that he, too, could possess a bronze skin and that splendid patch of hair emblazoned across his chest. Instead he was imprisoned in his utterly characterless body, crowned by his utterly characterless face. Ever since childhood, Tad had heard people tell his mother, my isn't Tad a pretty boy! He didn't want to be pretty! His sisters could be pretty, not he. He yearned for that distinctive masculinity that others seemed to possess—others like Gavin Pollard. Yes, he wished he looked like Gavin.

Gavin! Christ, he was due at his house in half an hour.

Tad stared glumly at his dark gray suit hanging in the closet. It was the same suit he'd worn that morning at the Snows. In his rush for the plane, there was no time to pick up some other clothes for Los Angeles. He'd have to show up at Gavin's looking like a Mormon missionary who was out tracting. Gavin would needle the hell out of him! And Pye! How she loved to chide him.

In the bedroom the six o'clock news was just starting, and Tad realized how desperately he wished that he were home. Whenever he visited Los Angeles, no matter how much he fantasized about his freedom, this was the time of day when the loneliness always hit him, and he hated himself for succumbing to it. Downstairs in the lobby the bars would be growing crowded with men and women, huddled together over their drinks, laying their plans for the evening. Their day would be beginning and his would usually be ending.

If he were home now, Nancy and the kids would just be sitting down to dinner. They would be bowing their heads and one of the kids, Dana probably, would say the blessing over the food in his sweet little voice, faltering over the key words but getting through it nonetheless. The house would smell of meat loaf or lamb and Nancy would be doling out the portions, urging the children in that softly melodic tone of voice to eat slowly and not to neglect their vegetables. Damn, he missed them! He absolutely ached for them. It had always amazed him how, with three small kids underfoot, Nancy never lost her implacable calm or her gentle smile. It was as though she was totally in mesh with her designated role in life as wife, mother, upholder of the faith. She was at peace with her expectations, knowing precisely who she was and why she had been placed there. Tad had always respected that wellspring of serenity, even yearned that he, too, could share it. Yet it seemed beyond his grasp. He had never felt the peace.

Even his teachers had noticed it. "You won't skid if you stay in your rut," his fourth-grade teacher had advised him. It was meant to be helpful counsel but it terrified him. He didn't want to skid, yet how he feared the rut!

He walked quickly to the telephone and dialed room service.

"This is Mr. Hastings in twelve twenty-two. Please send up a double vodka on the rocks. Yes, with a twist. How long will it take? . . ."

Tonight he would definitely need one for the road.

☐ He had always coveted Gavin Pollard's house, yet it represented in every sense the antithesis of his own tastes and predilections. Tad's home was built to accommodate a growing family. The dining- and living-room areas were cramped; most of the available space was allotted to bedrooms. Stuffed into every nook and cranny were toys, high chairs and other paraphernalia of childrearing. There was a pervasive aroma of talcum and candy. It was a good LDS house.

Gavin's, by contrast, was a celebration of bachelorhood. It was a large house, really, with a fine expanse of living room and a handsome den that smelled of books and leather. Tad remembered his surprise in discovering the house contained only one bedroom—an enormous bedroom, to be sure. Gavin had purchased the house a year earlier from a film producer who had fallen on lean times. Shortly after completing its renovation, he had proudly shown it off to Tad. "It's just a rustic little place," Gavin warned him modestly.

Rustic! A year later Tad still had to chortle over his friend's disclaimer. The place had been meticulously done over so that everything would suggest country—lots of solid oak furniture, brass lamps, big brick fireplaces, paneled walls of buffed teakwood. Elegantly framed portrayals of fox hunts and other sport adorned the walls. In Gavin's bedroom was a great old fourposter, complete with canopy and patterned quilt, which faced a big fireplace of used brick.

It was "country," all right—Beverly Hills country. The place might have worked, Tad sensed, had not everything been too chic, too fussed over, too expensive. Tad wished he could have taken Gavin's decorator to the old pioneer homes of Utah—the stalwart two-story sandstone houses with their stubby stone fireplaces or the squat, rugged little stucco-covered saltboxes built to withstand blizzards and floods and infestations. Now that was rustic! Mormon rustic, Gavin would scoff, but a damn sight more authentic than Beverly Hills rustic.

On the other hand, the Mormon saltboxes didn't have the other accoutrements which Gavin valued so greatly—the tennis court out back, and the swimming pool, and next to that, the Jacuzzi. Tad himself had spent many hours enjoying these creature comforts. Indeed, his consistent ability to defeat Gavin on the tennis court was always a high point of his trips to Los Angeles, one of the few things he looked forward to. These victories and, of course, Pye.

The taxi had been twisting up Coldwater Canyon, rolling past the splendid pine trees which formed a rich green shield for the mansions that loomed behind. Turning onto a quiet lane, Tad directed the driver to the appropriate driveway, paid him and rang the bell. The Brazilian houseboy known simply as "Joe" responded immediately.

Tad found Gavin in the den, a telephone, as usual, clutched in his long fingers, signaling a greeting with his free hand. Across the room, veiled in a billowing cloud of cigar smoke, sat Pat Minafee, who extended his hand but did not smile or rise. Minafee had been the personal attorney and close friend to Gavin's father during the long years he had headed Suncorp, and now continued as Gavin's counselor. When old man Pollard had died nine months earlier, he no doubt had told his friend, "Take care of my son." Minafee dutifully was taking care, in his brusquely overprotective way.

Tad lowered himself into a big leather chair, as far removed as possible from the cigar smoke, just as Joe appeared with a glass of Pepsi-Cola, which he set down next to Tad. It was Tad's usual drink, Joe knew, but Tad would have ordered another vodka if given the opportunity. Gavin was still talking on the phone, an edge of impatience in his voice. He was dressed in a burgundy velour shirt, tan trousers and tennis sneakers. His handsome face looked rather haggard, the crease marks of fatigue seeming out of place on his fine, tan skin. Tad realized that Gavin Pollard was one of those people whose appearance, for better or worse, was totally revealing of themselves. Gavin was a thoroughbred and looked like one. There had been three generations of wealth to smooth his path, and it all showed—it showed in the fine bones of his face, in his lean-flanked, graceful body, even in his burnished brown hair which was wet from a recent shower and combed straight back. All of it suggested the patrician, and it occurred to Tad that, if the house was somehow "too perfect," so was its owner. Gavin's face would have benefited from some imperfection—a bump in his thin, straight nose, or a squint in his deep-set brown eyes. Because all his features came together so well, they presented, somehow, a sense of weakness, even fragility.

Gavin plunked down the phone. "Well, welcome, Elder Hastings. You look like you've been out converting the heathen."

Tad blanched, but grinned bravely. Suddenly his dark suit seemed warm and confining. "You summoned me so hastily I didn't even have the chance to get out of my lawyer's uniform."

"Well, it's good to see you, asshole." Gavin walked over to him and dispensed an affectionate pat on the back, plucking his glass and moving to the bar. He poured a vodka and ice and handed it to Tad. "Try this," Gavin said. "It's a new drink we Gentiles have invented to get us through times of turmoil. It's called Smirnoff."

Tad smiled gratefully and took a sip.

"What did Boroff have to say?" Minafee asked.

"He checked the SEC, Justice Department—everywhere. He came away empty-handed." Gavin turned toward Tad. "I asked Alvin Boroff, our Washington bureau chief, to see if he could learn anything about Alonzo Gaunt—anything that could help us."

Tad could feel the tension in the room. "Have your directors reacted to the revised deal?"

"A couple balked. They're worried about diluting the stock. The others still like the deal. The key to the whole thing is that old Gaunt is selling us nine terrific stations—the best or near best in their markets. Everyone wants Suncorp to diversify into radio and television—well, we're diversifying, and the price is right."

"The price is too right," Minafee growled, chewing on his cigar. "Something doesn't square." A florid, heavyset man, Minafee's curly, once-red hair had turned an orangish-gray. His standard expression, Tad felt, was that of a man who had spent his life turning over rocks, and taking perverse pleasure in the objects he found lurking below.

"It's Emory and Marva who've really surprised me," Gavin said, kicking off his sneakers and folding his long legs beneath him on the brown corduroy sofa. "Today was the paper's annual award luncheon to honor the clergymen who've performed the greatest service to their community. It's a real bullshit thing we do every year as a sop to Aunt Marva. My dad thought it would keep her happy before he found out nothing would keep her happy. Anyway, I expected Marva to come at me like a tigress over the change in the Pacific deal. It's just the kind of opening she would leap at, but she didn't say a thing. She just smiled benignly as if I were her favorite nephew."

"She may be saving her ammunition for the next board meeting," Minafee said.

Tad had never met Emory Pollard or his wife, Marva, but he knew they were a thorn in Gavin's side. Emory was the younger brother of Gavin's father, Nicholas Pollard. In keeping with the

ironclad rules of primogeniture, he had been denied the top position at Suncorp when their father died. He had instead become
a rather notorious playboy until marrying Marva O'Connell, an
ambitious, strong-willed woman who straightened out Emory and
saw to it that he used his ten percent share of Suncorp to exercise
a strong and, according to Gavin, shrill voice against what she
considered the increasingly "liberal" position of its editorial
stance. Marva's idea of a liberal, Gavin complained, was anyone
born since Bismarck. Upon the death of Nicholas Pollard, Uncle
Emory, with Marva's prodding, launched a vigorous battle for the
presidency of Suncorp, a position which Nicholas had explicitly
intended for his son Gavin. Nicholas had assumed that his choice
of a successor would go uncontested, despite Marva's obvious
ambitions. What he hadn't counted on, however, was the changed
composition of the board of directors. As Suncorp continued its
aggressive expansion over the years, swallowing up newspapers,
magazines, book publishers and other diverse enterprises, its
board was steadily expanded to include top officers of acquired
companies as well as several bankers and Wall Street figures. It
was to these men that Emory and Marva had taken their case,
arguing fervently that Gavin Pollard was a lightweight, a playboy,
a liberal, a man who was clearly unqualified to fill a job of such
high responsibility as head of a far-flung media empire which
included the single most influential daily newspaper on the West
Coast. No, the appropriate successor to Nicholas Pollard, they
argued, was Emory Pollard. And, while both Emory and Gavin
were lining up support on the board, Gavin had been kept in a
holding pattern in the post of vice-president, a position he found
increasingly precarious.

Gavin and Minafee were still in animated conversation about
his aunt and uncle—a conversation Tad wished would end. "I
just want two days," Minafee was barking. "Two days to study the
new proposal, that's all."

Gavin lifted his lands in exasperation. "I don't have two days."

"Then get them."

Gavin turned toward Tad with a gesture of helplessness.
"Would you believe this? We've come up with a deal that is so
good my own dear aunt and uncle are afraid to attack it, and yet
my consigliere here is dead against it."

"I'm not against it," Minafee said. "I just want more time to look into it." Minafee's bloodshot eyes fixed on Tad now. "You brought us the deal, kid. Go back to Curry and get us two days. You have the leverage with him."

"I already took a stab at it," Tad said. "He turned me down. He wants to close the deal or he'll shop it elsewhere." He was tempted to say more, tempted to tell Gavin now about the will— to get it all out on the table. But peering at the bristling Minafee, he sensed this wasn't the time; no, he would tell Gavin when they were alone and let Gavin make the decision whether to pass the information along to Minafee. It wasn't really germane to this argument in any event.

"If he wants so bad to close the deal, why the fuck did he change it all around?" Minafee sent a yellow cloud of cigar smoke drifting in Tad's direction.

"He said it was Mr. Gaunt who changed the deal. Mr. Gaunt decided that if he were going to sell his stations he might as well sell the whole company. He's living in retirement in Hawaii. His wife died a few years ago and he's lost interest in business."

"Go back to him and say it's no deal unless we get two more days," Minafee snapped.

"What can you possibly hope to learn in two days?" Tad demanded as he tensely sipped his vodka. The moment the words escaped his lips he regretted them. He could see Minafee's already florid face redden.

"What I meant to say is, if there's anything about the deal that worries you, perhaps my law firm can look into it. . . . ."

"Look, kid, you brought the deal in. Don't try to stuff it down our throats."

"Take it easy," Gavin interjected, but Minafee was leaning forward in his chair, his big belly spilling over his belt.

"No, I don't want to take it easy!" Minafee exploded. "I want the kid here to take it easy. Him and his Saintly friend, Alonzo Gaunt."

"Let's not make this a religious war," Tad said.

"Remember, Minafee, Elder Hastings and I served as missionaries together, converting the savages of the South Pacific," Gavin said facetiously.

But Minafee was not to be sidetracked. "Goddamn Mormons,"

he grumbled, lighting his cigar anew. "They always look so pious, then end up busting your balls." He looked at Gavin in exasperation. "You weren't around during the Blanton deal, kid."

"What Blanton deal?"

Gavin shrugged. "Blanton was the principal newsprint supplier for our newspapers. My dad wanted to control his own paper resources so he made an offer for the company. After a lot of negotiating back and forth they agreed to an exchange of stock, only to find that the Blanton brothers had willed their holdings to the Mormon Church. That's how the Church ultimately ended up with twenty percent of Suncorp. It was really no big deal."

No big deal! Tad thought, struggling for his composure. He had never heard of the Blanton situation, but this was not the time to show it. His mind flashed to Curry's remarks about Gaunt and the will—". . . you and your friends in Utah are the last people who should worry about this deal." Those were his words, but what exactly did they mean? Was Curry alluding to the Blanton deal in some elliptical way? The similarity to the Pacific situation was remarkable in any event. The Blanton family had willed their stock to the Church, and now Alonzo Gaunt was about to follow the same pattern. And, once again, no one knew about it. No one except he and Curry—and Ellis Marmer. A bizarre coincidence! But was it only a coincidence? If this deal were consummated, the Gaunt and Blanton holdings combined would surely approach working control of Suncorp. But that was absurd, of course. The Church would never seek dominance of Suncorp. That had never been its objective in this or any other business transaction. What would be the purpose? No, the whole thing was a coincidence.

The phone rang and Gavin handed it to Minafee, who was now barking at someone at the other end of the line. Gavin had returned to the bar and was replenishing his and Minafee's drinks. Tad was grateful for the breathing time. He had to think things through carefully, one last time. He had a big decision to make. The right thing to do was to tell them both—tell them all he knew. Gavin was his friend, after all. In some ways he was the best friend Tad had ever had. Minafee would jump all over it. He would turn it into a Mormon plot. Minafee would rub Gavin's nose in it. Gavin would become scared enough to agree to a delay and then Tad would have to go back to Curry, hat in hand, to beg for an extension which wouldn't come. Curry and Gaunt could easily find another buyer.

His first impulse was correct, after all. It really came down to a question of protecting Gavin. If this deal went through he would surely become president of Suncorp. Gavin would benefit richly and so would Tad. The most important task was to go home and find out what Ellis Marmer knew about it. Then he would tell all he had learned to Gavin, placing it in its proper context.

Minafee slammed the phone down. Tad felt a churning in his stomach. He got up and walked down the hallway to the bathroom. He bent over the sink and cupped the cold water in his hands, sloshing it over his face. The coolness of the water refreshed him. He dabbed his face with a towel.

And then, for no reason he could reasonably discern, the image of Dana Sloat flashed before him. What did *he* know about all this? The one thing he could never get out of his mind was his instinctual feeling, after telling his father-in-law about the Pacific deal, that Sloat knew it all—that he knew the details of the situation even before Tad explained them to him. Yes, Sloat knew—but how?

Unless—Tad's mind began to whirl with the possibilities—unless Tad was the Trojan horse in the situation. Unless Tad, using his well-known relationship with Gavin Pollard, was being manipulated to set up this whole deal. Manipulated by Dana Sloat for reasons of his own.

Christ, all this was stupid, Tad told himself. He was doing exactly the things he feared Minafee would do. He was conjuring up conspiracies and paranoid plots. He was behaving like a damned fool, letting himself succumb to these wild imaginings.

His shirt was damp with sweat. He bent over to dab water on his face again, and then he realized what was happening. He was helpless to do anything about it. He was throwing up.

☐ When Tad returned to the den, the room was empty. The stale aroma of cigar smoke hung in the air, but there was otherwise no trace of Minafee or Gavin. It was like one of those nightmares where suddenly you open your eyes and all the bad guys have magically evaporated.

Tad walked to the bar and poured some Perrier water. He drank it slowly, assuaging his angry stomach.

"Mr. Tad."

Joe was standing there, holding white tennis shorts and a shirt. "Mr. Gavin is changing for tennis. He ask me to bring you these."

Tad shook his head and accepted the garments being handed to him. Yes, this was a typical Gavin switch: One moment he could be in the midst of a critical business meeting and then suddenly it was time for tennis—everything else would have to stop.

That was, Tad supposed, one of the prerogatives of great wealth. When one wears the armor of the Pollard fortune, matters that seem cosmic to others shrink to a lesser perspective.

Tad was grateful today for his friend's quixotic nature. He'd had his fill of the Pacific deal. It felt wonderful to peel off the damned gray suit, draping it over the back of a bar chair. He cursed to himself as he tried to squeeze into Gavin's tennis shorts, sucking in his stomach as he struggled. He'd have to watch his desserts, Tad cautioned himself. Nancy's cooking. On the other hand, Gavin had the build of a goddamn ballet dancer—it wasn't fair to hold him as a standard.

"Don't rupture yourself, Elder Hastings."

Gavin, resplendent in a brown velour warm-up suit, was holding two metal rackets.

With one last great effort, Tad zipped himself into the shorts. "You're trying to demoralize me before we even start to play."

"I need all the help I can get."

They played a long, hard-fought set, under the lights, and were tied at four games apiece when Tad became aware that his racket had begun to feel very heavy; each stroke seemed a major exertion. Amid the brilliant incandescence, Gavin's figure blurred to liquid, darting everywhere, retrieving everything, his shots whistling by him with precision. He tried to make a contest of it but it was hopeless. Gavin ran off the last two games, then leaped over the net with a whoop of delight and flung his arm around Tad's shoulders. "Don't look so stricken, asshole. This is the first set I've won in months."

"I just ran out of juice."

"It's your dissolute life-style."

They turned off the lights which illuminated the court, and

walked back toward the house. The garden smelled of jasmine. Tad stopped and breathed deeply, feeling weary but strangely tranquil. Only that morning he had been trudging through the snow and now, here he was, strolling through this lovely garden, where even the warm night air seemed beguilingly seductive. It was definitely a change for the better.

Tad showered, then put on a warm-up suit he'd borrowed from Gavin. As he combed his hair he heard the familiar laughter, playful, girlish, sonorous. How he'd longed to hear that laugh!

He watched them from the window, standing there in the garden. They were beautiful, both of them—slim and coltish, chattering together like two schoolgirls. Melody was the bigger of the two, a tall girl with a full figure and long silky black hair. Her striking jade-green eyes peered from her tanned, almost amber face. As usual, she was talking—talking endlessly and exuberantly. By contrast, Pye seemed slight—small-boned and pert. There was a piquant quality to her face, with its upturned nose, wide cheekbones and impish blue eyes. Compared with Melody's high color, Pye's presence conveyed whiteness—white skin, white teeth, white dress and long straw-colored hair that curled around her shoulders.

Gavin had been dating Melody for about a year; she in turn had introduced Tad to Pye. Friends since their teen years in Bangor, Maine, both women had dabbled briefly in modeling, but had hated it. Melody had studied design, and had just begun to make a living at it. Pye was an assistant film editor, working mostly on what she described as "shlocky" low-budget films. Her real name was Patricia Ives, but somehow the girlhood nickname Pye had stuck and Tad rather liked it. He'd been enamored of her from the moment of their first meeting, and to his delight and amazement, it was reciprocal. They had been lovers since the first night and he had seen her every time he came to Los Angeles—which was as often as possible.

Tad had long harbored his secret fantasies about meeting a girl and having a passionate affair, but he had never thought it would happen; indeed, he'd hoped it wouldn't. Pye, to be sure, was far removed from his "fantasy girl." He'd dreamt of a dark, almond-eyed buxom girl with black hair, tawny skin and an utterly submissive nature who would do his every bidding. Pye was blond, with delicate, girlish breasts, and had about her a fierce independence which awed him. In their conversation, as in their sex, she was the leader. She was the one who did things to him, and she wouldn't have it any other way; nor would he. Pye was the polar opposite of his wife. Nancy's world was children. Pye didn't want to have any. Nancy's obsession was the Church. Pye was a self-exiled Roman Catholic who disdained religion in every form. Nancy was utterly unimaginative when it came to sex: It was something to which she submitted in fulfilling her Mormon duty to procreate. To Pye, sex was an unending source of creativity; if you did it the same way twice, there was something wrong with you.

Standing now at the window, watching Pye laugh at one of Melody's nonstop jokes, Tad realized how much he wanted her. It was an urge from his viscera—not one he could control. And to think, only hours earlier he'd found himself yearning for his wife and kids, pining to be back in Salt Lake. How could he be such a sentimental fool!

When he joined them in the garden, she kissed him, and so did Melody. Gavin appeared from nowhere holding a bottle of champagne, Joe at his heels with a tray of glasses and caviar. They sat in the garden amid the scent of jasmine and orange blossoms. Tad could feel his moist scalp tingling in the night air, which had grown cool now, the champagne dissolving the last vestiges of tension. As always when they all were together, the conversation seemed to flow effortlessly. Melody was describing with relish how she'd ripped off a French firm's design and sold it to a Los Angeles jeans manufacturer at a handsome profit. And then Pye described her day-long labors in editing a soft-core sex film to qualify it for the code, snipping away deftly at genitalia and pubic hair as her producer grimaced in agony, watching his potential profits tumbling into the refuse bin. Tad found himself laughing heartily, and he saw Gavin laughing, too. It was as if the problems of the day had never existed for either of them. Observing his friend, Tad realized yet again that Gavin Pollard dwelled in a lofty sanctuary that was beyond the reach of mundane difficulties. They could briefly graze him and even taunt him, but in the end he would remain untouched, his world intact. The notion now of taking him aside and confiding the details of the meeting with

Curry seemed absurdly out of place. Gavin really didn't care. He just wanted to be president of the company, and he would get the presidency, just like he got everything else in life he wanted. Indeed, sitting here in this magical setting, the champagne lulling his brain, a beautiful girl on either side, Tad was amazed that he could have subjected himself to his earlier paranoia about Sloat, about Nancy, about his own Church—all of it. How childish to think that they were all using him, exploiting him. It embarrassed him that he could have entertained such bizarre notions. It all seemed so remote now—remote and unimportant.

They went in for dinner at nine, all of them weaving slightly from the champagne. A lavish buffet of cold lobster, crab and Caesar salad had been prepared—all delicacies Tad never ate except at Gavin's house, and he savored them.

There was wine now, a delicate white wine, frosty cold, which prickled his tongue as he drank. Thirsty from tennis, he finished three glasses before he realized the edges had begun to blur, voices merging into a happy cacophony of laughs and tinkles.

Hours later, nursing his hangover, he tried to dissect the conversation, to analyze at what point the mood had soured. It had all been so cheerfully convivial and then suddenly, inexplicably, it had grown serious, even nasty.

They had been telling jokes—that much he remembered. Gavin had told one about the cleric in the Vatican who came running up to the pope. "I have good news and bad news, your Holiness," the cleric said. "The good news is that God is on the telephone."

The pope smiled beatifically. "That is wonderful, my son."

"The bad news is that He's calling from Salt Lake City."

It was a harmless joke, a joke about Mormon conceit which was also intended, Tad knew, to give him the needle. The two girls had laughed appreciatively, but Tad had not, sitting there with a dour expression on his face. After all of Minafee's barbs that afternoon, he had had his fill of Gentile humor.

"Tad didn't think that one was funny," Melody said, noticing his sudden change of mood.

"Come on, Elder," Gavin said, prodding him further. "You're outside the Zion Curtain now—you can afford a laugh at the expense of the brethren."

But it was Pye, surprisingly, who'd really dug in the scalpel. "Tad's problem is that the joke pokes fun at his superiority complex. After all, Mormons believe that they, and only they, can speak directly to God. Following that logic, there's no reason at all for God to call the pope from Salt Lake. Why should He waste his time?"

"Do Mormons really believe they talk to God?" Melody asked, incredulous.

"It's basic doctrine," Tad snapped. "Everyone knows about divine revelation."

"I think that's weird," Melody replied with a suppressed giggle.

"God's chosen people," Gavin said, his voice heavy with irony.

"If they're the chosen people, why isn't God nicer to them?" Melody persisted. "Why aren't they in better shape than the rest of us?"

"We are," Tad said, seeing the trap, yet determined, in his alcoholic fog, to plunge ahead anyway. "Have you ever spent time in Utah, Melody?"

"Only to ski for a few days. . . ."

"Look around sometime. Compare it to Los Angeles. You'll find polite, decent people. People who value education and hard work. People who care for their own, and don't look to the government to hold them up. You'll find cities that are clean and safe. And prosperous. Yes, the Good Lord has been very kind to the Mormon people. Very kind, indeed."

"If He were any kinder, they'd take over the whole goddamn world," Gavin said.

"I'll say one thing—you people really stick together," Melody said.

"We've stuck together for one hundred fifty years," Tad said. "If we hadn't we would have been wiped out back in Missouri. And again in Illinois. And in Utah, for sure. Our people were strong and brave and they learned how to stick together."

"That sounds awful close to that old master race shit," Pye snapped, her eyes flashing.

"Now wait a minute, Pye," Gavin interrupted. "Tad does have a point here. I mean, those old Mormon pioneers must have been made of pretty tough stuff. How else could they have tended their farms all day, and their ten or fifteen wives all night?"

Pye smiled. "You'd have liked that, wouldn't you, Gavin? You'd have loved having thirty wives like Brigham Young trying to crawl into your old Mormon underwear."

"What's Mormon underwear?" Melody asked.

"It's something the master race wears," Pye shot back.

Tad bristled, but remained silent. He understood that he was being put on; indeed, it was more an assault than a put-on, but he was too drunk to tell the difference. He had dug himself a hole and he had to get out of it. He had to get out of it fast. If only he hadn't gotten so bloody drunk!

Tad saw Pye sitting there, stony-faced, averting his gaze. Gavin was peering at him, eyebrows cocked, prodding him, coaxing.

All right—he'd do it. He was drunk enough.

Tad lurched to his feet and suddenly stripped off the jogging suit, standing before them now in his floppy, old-fashioned union suit, seeing their startled expressions. He bowed deeply, then turned and, pulling the flaps aside, he mooned them. He did it calmly, almost ceremonially. And when he was finished he blandly seated himself at the table again, as though he had simply excused himself to fetch a napkin.

Gavin's face was reddened with laughter. Melody clapped her hands in delight. Even Pye, despite her best efforts, was smiling broadly now, her puckish eyes beaming with surprise.

"I don't care what any of you Mormon-baiters say—I think Tad's cute," Melody said. "And he has a cute tushy, too."

"I'm sorry I've been needling you," Gavin said. "Maybe it was too much wine and too much Minafee."

They all rose and walked toward the den. Tad felt Gavin's arm around his shoulders. They were all with him again. The evening wouldn't be ruined. He was grateful for that. Yet he was mortified: How could he do such a thing? He had never done anything like that in his life. Never. He and Nancy were so modest they even got undressed in the dark. And here he was, revealing himself to two girls and Gavin!

He had to stop drinking. It had gotten out of hand—Tad knew that now.

"You're a good sport, Elder Hastings," Gavin was telling him as they reached the den. "Besides, I better be nice to you. The way things are going, who knows, I may end up working for you!"

Tad stared into Gavin's eyes. He knew he meant it good-naturedly. But the words stabbed at him nonetheless.

□ Tad awoke with a start, in a sudden panic of disorientation. He sat up, his eyes probing the blackness for some familiar sign or object. Then he felt the throb in his head and the swelling of nausea and lay back again. He could hear the soft breathing next to him and his hand felt the warmth of her thigh. All right, he was at Pye's, he could remember that now. He'd had too much alcohol—that was what the headache was all about. His eyes could perceive the time—four o'clock. He had made a reservation back to Salt Lake City on the eight o'clock plane; there was plenty of time to get some more sleep.

He closed his eyes. He heard Pye moan softly and turn over in her sleep, could feel the humid warmth of her body under the blanket. A moment earlier, in his dream, he had been sitting with Pye before Isaac Hamblin in his steamy sitting room in Tonga. They were both naked. He had come upon them making love, and he was shouting at them now, condemning them to a life of misery for their wickedness. Mortified, Tad was sitting there, his penis still erect, Hamblin pointing to it, his voice like distant thunder. "Foolish boy," the Mission President roared, shaking his finger menacingly. "Your carnal urges have forfeited your place in the Celestial Kingdom. You have surrendered your place in the immortal order for a moment's lustful gratification." Then he heard Pye's mocking laughter, and he was suddenly awake, his face damp with sweat.

A bizarre dream. It had been eight years since Tonga, yet the fat Bishop still materialized in his nightmares, a recurring phantom. Dreams play such gruesome games in your head, Tad thought. The idea of Pye and Hamblin confronting each other! Only in a nightmare. Yes, he could imagine her laughing mockingly at his interminable admonitions, and at Lorenzo, too.

She had laughed at Tad tonight—she had never done that before. After they had left Gavin's place, he sensed she was still angry over his remarks during dinner. "I hate it when you sound self-righteous," she said, and he had apologized again, although he couldn't really recall what it was he'd said to offend her. Nonetheless, he'd tried to explain. When you are raised in the Church there are certain things implanted upon layers of your subconscious.

Pye had countered: "I hated going to church when I was a child. I hated the Catholic ritual, the cant. I think I'm a better person because I'm rid of all that. I saw the way my friends had been brought up, and I simply turned my back on my past."

"You're different," Tad argued. "When you were a kid, not all your friends were Catholics. Not all your teachers, not all your parents' friends. When I was a little boy I never knew there was anyone in the whole world who wasn't a Mormon."

Tad had not intended that remark to be funny. He was startled when Pye suddenly started laughing—pleased at first to see her mood lighten, but then realizing she was laughing at *him* again, not at something witty he had said.

"You're brainwashed—that's what you're telling me," Pye said. "You're actually admitting it!"

"Shut up, Pye. You've had your fun. Let's change the subject."

"Never in my life did I ever think I would have a lover who admitted he was brainwashed."

Tad felt his temper rising, started to say something but thought better of it. He'd said enough tonight. He was weary of it all. He hadn't wanted to fight with Pye but, rather, make love to her. There had always been such an intense closeness—a wondrous intimacy. They were like two people who were in total touch. Or were they? There was always that small area of their consciousness where an invisible wall separated them, invisible and insurmountable. They had avoided confronting it, but it was there now, looming menacingly.

Tad felt a sudden sadness. No woman could ever truly understand him except an LDS woman. That is what it was all about. Perhaps it was time he'd learned it and faced it. Damn, he was good at avoiding the truth! A positive genius!

When finally they'd made love, it was not the way it usually was between them. It was perfunctory, almost mechanical. Pye had always been an imaginative lover, yet tonight, after he had climaxed inside her, he knew she was not with him. He tried to massage that special little part of her that had always brought her pleasure, but she took his hand away, and moments later, she was asleep.

Now Tad sat up in bed again, feeling the throb of his hangover. There was no way he would get back to sleep. If he stayed in bed his mind would simply replay the events of the evening over and over again. He didn't want to think about any of it anymore.

Moving quietly so as not to wake Pye, Tad felt around in the dark for his clothing. As he got dressed, he bumped the table sharply, but the sound of Pye's soft breathing continued. He would leave a note for her.

He put on the light in the kitchen and started to write.

"Darling, I couldn't sleep so I'm going back to the hotel, then to the airport. I'm sorry again I acted like such an asshole. Maybe I was angry. Maybe I was just scared."

He wanted to write more but it didn't come. He wanted to write, "This isn't going to work with us; we shouldn't be seeing each other any more, trying to push it," but instead he just wrote, "Much love, Tad."

He looked back into the bedroom. Pye's face had such a childlike sweetness, lying against the pillow. He started to enter the bedroom, yearning to kiss her, but restrained himself. Instead, he went to the front door and opened it.

Standing in the darkness, he knew he had betrayed them. All of them. Never before had he felt the utter loneliness that comes with betrayal.

IT had been Eliza's plan to work late at the office, burying herself and her concerns amid the self-replenishing mass of correspondence and memoranda which, at any given moment, always threatened to overwhelm her staff in a tidal flood of paper. Eliza welcomed that time in early evening when the phone calls and streams of visitors would abate and she could sit alone in her office with her dictation machine, sifting through the bureaucratic effluvia which her Church, like most large organizations, seemed to spew forth with such unrelenting ardor. If she focused on the correspondence, Eliza reasoned, it would keep her mind from dwelling further on the meeting, which, only an hour from now, would be getting off to its uncertain start—a prospect which filled her with apprehension. The image of Grace Turley's face, contorted with guilt, uttering her vague warnings, still hovered before her.

Well, the warnings were vague no longer. By midafternoon Eliza had talked to friends around the state, their voices filled with alarm and compassion, and she knew now what she was confronting. They were not just playing games, Sloat and his friends. It was war. How foolish it was of Sloat to proceed in such a secretive, backhanded fashion. She had too many allies in the outposts of Mormondom for them to get away with maneuvers of this sort.

But secrecy was Sloat's style—that was vividly apparent—and one short hour from now she would go forth and deal with it. His intrigues had entrapped her in this sad and frightening chain of events. Had she been more alert—indeed more forceful in following her own initial instincts—she could have thwarted him, but she had passed that point now. Her course had been set and she would pursue it to its bitter culmination.

For a fleeting moment, in the doldrums of early afternoon, she had flirted with the notion of simply turning her back on the whole mess. She would drive to Turner's office, grasp him by the hand and head for the airport to take the next plane to Honolulu or Paris or Rio. She would let the brethren wallow in their squalid machinations. All this trickery and treachery had nothing to do with the true concerns of the Church, which had consumed her passions and energies these many long years—the nurturing, the teaching, the prayerful uplifting of men's minds and souls. They were all obsessed with their power plays; very well, but these were of no concern to her.

She had phoned Turner and they'd talked for half an hour. As always, he'd been loving and wise, and after speaking with him, she'd decided not to run away from it, no matter how galling a confrontation awaited her. Running away was simply not in her nature.

And there was so much still to be accomplished in the Relief Society. How could the brethren fail to understand? The Relief Society was not just another arm of the Church. It was a true sisterhood in every sense of the word, and Eliza felt a spiritual tie to each of the two million members who comprised its proud ranks. No other organization in the world could galvanize the collective energies and goodwill of so many souls so quickly.

"The Church was never perfectly organized until the women were organized," their Prophet, Joseph Smith, had declared in 1842, and his words *were* prophetic. When times were darkest, her sisters had salvaged the cause. Spurred on by the Relief Society, the Mormon women of the frontier had become doctors, nurses, factory managers, hospital administrators—achievements unthinkable to Gentile women in the East. How proud they had been of their accomplishments, and how scornful they would be if they could see how their granddaughters and great-granddaughters had retreated to the safe confines of domesticity. The brethren had gotten what they needed from their women and now wanted quiet, passive wives—conscientious homebodies—and the sisters had gone along. Eliza knew she had been part of that retreat, but it was not too late to strike a balance. Now, more than ever, there was so much that could be done. If only she had the chance!

Eliza rose from her desk and moved across her big rectangular office. She had spent up to twelve hours a day, six days a week in this room for so many years, it seemed more like her living room than a place of work. Yet she had deliberately kept the large room simple, almost austere. She wanted her office, indeed the Relief Society building as a whole, to reflect the notion of work, not female frivolity.

It was a unique place, this building, a square, sturdy three-story structure crouching, dour and businesslike, across the street from the great Temple. Like the Temple, it, too, was, in a sense, a sacred place—a symbol of her sisters' achievements and a repository of their aspirations. Each year some eighty thousand Mormon women streamed through its portals seeking information and inspiration. This was *their* place, Eliza felt. She had always found solace in the quiet dignity of the high-ceilinged public rooms, the graceful archways leading from one to the next, each room yielding its own special surprises. The walls were emblazoned with great quilts from Finland and Holland, depicting, in brilliant colors and graceful patterns, scenes of work, play and prayer. Adorning the windows were intricate macrame hangings, and beside them, trapunto quilting from Polynesia. Some new exhibits of delicate needlework had just arrived from the São Paulo Stake and Eliza inspected the napkins and handkerchiefs admiringly. In a glass case were drawings and statuettes from Nauvoo showing the rigors of life in the early Mormon settlements. Across the broad room were a series of exhibits illustrating ingenious ways in which a two-year supply of emergency foodstuffs could be stored unobtrusively within a small home. A handsome oak coffee table served also as a secret storage tank for fifty-five gallons of water. A wrought-iron lamp, when turned over, revealed a storage area for soap and canned goods. Another lamp doubled as a Bude burner for emergency cooking. The proximity of these exhibits to the Nauvoo displays was designed to remind the visitors that, in any emergency, there must be enough food for survival without turning to the government or to Gentiles. The LDS community could, as always, stand alone.

"Good evening, Sister Eliza."

The voice, husky and vibrant, resounded through the empty room. It couldn't have startled Eliza more had it been a sudden clap of thunder.

"I hope I didn't frighten you," the intruder said. "I was hoping to find you here tonight. I thought I'd take the chance."

She was a slight woman in her fifties, whose birdlike body did not look like it could support such a formidable voice. The face, with its piercing blue eyes was a familiar one: Eliza knew she had met this woman somewhere, sometime.

"Truthfully, you did give me quite a shock. I thought the building was empty."

"You don't know who I am, do you?" There was a glint of amusement in her eyes as she posed the question. Her visitor, whoever she was, bore the calm self-assurance of someone rich and celebrated.

And then it clicked in Eliza's mind. Of course!

She had seen this woman on many occasions, all of them large functions where hundreds of hands were shaken and hundreds of faces were paraded before her. But hers was also a special face— a face that had peered out at her from countless newspaper photographs and Church publications. Indeed, she was probably the only LDS woman whose countenance was better known throughout Mormondom than was Eliza's.

"I am surprised and delighted, Sister Cora," Eliza said, shaking her hand warmly.

"And I, too, am delighted."

There was a quality in this woman, a certain frontier strength and resourcefulness, which Eliza instinctively admired, yet her attire, indeed her whole demeanor, bespoke wealth and urbanity. She wore an elegantly patterned suit of gray silk; a string of expensive pearls hung from her neck. Her silver hair was swept back in a twist in contrast to the bouffant styles which most visitors to these halls still wore.

Cora Snow's eyes were scanning the room with avid curiosity. "I've been looking at your exhibits—I hope you don't mind. There are so many people visiting *my* building, I've never had the chance to come over and visit *yours*." She turned to Eliza with a quick smile.

"Both buildings are symbols of achievement," Eliza replied. "They give our people something to take pride in."

"I hope so," Cora Snow said, as she strode across the room, inspecting the colorful quilting. Though she moved in a masculine, rolling stride, her eyes shone with a true kindliness when she smiled. As with so many strong-willed women, Eliza thought, there was a complex androgyny to her nature. "In a way, Sister Eliza, we're working the same side of the street, you know. It all comes down to show business, whether one is selling God or entertainment. They're both growth industries, my marketing analysts tell me."

"I never heard it put quite that way," Eliza said.

Cora Snow turned to face her. "What you really mean is that you've never heard it put in such a coarse way. I'm afraid that's a weakness of mine. I'm basically a rather coarse woman." The delicate Brazilian napkins all but disappeared in her strong hands.

"Women who deal in the world of affairs learn to express themselves more bluntly than homemakers."

Cora Snow nodded. "That is quite true. In my own case, I have learned the best way to survive is for there to be two Cora Snows. There is the public Cora Snow who wears her hair in a bun and says very little as she follows her husband around. And then there is the private Cora Snow who runs the business and raises her voice and even curses from time to time."

Eliza smiled. "I find that very disarming."

"Not many people do. Some of the men who do business with me call me 'Snowballs.' They don't think I know that, of course."

Eliza raised her eyebrows. "I'm sure they say it in admiration, Sister Cora."

"Not entirely." Cora Snow was prowling among the food-storage exhibits with their hidden compartments and camouflaged Bude burners. "Very ingenious," she said softly, turning toward Eliza once again. "Your Relief Society women made all these things?"

"Women from all over the world."

"It's all quite wonderful, really it is." Cora Snow paused for a moment, as though weighing her words. "But doesn't it all rankle you a little bit? Just a little?"

"Rankle?"

"Somehow I can't help thinking about the good little sisters out there, busying themselves with all their dozens of projects: handicrafts and teaching and family preparedness and cultural refinement and on and on. All of them on this treadmill, frantically doing all these assigned tasks that will keep them as busy and obedient as the brethren want them to be."

"I think you misunderstand the purposes . . ."

"With all respect, Sister Eliza, I think I really *do* understand the purpose. Coming in this evening I passed a bulletin board, which lists all the things a good LDS housewife is supposed to strive for. It lists work. It lists service. It lists consecration. All sorts of things like that. I looked at it and I said to myself, Fine, but what are the women going to get out of all this? How about *their* needs?"

"Do you remember the admonition we were all raised on? 'Sacrifice brings forth the blessings of heaven. . . .' "

"There's nothing wrong with that admonition—it's just that the sacrifice has become a little one-sided," Cora Snow said, standing before her now. "Tell me, Eliza, do you happen to know a woman named Augusta Cobb?"

"I have never met her. I know of her."

"This may surprise you, but Gussie and I have become quite close. It happened by accident, really. I found a copy of her magazine left at the office one day. Anyway, I picked it up and found that it both shocked and fascinated me. I sent for some other copies, then I sent for Gussie. We started meeting for lunch now and then. Obviously we never met in the office or anywhere we could be recognized. But Gussie became my teacher, you might say. Do you find that strange?"

Eliza shook her head. How curious it all is, she thought—all the furtive lines of communication, the crossed channels. Especially with the Cobbs. How often have their names popped up in unexpected ways. And now with Cora Snow!

"No, I don't really find it strange," Eliza said. "Not strange at all."

Cora Snow cocked her eyebrow. "Some of my children's fans might find it strange, don't you agree? They'd find it positively alarming that I am consorting with an excommunicated Mormon. . . ."

"I think that's a safe assumption."

"Well, they'll never know. My opinions belong to me, not to the teenyboppers who watch our shows."

"And your family? Do they know?"

"Mine is not exactly the sort of family you'd bring together for a philosophical chat," Cora Snow said. "My husband, Vernon, pops Valiums all day long. He's so mellow, bless his heart, he thinks blinking is hard work. I love him, but that's Vernon. Jeb is a good boy—at least he's been a good boy for the last two years, since I told him I'd bash his head in if I ever caught him snorting coke again. But Jeb's not what you'd call an intellectual—I wouldn't want to burden his brain with anything as threatening as an idea. Then there's my daughter Charity. I gave her a copy of Gussie Cobb's magazine to read once, and she came back to me and fluttered her baby blue eyes and said, 'Ma, these people are Communists—they should be put in jail.' "

Eliza smiled knowingly. "I guess it's pretty lonely for you out there."

"There are a lot of other women lonelier than I am," Cora Snow said. "I have my business. I have money. I travel. I have my friends. But my heart goes out to all our sisters who think of themselves as wicked when they come to the realization that all of life's satisfactions cannot flow from their children and their handicrafts. They are the ones to feel sorry for."

"There is a restlessness, as I'm sure you know. A great restlessness among our sisters. It's not something the brethren are anxious to acknowledge."

"That is the reason I am here, Eliza."

Of course, that is exactly why she is here, Eliza told herself. She knows about it—about the meeting planned for tonight, about the hierarchy's response to it. It is not a mere accident that this powerful, indeed renowned, woman happened to drop by tonight of all nights. But why would it interest her? What role does she plan to play in this maze of moves and countermoves?

Eliza now led the way into her office where Cora Snow seated herself on the dark green sofa. Eliza faced her in the wicker chair she customarily occupied when entertaining visitors. There was a chill in the office, as was often the case in the evening hours when the thermostats were lowered. Eliza tightened her cardigan around her shoulders. She noticed that Cora Snow, attired in her thin silk suit, seemed oblivious to the chill.

"I wish I could offer you something," Eliza said, after they had settled themselves. "Perhaps I could find some juice . . ."

But Cora Snow did not seem to hear. Eliza felt her gaze upon her once again, shrewdly assessive. "You surprise me, Eliza. You truly do."

"Surprise you?"

"Forgive me for saying so, but I expected to find a different sort of woman. Someone more rigid, more dogmatic."

"Perhaps you would have found that woman a year ago. Even a month ago. Many things have changed in my life. Things that have shaken and surprised me."

"I've talked about my children, Eliza. What about yours? Have they shared these changes you speak of?"

Eliza sighed. "It is harder with grown children, of course. They are spread all around the world, one in England, one in Australia. I had always felt a real closeness with my two daughters, but that was in the earlier years when my late husband and I still told each other we had a good marriage. As for my son, Tad, I'm afraid there has always been a distance. I've tried so hard to bridge it, but I'm resigned to it now. That doesn't ease the sense of loss, of course. I've tried to figure out the reason why this chasm exists between us. I've laid out all the obvious reasons: Perhaps I failed him. Perhaps his father failed him. Perhaps it was our sham of a marriage. We never really know the answers, do we? We are left with our failed expectations and our self-reproach but we are never left with answers."

"The trap, Eliza, is to blame ourselves. The trap is to think, Oh, if only I had been the perfect Mother of Zion and had stayed home and nurtured my children all day long, they all would have turned out perfectly. I used to tell myself that. I caught myself apologizing to people for having a career, instead of staying home with the kids. And then one day I said to myself, What am I apologizing for? The only reason I ever got involved in business to begin with was to save us from going broke. Mormon women are always going around apologizing for their intelligence. It's like a racial disease."

Eliza smiled. "Surely you remember Brigham Young's explanation of how he handled his wives. 'I do not believe in making my authority as a husband known by brute force but by my superior intelligence.' That's what he said."

"Well, he married fifty-five dummies who believed him."

The two women laughed. How curious, Eliza thought, that she

would feel so comfortable with this rather arch woman with her husky voice and masculine stride. Here she was, exchanging confidences more freely with someone she'd known only a matter of minutes than with friends she'd had for decades. There was, indeed, a fierce candor to Cora Snow that inspired such intimacy.

"Eliza, I want to talk to you seriously now," Cora said, folding her arms on her crossed legs, her eyes narrowing to a stern, businesslike gaze. This was, no doubt, the way Cora Snow looked when she presided over her business meetings, Eliza thought. She had finished chatting now. It was time for Snowballs to assert herself. "I am here because of the meeting tonight," Cora Snow said.

"I suppose you must know of the plan that our brethren have concocted? . . ."

"They're going to sandbag you, Eliza."

Eliza smiled ruefully. "I've learned there will be a disruption. I know Dana Sloat and the others have decided that much. I think it's a tragedy. They will polarize the women at a time when we most need harmony. . . ."

"They only understand power, Eliza. They are defending the patriarchy. Their whole society, as they see it, rests on that system. God tells the Prophet what to do and the Prophet tells the men of the priesthood what to do and they tell their women what to do. And if the women start rebelling, then where will it stop?"

"But rebellion is not the purpose of this meeting. . . ."

"Don't be naive, Eliza. The brethren believe their women want power. And they intend to keep it away from them."

"I sensed this would happen. I tried to postpone the meeting. . . ."

"Yes, but they're just as glad you failed. They want you out of the way, Eliza. You're too independent and too well known. Your following is much wider than theirs. You were just a time bomb in their eyes. A time bomb that would go off sooner or later."

Eliza heard herself gasp. There—Cora Snow had finally said what she'd been afraid to tell herself. The brethren wanted her out of her job. It was as simple as that. Cora had dug right to the truth that Eliza herself had so nimbly been avoiding. Eliza lowered her eyes, her fingers twisting the several loose threads at the bottom of her cardigan. "If that's the case, then I suppose I'm a lost cause, Cora. Why would you want to involve yourself in a lost cause?"

Cora Snow shook her head impatiently. "Let me explain some things, Eliza. When Gussie Cobb told me what was going to happen tonight, something went off inside my head. I guess it's been coming for a long time. My own time bomb, you might say. So I decided on impulse to come over here and shake your hand and tell you that, no matter what happens tonight, it's not the end. Not at all. The fight is only starting, Eliza. You're the one who can unite the sisters, who can make them see the light. Gussie can't do it. I can't do it. Only you can do it. But it's got to be done. If it takes money, I'll put up the money. Hell, Eliza, I'm negotiating a three-million-dollar loan from the Church—nothing would give me more pleasure than to take a million dollars of that and put it right back into the fight!"

"Fight the Church with its own money?"

"Damned right. They'd never know. And it's going to take money, Eliza. Money and patience. We've got years of lethargy to make up for and generations of brainwashing."

"And you would devote yourself to this fight? Yourself and your money?"

"The more important question is whether *you* would. It would mean working outside the structure of the Church, Eliza. It would be an entirely new experience for you."

Eliza felt a gnawing apprehension. Cora Snow was building toward something. Her intuition told her it was something out of the ordinary, even startling. "What sort of 'new experience'?" she asked.

Cora Snow took a deep breath and straightened herself. "I would like you to run for public office, Eliza."

"Surely you're joking?"

". . . More specifically, for the United States Senate." Cora held up her hand as if to ward off the protestations she knew would be forthcoming. "Now, I know that may seem outrageous to you, but it's not anything of the sort. Our junior senator, Ezra Hurlbut, is up for reelection next year. Everyone in this state knows he's incompetent. His seat is vulnerable. I think you should enter the race."

"You astonish me, Cora. I know nothing about politics. . . ."

"Neither does Ezra Hurlbut. But think of all the things you have going for you. You have a following around the state. Everyone knows you and respects you. Your campaign would be well financed. The sisters would all work hard for you. It would be good for them, too. It would bring them out into the real world."

"I understand what you are saying, Cora, but still . . ."

". . . Ezra Hurlbut wouldn't stand a chance. You'd take him totally by surprise."

No, it wasn't madness, Eliza told herself. There was a certain logic to Cora's seemingly strange proposal. This was a practical woman, not a dreamer. It's just that it took her so much by surprise. There was so much for her to assimilate—so much that was new and confounding.

"I need time to think about all this, Cora. Please understand."

"Just don't dismiss it hastily, Eliza. It's too important."

"I won't. That much I promise."

Cora rose. "Thank you, Eliza. Then there are things we can look forward to, after all."

Eliza got to her feet. "There is something I would like to ask of you, Cora. If you feel this strongly, there is a way to demonstrate it. Come with me tonight. Walk with me into that hall. Let the sisters see you and know where you stand. It would mean so much."

Cora Snow shook her head. "I'm sorry. I cannot afford to go to war with the Church. Not openly. They are involved in every nook and cranny of the business community—banking, real estate, insurance. As big a company as I have, they could crush me like an ant. I have my children to think about. Their careers. Hell, maybe it's not that at all. Maybe it's my own greed. I'm just not willing to take the risk, Eliza."

Eliza nodded soberly. "I'm sorry, Cora. I shouldn't have asked."

"No, you were absolutely right to. . . ."

Eliza moved to the closet to retrieve her coat. "I'd better be going. They'll be waiting for me in the hall. . . ."

The two women walked together through the deserted corridors, Cora walking silently, lost in her own thoughts. "Eliza, do you remember that hymn we used to sing as children?" Cora asked suddenly. " 'Freedom's Daughter,' it was called."

"Yes, I think so."

"It was very nice, that hymn. One of the few that had something to instruct us."

And then suddenly Cora Snow started to sing. Her deep, husky voice blasted the somber silence of the marble halls like a sudden clarion call.

> "Freedom's daughter, rouse from slumber
> See the curtains are withdrawn. . . ."

Eliza looked over at her and smiled—yes, she remembered the words after all. If Cora Snow would sing, well she would sing with her.

> ". . . which so long thy mind hath shrouded
> Lo thy day begins to dawn. . . ."

They walked toward the street, singing together, their spirits joined.

> "Who'd ever think that Utah
>   Would stir the world so much?
> Who'd ever think the Mormons
>   were widely known as such?
> I hardly dare to scribble
>   or such a subject touch
> For all are talking of Utah
>
> Hurrah! Hurrah! We Mormons have the name
> Hurrah! Hurrah! We're on the road to fame
> No matter what they style us
>   it's all about the same
>
> They say they'll send an army
>   to set us Mormons right
> Regenerate all Utah
>   and show us Christian light
> Release our wives and daughters
>   and put us men to flight
> For all are talking of Utah

I now will tell you something
 you never thought of yet
We bees are nearly filling
 the hives of Deseret
If hurt, we'll sting together
 and gather all we get
For all are talking of Utah!"

Josiah Bingham's baritone was surprisingly buoyant for a man of eighty-two, his eyes twinkling behind his rimless glasses, his bald head glistening with perspiration, his gnarled, stubby fingers plucking the guitar in accompaniment. His audience consisted of only three people, two of them children, but this did not inhibit the vigor of his performance. Augusta Cobb saw the rapt fascination on the faces of her two boys as they listened to his songs, sprawled on the rough wooden floor in front of their great-grandfather's chair. He had been singing for the better part of an hour, seated there in red flannel shirt and suspenders, switching periodically from guitar to banjo to mandolin, gliding from song to song, his left foot beating out the steady rhythm, his still sprightly voice straining only occasionally to reach a high note. Behind him, the warming fire crackled in the great fireplace of swept worn brick, burning embers periodically dancing across the hearth. The songs were stories in themselves, some sad and some funny, their lyrics pouring from him in an unending stream. At the end of each song the boys would clap their hands, imploring him for another encore.

It was a ritual of Christmas, these visits to Grandpa Josiah—one of the few family rituals that survived her excommunication and, as such, one Gussie revered. Most of her relatives and those of her husband Hiram had long since made their attitudes abundantly clear: The Cobbs were apostates, enemies of the Church and, as such, embarrassments to their families. Even their parents had cut them off from family observances.

These ruptures saddened Gussie; it struck her as marvelously ironic that Grandpa Josiah would prove to be the dent in the solid wall of familial disfavor. As a girl, she'd thought this burly, moon-faced man to be hopelessly gruff in his mannerisms and eccentric in his behavior. She recalled her mother's utter consternation when Josiah, upon reaching his forty-sixth birthday, impulsively retired as a painting contractor, announcing his intention to become a full-time troubadour—an unconscionable deviation from the work ethic. Far from being the pathetic drifter all had thought him to be, Josiah, Gussie discovered with some delight, was truly a highly skilled musician who sang his songs with great verve, savoring every barb of irony and frontier humor. Though his hands showed a slight tremble, his mastery over his instruments was prodigious. Gussie's sons, Eric, who was seven, and Ethan, a year younger, would stare hypnotically at his callused fingers as they pranced over the strings.

He lived thirty miles outside Salt Lake in an old saltbox house of faded adobe brick, the house itself a pioneer relic, with its broad front porch and peculiar lean-to contours, its two brick chimneys propping it up at either end. Built in the 1880s, the house, Grandpa Josiah explained, was constructed according to the specifications Brigham Young had laid down to his followers. Old Brigham was a great one for specifications, whether it came to churches, homes or even women's attire.

And with that, Josiah picked up his banjo and started to sing once again:

> "Old Brigham Young was a stout man once
> But now he is thin and old
> And I love to state there's no hair on his pate
> Which once wore a covering of gold
> For his youngest wives won't have white wool
> And his old ones won't take red
> So in tearing it out they have taken turnabout
> Til they've pulled all the wool from his head."

"Grandpa," Ethan said, his small, pink face screwed up pensively, "why did the Mormons always sing so much?"

"Stupid question," Eric grumbled, as he usually did when his younger brother said anything.

Josiah plucked a chord on his banjo and pondered the question. "When people have lots of troubles they can either be silent or they can sing. Mormons were never very good at being silent."

"Why did they have so many troubles?"

Their great-granfather's eyes twinkled. "Because they were always trying to do very difficult things. Like starting a new religion. Or settling in places where the people distrusted them. Or traveling across a continent."

"Mommy doesn't like Mormons," Ethan blurted suddenly. "Do you like them?"

"Now, wait a minute," Gussie interrupted. "Your father and I have never said we don't like the Mormon people. We *are* the Mormon people—all of us. We're very proud of that fact. We just disagree with certain policies of the Church. . . ."

Josiah hit a chord again, and started to sing:

> ". . . For Mormons say it scriptural
> and Mormons say it true.
> And none can preach the gospel
> like the Mormons do. . . ."

"What are policies?" Ethan asked, undeterred.

"Policies are things you don't talk about at Christmastime," his great-grandfather answered cheerfully. "Santa Claus never talks about policies." He turned to Gussie. "Did you ever hear Santa Claus mention a policy?"

Gussie shrugged. "Never once that I can recall."

He turned back to the boys. "Now, let me ask *you* boys a question. Did you ever hear of handcarts?"

Both shook their heads.

"Handcarts were these little things the size of apple carts that my grandfather and thousands like him pulled all the way across the country. They put everything they owned onto them and then they pulled as hard and as long as they could."

"Were there motors in them?" Eric asked.

"Not even power steering," Josiah grinned. "There was nothing in them but Mormon muscle. Talk about troubles—handcarts were a lot of trouble. I can sing you a song about them."

As he started singing the "Handcart Song," which Gussie had heard on many occasions, she got up and made her way to his small kitchen, pouring herself a glass of apple juice from his ancient refrigerator. The fridge, she noticed, was alarmingly empty —a container of milk, some butter, an egg. She wondered how an old man who lived alone like Josiah fended for himself, whether he cooked or went out to dinner, whether he was lonely or still had many friends. Hearing him singing in the living room, she felt a great welling of affection for this venerable troubadour who tried so hard to give her sons a sense of family, and a sense of history.

History! What a strangely fragile mythology was encompassed by that word. Perhaps Josiah had the right idea: Perhaps history was best reduced to the melodic simplicity of a song, stripped of all its complexities and contradictions—a song time has embedded on our memories. She and Hiram these last several years had constantly done battle with history and somehow, at this point in time, she felt debilitated by their labors. They had struggled so hard to retell the Mormon experience—to relate it as it really happened, not as the myth-makers had imagined it. And yet, through it all, she had come away with the overriding feeling that she was saying things people really didn't want to hear. The myth had indeed become the truth, or at least the only truth anyone wished to know.

She and Hiram had embarked on their effort soon after the BYU incident, working separately and together, each starting down his or her own path of reading and research, prompted by a very simple desire: the desire to understand their past—all of their pasts.

They had begun at the beginning, with Joseph Smith, a semiliterate farm boy in western New York State, who maintained, at the age of eighteen, that he was receiving visits from an "angel" named Moroni, a messenger of God, who commanded him to unearth a stone box containing plates of gold. Though these plates were lettered in hieroglyphics, Joseph Smith would be able to translate them through use of two transparent stones, the Urim and Thummim, attached like eyeglasses to a breastplate which had been buried with the plates in the vicinity of Smith's residence. The plates, once translated, would convey the true story of how a band of Hebrews in 600 B.C. escaped Jerusalem prior to the Babylonian invasion, traveled to the Indian Ocean, built a boat and journeyed to the west coast of the Americas. Following his Crucifixion, Christ appeared in America to organize His church and unite the Hebrews, who had divided into two peoples, the Nephites and Lamanites. After Christ's appearance the two peoples lived in righteousness and harmony for two hundred years. Warfare disrupted the new civilization once again by A.D. 421, and Moroni, the last Prophet, buried the records of his people. Ultimately Joseph Smith was to name them the Book of Mormon after Moroni's father.

Threading their way back through Joseph Smith's own personal accounts of his visions and through the testimonies and affidavits of his contemporaries, Gussie and Hiram were incredulous that one of the world's great religions could be constructed on such a tenuous cornerstone. Here was a youth of erratic reputation who had been arrested at the age of nineteen for convincing an aged farmer that he could locate a lost Spanish silver mine, who as a teenager was obsessed with crystal gazing and treasure hunting and who had never produced a single witness to his many celestial visitations—yet none of it mattered. Joseph Smith was the self-proclaimed Prophet of God, and he had his own holy book to show for it.

And what an odd book it was. Though Joseph Smith insisted on his title page that he had translated the book literally from its original, as did his two helpers, their text, with its bizarre syntax, incomplete sentences, rambling circumstantial gerund phrases and incessant digressions, bore no relation to the concise, tightly structured ancient Egyptian or Semitic texts it was supposed to exemplify. Further, in comparing the Book of Mormon with the King James Version of the Bible, Gussie Cobb found hundreds of New Testament phrases reproduced intact. The "story," meanwhile, bore a resemblance to the plot of a romantic manuscript of the period written by a Presbyterian minister named Solomon Spaulding which appeared to have found its way into Smith's hands. In content, it reflected such contemporary concerns of Smith's period as the origin of the American Indian, questions of predestination and baptism, the smoldering issue of anti-Catholicism—all issues swirling around western New York State in the early 1830s, not those of a millenium ago when the book was supposedly composed.

In the view of Hiram and Gussie Cobb, the Book of Mormon was a fabrication, the product of a fertile imagination, not a long-buried relic of ancient times as Smith maintained. If the text had, in fact, been written by one of the Lost Tribes of Israel, why was it recorded in Egyptian hieroglyphics, as Smith maintained, rather than in Hebrew or Chaldean? Why had the book been inscribed on gold rather than papyrus? Why, too, had no one ever seen the plates except for the Prophet and his three closest aides, who were, indeed, a motley crew: One of them believed ardently in witchcraft; another insisted he had traveled to the moon and back and held personal meetings with both Jesus Christ and the Devil.

It was a tribute to Joseph Smith's persuasiveness that his new movement began to thrive despite its awkward beginnings. The times seemed hospitable, to be sure. The newly settled peoples of rural, mid-nineteenth-century America, impatient with the Old World religions, stood willing to embrace a whole range of exotic new sects, such as the Shakers, the Footwashers, the Campbellites and the Hard Shell. Gathering around him a band of avid disciples, Joseph Smith doggedly continued to expand his flock, shifting his center of activity from New York to the more fertile ground of Kirtland, Ohio, near present-day Cleveland; then, in 1839, settling still farther west in a tiny Illinois village on the east bank of the Mississippi called Commerce, a name he promptly changed to Nauvoo. Nauvoo, he explained imaginatively, was a Hebrew word for "beautiful plantation."

As he pushed westward, his following grew and so did his problems. In Kirtland, Smith and his associate, Sidney Rigdon, were arrested on charges that they had printed their own banknotes to solve their community's financial problems. In Jackson County, Missouri, the Gentiles stoned their homes and assaulted their children. In Independence, Missouri, a mob of three hundred tarred and feathered two Mormon Bishops and drove scores of Mormons from their homes. At Haun's Mill in western Missouri, some two hundred forty Gentiles surrounded a Mormon enclave, slaughtering seventeen defenseless Saints and wounding twelve. At Morley's Settlement, near Nauvoo, a mob launched a night attack, burning twenty-nine homes.

The wave of anti-Mormon violence continued unabated until, in 1844, an angry mob in Carthage, Illinois, stormed a jail where Joseph Smith was himself imprisoned, and shot the Prophet to death.

In studying the Mormon past, Gussie and Hiram tried to analyze this incessant persecution, since it played such a key role in
the formation of the Mormon character—its discipline, its militancy, its secrecy. Was it simply a question of religious bigotry, as
Joseph Smith insisted, or were there other contributing factors?

In part, the persecution seemed to stem from Mormon beliefs,
in part from Mormon solidarity. By claiming they had direct access to God through their Prophet, and hence to divine revelation,
the newcomers posed a threat to established churches. This threat
was compounded by the Mormons' aggressive proselytizing. Yet,
while reaching out for new followers, the Saints also practiced an
intense tribalism, remaining within their own enclaves of settlement, patronizing only Mormon merchants and voting as a bloc
for local candidates.

As their communities grew, their Gentile neighbors increasingly sensed that the newcomers considered themselves a nation
unto themselves, not answerable to existing laws and customs.
They listened to the pronouncements of Parley Pratt, a Mormon
Apostle, stating, "The Kingdom of God is the only legal government. Within ten years, the people of the country who are not
Mormons will be entirely subdued by the Latter-day Saints or
swept from the face of the earth."

To which Joseph Smith himself added: "I will consecrate the
riches of the Gentiles unto my people which are the House of
Israel." As if to fortify this Mormon militancy, the Prophet was
fond of appearing in public in full military regalia, replete with
braided blue uniform, sword and high boots, his Napoleonic hat
topped with ostrich feathers. With hundreds of new Mormon converts from abroad streaming into Nauvoo every month—the "off-
scourings of Europe," their Gentile neighbors complained—the
Prophet greatly expanded the size of his Army of Zion to some six
thousand men. Many of the newcomers also joined the Danites,
who swept down upon neighboring communities, wreaking acts
of "vengeance" upon Gentile persecutors. Their leader, Sampson
Avard, assured his followers that Church leaders condoned their
acts of terrorism.

Confronted with this militancy, a growing paranoia stretched
across the frontier countryside—a paranoia which intensified
with the discovery that the Mormons had started embracing the

institution of plural marriage. Polygamy seemed to strike even more fear in Gentile hearts than did terrorist bands, representing a direct assault upon established notions of family structure and sexual mores.

It was in 1843 that Joseph Smith revealed to his astonished followers that he had been overtaken with a divine revelation recognizing plural marriage, but there was considerable evidence that the Prophet had quietly taken as many as thirty wives prior to that, all over the fervent opposition of his first wife, Emma. Many of his new wives were teenagers. Indeed the wording of his revelation seemed to go out of its way to sanctify this practice: "... And if he have ten virgins given unto him by this law, he cannot commit adultery, for they belong to him and they are given unto him; therefore he is justified."

Some of his most prominent followers had trouble swallowing this "justification." Oliver Cowdery, the former schoolteacher who supposedly translated most of the Book of Mormon, angrily left Nauvoo, charging his Prophet and friend of fourteen years was conducting "adulterous relations." Dr. John C. Bennett, the former adjutant general of the State of Illinois, who was Joseph Smith's most prominent convert, resigned as mayor of Nauvoo amid a fusillade of charges that Church leaders spent most of their time competing for nubile young wives. Bennett wrote one article relating how a young convert named Martha Brotherton, who only three weeks earlier had arrived from England, found herself locked in a room above a grocery store with Joseph Smith and Brigham Young. Young, having locked the door and drawn the curtains, told her he planned to marry her. When she resisted, Smith advised, "Well, Martha, just go ahead and do as Brigham wants—he's the best man in the world, except me." Miss Brotherton fled the next morning to St. Louis, her life as a Saint quickly terminated.

Bennett's tales of "licentious conduct" were supported by another prominent defector, William Law, a wealthy Canadian convert who had provided the principal financial backing for the Church. Law went to the trouble of leasing a printing press to publish articles denouncing the Prophet he had so long admired. Joseph Smith, Law wrote, levied illegal fees whenever property was bought or sold, engaged in bizarre financial manipulations and was so out of control sexually he was turning Nauvoo into a "whoredom." All attractive young Mormon converts arriving in Nauvoo from abroad were required to sleep with the Prophet, Law wrote.

Though most leaders might have shrunk before these charges, Joseph Smith became all the more flamboyant. He hastily excommunicated Cowdery and other dissidents, and sent his Nauvoo legion to wreck Law's printing press. Deciding the time had come to expand his "Kingdom of God," he announced his intention to run for the presidency of the United States against James K. Polk and Henry Clay. At his nominating convention, the Prophet called for the abolition of slavery and extended an "invitation" to Canada and Mexico to join the union.

To insure his power base, Smith also convened the clandestine group called the Council of Fifty, which was ultimately to consist of fifty Mormon "princes" stationed around the world who would preside over his "Kingdom of God." Hence, at the very time he was running for the presidency, Joseph Smith, in a secret ceremony, also was ordaining himself King.

The Prophet's increasingly erratic actions brought prompt response from the Gentile community. In 1844, Governor Thomas Ford of Illinois ordered Joseph Smith's arrest on a variety of charges, including his cavalier destruction of William Law's printing press. The Prophet desperately feared arrest: Only his legion could truly guarantee his safety, he insisted, but the governor personally visited Smith's jail cell, promising protection from his enemies. Once Governor Ford had departed, a band of one hundred men, their faces blackened, scaled the fence surrounding the jail. Guards offered but token resistance.

When he heard the approaching mob, Joseph Smith, who was drinking wine in his cell with his brother, grabbed a six-barrel pistol which had been smuggled to him earlier in the day. His attackers were greeted with a fusillade as they burst into his cell. Seeing his brother crumple to the floor, Joseph Smith flung away his gun and made one final effort to save himself by escaping through a window, but as he reached the ledge, bullets exploded around him. "Is there no help for the widow's son?" he cried as the bullets hit him. He doubled up and fell onto the ground.

Though the killing of their leader sent a shock wave through the Mormon community, the people of the "City of Joseph" seemed to draw together rather than splinter, as enemies of the Church had presumed.

The Saints had their martyr now. They also had their iron discipline that always had saved them in the past, and they had their secret Council of Fifty to enforce that discipline until a successor could be selected.

The logical contender seemed to be Sidney Rigdon, who had been Smith's principal counselor. His rival was a strong, stolid young carpenter named Brigham Young. Appealing for support, Rigdon and Young each addressed a great outdoor meeting of eight thousand Saints in an open grove overlooking the Mississippi. Rigdon's address was well received, but Young exercised a spellbinding hold over his audience. As he spoke, he seemed to assume a greater stature, and his voice sounded astoundingly similar to that of the fallen Prophet. To the faithful Saints, Young's performance was a miracle. As the Apostles of the Church witnessed his charismatic hold and heard his words ringing across the open grove, they knew he must be their Prophet.

Gussie Cobb remembered that during her school days a sense of awe would always settle over the classroom when Brigham Young's name was invoked. To the Mormon schoolchildren he was George Washington, Thomas Jefferson and Abraham Lincoln rolled into one. He was truly the founder of the Mormon nation. He was the ultimate spiritual leader, the embodiment of God's will on earth.

And even now, as Gussie reread the histories and journals of that period, that sense of awe still gripped her. Here was a man who was, indeed, bigger than life, a man capable of staring out at the bleakness of the Salt Lake Valley and stating, "This a good place to make Saints; it is the place that the Lord has appointed."

Certainly, Salt Lake, grim as it was, presented a more hospitable environment than Missouri, where, even after Joseph Smith's murder, clashes between the Mormons and Gentile marauders increased by the week. Still new charges of counterfeiting and other crimes were brought against Mormon leaders, including Brigham Young. Rumors were rampant that federal troops would be brought in to disperse the Mormon community. The time for exodus was clearly at hand.

The decision to go as far as Utah, however, was greeted with disbelief. The trek Brigham Young was proposing to his flock seemed like a voyage into outer space. The Great Basin was more than one thousand miles from the western fringes of frontier settlement along the Missouri. Sparsely populated Oregon and California lay almost as far beyond. The trek would take more than twice the time consumed by the journey from Boston to London by sea.

Brigham Young spoke of the Great Basin as offering a "blessed isolation," but others in his advance party found it less blessed.

Most of the visible farmland was highly alkaline or saline. There was virtually no timber. Annual rainfall was slight, averaging only ten to twelve inches. The Utes, Paiutes, and Shoshone seemed less than exuberant about receiving new settlers. Vital supplies would have to be brought in over mountains and deserts. Why not push on to California? some of Young's confidants urged. Reports were already filtering back about California's lushness and mineral wealth.

But Brigham Young was, as usual, adamant. "This is the place whereon we will plant our feet and where the Lord's people will dwell," he intoned. He was so gravely ill from Rocky Mountain spotted (tick) fever he could barely raise himself from his pallet, and yet, he sensed that "the spirit of light hovered over the valley."

In the spring of 1846, the Great Trek began. With their new Prophet in the lead, an incredible caravan encompassing hundreds of wagons and twelve thousand Saints strung itself out along one hundred twenty miles of prairie. It was perhaps the largest mass migration in American history, and also the most ill-prepared. The Mormons were farmers and artisans, not frontiersmen. Unlike other pioneers, they had consulted neither guides nor professional outfitters. The haste of their departure had left most penniless: "We have sold our place for a trifle to a Baptist minister," wrote one traveler. "All we got was a cow and two pairs of steers, worth sixty dollars in trade."

Their leader spurred them on with Biblical rhetoric. The flight of the Saints, he said, was a reenactment of the exodus from Egypt under Moses. They were voyaging to the Promised Land. They were blessed by God.

Within weeks of their departure, Brigham Young knew his Saints were in desperate straits. Progress was slower than he had calculated. Food was already growing critically scarce. What had once been the proud Armies of Zion had become a sad band of starving paupers.

Wherever they found settlements along the way, the Saints stopped to do odd jobs or simply to beg or steal food. Mormon bands played at funerals and wakes. And as winter finally closed its deadly vise, the Saints were ill-equipped. In Iowa alone two hundred Mormon travelers died of cold and hunger.

Doggedly, they pushed on. Late that winter, the first advance parties began trickling into the Great Basin. Within three months, two thousand people had arrived, with the newcomers quickly regimented in paramilitary fashion into wards and stakes— "stakes in the tents of Zion." A Bishop took charge of each ward and a President of each stake. Atop them all sat the Council of Fifty, supervising the rationing of food and the allocation of land and other resources. Crops were planted, homes started, streets laid out. But when the first crops failed and Indians and wolves decimated the livestock, the hungry settlers found themselves eating thistle tops, tree bark and crow, and wondering about their Prophet's vision of "protection and safety."

Their luck began to change. In 1848, when hordes of black, goggle-eyed crickets swarmed over the first crop of sprouting grain, flocks of sea gulls rose magically from the Great Salt Lake and devoured the locusts. A "providential intervention," declared Brigham Young. An even more astonishing intervention was about to save his poverty-stricken people: News of gold strikes in California had reached the East Coast, and fortune seekers by the thousands began to descend on the Mormon colony, all of them eager to trade for provisions and continue their trek. Another prophecy fulfilled, said Brigham Young.

As Mormon fortunes improved, the Prophet turned his fierce energies to the task of forging his Kingdom. Not a detail, however minor, escaped his attention. A solidly built man, five feet ten inches in height, with unwavering steel-gray eyes and a frontiersman's blustery vigor, Brigham Young was as practical and businesslike as Joseph Smith was erratic and romantic. Typically, while Smith loved to display himself in gaudy uniforms, his successor favored plain dark suits. Smith could confess to his disciples, "Brethren and Sisters, I got drunk last week and fell in a ditch, . . ." but Young kept himself aloof from his followers—an austere symbol of authority. Smith was the consummate mystic, and yet an egalitarian. Brigham Young believed in power and hierarchy.

Like most authoritarian leaders, Brigham Young harbored a deep distrust of his own people. "Every government lays the foundation of its own downfall when it permits what are called democratic elections," he declared. In a theocracy, there's nothing wrong with voting provided everyone votes for the same candidate: "Let us all vote one way and think and act one way, and keep the commandments of God."

And so it was in the Mormon Kingdom. The Church decided which candidates would run for office; anyone choosing to run without Church approval was instantaneously excommunicated. There was one political party, the People's Party, which would select candidates for local office as well as Utah's lone delegate to Congress. The Church organized and ran the schools, commanded the military, dispensed public lands, operated the courts and even coined money, stamped Holiness to the Lord.

There was little tolerance of those who bridled under the tight reins of theocratic rule. A corps of enforcers, including many of the old Danites from Missouri, stood ready to protect their leaders and punish dissenters. Mormons who indicated a desire to leave Utah faced confiscation of their property, not to mention physical assault.

Nor did the representatives dispatched by Washington to its new territory escape the wrath of the "enforcers." Federal judges, Indian agents and other officials were ignored and sometimes threatened, and federal grants for construction of public buildings were simply appropriated by the Church.

In his orations, Brigham Young made no effort to conceal his defiance. "The Mormon people," he stated, "are free and independent from all other kingdoms." Like Joseph Smith before him, Young believed that the federal government would ultimately crumble, permitting his self-proclaimed "State of Deseret" to fill the power void. "The Government known as the United States has become like water spilled on the ground," he told his followers. "It is a regime controlled by imbecility."

To be sure, there was a great deal of false swagger in Brigham

Young's militancy. While hurling epithets at Washington, he recognized at the same time how desperately his still-fragile nation needed federal economic and military assistance. Indeed, the Prophet at one point dispatched representatives requesting admission to the Union, defining as Mormon territory some two hundred thousand square miles comprising Utah and Nevada, plus large hunks of California, Idaho, Wyoming, Colorado, Oregon and New Mexico. When these fanciful claims were rejected, David H. Burr, the official surveyor general dispatched by Washington, sent back word that "my life is in danger . . . I have been cursed and denounced in public meetings . . . The U.S. courts have been broken into. The fact is these people repudiate the authority of the U.S. and are in open rebellion against the government." In 1857, President James Buchanan dispatched a force of federal soldiers to get Brigham Young back into line. The long-feared confrontation was at hand.

The fates were again on the side of the Mormons, however. The eighteen hundred federal soldiers ran into fierce winter weather and were stranded at Fort Bridger at the eastern entrance to the territory. Wagon trains sent to supply the stranded troops were attacked and burned by Mormon raiders, leaving the soldiers on the brink of starvation.

Confronted with this ugly stalemate, both Buchanan and the Prophet decided on a policy of accommodation. Since the president was suffering heavy criticism for the failure of the Utah Expedition to achieve its objectives, it was agreed that his troops would be allowed to march through Salt Lake City and establish a position forty miles away. Their mission would be to ensure the rights of federal appointees. The Mormons who had fled south, fearing war, returned quietly to their farms and homes.

After all of the posturing and rhetoric, the "semioccupation" was surprisingly serene. The Mormons relished the financial benefits that flowed from presence of the federal troops. A Mormon shadow government ran the affairs of Deseret, despite the facade of intervention. In 1861, the new president, Abraham Lincoln, sent an intermediary to Brigham Young with a terse offer: "If he will let me alone I will let him alone." To Lincoln, the slaves, not the Saints, now posed the gravest problem to the Union. Federal troops in Utah were promptly withdrawn.

The conflicts with Washington had convinced the Prophet to redouble his efforts to increase the Mormon population and fortify its sagging economy.

In 1850, the Utah legislature officially incorporated a Perpetual Emigrating Company to spur a new influx, and missionaries fanned out across Western Europe to begin their quest.

The new campaign, Brigham Young decreed, would be run with vigor and discipline. British and Scandinavian immigrants were assembled at Liverpool where they were met by a President and two Counselors who herded them aboard waiting vessels and supervised their voyage to Zion.

Charles Dickens, the novelist-chronicler, was a startled observer of one Mormon departure: "They had not been a couple of hours on board when they had established their own police, made their own regulations and set their own watches at all the hatchways. Before nine o'clock the ship was as orderly and quiet as a man-of-war."

When they arrived in Utah after their tortuous journey, the newcomers were apportioned to local Bishops at "placement meetings." A Bishop from one town would call out, "I'll take five brick-layers, two carpenters, a tinman and eight farm servants," and there was no question but that the new arrivals would go to their assigned stations. With the increased flow of immigration, Brigham Young became more selective about whom he would accept, sending lists of needed craftsmen to his missionaries. Metal and textile workers as well as potters were to be recruited most vigorously, the Prophet instructed. Workers in these desired fields were presented a rather glowing picture of the trip that awaited them, promising "roads, bridges, ferry-boats, stopping places to rest." One proselytizing pamphlet stated that vegetation in Utah "flourishes with magical rapidity." Within a month of planting, potatoes would grow to eight inches and corn to four feet, it said.

Though word began to seep back that Zion was not all it purported to be, Utah's population soared from 40,200 to 86,700 in the decade between 1860 and 1870. The flow of immigration reached such a level that the Church found itself hard-pressed to subsidize the influx. As one method of reducing expenses, Brigham Young came up with a scheme that startled his closest advisers: Instead of offering converts the usual wagons and teams for the final leg of their voyage, they would be given small handcarts. If newcomers wanted to reach the Promised Land, they would have to walk.

The two-wheeled wooden carts had projecting staffs of hickory or oak. The owners were to haul them like oxen.

In a letter to Elder F. D. Richards in Liverpool, Brigham Young estimated that the faithful would be able to average fifteen miles a day with their carts. "The little ones and the sick, if there are any, can be carried in the carts, but there will be none sick in a little time after they get started."

The Prophet's ambiguous prediction proved accurate. Though the first two companies of handcarts arrived safely in Utah, two others bogged down in bad weather. One Gentile traveler recorded in his journal coming upon a mile-long chain of the carts, most of them pulled by women. He also noted the sad procession of the sick and aged, mothers holding babies, men supporting themselves on canes, walking behind them. Of the thousand seventy-six converts in the final two handcart trains, over two hundred died. "Three out of four were frozen when we arrived in Salt Lake City," one immigrant recorded in his journal. "My mother was dead in the wagon. Bishop Hardy had taken us to a home in his ward and the sisters brought us food. We had to be careful and not eat too much as it might kill us we were so hungry."

The handcart scandal brought immigration to a temporary halt, and many of Brigham Young's budding new industries soon began to founder from the lack of skilled workers. The woolen mill was dismantled. A blast furnace for manufacturing iron was shut down. A much-heralded sugar industry was abandoned when it was found cane couldn't be grown. The pottery works failed to meet its production quota. The Prophet had pledged self-sufficiency to his people, stating, "We do not intend to have any trade or commerce with the Gentile world," but his promises proved optimistic. To make matters worse, Mormon businessmen had to watch with jealous eyes as a small band of Gentiles in Utah amassed considerable fortunes from mining gold, silver and copper—an industry the Prophet disdained. Their resentments were heightened by Brigham Young's own soaring fortunes. The

Prophet borrowed substantial interest-free funds from the Church, and, though secretive about his personal affairs, he died a millionaire.

The discord generated by financial jealousies was minor, however, compared with the continuing problems stirred by plural marriage. Having witnessed the dismantling of Nauvoo, some of the Saints hoped that polygamy would be banished in Utah, or at least discouraged, but their hopes were soon dashed. Once the initial chaos of settlement and the fears of federal invasion were overcome, Mormon men turned with renewed vigor to their most controversial and divisive custom.

The Prophet's own attitudes and public postures were a curious mixture of piety and overt sexuality. While presiding over his bevy of wives, he demanded that women garb themselves in the most conservative clothing, and would even visit his wives at their sewing machines during the day to inspect the stitching of modest skirts and bodices. When the older of his fifty-six children went out for the evening, he insisted on inspecting their attire, admonishing them to be home before ten. Though he enjoyed music and dance, he condoned only the cotillion and quadrille, contending that others were too sexual. He ordered construction of the biggest theater west of Chicago, which was opened amid great fanfare in 1862, but he personally exercised the role of censor over its performances. Seated in the middle of the parquet in his own reserved rocking chair, Brigham Young often munched apples during a performance and occasionally fell asleep, but once, glimpsing the wardrobe of a visiting ballet company, he closed the show until the dancers could be recostumed in floor-length dresses.

Armed with this commitment to public piety, the Prophet did all he could to foster the notion that plural marriage in fact embodied this precept. Under his direction, a resolution was introduced into Congress stating, "Polygamy is the only reliable safeguard of female virtue and innocence . . . the only sure protection against the fearful sin of prostitution."

Remarkably, he even convinced most of his female Saints that he was correct. Some of the women's diaries argued that polygamous wives were pursuing a loftier morality, since they had intercourse with their husbands only for purposes of procreation, while monogamous wives constantly had to satisfy their husbands' carnal urges. By the late 1870s, between fifteen and twenty percent of all Mormon households were polygamous, with the incidence rising at the upper reaches of the socioeconomic ladder. While the ordinary farmer had neither the time nor patience to support several women, the affluent merchant or lawyer would reward each new stage of his prosperity by taking a new wife.

Despite the spiritual sanctification of plural marriage, many households were wracked by constant domestic strife, as wives quarreled over money and attention. Brigham Young himself occasionally saw fit to denounce the "whiners" among polygamous wives during his ringing Tabernacle sermons.

Like many others in his flock, the Prophet tried to reduce domestic tension by marrying clusters of sisters, two or three at a time, on the dubious presumption the women would get along better. He provided separate rooms for his wives, posting a chalk mark on the door of the individual with whom he wished to spend the evening. There were gaps of as long as fifteen years between the births of the children of some of his wives, indicating that he divided his attentions faithfully. Less affluent polygamists would stack their wives in bunk beds, visiting whichever bunk they chose.

If the women proved occasionally quarrelsome about these arrangements, their rancor was mild compared with that of the brethren. Competition over prospective wives flared into sporadic violence, as the older men in the hierarchy plucked lissome young women from the arms of their youthful suitors. One elderly Bishop ordered a Mormon youth castrated because he had the misfortune of being engaged to a girl whom the Bishop fancied. Another Bishop ordered a rival's throat cut from ear to ear. Most often, clashes such as these were resolved more decorously in the quiet offices of a General Authority, as were other moral concerns. At one General Conference, a General Authority caused a shocked hush by cautioning his older colleagues against excessive competition with their younger brothers, adding, "Some of the brethren are bringing on premature decay and an early death by the too frequent use of sexual intercourse."

Predictably, the Mormons' marital customs did not escape the attentions of the outside world. A steady stream of journalists from the East and Europe trekked to Utah to record their impressions. Congressmen introduced a succession of bills barring plural marriage, heaping their best oratorical flourishes upon the Prophet and his fellow transgressors. Evangelists and yellow journalists clamored onto the crusade. On August 8, 1873, when Brigham Young's twenty-seventh wife, Ann Eliza, defected from his household and submitted to an angry interview, the *New York Herald* spread the headline across page 1: THE PROPHET OF UTAH AS A LOVER. Taking to the hustings, Ann Eliza claimed the Prophet's wives were a miserable lot and their children resentful and lonely. Mormon men really hated their women, she said; even the revered Apostle, Heber Kimball, referred to his wives as "cows."

By the end of the 1870s, the Supreme Court indicated its intent to uphold the new antipolygamy laws and a new force of federal marshals was formed to enforce the rules, even if it meant searching for offenders "haystack by haystack." The end of an era was at hand. In 1877, Brigham Young died suddenly of a ruptured appendix and thus was saved from witnessing the sorry spectacle of Church leaders going underground with their wives or fleeing to Mexico and Canada. The Prophet's successor, John Taylor, himself a polygamist, led a migrant life, moving from home to home, dying in 1887, a martyr to his fellow polygamists. With the passage of the Edmunds-Tucker Act in 1887, the Church corporation was officially dissolved, its property confiscated. Not until 1890, when a more moderate Church President, Wilford Woodruff, agreed to submit to federal authority, was Church property returned by a joint resolution of Congress. Finally, in 1894, an enabling act was passed permitting repentant Utah to form a state government.

The Church was intact once again, but much had changed. With statehood, the goal of a unique Mormon nation, separate and apart, had been set aside. The institutions of theocracy and polygamy they had fought so hard to sustain were buried.

But not the dream. Brigham Young still cast his long shadow over his Kingdom. He had succeeded in planting a new Zion in the wilderness of the Great Basin. He had presided over one of history's great ingatherings, and had run his theocratic regime for three decades as though the tides of democracy and secularism were not lapping at his very boundaries. He had imbued his people with a will that had endured the rigors of poverty and persecution and that would now be tested by an affluence and security on a scale he could never, in his wildest expectations, have imagined.

"We are going some day to possess the earth because it belongs to Jesus Christ and he belongs to us and we to him," declared Brigham Young's successor, John Taylor. And though the Mormon people had made their temporary accommodations to statehood and federal power, the dream of Zion lived on.

☐ When Gussie returned to the living room, Josiah Bingham was kneeling before the fireplace, jostling its embers back to life. Her children were nowhere to be seen.

"They finally got bored," the old man said when he saw her. "I don't blame them."

"Don't be ridiculous, Grandpa. You were absolutely wonderful."

"Not quite ready for Broadway," he said, tossing another log, the sparks leaping in all directions. "And why are you so preoccupied this fine evening?"

"Preoccupied?" Gussie blushed.

"At least you're consistent, Gussie. You were a very serious little girl. Now you're a very serious young woman."

"I really have no right to be preoccupied, Grandpa. You've been so kind to the boys and to me. It means so much to us—especially because of how it is with the rest of the family. . . ."

Josiah glanced at her over his shoulder. "Don't people pick strange ways to prove their righteousness?"

"Strange and hurtful ways."

"Well, I got plenty of it in my time, after I quit my business. Among our people, giving up your job is as bad as giving up your religion."

Gussie managed a smile.

Josiah groaned as he straightened up, rubbing his hip with his big hand. He stood facing Gussie, his back to the fire, which was now raging once more. "If an old man may be permitted a word of advice, Gussie . . ."

"Of course you are permitted . . ."

". . . Just don't take it all too seriously. Any of it. Not just the family stuff, but all the rest—the work, the magazine, the politics. I know you and Hiram feel very strongly about these things, but when you get to be my age, life takes on a different perspective. It becomes much harder to get angry."

"My heart says you're right, Grandpa. Really it does. But I *still* get very angry. I stand back from it all and see the two of us, Hiram and me, tilting at windmills, fighting with all our strength. And to what end?"

Josiah looked at her quizzically. "That's a good question, Gussie. Do you care to answer it?"

Gussie shrugged and was silent for a moment. In the next room she heard the voices of her two sons scrapping over something. "Oh, it's hard to say, Grandpa. I suppose . . . well, I suppose we just want people to realize they are free, that's all."

". . . Free?"

"Free to do what they want with their lives, not what the brethren expects of them. Even free to be troubadours, if that's what they want."

"I see," Josiah said, rubbing his haunches where the fire was warming him.

The boys burst into the room, in a sudden clamor of shouts and confusion. Ethan's overalls were unhooked and Eric was missing a shoe. Gussie smiled helplessly at Josiah, then proceeded with the task of assembling their clothing and zipping them into their parkas. The boys hugged their great-grandfather and Ethan planted a kiss on his gnarled chin.

They were at the door when Gussie felt Josiah's hand on her arm and saw him smiling at her wistfully, his two gold teeth glinting in the dim light.

"Well, keep at 'em, Gussie," Josiah Bingham said.

". . . At what, Grandpa?"

"The windmills." He winked.

"Sure. Thank you, Grandpa." She kissed him and felt his warmth against her.

ENTERING through the stage door and standing now in the backstage shadows, Eliza knew precisely what had happened. She could tell by the sound. When one spends a lifetime attending meetings and giving speeches, crowd sounds become a language of their own. Without seeing a single face, she could differentiate the restless audiences from the happy ones, the angry crowds from the sympathetic. It's all in the hum, the interplay of murmurs and titters, the subtle frequencies and amplitudes. Eliza had heard them all. She had addressed college audiences so hostile the tension was almost tactile. And she had spoken to groups so passive she'd become convinced that everyone had died during the course of her remarks.

Tonight's din, she calculated, was combative, expectant, not quite angry but ready for battle. And from the decibel level, she could tell the crowd was vastly greater than the two hundred fifty women she had expected. The hall, she knew, seated about one thousand—vastly too large for their meeting but the best available.

Moving unnoticed to the doorway at stage left, Eliza gasped when she saw them all.

Every seat was taken and the crowd filled the aisles and spilled into the lobby beyond, bodies packed shoulder to shoulder, an absolute sea of femininity. Yes, they'd really done it right, Eliza thought.

It was Helen Taylor who saw her first, moving quickly to her side.

"I've been circulating around the hall, Eliza. They've come from all over the state. Some even came from Idaho, Arizona and California. It's incredible."

Eliza could see that glassy-eyed look of incipient panic in her fine, intelligent face.

242

"The word went out from Church Headquarters yesterday morning," Eliza said. "I learned that every Bishop was instructed to send four representatives to pack the meeting. Women who could be counted upon to defend the faith."

"How can you be so calm, Eliza?"

Calm! That infuriating word again. If there was one word that was inappropriate at this moment it was calm. How she longed to confront Dana Sloat and tell him what she thought of him. She could never forgive Tad for bringing that soulless sonofabitch into the womb of her family.

"What do you think we should do, Eliza? Should we try to start the meeting anyway?" Amelia Stubbs was standing with them now, her face ashen. "These people really give me the cold sweats."

"They'll just hoot every speaker and vote down every resolution," Helen Taylor said. "What's the point?"

"We've got to do something. Everyone's getting restless."

They heard the chanting now, faint at first, a few voices in the huge throng, then gaining strength. The words were slurred but, as the decibel level rose, the sound crystallized:

"We don't need the ERA
Through the Lord we've found the way...."

Amelia Stubbs grimaced with frustration. "They're still fighting the old battles, Eliza."

Struggling to contain her rage, Eliza scanned the rows of chanting women, their faces contorted, mouths gaping, chests heaving from the exertion. There was a tinge of hysteria in their expressions, and also in the cacophony of voices as their chant grew ever louder, pulsing against the walls of the vast hall like bursts of thunder. Were these truly her sisters? Eliza asked herself. Were these the women for whom she'd fought all these years? It was as if her career, her entire life, was fluttering before her in a nightmare collage of distorted shapes and chaotic sounds—a collage without substance or meaning.

Helen Taylor was peering at her through frightened eyes. "We're going to have to deal with them soon. It's not a crowd anymore. It's more like an angry mob."

"She's right." The familiar voice came from directly behind her. Turning, Eliza saw Cora Snow standing there, surveying the throng. "I know, Eliza—I tried. I got into my car and rode a few blocks. But I couldn't go home and let you face these hussies alone." Her thin face creased into a pained smile.

"Aren't you Cora Snow?" blurted Amelia Stubbs.

"The very same."

"What are *you* doing here?"

"I'm sure I'll be asking myself that question in the morning," she replied, turning back to Eliza. "Well, Eliza, shall we do this thing before I change my mind?"

Eliza was staring at her, incredulous. Cora put her hand on her arm and said, "I have a feeling if we don't try to cool them off right now, there'll be no cooling them at all."

Eliza knew she was right. She could hear the noise level soaring ever higher. They had run out of time.

The two women walked onto the stage side by side. The noise seemed to rise at first, then subsided into an expectant lull.

Reaching the podium, Cora tapped the microphone with her thumb, sending a loud thumping sound across the hall.

"Sisters!" Her husky, vibrant voice failed to settle the din.

"Shut up, all of you!" Cora commanded.

A surprised hush gripped the room.

"My name is Cora Snow, Sisters. I happen to be the mother of two teenage millionaires."

A rumble of laughter started building, transforming itself into applause. "You know the person at my side. Eliza Hastings needs no introduction. She's better than we deserve."

There was another, even stronger, wave of applause.

All right, Eliza told herself. Cora Snow has the audience with her now, and she's not going to let them off the hook.

"Now you may very well be wondering, what's Cora Snow doing up there tonight?" Cora continued, her voice knifing through the continuing murmur. "As you may know, I am not much for meetings or politics or any of that. All my life I've been interested in building my business, not changing the world. I certainly had not planned to come here tonight. It's just that I was talking with my friend Eliza, here, and began to get angry. Now, I don't like being angry. It makes me very angry, being angry."

The women were laughing again. Eliza saw the row upon row

of faces, smiling appreciatively, riding on Cora Snow's every word. The hostility she had sensed before seemed to be dissolving.

"So I said to myself, okay, I'll go to that meeting. I'll go there and stand beside Eliza Hastings while she tells you some things that need saying. I'll go there because I believe in Eliza."

Eliza saw Cora step aside suddenly, surrendering the microphone to her. The auditorium was hushed.

"Let me make it quite clear, Sisters, we are not here to start this meeting," Eliza said, bending over the microphone. "We are here to end it. A tragic mistake was made here this evening. It's no great mystery how it came about." The murmur started again, the women buzzing among themselves in confusion.

"The whole incident," Eliza said, "reminds me of another meeting that took place one century ago just down the street. At the time, the brethren were scared out of their wits because the laws against plural marriage were being enforced. So headquarters gave the signal and suddenly there was this great mass meeting—thousands of women packing the old Salt Lake Theater, shouting their praise of polygamy, promising to defend it to the death. Now I ask you, Sisters, do you believe those women really and truly condoned the idea of sharing their husbands with other women?"

The auditorium resounded with shouts, most of the women yelling "No," but their voices were countered by a smaller but louder chorus of "Yes."

Cora Snow took the microphone again. "Let me say something Eliza is too polite to say," she snapped. "Anyone who answers yes to that question is a damned fool." There were a few shouts of protest, but Cora plunged ahead. "My great-grandmother was a plural wife, Sisters. Her husband could barely provide for her, yet he had six other wives. When I was a teenager I read her diary —read how much she hated her life, the degradation, the cruelty. Yet when the Bishop told her to attend that meeting Eliza just mentioned, she was there—defending an institution she loathed. She crowded into that theater just like you crowded into this theater tonight. Because you were told to do so. That's the only reason most of you are here, Sisters—because someone told you what to do and you're all a bunch of sheep. . . ."

Eliza expected a real roar of protest now, but, to her astonishment, there was only nervous rustling, a mounting uneasiness, like a great animal trying to decide how to fend off an unexpected assailant. Cora Snow had backed away from the podium once again, as though surprised by the intensity of her own words. Eliza knew she had to bring this to a close quickly now. She had to dispatch the crowd before it turned on them.

"Sisters, as I said before, tonight's meeting was a tragic mistake —perhaps a series of tragic mistakes. The reason most of you are here tonight, as Cora said, is that your Bishop *told* you to be here. All right, we're not saying, don't listen to your Bishop or don't listen to your husband. We are simply saying listen to your heart. That's what I've learned tonight. I hope you've learned that, too.

"Now, if you agree with me, I suggest a very simple way of demonstrating it. Just rise from your seat and walk quietly to the nearest exit. Return to your homes and forget this thing ever happened. Forget you ever came. But next time somebody tells you what to do, listen to your hearts."

Eliza stepped back from the podium and stood beside Cora Snow, staring into the faces before them. The crowd was motionless. Then, as if on some rehearsed cue, hundreds of women got to their feet and started filing toward the exits in a great silent throng. The only sound was that of shuffling feet. All the raucous voices of a few moments earlier were suddenly stilled.

It was over.

□ At the edge of the stage, Turner Mead awaited her, standing in the shadows in his dark blue suit. Eliza darted to him and he put his arms around her.

"... Turner, I never ..."

"I just wondered if you'd like a ride home," he said softly.

"I would like one very much."

Later, in the car, Turner grasped her hand and said, "You were really quite wonderful out there tonight, Eliza."

"I was so lucky Cora Snow was with me. I don't know what would have happened ..."

"No, she'd talked her way into a corner and then you turned them around. You won, Eliza."

Eliza glanced at him wearily, then out at the darkened shops along Main Street. There was not a soul on the street, which only hours earlier had been surging with Christmas shoppers. "We didn't win tonight. The brethren won. They destroyed the meeting and accomplished exactly what they wanted."

"Don't judge yourself too harshly, Eliza."

"No, darling, if anything, I've been too easy on myself, not too harsh. Until today part of me was still convinced things were the way they used to be: The Church was still the same, the Relief Society was still the same. It took Cora Snow finally to make me hear the cold truth. The brethren want me out. It's as simple as that."

"You're just tired, darling. Tired and discouraged."

"No, she's right, Turner. They want me out of their way, and I want out, too. Truly I do. It's all changed. It's lost its meaning for me."

He clasped her hand more tightly. "You know I love you, Eliza. I hate to hear you throw away all you've worked for."

She moved over in the seat so that her body was against his. "It's strange, darling, I'm the one who's always advised others to be decisive, and now I've had such trouble heeding my own advice."

They had stopped at a light on the deserted street. Turner stared straight ahead, gathering his resolve. Then he turned to her suddenly. "Well *I've* taken your advice, Eliza."

"My advice? . . ."

"Tonight you told those women to listen to their hearts, remember?"

"Did I say that? Pretty banal, I'm afraid."

"True, but I've been listening, Eliza."

There was a wan smile on Eliza's lips. "And what does your heart have to say, darling?"

"That we've been living our lives foolishly. That it's wrong for us to live apart, to meet secretly, to pretend to the world that we barely know each other. It's all foolishness."

"It's something we have to do, Turner. The facade was necessary. . . ."

"It's not necessary anymore."

Eliza stared at him, her lips parted. "Turner, I'm not sure I'm hearing you correctly."

"I think you are."

". . . Are you proposing?"

"Does that shock you terribly?"

". . . Well it certainly takes my breath away."

"I don't want to rush you into anything, Eliza. I know there are many pressures on you."

"That's true."

". . . So I thought we'd delay our wedding perhaps to, say, the day after tomorrow."

"Thursday!" Eliza looked at him, wide-eyed.

"At the latest!"

"Turner, really! Even if we wanted to, we could never arrange a Temple wedding by Thursday."

"I don't envision a Temple wedding."

"What sort of wedding do you have in mind?"

"I think a hotel would be romantic. The Hotel Utah, perhaps. No, it's too stuffy—it would feel almost like the Temple. I've got it: the McCune Mansion! Do you know it, Eliza?"

"That big Victorian fortress on the hill?"

"Exactly. I'll bet we could take it over for a morning. It would be downright elegant, in a funky sort of way."

Eliza shook her head in bewilderment. "I don't believe this entire conversation. . . ."

Turner tightened his grip on her hand. A car behind them was sounding its horn. The light had turned green and they were still standing. Turner accelerated.

"Are you really sure you know what you're saying, Turner? I'm an awful lot of trouble, you know. At least the brethren seem to think so."

"I know you a lot better than the brethren."

She fell silent. He placed his arm around her. "What's the matter, Eliza?"

"Something just seems wrong. It's not you, dearest. You know how much I love you—that's exactly what's troubling me. It's as if I were being rewarded for losing my job, for leading my sisters down the wrong road, for bungling everything."

"You didn't bungle anything, Eliza."

"Well, something got bungled. Something terrible. And here I am, sitting in the ruins, and you feel sorry for me and want to help me in some way. And so you're asking me to marry you." Her hands fluttered in frustration. "It's just not the way it should be. . . ."

Turner twisted the steering wheel abruptly, swerving the car to the curb. It screeched to a stop in front of a darkened warehouse.

Eliza reacted in surprise as Turner faced her sternly. "Now look here, Eliza, let me make some things very clear to you. I'm not asking you to marry me because I feel sorry for you, nor to salve your hurt feelings about the Relief Society. To be frank about it, I don't give a damn about the Relief Society. Not a damn, do you understand?"

"Now I've got you angry with me."

"Damned right I'm angry with you!"

"Well, I'm also angry with me—I don't want both of us to be angry with me!"

"Well, then, stop talking like a sentimental fool, Eliza. Stop it instantly!" Turner's voice reverberated through the tiny car.

Eliza sat absolutely still. "What would you like me to say?" she asked softly after a moment.

Turner took a breath to calm himself. "There's going to be a wedding at the McCune Mansion Thursday," he said softly. "Are you planning to attend?"

Eliza hesitated for a few seconds. Then she leaned over and kissed him lightly on the lips. "I wouldn't miss it for the world," she said.

And she kept repeating those words over and over to herself throughout the rest of the night. She could not remember any words ever making her happier.

WEDNESDAY

The Portent

AUGUSTA Cobb awakened at five thirty. In the darkness she felt the sensation of sliding slowly from some great labyrinthine womb into the cold dawn, her sheets parting like leaves of marble.

The damned Nembutal! How she detested those insidious little yellow capsules. She had gone to bed early and endured a brief, tormented sleep, steeped in inchoate fears and baroque visions. Around midnight she found herself wide awake once more, staring at the little bottle of pills that sat seductively in her medicine cabinet. Whatever happened, she wondered, to the innocence of sleep which left children with that morning glow?

She swallowed a capsule, and though sleep gripped her once again, it was a drugged sleep, locked in some cold, distant place, devoid of dreams or sensation. She always told herself the next morning it wasn't worth it—not worth the numbed disorientation and, later, the strange edge on her emotions. These last few weeks she had been taking the pills two or three times a week, hiding them from Hiram. . . .

Oh, Lord—Hiram!

Even before turning on the lamp she knew his place was empty. Suddenly the drowsiness evaporated and her senses were screaming. She was staring at the place where he should be sleeping, her panic welling.

She should have called the police at midnight! Her instincts had told her to do so. She'd hovered over the phone, her hand poised at the dial. If only she had placed the call and alerted them, instead of taking that damnable pill!

Hiram, she knew, would have been furious. These last few weeks he had come home after midnight several times. He'd been so busy, so distracted. The piece he'd been preparing about the polygamist cults had consumed his energies. Interviews with people who'd dropped out of those cults—deviant, frightened people—had taken place at odd hours in strange places. The previous day, too, Hiram had told her he was working on a special project for Turner Mead. That could also account for his absence.

But, in the past, whenever he'd have a late meeting she would awaken in the predawn hours and hear his soft breathing and feel his warmth next to her. He would always be there. Where was he now!

Gussie made her way to the kitchen and put on some tea. Her mind wrestled with the possibilities. She could wait a couple of hours. Surely he would call. It would turn out that he was in some remote corner of the state, meeting with some renegade polygamist. They would laugh about it later, and he would regale her and the kids with stories of the weirdos. How the children loved to listen to his exotic descriptions. To them, their father had become an explorer venturing into the great beyond, only to return with tales of his adventures. Sometimes he would even bring photographs which they would inspect in disbelief: A polygamist standing with his seven wives, all of them looking at the camera with oddly blank stares, their clothing a hundred years out of date, women in gingham, bearded men in big hats and crude overalls. He'd taken one shot of a group of children, eyes livid with fear, clustering together in the expectation that the Gadianton Robbers would, as predicted in the Book of Mormon, descend on them imminently, plundering their village.

Hiram had grown increasingly fond of these odd people, and that, Gussie sensed, carried with it great danger. There was a side to Hiram that was utterly naive. He was still the accountant, at home with columns of numbers, but obtuse in his insights into human character. He *wanted* so badly to trust people that he could overlook even the most blatant signs of mendacity.

No, Gussie did not trust these cultists. Their minds and mores resided in another era. Hiram would point to the faces in the photographs and talk about their innocence, but Gussie saw only an immutable emptiness.

It was after six. She stared at the phone expectantly. Surely he would call.

Enough. She would not allow any more time to go by. If he

were being held captive somewhere, the police might still be able to rescue him.

She took the receiver off its cradle, then slammed it down again.

What would she tell them? That her husband, Hiram Cobb, was off on some secret investigation of polygamous cults—that he might be a captive in some remote encampment? That he had been holding meetings with people who worked at the Little Cottonwood Genealogical Vaults trying to find out the background of Dana Sloat?

She could imagine the police officers, sitting in her living room, staring at her skeptically. When she'd reported an attempted arson several months earlier, she remembered the barely civil response of the two bulky officers who had come to their home. They were both big blond Mormons and she could sense their suspicion that she and Hiram were The Enemy, not the would-be arson victims. They did not help then and they would not help now.

Gussie felt suddenly overwhelmed by the sense of her own helplessness, her face wet with tears. No, she would not let herself sit here and cry, like some pathetic housewife. She would not let the children see her like this.

She started dialing. There was someone who would help.

WHEN the bedside phone started ringing, Turner Mead thought it was the alarm and was puzzled why the ringing persisted after he'd shut it off. He felt Eliza stirring next to him and saw her lovely hair splayed against the whiteness of the pillow.

"Is this Turner Mead?" The voice was unfamiliar to him.

"Yes." Turner saw the glimmers of first light through his window.

"My name is Hosea, sir. Hosea Cloor."

"It's very early, Mr. Cloor, . . ." Turner whispered.

"I am in charge of security for the Snow family, sir."

"Can this wait till later?"

"No, sir. I'm sorry." There was an almost servile politeness to the man's voice. "You are acquainted with a man named Hiram Cobb, sir?"

"What about Hiram Cobb?"

"He is missing, sir. His wife, Augusta Cobb, asked my employer to assist . . ."

Turner saw Eliza coming awake, turning onto her back, rubbing away the grogginess.

"Missing?"

"Yes, sir. I am calling you because it was my understanding Mr. Cobb was doing a job for you at the time of his disappearance."

Turner sat bolt upright in bed, clasping the phone more tightly. "Exactly what's your relationship with the Snow family?"

"The family employs a staff of eight security personnel, sir. For their tours and public appearances. I am in charge of that staff. Let's just say Mrs. Snow cares about the welfare of the Cobbs."

"What is it, dear?" Eliza asked softly.

"How long has Hiram been missing?" Turner said tensely.

"I would prefer to discuss these questions with you in person, sir."

Turner sucked in his breath, giving Eliza a helpless glance. "Forgive me, Mr. Cloor. It's very early—my mind is not exactly razor-sharp."

"I could be at your house in ten minutes, Mr. Mead," Hosea Cloor said. "Perhaps we could talk?. . ."

"Of course," Turner said. The phone went dead.

Eliza's worried eyes were fixed on his. "What is this all about?"

"I'm afraid to think," he said, climbing out of bed.

□ The moment Turner saw Hosea Cloor's massive figure in his doorway, he felt a stab of recognition. He'd never met Hosea before and yet the features were familiar. He was a hulking man, fair-skinned with thinning sandy hair, his forehead somehow too narrow for his large face, his eyes slightly too close together. As he introduced himself, he flexed his thick neck as though to protest the confinement imposed by his white shirt and black tie. His dark gray suit seemed more a uniform than a garment.

They were like Mormon clones, these men, Turner thought. They were part of the culture—loyal and diligent, and also ploddingly unimaginative.

They sat in the breakfast room and Hosea asked his questions in a voice awkwardly high for a man his size. When had he last heard from Hiram? Where had he called from? Had he indicated his next destination?

The questions droned on, as in a police interrogation, and Turner tried to be helpful, balancing cautiously in his mind that which he could say against that which was best left unsaid.

Turner surmised that when Hiram phoned he probably was in a restaurant or some public place because there was a faint hubbub in the background, and some music. Perhaps it was a bar. Their conversation had been brief. Hiram had promised to type out a short report and drop it by Turner's house in the next few days. When Turner arrived home late last night, he'd found the three typewritten pages under his front door—Hiram's typical compulsiveness.

That much Turner had volunteered to his interrogator—that much and nothing more. When he had finished, Hosea was still staring at him, clearly suspicious that he was holding back, as indeed he was.

"If you can think of anything else," Hosea said, collecting his notes and hefting his big body out of the narrow chair, "anything at all. There's so little to go on, Mr. Mead. Hiram had been meeting with these polygamists for his article. There are violent people among them. One can only assume he had an enemy. That's the only possibility."

"Isn't it also possible that he hasn't disappeared at all?" Turner asked. "He might have gone off on some project of his own. He's only been gone one night."

Hosea shook his head gravely. "In the past Hiram has always called quite faithfully, according to his wife. She has an intuition."

Even as he said good-bye to Hosea, Turner knew he shared that intuition. Something had happened to Hiram Cobb, that much was certain. And he, Turner Mead, bore a major burden of responsibility. The work Hiram was doing at the time of his disappearance did not involve polygamists, as Hosea thought. It involved Dana Sloat and the massacre at Mountain Meadows, and he had been working on it at Turner's instigation.

Turner hadn't told Hosea Cloor about any of that. If he'd mentioned the Little Cottonwood vaults he would have had to mention the name of Hiram's secret source there and that he had promised Hiram never to do. It had only been very reluctantly that Hiram had confided Lillian Thompson's identity to Turner. The reason, of course, was that Hiram had needed a favor. Lillian's son, Richard Thompson, was trying to get a start as a photographer and Hiram hoped Turner might help the boy. That much Turner had done.

Now Turner would have to telephone this woman of the underground vaults. Lillian Thompson had unlocked many a mystery over the years from her perch at Little Cottonwood. If only she could shed some light on what had happened to Hiram.

As Turner picked up the phone he heard Eliza preparing breakfast in the kitchen. He replaced the receiver immediately. He did not want to involve Eliza in all this. Here it was, the very first morning of their new life together, and he was suddenly embroiled in this ugly business. He would not let it loom between them. There were the plans for their wedding to discuss over breakfast—so much to do in so short a time. If she had any questions about Hiram he would do his best to minimize the situation for the present. There would be abundant time later to explain the rest to her—especially the business about Sloat and Mountain Meadows.

Turner wondered how Sloat fit into this latest puzzle. Could it be possible that he was somehow involved in Hiram's disappearance? Could he, in his intimidating ubiquity, have picked up the trail?

Turner felt a sudden welling of exasperation. What in God's name is happening to my Church? he asked himself. What is happening to this once pristine sanctuary of decency and morality? How could he even be thinking these things and asking these questions?

He heard Eliza calling now and steeled himself. All right, he would sit down and put all this out of his mind. They would have a peaceful breakfast together and would set their wedding plans.

Then he would go to the office and make that telephone call.

H IRAM Cobb had fought sleep for more hours than he could remember. He would begin to nod off, lulled by the bucking and lurching of the old pickup truck as it sped along the highway, but then a sudden jolt would snap him awake again. It was a sadistically uncomfortable little truck, which listed to one side awkwardly, and its shocks had long since rusted beyond the point of futility. Hiram could feel two springs gnawing against the thin plastic of his seat, as though preparing its direct assault upon his posterior.

He was determined to stay alert. The succession of events seemed so unexpected, even comical, he wanted to record in his mind every word and action. When these bizarre people finally let him go, realizing the error they had committed, he would set it all down precisely as it had happened. His readers would love it; their curiosity about the polygamist cults was insatiable. And, though the giant Viking who sat next to him, driving stoically, hour after hour, had not acknowledged where they were heading, Hiram didn't need to be told. This blond-haired hulk in his tattered denim overalls could only be one of them. It was written all over his dinotherian features.

If only he would talk! Hiram had tried several times to entice him into conversation but he couldn't overcome the reticence. The man was intensely self-conscious about his tentative command of language; that was part of the problem. But Hiram also had the impression that Penrose, as he had called himself, had been specifically instructed to say nothing, and he did as he was told.

What was it really all about? That was the real question nagging at Hiram. Why had Penrose been sent for him, and by whom?

He had first become aware of him after slipping the pages of his report under Turner Mead's front door. It was about ten-thirty, and the snowflakes were glinting in the dim light of the street-

260

lamp. He saw the pickup parked down the block but thought
nothing of it until he started driving, the truck following him at a
cautious distance. And then he wondered if there hadn't been a
truck parked outside his home. Could it have followed him to
Turner Mead's and be trailing him still?

Alarmed, Hiram veered sharply down a side street and pulled
to the curb, holding his breath as the seconds passed. The pickup
had vanished. His pursuer had given up the chase. Hiram heard
his own breath come in quick bursts now, as if he'd just been
sprinting. And then suddenly, the lights were blazing upon him,
the truck bearing down fast. Hiram desperately floored the gas
pedal, feeling his Toyota protesting the urgency of his response.
The aged car spurted forward, but it was too late. The pickup had
darted in front of him, forcing him against the curb.

From the perspective of his little Toyota, Penrose had seemed
ten feet tall as he leaped from his truck and towered above him,
moving in quick, awkward motions as though demanding of his
unwieldy limbs movements which were beyond their level of
performance. "You are Hiram Cobb?" he asked, bending down so
that his face was inches from Hiram's. Though an enormous man,
he had the soft, pink skin of a small boy. His hair was long and
flaxen.

"Yes, I am. What is the meaning of this?"

"You are to come with me, Mr. Cobb," the big man said, pronouncing his words slowly as though he were translating them
from an alien tongue.

"Who are you? What's your name?"

"My name is Penrose," he said as he opened the door of the
Toyota and placed his large hand around Hiram's arm, totally
enclosing it. The big man guided him out of his car and into the
pickup, and though he was trying to be gentle, it was clear he
possessed the physical resources to enforce his will.

"I can't just leave," Hiram protested. "I have to call my wife."

Penrose climbed into the driver's seat, and the truck started
rolling. "When we get there, perhaps."

"Get where? How long will it take?"

"Many hours," Penrose replied, and that was all he said, lapsing into a silence that had indeed lasted many hours.

And so they drove. From the road signs, Hiram could calculate roughly where they were headed. He knew the locations of the major Fundamentalist enclaves, and as he charted their progress, he crossed off the possibilities in his mind. They were not heading for Colorado City. That was a relief. He had visited that community briefly a year ago, and found its residents hollow-eyed and hostile. They had missed the turnoff for Short Creek—that, too, was a relief. He'd been told by a former resident that the highly inbred denizens of Short Creek had displayed increasingly violent responses toward the outside world.

New Nauvoo! That was the most probable destination. Hiram felt an edge of anticipation. Few, if any, outsiders had ever visited New Nauvoo, which was reputed to be the most prosperous of all the settlements. None of Hiram's sources was able to explain the source of New Nauvoo's affluence, but certainly one important clue lay in the information he'd reported to Turner Mead only that previous day—that its leader was Dawson Sloat, the only son of the Church's new First Counselor. Dawson had always been described in his official biographies as "a businessman in Australia." The Utah–Arizona border was a long way from Down Under. If only he could get Penrose to talk. What fascinating insights he could supply about these mysteries.

"I've heard New Nauvoo is a fine community," Hiram said with studied nonchalance, hoping to evoke a response from his captor, whose unyielding features seemed carved in granite.

Penrose glanced at him quickly, his eyes glazed with weariness, but did not respond.

I'll give it one more try, Hiram told himself. Just one more.

"Dawson Sloat is a fine man, I've been told." He saw Penrose react now.

"Brother Sloat is a great leader," Penrose said ponderously.

"I am honored he wants to see me," Hiram said.

Penrose looked over at him once more, his expression noncommittal. "Yes," he said, returning his gaze to the road.

That was all he was going to elicit from this primitive, Hiram concluded, but at least he'd learned his destination. As they continued driving, Hiram struggled to reassemble in his mind all the random bits and pieces of information about Dawson in the hope they might shed some light on this curious expedition. Apparently he was a benevolent leader: There were no tales of violence, no rumors of mysterious disappearances such as marked some of the other Fundamentalist colonies. Thank God for that. As Dana Sloat's son, he was probably better educated and more intelligent than the other cultists. That, no doubt, helped account for the settlement's prosperity—that plus indirect aid from Dana Sloat himself, perhaps. But he could not recall any physical descriptions of young Sloat, nor any specific accounts of his habits or mannerisms.

The picture was a vague one. Alone among the polygamous enclaves, New Nauvoo had remained a mystery, and so had its leader. And here he was, on the day before Christmas, bouncing along a road leading to Arizona in this miserable pickup truck to see this mystery man!

But why?

If only I could get a call through to Gussie, Hiram thought. She would worry terribly if he was not at her side in the morning. She had seemed so jittery lately. Surely Dawson Sloat would allow him to place the call.

It was almost four in the morning when the pickup finally turned off the highway and plunged down a dirt road. The flat landscape seemed like an ebony sea. Hiram's bones ached from the unceasing jolts and lurches and his mind felt heavy with fatigue. He had fallen into a drowsy stupor when suddenly he felt two strong hands upon him and realized the truck had finally stopped. He could make out the faces of two men, both bearded, grasping him, forcing him out into the night, his stiff limbs struggling to regain their feeling. The men were moving quickly, one on each side of him, holding him under his shoulders so his feet barely grazed the ground. There were no voices, only the eerie silence broken by the harsh crunch of boot against gravel. One man released him now and the other was pushing him through a doorway into a dark shack, which smelled like an abandoned cellar. Hiram was holding back, resisting his forward thrust, afraid of colliding with an unseen object in the blackness, but the two men seemed to know exactly what they were doing. He felt a weight on his shoulders and he sank into a hard wooden chair, hearing the snic of handcuffs and feeling the cold metal against his wrists. "That's really unnecessary," Hiram protested. "I have no place to go."

But the men said nothing. They locked the cuffs and Hiram heard the door close behind them. He was alone.

It was cold in the shack, Hiram realized now. Cold and utterly black. He felt a profound disorientation, as though his body were free-floating through a yawning void. His mind seemed clouded, his ideas unformed, like arabesques tantalizing him with their intricate vagueries. Once his eyes became accustomed to the darkness, he reassured himself, he could begin to recognize specific objects and these would anchor his perceptions, but with each passing minute Hiram realized that the darkness was uncompromising. New images paraded before him. He was manacled to the prow of a ship, cleaving the dark waters, plunging ever forward to the outer reaches of time and space.

He awoke to a shrill, ethereal sound, distant but ominous in its insistence. The shack was still dark but he could begin to make out the outlines of his chair and the table that stood adjacent, and even the glint of the handcuffs which were cutting into his wrists, numbing his hands. They would come for him soon, he told himself. He would meet Dawson and would find out what lay behind all this. Perhaps Dawson had heard of his investigation and wanted to speak to him about it. Perhaps he had even read Hiram's writings and desired to share his viewpoints. These were curious people, these fundamentalists, throwbacks to a distant epoch. They would not simply telephone or write someone and express their need to establish contact. They would send a Penrose and simply annex you—that was well within their pattern of behavior.

If only Dawson would come soon. He was freezing within his parka. He had not bothered to put on a sweater last night for his short excursion to Turner's house. He never thought he'd end up handcuffed to a chair in the middle of nowhere.

There it was again—the shrill, grating sound, like chalk against a blackboard. It was like a distant whistling, except there were lots of creatures whistling, their notes converging into a harsh dissonance. It was growing louder now, coming from all directions. The shack seemed to be surrounded with these whistling creatures, all of them holding a single lingering note which melded into an eerie cacophony. Could they be insects? Some odd form of locust, perhaps?

The Whistlers! Hiram jolted upright in his chair as his mind suddenly connected his fleeting thoughts and images. What the hell were they called? The Nauvoo Whittling and Whistling Brigade! The very name started his heart thumping, his hands straining against the handcuffs that entrapped him. He remembered the oddly elliptical way in which the settlers' diaries in Illinois always referred to the Whistlers, as though the very mention of their name struck terror in their hearts.

They were gangs of children and teenagers, Hiram remembered, savage and feral. Their inspiration came from the adult "enforcers"—the Danites and Mean Devils and Destroying Angels. Their prey, Hiram knew, was not limited to those who attacked or persecuted the Saints. The Whistlers, in particular, would descend like packs of jackals on a Gentile traveler, literally terrorizing him to death with their well-honed tools of torment.

Snap out of it! Hiram demanded. This is not 1844; it's Arizona, not Illinois. This is no time to conjure up grotesque images from the past. That's the trouble with steeping oneself in history, Hiram told himself—the past becomes a sort of inner dialogue that haunts one's perceptions and distorts vision. It is a curse to have read too much and to have known too much. Even the most ordinary events take on fearsome meanings that would elude any normal individual. If only he weren't locked to this damned chair! If he could just walk around the room and get his circulation going once again, then these hallucinations would dissolve from his mind.

The sudden thump of the door bursting open caused Hiram's body to lunge forward in surprise, the chair scraping along the floor as he dragged it with him. Blinking desperately, Hiram saw two figures materializing out of the darkness, felt them leaning over him, smelled their sour breath and heard the sound of their exertion. They were lifting his chair and him as well, moving him swiftly through the door.

"Get me out of these damned handcuffs," Hiram called out to them, but he heard his own words slurred into incoherence. It made no difference. The men were not listening to him, nor were they talking. He felt his knee smash against the doorjamb as they shoved him outside, felt the sudden breeze now. The air had that dank heaviness that preceded first light, and Hiram felt he was drifting through layers of ink. The moon was a dim sliver hovering low in the sky as though to conceal its insignificance. He could see other shapes hovering around him in the darkness, a circle of spectral shadows. They had set him down with a jarring thud and he could hear the whistling again, growing louder now. They were all around him in the darkness, emitting their shrill, discordant sounds, coming always closer, tightening the circle. He could hear their footsteps, too, the soft tread of boots against the coarse gravel.

A match was lit and suddenly, with a deafening whoom! flames exploded in front of him, burgeoning like angry fingers grasping at the night. Hiram could hear the myriad little explosions of the twigs and branches consumed within the detonating flames, and his eyes, hooded by the darkness, were assaulted by the sudden fierce onslaught of light. And in the background the whistling was growing ever louder and he knew that his first instincts had not been idle hallucinations—some bizarre ritual was about to unfold, some strange rite of these preposterous people who had crept out of a time warp and set upon him.

The shapes were all around him now, their figures liquid in the refracted firelight. Hiram's eyes could see the flash of the long knives as they whittled away on their sticks, fashioning them into spears for the final ritualistic assault. He knew it all now, like some terrible nightmare playing back to him.

"Stop it!" Hiram shouted. "Stop this madness!"

The whistling stopped. He could see the circle of faces around him. They were youngsters mostly, some of them as young as ten or eleven, with hungry eyes and thin faces, like coyotes.

"Who is the leader here? Step forward so I can address you!"

"I am the leader." It was a man's voice that came from the darkness beyond the circle of Whistlers.

"I want an explanation for all this. My name is Hiram Cobb. I am not some drifter you've brought in off the road whom you can tie up and terrorize."

"I know who you are," the voice said. "You are an apostate. You have failed to keep your covenants. You have courted Satan. Your fate now rests in the hands of the Avenging Angels."

The man who spoke seemed to be sitting, unlike the others, like some tribal leader upon his throne. His voice had a hypnotic timbre to it.

Hiram felt himself gripped by true terror. All that had happened till now seemed oddly ethereal. He'd felt distanced from it as though it were happening to someone else, somewhere else, and he'd been a mere spectator to this madness. But there was something about that messianic voice that was more profoundly menacing than anything that had gone before. It was a fanatic's voice and it conveyed a fanatic's authority. And suddenly the entire tableau that lay before him—the bonfire, the shrill whistling, the encircling shapes, the sharp jutting sticks—all of it crystallized into a single nightmare vision.

"Tell these children to return to bed," Hiram called out, trying to disguise the terror that was choking off his words, but on some unspoken signal, the circle around him tightened yet again. They were struggling with what looked like a large barrel, tilting it, its murky black contents spilling out with a hissing sound upon the ground in an ever-widening puddle. Smoke rose from the thick fluid as it hit the chill night air.

He heard the click of the handcuffs being unfastened, felt the aching numbness in his hands and arms as he tried to move them. There were men hoisting him roughly out of the chair and Hiram gasped as he saw the knives flashing toward him, heard the sound of ripping cloth, then suddenly felt the stab of cold air against his skin. They were slicing away his clothes, manipulating him like a rag doll, yanking arms and legs, pulling him first one way, then another, tearing away his boots, ripping off his shirt. He felt a sudden jab of pain as, with one great swipe, a knife chopped through the buttons of his trousers, the edge penetrating the soft skin around his belly.

"Goddamn bastards," Hiram spat out as he saw the blood seeping out below his navel. He tried to lunge but felt the strong hands upon him, like iron clamps, then felt another searing pain as his briefs were torn from his body like ribbon from a package. They were proceeding with mute efficiency about their task, like hunters skinning their prey. Suddenly he was off the ground and felt their hot breath upon him as they moved him through the night air, closer, ever closer to the fire. He tried to cry out but his mouth was dry with terror. There was shouting all around him now, all of them yelping sharp, savage cries which lacerated the night.

Hiram felt himself thrust onto the ground, his body recoiling against the hot, sticky substance, hearing himself cry out from the burning agony. He tried desperately to roll away from it, but the thick, tarry stuff was all over, the hands rolling him in it, holding down his flailing arms and legs. His nostrils exploding with the sweet, tarry smell and then the acrid scent of burning flesh—his own burning flesh! He arched his back but felt the sharp sticks prodding him, poking at his body with their needlelike points, and he saw their faces all around him now, savage jackal-like faces reddened by the glow of the firelight, mouths gaping, screaming in the night, eyes burning with bloodlust, a circle of child-devils mesmerized by this Mephistophelian ritual. The images were all merging together now as he was losing vision. Strong hands were holding his head down in the muck and he could feel the tarry stuff all over his hair, blistering the skin on his face and neck, and he kept blinking desperately to keep his eyes clear but it was seeping in. It was becoming a lunatic collage of reds and blacks and grays, as he felt himself being turned over, tasting the awful stuff, thick, molasses-sweet, searing his lips and tongue. Then there was no sensation at all in his mouth and he could no longer cry out. They were still rolling him over and he could see a sudden feather-light curtain of white descend on him. For a single, fleeting moment he imagined himself on a mountaintop, buried in the soothing coolness of virgin snow, feeling its clean, sweet moisture all over him. His body was sliding away from him, sliding off into the snow, removed from its agonies. At peace.

It became clear to him then, a sudden moment of agonized clarity.

These bloody fools! They were doing it wrong! He could feel himself encased in the solid wall of burning tar, his blistered skin screaming for release. There was no sensation in his body. His brain commanded his limbs to move, but there was no sensation anywhere, as if his body had simply surrendered to the pain and gone away. His eyes and ears were going fast now. He tried to scream at them—they were doing it wrong!—but his tongue was encased in the burning slime. They were tarring and feathering him as they did at Nauvoo to marauding Gentiles, to thieves and apostates and others deemed dangerous by the Defenders of the Faith, but they were doing it wrong. They were suffocating him!

More than anything else, Hiram felt rage. Rage against their bigotry, their incompetence, their savagery.

They were killing him, these barbaric fools! They were killing him and they didn't even mean to.

He was back on the mountaintop now. Back in the virgin snow, the soothing whiteness all around him.

IT had been one of those bone-rattling flights where the plane kept shuddering and plummeting like a kite caught in crosswinds. Weary, his spirits low, Tad felt imprisoned in this absurd aluminum tube, hearing it groan and rattle as if to protest its fate, and he wished he could join its lament. The pilot's voice, with condescending calm, urged the passengers to remain in their seats and unfurled a sorry repertoire of white-knuckle jokes. Compounding Tad's discomfort, the stewardess laid before him a sulfurous omelet which looked as though it had emerged from an excavation, not an oven.

The snowcapped peaks seemed alarmingly close as the plane slammed through the thick clouds, the Great Basin suddenly revealing itself below, a landscape frozen in white. Walking through the airport parking lot, the air, numbingly cold after the benign temperatures of Los Angeles, snapped his senses back to full alert. He was aware of an aching need to see Nancy and the children. He wanted to be home again. Yet first, he knew full well, there was the business involving Ellis Marmer and the Pacific situation.

Arriving in his office, he told Marmer's secretary that he needed to see him, then placed a call to Gavin to be sure there'd been no new developments this morning. Gavin seemed downright cheerful. Minafee had calmed down, he said. "Just to keep him happy I've moved up the Alvin Boroff series."

"What series?"

"The stories about the political influence of the Mormon Church—Minafee's favorite whipping boy. The series will start tomorrow. Read it, Tad. You might learn something."

Smiling to himself, Tad hung up. He didn't care about Boroff's series. As far as Tad was concerned, he could expose anything he wanted to.

270

Ten minutes later Marmer's secretary buzzed him. All right, Tad told himself, you're just going to get one shot at him. Make the most of it.

Dwarfed behind the immensity of his oak desk, the old man looked as frail as ever, his thin veined hand shaking as he beckoned him in. His dark gray suit, with its old-fashioned padded shoulders, looked several sizes too big for him. Marmer was not above using his seeming decrepitude to his own advantage, Tad knew, in fending off the demands of clients and employees.

"Good morning, Hastings," Marmer said, peering over his thick spectacles. "The timing of your return is fortuitous."

"Sir? . . ."

"News of the Suncorp deal just came over the Dow Jones ticker five minutes ago."

"They announced the deal?"

". . . announced they had concluded negotiations to acquire Pacific in an exchange of stock."

Tad felt a sudden release, as though a great muscle had just unknotted. "The last meetings had been somewhat difficult, sir."

"Job well done," Marmer said, as his eyes returned to the papers before him, his manner dismissive. The deal had been closed. Marmer had offered his brief felicitations. The audience was over.

"Sir, could we have a few words? There were certain aspects of the negotiation . . ."

Marmer's rheumy eyes peered over his glasses. "Sit down," he said crisply.

"There was a question of professional ethics, sir, that's been troubling me." Tad felt like an embarrassed schoolboy seated before an impatient principal.

"What was the issue?"

"An issue of disclosure. The Suncorp management, I discovered, had not been aware of the terms of Mr. Gaunt's will. They had no knowledge the Church will soon own his shares." Tad shifted his position uneasily. His real concerns, of course, were not those he was propounding, but rather the stratagems that lay beyond. He was fencing with someone whose skills at this sort of thing were vastly superior to his own.

"And did you inform them of the will?" Marmer's words came sharply.

"No, sir."

"Appropriately not. All the relevant documents were at their disposal, correct?"

"Yes. All except the Gaunt will."

"You were representing Pacific in this negotiation. Isn't that right?"

Tad felt the sulfurous omelet wallowing in the recesses of his digestive tract. "Since I also brought Gavin Pollard into the negotiation I was acting implicitly on his behalf."

Marmer removed his glasses impatiently, placing them on the papers before him. "Your primary client was Pacific, Hastings. Your fee will be paid by Pacific."

"That is true, sir."

So far, so good, Tad told himself. He was learning what he needed to know. Marmer was growing a bit skittish, but at least Tad had confirmed his suspicion that Ellis Marmer had indeed known the terms of the Gaunt will and had deliberately kept him in the dark. That was half of the puzzle. Now if there was only some way of solving the other half—the important half.

"I am still concerned, sir, that when the Suncorp people find out about the will there might be a degree of alarm," Tad said.

"Mmmh," Marmer murmured ambiguously.

"I mean, if you add the Gaunt shares to the bloc already owned by the Church through the Blanton company acquisition a decade ago, the Church conceivably could have working control of the company."

"I don't really think anyone at Suncorp will burden themselves with that much arithmetic, do you, Hastings? Besides, even if they did, there's no way anyone could squeeze out of that deal. It's locked tight as a drum."

"I don't quite understand . . ."

"It's not important that you do," Marmer snapped with finality. "You know, Hastings, this firm has always represented Church Headquarters in much of its legal dealings. Never quite on a scale with the Fielding firm, of course, or even with the Wiggins office."

"Yes, sir."

"I just wanted you to know that it looks like this office will be getting a much greater share of the business now. Much greater."

"I am pleased, sir." Tad gathered his courage. All right, if he's going to penetrate this veil of propriety, now's the time to try. "And, in that context, sir, I wanted to express my gratitude to you for entrusting me with this assignment. To you and to Mr. Sloat."

Marmer was staring at him impassively. The old man, Tad figured, was asking himself, does the kid know what he's saying or is he just running off at the mouth? Seated imperiously behind his desk, Marmer looked like an old portrait in oil that had dropped from its frame—the portrait of The Founder that always adorns the reception rooms of important corporations. His was an intimidating presence.

Marmer cleared his throat. "We both knew you were the logical man for the job, given your unique relationship to the principals of this transaction," Marmer said crisply. "Brother Sloat and I both recognized that fact."

At last! Tad heard the words he'd been probing for. He had bluffed the old man into confirming what his darkest intuition had informed him from the outset.

"I think you're going to have an excellent future with this firm," Ellis Marmer continued, pushing himself back from his desk, rising from his chair and walking over to where Tad stood. He extended his thin hand and Tad took it, feeling the old man's skin, soft and cool against his. "Yes, Hastings, a really bright future. I shall be recommending to my colleagues the consideration of a partnership. Yes, you have progressed excellently—you should be a very happy young man."

"Thank you, sir," Tad said, surprised by the sudden surge of excitement his words evoked. "I appreciate your confidence." He started to say something more, but then thought better of it, as Marmer tightened his grip, to punctuate his meaning. But Tad understood him quite well. Keep your eyes straight ahead and your mouth shut, he was saying. The inner circle is beckoning to you—the circle of money and power and ecclesiastic prestige. It would all be there for you if only you do your job and keep to the straight and narrow. Tad could never remember an instance where Ellis Marmer had ever gotten to his feet to shake the hand of a junior attorney, no less to offer his congratulations. It was not just a courtesy, it was a benediction.

And indeed he deserved it. He'd brought it off, hadn't he? They'd known all along that he would do what was expected of him.

So standing now opposite Ellis Marmer, having received his benediction, Tad realized it all came down once again to that same nasty question, the same question he'd asked himself so often these past few hours, these past few years. Whom did he belong to, anyway?

EZRA Hurlbut was elated. He had spent much of the morning at Church Headquarters and marveled at the energy and resolve that had been infused into the staff by the new administration. As Utah's junior Republican senator, Hurlbut customarily paid homage to senior Church officials when visiting Salt Lake, especially over the Christmas holidays. He made it a point to drop off a gift to the President's secretary, Edith Snipp, and exchange pleasantries with Bill Chadwick and other senior staff members. Church Headquarters, Hurlbut knew, represented a key part of his constituency. Its officialdom, once cultivated and secured, was like a firm anchor of support in the always treacherous political seas.

His most important business this morning, however, was Dana Sloat. The Church's newly installed First Counselor had summoned him to a meeting, which usually meant a terse ten-minute confrontation—that was Sloat's style. This morning, however, Hurlbut was both surprised and flattered to find himself swept up in a whirlwind of meetings and consultations dealing with a broad range of temporal affairs. Sloat presided over the meetings with his usual firm hand. Every fifteen or twenty minutes a new cluster of dark-suited men were ushered into the First Counselor's office and arrayed around the conference table. After the second or third such meeting, Sloat's strategy had made itself apparent to Hurlbut: What he was already doing was introducing his corporate whiz kids into the tired substrata of the Church hierarchy, building what the business magazines like to call a "management team." And Sloat seemed eager that Hurlbut consider himself part of that team. Virtually every problem that was reviewed had a governmental or political aspect to it, and Sloat was careful to defer to the junior senator from Utah for his comments on those areas. At the end of every meeting Sloat would enunciate his conclusions and instructions, like a general dispensing his marching orders.

Promptly at eleven o'clock Sloat terminated a meeting on tax planning, checked his schedule and turned to Hurlbut. "The President will be extending his Christmas greetings to senior staff, Senator. I'm sure he'd enjoy seeing you."

"It would be a great honor."

Moments later Hurlbut entered the sacrosanct office of the Prophet, where he'd never before been invited. Crossing the threshold, a numbed awe overtook him. Several other officials had preceded him, lined up informally, but Hurlbut was too concerned with his own fluttery stomach to notice their identity. How odd, he thought as the line progressed, that he would be affected this strongly. He had been on reception lines for the President of the United States and other heads of state without any loss of equanimity. Yet the slight, gray-haired man who now came into view was not merely a head of state. He was, more importantly, his spiritual leader; he was the Apostle of Jesus Christ, the Lord's divine spokesman on earth. Approaching him, Hurlbut sensed a glow about this man, a divine emanation. Samuel Heber Bryce was his sovereign. That in itself was awe-inspiring.

"I am honored to meet you, President," Hurlbut said, shaking the small, smooth hand that had been extended to him.

Dana Sloat was at his side, performing the introductions.

"You have done good work in the Congress, Senator Hurlbut," President Bryce said in a soft, reedy voice that sounded hoarse from the week's speechmaking.

"Thank you, sir." Though the Prophet's face seemed drawn, his skin wrinkled like ancient parchment, there was an astuteness to his gaze which added to his aura of dominion.

"The Senator has been good enough to sit in on our meetings this morning to lend us his expertise," Sloat said. Even Sloat, Hurlbut noticed, seemed to be gentler and more reverent in his presence.

"Your counsel is gratefully received," the Prophet said. "You know, Senator, the tasks confronting the First Presidency are unyielding in their complexity."

"I'm sure that is true, sir." Hurlbut felt the line stirring impatiently behind him, but the Prophet seemed eager to pursue their conversation. "On the plane home yesterday, Senator, I was reviewing appeals of excommunications. I found myself dealing not simply with interpretation of Scripture, but also grooming standards, hypnotism, sealings, Sabbath observances, sensitivity training, donation of one's body parts to science and so forth. We live in times of great turbulence."

"That is why the Good Lord has placed a seer amongst us," Dana Sloat said tactfully.

Hurlbut saw the First President smile faintly, and then felt himself being propelled along the reception line, greeting several other senior members of the hierarchy who had gathered to add their Christmas felicities.

Moments later he was back in Sloat's office, seated before his desk. Sloat folded his tall, angular body into his leather chair.

"This was an inspiring morning," Hurlbut said. "I am grateful to you for letting me experience it. If I can be of further service, please do not hesitate . . ."

Hurlbut heard Sloat crack his knuckles. "There is one other item," Sloat said, his eyes locking on him. "I noticed you've avoided any mention of my remarks in Washington last week. Surely there has been some reaction by now."

Hurlbut had hoped, in the press of business, that the First Counselor would not get around to that subject. Sloat's speech at the prayer breakfast had stirred grave concern among the brethren in Washington who held high government position. They were prepared to do Sloat's bidding, but were nonetheless alarmed that the First Counselor was moving too fast, that he failed to comprehend the sensitivity of their position. Hurlbut was reluctant to mention these reservations now, however. Sloat was an impatient man, he knew. Impatient and imperious. He would jump on something like this as a breach of discipline.

"The reaction was uniformly positive," Hurlbut lied, choosing his words carefully. "The brethren realize the Church is entering a new era of leadership and dedication."

Sloat nodded warily. "You and I both know, Senator, that there's a tendency in Washington to get cautious and self-protective. It's a disease of bureaucracy. I want your help, Senator, in reiterating to our brothers that the Church intends to take a bolder posture in government."

"I quite agree, sir. The only concern our brothers have is to be publicly singled out as Mormons. They feel they can be more effective if they can work quietly, behind the scenes.

Hurlbut saw the tall man rubbing his hands impatiently. There was silence in the room as he considered his reply. The only sound was the cracking of his knuckles.

"I feel that concern can be used as an excuse for inaction," Sloat replied.

"There are specific fears, sir. The Pollard newspapers in California, for example, are planning a series of articles on the Church. The articles would contain a list of senior officials . . ."

Hurlbut heard his voice quavering, and tried to steady himself. Just before getting on his plane this morning, he'd learned that the stories planned to single him out as the LDS front man in Washington and as the pivot in the anti-ERA campaign. The news had filled him with dread.

"Tell the brothers not to worry about those articles," Sloat cut in quickly.

"Sir, I don't think you realize the potential damage they could cause in undermining our effectiveness. . . ."

". . . I said don't worry about it."

"Sir?"

"The Church has acquired control of the Suncorp company, which owns those newspapers. They won't be running any stories we don't want them to run."

Hurlbut's breath escaped him in a sudden rush of awe and relief. "That is very good to hear." He knew that Suncorp was one of the biggest media conglomerates in the nation. Had Sloat, in only his first week in office, actually managed to bring off a coup of such magnitude? Perhaps the wild rumors were correct after all—the rumors of corporate maneuverings and acquisitions. Hurlbut had tended to dismiss the rumors from his mind; they were the sorts of stories that always followed a figure as controversial and secretive as Dana Sloat. But maybe they were all correct.

The tall, lanky man who sat before him, with his guarded, furtive eyes, was a true leader. A visionary. Though a man of business, he saw himself in the mode of a Brigham Young or a Joseph Smith—that much Hurlbut sensed. He had inherited their mantle and their dream: the dream of a Mormon empire. And he wanted a trusted ally—that had been made abundantly clear this morning. Hurlbut felt himself swell with excitement. What a privilege. What an opportunity! This man seated before him was clearly destined for power and greatness, and Hurlbut would be at his side. Who knows how far they could travel together?

"You and I both know, Senator, that there are parallels between Washington and Salt Lake," Sloat intoned, swiveling his chair to one side, hefting one long leg over a desk drawer that was slightly ajar, his gaze distant now. "Both are great power centers. Both profess to be run in accordance with democratic precepts. Yet both operate on the basis of political oligopoly. Both systems are run by a favored few who minister to the needs of the multitude. Do you agree, Senator?"

"Yes, I do."

"I have looked into your background, Hurlbut. Your family was much like mine. A good old Mormon family, but always outside the circle of power. Never considered quite good enough to gain acceptance by the hierarchy."

"That is a problem I have labored to overcome, sir." Hurlbut was surprised to hear the First Counselor in such an expansive mood. Never before had his remarks penetrated beyond the impersonal surface of politics and policy.

"I, too, Senator. I built my companies despite the inner circle, not because of them. I am one of the first Mormon businessmen to reach far beyond the boundaries of traditional LDS power. I showed them what could be done. I contributed millions to their universities, their hospitals, their charities, before they granted me even the most rudimentary recognition."

"I have observed all that with great admiration, sir."

Hurlbut was distracted by the buzzing of the intercom, but Sloat did not seem to notice. "My name wasn't Smith or Fielding or Grant or Cannon, Senator. My forebears weren't dispensed land or mineral rights or other favors by Brigham Young, despite their faithful service to him. They were shunted aside as political embarrassments. . . ."

The buzzing continued. Exasperated, Sloat grasped the phone to his ear. "I did not answer your buzzer because I had asked not to be interrupted," Sloat said sharply. Hurlbut saw him listen for a moment, then angrily punch a button on his console.

"Yes, Dawson, . . ." he said.

Hurlbut checked his watch. It was approaching noon. There were several appointments he had made on the assumption that his meeting with Sloat would take the customary ten or fifteen minutes. Now that Sloat was in such an expansive mood, perhaps their conversation would linger through lunch and into the afternoon. He had never expected to find him like this—it was a new Sloat revealing himself to him, a more human, compelling Dana Sloat reaching out to form a bond of power and even friendship. No, he had never anticipated that the morning might take this turn. If only he could slip out for a few moments and cancel his other scheduled meetings for the day . . .

Hurlbut rose from his chair, glancing over at Sloat to signal he would be leaving for just a moment, but then sank down again. Sloat's face, which moments before displayed a new openness, had frozen into an angry mask, its color suddenly drained. Hurlbut stared at him, incredulous at the transformation. Sloat was listening intently to his caller. "How dare you, Dawson?" Hurlbut heard him say, his voice filled with rage. "How dare you!"

Sloat's gaze met his. "I must ask you to leave me now," Sloat said, holding the receiver away from him. In his mind, Hurlbut had simply ceased to exist.

"Of course, sir," Hurlbut said, rising quickly, extending his hand, but Sloat did not take it. His attention was riveted on his telephone conversation.

Hurlbut felt his own anger rising now. What right had this man to dismiss a United States senator as if he were an office boy? To think that he could have presumed this man capable of friendship —no such thing! Had the arrogance of power so quickly overtaken him? Well, Sloat might hold great power but even he was vulnerable.

THE impulse had overtaken her unexpectedly as she was driving to her office and, though she had dismissed it from her thoughts, it kept nagging at her. This was to be such a frenetic day—so much to be started, so much to be brought to a close—there was really no time to indulge herself. Important decisions had crystallized in her mind and she had determined to act on them. And yet, amidst it all, she had a gnawing desire to see her son. It had surprised her, and it was clear from the hesitation in his voice, it had surprised Tad equally, as though she were the last person he'd expected to hear from. Many weeks had passed since they had last seen each other, many months since they'd had a serious talk, with no one else present. Many months? Eliza asked herself, feeling a pall of guilt. Perhaps many years. When she had called him at the office, she could hear his uncertainty, so she'd cut through it quickly. "I'd like to have lunch with you today, Tad. I'll meet you at Bratton's at twelve fifteen."

"Sure," Tad had responded, but then mumbled something about being exhausted as a result of getting up at dawn to catch a flight from Los Angeles. She could tell he wanted to get off the hook, but Tad *always* wanted to get off the hook, no matter what the issue at hand. Even as a child she could recall him wavering uncertainly before every decision, stepping forward one moment, pulling back the next. How odd it was, Eliza reflected, that her daughters, Anne and Catherine, had been imbued with the traits she would have desired for her son. As children, both girls had been as self-assured as Tad was timorous, as assertive as he was passive. Even physically, the girls had been large for their age, while Tad was small and skinny, his features displaying an almost feminine delicacy which made him acutely uncomfortable.

Standing in the crowded foyer of the restaurant, she saw Tad seated alone at a corner table, looking preoccupied and vulnerable, and Eliza realized how much her son, at age twenty-eight, was still the child she had nurtured. He was slumped in his chair, his pale blue eyes staring off into space, his brow furrowed above his lean, handsome face which still bore the smooth lines of adolescence. Eliza had to stand still for a moment amid the jostling crowd, struggling to contain her surging desire to rush to him and clasp him to her as she would a small boy. How she longed to tell him all the simple, prosaic, motherly things—I love you, Tad, no matter what you say or do or how deeply you disappoint me, or yourself for that matter. You are my son and we belong to each other and need each other irrespective of the tensions and angers of the past. None of that means anything anymore. Why let it contaminate the present?

Of course, she couldn't say these things. They would fluster and embarrass him and would cast a cloud over their luncheon. No, she would pull herself together and walk up to his table calmly, as though they had just seen each other the previous day and were picking up where they left off.

"Do you have a reservation, madam?" the headwaiter asked, looking intensely harried. Indeed, everyone around her, Eliza thought, bore that look of skittish agitation that marked the holidays. The noise level of the restaurant, as at most other public places, seemed to rise with the holiday fervor, as though customers felt impelled to talk louder and faster to meet the heightened demands upon their time.

She was standing over the table before Tad noticed her, lurching quickly to his feet. He leaned forward and Eliza offered her cheek for their ceremonial kiss, feeling his moist lips grazing her flesh.

They struggled through the opening amenities. Yes, his sisters were fine, Eliza reported. She had received a Christmas card and accompanying letter from Anne, stating that she was enjoying her life in Australia, that her husband was well, as were her two young children. Catherine, Eliza said, had phoned from London the previous week and sounded ebullient. "I had the distinct suspicion from her tone of voice that she was in love," Eliza said. "If she follows her previous pattern I should be receiving a letter in the next few weeks which begins, 'I have met the most wonderful man and his name is . . .' "

When the waitress arrived Eliza ordered a shrimp salad while Tad scoured the menu with that same small-boy indecisiveness that he always displayed when they'd eaten out. "The Dover sole looks very good, dear," Eliza offered, knowing his predilection for the dish, and Tad, as expected, nodded gravely and said, yes, he'd like the sole. His eyes, she saw now, were reddened and weary and his dark suit looked as though he'd slept in it.

"Did everything go well in Los Angeles?" she asked.

"We closed the deal," he said blandly. "I got that one off my back."

"Good for you," Eliza said, puzzled by his lack of enthusiasm. "Do you want to tell me about it?"

Tad grimaced. "I've been living with it night and day, Mother. I'd just as soon talk about something else."

Very well, Eliza told herself. Tad was being as diffident as usual. She might as well dive in.

"Tad, I'm glad we could have this lunch today. We don't get many opportunities to talk to each other. I want to tell you about some things that are happening to me, dear."

"What things?" She felt his pale eyes upon her.

"Well, I really don't know where to start. I wish Turner were here to issue a press release. . . ."

"Turner? . . ."

"Turner Mead. He's Director of Public Communications for the Church, dear. He's also the man I'm going to marry."

Tad stiffened. "Would you say that again, Mother?"

"I'm going to be married, son."

". . . Married!"

"Precisely."

"When?" Tad was gaping like someone who had just witnessed an astonishing preternatural act.

"Tomorrow morning at eleven. I hope you can make it."

Tad hunched forward in his chair. "You *are* joking, aren't you?"

"Why, Tad, why should I joke about something like this? Do you think your mother has reached too advanced a state of decrepitude to undertake another marriage? Is that it?"

Tad's face flamed with embarrassment as he continued staring at her. ". . . I didn't mean . . . it's just . . . When did you decide?"

Eliza folded her hands, realizing she was enjoying this. "We decided last night."

Tad's head shuddered, like someone clearing the cobwebs. "Now I *know* you're joking."

"We've known each other a long time and we suddenly realized it's something we both wanted to do."

"This is absolutely amazing. Do Catherine and Anne know?"

"I thought I'd call them this afternoon. I wanted to tell you first. Too bad they can't attend. I would love to have all of you there at the mansion. . . ."

". . . The mansion? . . ."

"We're being married at the McCune Mansion. No one lives there anymore, as you know. You can lease it for a day or an afternoon."

"Not a Temple wedding?" There was a hint of indignation in Tad's voice.

"No, there isn't time. The marriage will be sealed in the Temple next month. Both Turner and I prefer it this way."

"Well, I'll be darned."

Eliza saw him retreating into himself. It both surprised and amused her that his reaction would be this intense. She couldn't remember ever before seeing him react so keenly to something she had said, a response that was a pleasant contrast to his look of pained forbearance which customarily marked their colloquies.

"I really didn't expect you to be this confounded, Tad."

Tad shrugged. "Maybe it's just that I never thought about it. About your remarrying, I mean. It seems Dad died so recently. . . ."

"But our marriage died a long time ago, son. You know that as well as I. It just slipped from our grasp. We were like two people struggling to hold onto something which kept eluding us. I'm certain we both had our faults, Tad. We were both responsible."

They lapsed into a pained silence, punctured moments later by their waitress who set the plates before them with a frenzied alacrity. Eliza grasped her glass of water to protect it from the assault.

Tad eyed his sole hungrily, holding his knife and fork. "Well, Nancy and I will be there, all right," Tad said, cutting into his fish.

". . . Be there?"

"At the McCune Mansion."

"Splendid."

"How will the other guests feel? Won't the brethren be taken aback, watching their senior woman official of the Church married in a civil ceremony?"

"I don't really care what the brethren think," she said firmly. "As a matter of fact, Tad, the brethren and their opinions no longer play a role in my life."

Tad's gaze was upon her once again. "Sorry, Mother? . . ."

"I made a decision last night," Eliza said. "I'm going to ask to be released from my position in the Church. I've considered it very carefully and I know it's what I want to do."

"You're going to quit the Relief Society?"

"Exactly, Tad." Eliza was resolutely digging into her salad, but the lettuce resisted as though it had the consistency of fiberglass.

Tad sucked in his breath. "Forgive me if this seems disrespectful, Mother, but it sounds like some sort of midlife crisis."

Eliza emitted a short burst of laughter before she managed to contain herself. "That's priceless, Tad. That really is. I think you've been reading too many books of popular psychology."

Tad blushed. "I didn't mean it as humor."

She put her hand on his arm. "I'm sorry, son. Really I am. When you said that, it just struck me as terribly amusing. . . ."

"Why would you want to leave your job?"

"It's so complicated, Tad. I haven't got to the point where I can simply cite a nice crisp reason. There are many changes taking place in the Church and I sense that I'm just not part of those changes. The Relief Society has been not so much a career as a conviction. Now I sense myself losing that conviction. It's like staring at a beautiful sunset. You keep staring at it and suddenly it's not there anymore. The beauty of your vision has vanished and you are staring into darkness."

"Does this have anything to do with Sloat? Is that it?"

No, she wouldn't deal with that now, Eliza instantly decided. Dana Sloat had caused enough friction in their life without reviving all of it at this time.

"It goes beyond Sloat," she replied simply. "As I said, it's all very complicated."

Tad pushed his plate away. She could see the hurt in his eyes.

"You're very disappointed in me, aren't you, Tad? I'm sorry you feel that way. Truly I am."

Staring down, Tad shook his head slowly. "No, Mother, it's not that."

"What is it then?"

"I'm disappointed in myself, not you."

"I'm afraid I don't understand."

Tad stared glumly at his abandoned food. "You've always been right about Sloat, Mother. I understand that now. Do you remember that awful business at BYU? The business with the spy ring?"

"Of course I do."

"Well, I'm right in the middle of another mess now. It reminds me so much of BYU, I shudder to think of it. And Sloat's put me there. He's put me right in the middle."

Eliza pursed her lips tensely. It astonished her that Tad would mention the so-called "spy ring" now—an incident she had thought was long buried. When Eliza had learned that her son had been one of the BYU students who were taping lectures of suspected "radical" teachers, she had confronted him, demanding an explanation for his actions. Tad had protested meekly that he'd not really been part of the ring, that he'd merely been manipulated into taping that one lecture. Furious, Eliza insisted that, though he had played a minor role in the whole dishonorable scheme, he still had an obligation to expose it to his professors. He had let everyone down. They had quarreled bitterly, and though the subject had never again been mentioned, she knew the scars remained.

"Can you explain what you mean, Tad?"

Tad lifted his hands in a gesture of frustration. "The circumstances are so similar, Mother—similar but different. The bottom line is Sloat has put me in the middle of an ugly situation. A lot is at stake—a lot of money, the trust of my closest friend. And I feel like I'm still sitting their stupidly holding that tape recorder, scared to tell anyone about it, knowing somehow that I'm going to be the fall guy. I know it, but I can't seem to do anything about it."

Sitting across from her son, Eliza felt a welling of compassion. For the first time in so many long years he was reaching out to her. They were talking as mother and son once again. If only she could find a way of helping him, and of understanding what had happened. If only she could lead him across that shadow line that had always restrained him in the past, that invisible barrier that had always crippled his resolve.

"Is there something wrong, sir?"

They both looked up. The waitress was standing there, her eyes fixed on his abandoned fish. Lost in his thoughts, Tad shrugged and did not reply.

"The fish is fine," Eliza told her.

"I would be glad to replace it if it's not satisfactory." Eliza stared indignantly at this stolidly conscientious Mormon matron who stood over them, desperate that she go away before the mood was broken.

"My son has no appetite, that's all," Eliza said firmly.

"I'm sorry—no appetite," Tad repeated.

Discouraged at last, the waitress took the plate and left.

"Would you like to explain some of the particulars?" Eliza asked him. "Sometimes it helps just to hear yourself discuss things aloud. It clarifies your thoughts."

But Tad was shaking his head uneasily. Eliza's instincts were correct; the mood had been shattered. Tad had gotten right to the line once more and had retreated.

"I don't want to go into that now," he said, his voice a virtual whisper. "There are certain things I just have to figure through for myself. No one else can help."

Their eyes met: She saw those handsome blue eyes—so handsome and so weak. "Of course, darling," she said reassuringly. "Just remember, though, if you want to talk . . ."

She signaled the waitress, who was upon them instantaneously. She ordered two portions of Snelgrove's Ice Cream, which they consumed eagerly. She paid the check, and outside, he offered his congratulations once again. "I really look forward to meeting this Turner Mead," Tad said earnestly, but she saw there was a distance in his gaze. That curtain of impersonality had descended once again. They had come together for an evanescent moment; once again they were apart.

Strolling back to her office through the midday crowds, she was overtaken with a sadness she'd felt often when dealing with her son. There was, she felt, so much love hovering in the recesses of his being, yet all of it so repressed, so bottled up.

She wondered why. Was it something she had inadvertently done to him as a child? Was it something his father had done? It was such an intricate, frustrating task, guiding a boy to manhood, trying always to strike that delicate balance between masculinity and gentleness, between courage and love. Maybe they'd botched it somehow.

Or was it something broader—the culture, the Church, the whole value system in which he was raised? Was that where the flaw lay? Perhaps she had made a terrible mistake bringing up her son in a closed society, sealed off from conflict and dissent. Possibly that was why he seemed so pathetically helpless in dealing with the sorts of questions facing him now—questions of character and authority. What an extraordinary paradox, Eliza mused, that whatever the strictures of a church, however all-encompassing its dicta, issues of morality remain so intensely personal. The bitter struggles of right versus wrong are always fought on the lonely battlefield of one's own heart.

Yes, she had made mistakes with Tad—serious ones. And with herself, too. At least she could now deal with her own mistakes. She could no longer help her son, but it was not too late to help herself.

"**E**LIZA, thank God I was able to reach you."

She had just returned to her office when the call from Turner Mead came through. She'd had an intuition he'd be calling.

"Where are you, Turner? Your voice sounds far away."

"I'm at Bountiful. Sky Park. I'm getting on a plane in just a few minutes, Eliza."

Eliza felt her panic rising. "Where are you going?"

"I'm going to try and find Hiram. There's been some more information, darling. I think I know where he is. If I'm right there's a good chance I can bring him back quietly and peacefully. At least I have to try, Eliza. I feel responsible."

"Can't the police do it?" Eliza protested. "There must be someone . . ."

"Trust me, Eliza. This is something I have to do. Believe me, I don't want to go any more than you want me to. But it'll be okay, really it will. I'll be traveling with Hosea Cloor, the man who came by this morning. We'll be using the Snows' private plane. I'll be back tonight."

Despite his assurances, she could hear the anxiety in his voice. She sagged in her chair. Turner was explaining other facts, assuring her of his precautions, but she didn't need to hear any more. Her mind, only moments earlier, had been steeped in plans for their wedding, their honeymoon. And now it all seemed so tentative.

Turner was off to find Hiram. Yes, of course that is what he would have to do.

289

STARING down from his seat directly behind the pilot, Turner Mead watched the stark landscape below redden in the day's afterglow. When they'd taken off forty-five minutes earlier in the small Aero Commander, the countryside had been swathed in white, but they were flying into high desert now, the endless stretches of bleak, rocky landscape broken only occasionally by tiny patches of cultivated land and, here and there, a few isolated houses, their corrugated aluminum roofs glinting in the late sun. These were, Turner knew, the outer reaches of the LDS Kingdom, remote and inviolate. Turner treasured these distant throwbacks to frontier Mormondom that still withstood the urban intrusion, the smogbound sprawl of Salt Lake, but today it seemed like a barren, unyielding lunar landscape—surely the last place he wished to be. The place he wanted to be was at Eliza's side, not in this cramped six-seater which kept shuddering and fishtailing through the rough air on its way to an uncertain destination.

At his right sat Hosea's massive body, spilling out from the narrow confines of his seat, his eyes darting incessantly from the vista below to the map which lay open on his lap. The craft he was flying, which was owned by the Snow family, had been placed at their disposal by Cora Snow with the one admonition: "Find him!"

Well, they would try, but Turner felt the vague dread that had lodged itself in the pit of his stomach. Here they were, ten thousand feet above a horizon of utter desolation, searching for a community which wasn't even on any official map but existed only as a small X which Hosea himself had marked. It was not a precise location, Hosea had stressed before they had left. He could not guarantee they'd find New Nauvoo, nor, if they found it, that they would receive a friendly reception. Indeed, the big man had made it very clear, given the chancy circumstances, that only he

290

should attempt the mission, not Turner Mead. He was trained for trouble, Hosea emphasized. But Cora Snow had pointed out that Turner's prestige and gifts of diplomacy might be the key factor in gaining Hiram's freedom, if indeed he was being held captive, and Turner knew she was right. It was appropriate that he accompany him. If they failed, he could never forgive himself for not being there. Besides, it was because of Turner that the mission had been instigated—Turner and Lillian Thompson.

His meeting with Lillian in the lounge called The Tie Breaker at Big Cottonwood that morning had been a grim enactment of his worst imaginings. From their first moment together, he saw the troubled look in her dark eyes. She'd been a terrible fool, she said, fighting back the tears. Hiram Cobb was the last person she ever would want to harm. He was a wonderful, courageous man. It's just that she wanted so desperately to help her son Richard. After she had discovered the truth about Dana Sloat's background, it occurred to her that the information could possibly help Richard as well as Hiram. After all, Hiram had said he was going to convey the information only to one man; he wasn't even going to publish it. There would be no harm in placing one phone call —to Dawson Sloat. Surely Dawson Sloat would be interested in knowing that the secret file had been discovered and he would, in return, be willing to serve as a pipeline to his father.

Dawson knew her son, Lillian explained; indeed, during the two years Richard had lived at New Nauvoo, he had looked up to Dawson Sloat as his spiritual leader. After being sent home as a missionary, Richard had failed everywhere else, but he liked New Nauvoo and he venerated Dawson. His letters spoke glowingly of the closeness, the spirituality. Then eight months ago his letters had stopped abruptly, and one gray evening, Richard appeared on her doorstep, a forlorn figure dressed in rags. There had been trouble at New Nauvoo, he explained sadly. He'd fallen in love with a girl his age and wanted to marry her, but the girl had already been claimed by an older man, a polygamist, as his future fifth wife. Dawson had been very nice about it, but also very firm. The girl belonged to someone else, he said. Richard would have to wait for another. Heartbroken, Richard decided to leave.

Three weeks after his return to Salt Lake, Lillian got the call she'd always most feared. It was her son, choking on his own panic, calling from the police station. He had been arrested for dealing dope. Please help me, Mother, he cried. Please help.

Lillian knew only one person who could help. She'd been reading about him in the newspaper every day. Dana Sloat could help, and the way to reach him was through Dawson. It was a simple plan that could do no one any harm.

Sitting with Lillian in the lounge, listening to her words, it became vividly clear to Turner what had happened to Hiram Cobb. It also became clear that Turner was as responsible as was Lillian. He had, after all, encouraged Hiram to glean the information. He could easily have called him off had he not been so eager to learn the truth about Sloat. Yes, it was Turner's responsibility that Hiram was in this mess, and it was Turner's responsibility to get him out of it.

"Look there!" It was Hosea's excited, raspy voice coming from the front of the plane. Peering down, Turner saw that the flat, dusty plains were giving way to rocky plateaus. "We're getting close to the Utah–Arizona border," Hosea said, eyes fixed on his map once again. "They call this area the Arizona Strip."

Just southward, Turner knew, lay the majesty of the Grand Canyon. The tourists would be swarming, antlike, over its road and trails, yet here, a small distance to the north, there were no travelers, indeed no roads. Turner saw some animals that looked like wild burros gnawing on the sparse grass, and, some distance away, a few head of cattle were grazing on barren fields.

"The homesteaders never could settle this Godforsaken place," Hosea said, his eyes searching. "You can see the abandoned homes. Just lost dreams. No one could ever make it here. Only at New Nauvoo. It just goes to show what a man can do if he has four or five wives to take care of him." Hosea glanced back at Turner, then continued, his expression serious. "I grew up in one of these places. Colorado City. My ma ran away from the place when I was twelve. All I can remember is quarreling women and dust and heat and my father beating the hell out of me for not digging enough potatoes. Sure was grateful to my ma for taking me away from those people. They were mean as hell."

"Uh, oh, I think we have something," Turner said as the rows of dots on the barren horizon began materializing into shapes he could recognize as homes. Hosea saw them, too.

"It's a settlement," he explained, eyes shifting quickly to the map. "This is northeast of where I had it figured, but anything is possible. You want me to go in low or shall we try and pay them a surprise visit?"

"Makes no difference. They'll know we're coming."

Hosea dipped a wing and put the nose down. The small craft plummeted five hundred feet and Turner felt his stomach lurch. He clasped the arms of his seat tensely. "Damnable air pockets," Hosea snarled, as he steadied the plane once again. "Desert air —never know what you're going to hit."

Turner could make out the houses now, mostly wooden shacks with aluminum roofs to trap the occasional rainfall, but as they drew closer, Turner could see something was wrong. The houses were in total disrepair. There were no farm animals or signs of cultivation. And there were no people—absolutely not a soul.

"If that's your town, they're in sad shape," Hosea said, nervously scrutinizing his map. "That's a ghost town. We've got to look west of here."

They gained altitude and continued their search, flying first toward the west, then shifting north, then doubling back once again—like a great metal beast stalking its prey. The arid, lifeless monotony of the landscape and the droning vibration of the engines made Turner more uneasy. He closed his eyes, trying to think of Eliza, how lovely she was that morning, sitting there across the breakfast table, chatting about their wedding. Their wedding! The notion still seemed abstract to him, like some blissful event happening to someone else. He was actually marrying Eliza Hastings! They would be able to go home together every night, to have breakfast every morning, to appear openly together as husband and wife.

He thought of the terror in her voice when he phoned her. "Don't go, Turner. Let the police find him. Please don't go." He had tried to explain to her his sense of personal responsibility. This was something he had to do. Besides, these people were not dangerous. He would be back by nightfall and they would have the evening together. That was a promise.

But now, opening his eyes again, Turner regretted the false promise. The colors below were deepening to reds and maroons with the approach of twilight. They were doubling back and forth and Turner could see the worry etched on Hosea's face.

And he felt a jolt of resentment. What an ugly irony that, at this moment in his life—a life that contained more than its share of self-denial—he would find himself in this fragile craft shuddering amid the desert winds, headed for a place that seemed not even to exist.

"It's getting tougher," Hosea called back to him. "The shadows get longer, and you could miss an entire village."

The plane turned to the south again, its wings buffeted by the bumpy air. Turner rubbed his tired eyes and considered what a pleasant relief it must be to be able to swear—to give vent to an absolutely withering chain of angry, colorful, virulent expletives. All his life he had trained himself never to utter one of those words, but by God that's one of the things he would change. He would teach himself to swear with the best of them.

He peered absently toward the ground again and came forward in his seat: There it was, partially shrouded by the lengthening shadows of the rocky hills.

"Hosea . . ."

"Yes, I see it."

The town was nestled between rocky outcroppings that scarred the red mountains. Hosea turned abruptly to catch a second look, losing altitude quickly, engines whining their protest. They swept across the chain of hills, then doubled back, much lower this time. The translucent sky was deepening to green at the horizon. And suddenly there it was again, hiding among the long shadows and the purple fingers of the sagebrush. It was all hurtling by, but they could see the clusters of houses, some wooden but some of stalwart stone and brick, now the broad gravel road that served as the main street, with houses lining either side, and also farmhouses tucked among the surrounding hills and gullies. There were fields under cultivation and farm animals grazing. They could even see a little stream twisting down the hillside. Several trucks and vans were visible along the main street, but there were no people—no one at all. The main street terminated at the foot of a jagged rocky hillside, and seeing it, Hosea pulled up and ascended once again.

"No doubt about it," Turner said. "If there is a place called New Nauvoo, that's got to be it."

"I wish we'd found it an hour ago," Hosea shouted. "Even if I find a place that's smooth enough to land we'll never get out again tonight. Not without runway lights. We could fly back to Salt Lake and try again tomorrow. But if they're holding Hiram Cobb captive . . ."

"If they've got Hiram we've only made it worse by flying low over the town," Turner put in. "They might get panicked."

Hosea nodded gravely. "Mrs. Snow would want us to go in tonight. That's what she would want." He studied the landscape. "That gravel road looks pretty straight once it gets out of town. I might be able to get us down, but it could be a long night down there."

"Let's give it a closer look," Turner said.

A few miles to the north the road widened and Hosea brought them in low, casting his apprehensive gaze over the terrain. Turner heard him mumbling under his breath. When they had pulled up, he turned back to him once more.

"I'm not one of these whiz-kid bush pilots," Hosea grumbled.

"Give it your best shot," Turner said, sensing immediately the foolishness of his comment. His "best shot" would be their only shot.

Hosea shrugged in resignation and banked sharply. They were plunging earthward again, engines whining, the craft lurching to one side, then righting itself. Turner tugged his seat belt tighter, feeling the moisture on his palms. The plane was hovering just above the ground, brush racing past them in a surreal blur. They slammed down onto the gravel now, bouncing once, twice, veering suddenly. Turner heard the rocks hammering against the underside of the craft, glimpsed Hosea grappling urgently with the controls, all of it reminding him of some preposterous amusement park ride, careening along in their fragile aluminum tube, landscape hurtling by, everything out of control. And suddenly they were slowing and the terrible noise had stopped and so had the jolting.

When they had come to a stop neither of them said anything. Turner heard his own breath coming in short bursts and saw the clouds of dust settling around them like a great red mist.

"Thank the Lord," Hosea murmured finally.

"Good job," Turner told him.

"I just hope I can get us up again. I'd better check to see there's no damage." Hosea reached into a side compartment and Turner was surprised to see him remove a rifle.

"You're not planning to go out there with weapons?"

Hosea stared back at him stonily.

"I'm certain these people have enough weapons to arm a Marine division," Turner said. "I'm told these colonies are like armed camps."

"We must be able to defend ourselves," Hosea protested.

Turner swallowed hard. He could see the fear written across his companion's face. Surely their reception committee would also notice it. It was as though Hosea felt he was returning to Colorado City.

"One of us should stay with the plane," Turner said. "Besides if I walk to town alone it may seem less threatening." Hosea started to protest, but Turner raised his hand. "If there's trouble you can radio for help."

Hosea seemed embarrassed, but relieved. "At least take some flares with you. If there's trouble, fire one of them and I'll get on that radio in a flash."

They both deplaned, peering around them uneasily, like astronauts leaving their spaceship. The bleak rocky vistas that spread out around them acquired a vague malevolence amid the maroon glow of twilight.

Turner shook hands grimly with Hosea, then turned, and started to walk. The only sound he heard was the steady crunch of the harsh gravel against his shoes. He felt vulnerable and very much alone. He passed a cluster of fuel storage tanks; other than that, nothing. But his eyes kept searching restlessly.

He walked for thirty minutes before the settlement rose like a mirage out of the stark wilderness, the rocky hills looming behind, framed by the red bars of sunset, like stripes on a flag. He walked past a wooden farmhouse, its windmill fluttering in the breeze. An aged pickup truck stood in front, but there were no signs of life, just the gravel road stretching ahead into the hills. The town seemed absolutely still.

All they know how to do is hide, Turner told himself in disgust as he kept walking, passing a patch of scrubby grass, a scattering of trees. The homes, rudimentary in construction, like pioneer cabins, were in good repair. There were curtains in the windows, even window boxes with flowers. Turner thought he saw a child's face staring from one window, but it darted away. The sound of a dog barking came from inside a house, and he thought he heard a baby's cry. A small black dog with white spots raced out from behind a van, but cowered, as though threatened by an alien scent.

Even the animals were playing hide-and-seek.

As the road twisted upward, the mountain ahead, with its angry sawtooth ridges, glowed an angry red against the fading horizon. The scrubbed-clean desert air carried a chill now, and Turner realized the absurd inadequacy of his business suit. Something scurried by his feet, startling him. He saw the jackrabbit, ears tucked back in terror, racing away. Otherwise, there was silence.

Reaching a rise in the road, he looked down into the main part of the settlement. Lights were blinking on, and there was the tang of burning sagebrush in the air. A distant sound reached his ears. It was music!

Yes, the sound was unmistakable now—there were fiddles and laughing voices. It was like a celebration. What could they be celebrating? Surely they'd heard the plane. They knew strangers were out here somewhere.

Turner's face darkened. He quickened his pace. As he neared the center of town, the houses grew larger, with broad porches and painted shutters. Some were sturdy, two-story stone houses, stolid frontier structures Turner had seen so often in the rustic precincts of Mormondom.

Then he saw them, all six of them. They were big men, wearing denim overalls and boots and broad-rimmed hats.

They were standing in the road, waiting for him.

SHE had summoned them to gather at four o'clock and yet now, only moments before the hour, she still had no idea what she would say to them. They had been, over these last few years, her closest associates and, in a sense, her dearest friends. She owed them an honest, lucid explanation—that much she knew. She had tried to jot down some thoughts and then gave up, gripped yet again by her overriding sense of futility. What did it all matter when the man who dominated her thoughts, who inhabited her innermost being, was even now roaming about some Godforsaken wilderness, questioning a barbarous cult about the whereabouts of Hiram Cobb? As the afternoon had progressed, hour by hour, Eliza was overtaken ever more strongly by the premonition that something terrible would happen to Turner, that their marriage would never take place—that it was total folly, as though some malevolent spirit out there were playing a terrible game with them, holding out the promise of euphoric bliss and then yanking it away again. The premonition angered as well as terrified her: She was not a woman given to random fears or superstitious forebodings.

She had tried to apply reason. Turner was, after all, a cautious and prudent man. He had been accompanied by a professional security man who was armed. Surely they would know how to cope with these strange people.

But none of it worked. She knew she had lost him. He had been torn from her just when their brightest hopes were to be realized.

If only she had dissuaded him. Lord knows, she had tried. She had done all she could, yet was left with the residual ache that it was not enough.

"Sister Eliza . . ."

It was her secretary, Rachel Loftus, poised by the door.

". . . The staff. . . . You asked me to assemble them at four. They are waiting outside."

Eliza flinched. Of course, the staff! She would have to tell them now. If only she could find the words. It would come as a surprise to them—that much Eliza knew. The only person she had informed was Rachel, whose kindly face was pale with distress. "Forgive me for intruding," Rachel said, pausing to marshal her thoughts, ". . . but the sisters think you've assembled them for a Christmas party. They have little gifts and flowers for you. They are anticipating a happy little Christmas message for them. Something inspirational. . . ."

Eliza sighed in frustration, and sank back in her chair. "Something inspirational! Good Lord, Rachel!"

The secretary flicked her hands helplessly. "If only you could postpone your decision, even for a few weeks. If you went away for a brief rest you might even change your mind. . . ."

Eliza shook her head in resignation. "No, dear Rachel, my son suggested the same thing. I must get this over with now and not let it linger."

Rachel dabbed the wetness from her cheek and then retreated quickly from the office. Moments later the women were streaming in, all twenty of them, chattering joyously among themselves, greeting Eliza, depositing their gifts upon her broad desk. Mustering all her resources of self-control, Eliza did her best to return their felicitations, her face frozen in a resolute smile. They had arranged themselves before her now and she surveyed the familiar faces. She loved them, as only one can love those who have shared so much of one's life—doing the work they had all believed to be most meaningful and fulfilling.

Now she must tell them as quickly and simply as possible.

"Sisters, I desperately wish I had some joyous message to enhance your Christmases, but I do not," she began, her eyes moving from one face to the next, as though instinctively searching for some hidden wellspring of strength and nurture. "What I must tell you is that I have decided to ask for my release as President of the Relief Society. It is a calling I cherish, but one which I cannot now pursue. With the advent of a new year a successor will no doubt be here in my stead. . . ."

Eliza saw the stricken look on the women before her. She

heard the cries of ". . . No, Sister. . . . Not so. . . . Surely you can't mean . . ." Eliza tried not to notice the tears already appearing in their eyes. No, she would not surrender to sentiment.

"It would be tempting to give you glib reasons for my decision. Glib and convenient. No one would be offended that way. No hurt feelings, no toes trampled upon. But I cannot do that.

"You see, two nights ago I found myself at a meeting in my home. I had thought it would be a fairly routine meeting but it wasn't. Suddenly I was sitting there, listening to my sisters tell me things I'd already heard but had chosen not to hear. They were awakening me, awakening ideas from deep within. Troubling ideas, some of them. Dangerous ideas, perhaps. But I am left with them, you see. I can no longer pretend they are not there.

"So you see, dear Sisters, I am out of step. I believe all that matters is how we live and how we love, day to day, and how God instructs and inspires us. I believe fervently that we must use the resources of our sisterhood to continue to progress as women and not permit ourselves to get shunted into a role that diminishes rather than fulfills us. I do not think it is important that we build a Kingdom or that we bring great armies of people into our Church or erect grand new Temples or absorb vast corporations."

Eliza fought for breath. The office seemed suddenly hot and claustrophobic. She saw their eyes upon her—sad and expectant —but the contours of their features were growing fuzzy.

"I feel a deep sense of disappointment, of course. A deep loss. That loss is offset by the fact that I am blessed with the love of a very dear and righteous man. I worried about that love at first, worried that without it I could not have had the courage to ask for my release, but I know now that is not true. My decision to leave was separate from all that."

Eliza felt her words choking off. Don't break down now, she prodded herself. You have gotten this far. See it through.

"You have all been like a family to me. I love you very much. God loves you, too. . . ."

Eliza stopped talking and sat down. She realized her head was swimming. She saw the sisters approach her, one by one, and heard their kind words of compassion, but their faces were indistinct, as were their voices. It was as though a veil had descended around her, locking her into her own emotions, isolating her from the kindnesses of those around her. She sensed their love, but she also knew she was alone.

Her office was empty once again. The air was stifling. Eliza went to the window, and breathed deeply. The snow was starting once more.

THE men came to a halt twenty feet away from Turner, inspecting him warily. Their expressionless gaze reminded him of zoo creatures viewing their unwanted visitors.

I will give it a try, Turner told himself, confronting his reception committee. "Good evening, Brothers," he said, pronouncing his words carefully like someone addressing those unfamiliar with the tongue.

The men did not respond.

"My name is Turner Mead, Brothers. The work I do is with the LDS Church. Your Church as well as mine."

Again, there was no sign of recognition. Could it be they've lost their ability to speak the English language? Turner asked himself. Was this whole exercise futile? He began to wish he'd taken Hosea with him after all.

From the corners of his eyes Turner could sense still others gathering around, edging cautiously toward the center of the gravel street. There were little towheads in overalls, men in rough farm clothes, women in long dresses with crinolined tucks, their hair pulled back and parted down the middle as in pioneer days. Their faces were devoid of lipstick or rouge. They were all standing there, a tableau frozen in time from an epoch long forgotten. They were watching, waiting. Turner felt their eyes upon him. He realized the music had stopped.

"You sure you know where you are?" The speaker was much taller than the others. With his full blond beard and flowing hair, he reminded Turner of a Viking.

"I am, of course, in New Nauvoo," Turner replied patiently.

"And why are you here?" The Viking spoke with the singsong rustic twang of rural Utah.

"To find a lost brother. I hope you can help me."

The big man stared at him grimly. "Come with me." Turning, he beckoned him to follow.

302

Turner fell in behind him, several of the others trailing at a comfortable distance.

As he walked, Turner realized his legs were rubbery. All that day he had felt a gnawing apprehension, but now it had finally congealed into open fear. He had not expected to be received with cordiality at New Nauvoo, of course, but there was something coldly rehearsed, even ritualistic, about their reception that chilled him. It was as if these men knew exactly who he was and how he was to be dealt with and were going about their tasks with practiced calm. And he wondered once again, why the music? Was that, too, part of some eerie ritual—a ritual that would soon involve him?

A new cluster of men arrayed themselves ahead, staring at him with the same steely detachment, like spectators at an event in which they had no direct interest. The big Viking was approaching a large house of gray stone that was taller than any of the others. He stood poised atop the great stone steps that terminated on a wide expanse of porch. The big oak door at the entrance stood open.

This is the time for aplomb, Turner told himself. He must not betray fear. His hosts would surely react as a horse to a skittish rider. Behind their rough frontier facades, these might very well be harmless folk, primitive in their customs and awkward in their manners. After all, their roots were the same as Turner's. They shared his genes, his faith. Indeed, in a sense, they were living lives which were truer to the ideals of their forebears than was Turner or any of his colleagues who dwelled amid the air-conditioned, concrete-and-steel grandiosity of Church Headquarters.

Yet they still frightened him. They scared him to death.

The big Viking motioned him through the great door, following close behind. It was dark in the front hallway, which smelled vaguely of candles and bergamot. They passed through an arched doorway into a large parlor, the shiny oak floors groaning slightly under their weight. In the dim light Turner caught glimpses of a spinning wheel, copper candle-sconces, a wide sofa, its dark velvet upholstery edged in lace, a rustic rocking chair of split timber, and, at the center of the room, a fireplace and hearth of old brick. On the walls were splendid daguerreotypes and a blue-and-white quilt of intricate patterns. The room and its furnishings were a perfect evocation of an old pioneer home.

"Be seated," the big man said, motioning toward the sofa. He himself remained standing, letting his breath out wearily like a man who bore a heavy burden.

Turner lowered himself onto the sofa. He started to say something, then fell silent. The big Viking remained by the door, shoulders squared, sentinel-like.

Several minutes passed. Through the gaps in the heavy curtains Turner saw that the day's last light was quickly fading before the encroaching shadows. Once darkness fell they would be stranded here for the night since the plane could not take off. He could hear sounds of people hurrying by, their muffled voices radiating excitement. Suddenly the music started again—guitars, banjos and fiddles. Turner recognized some of their melodies—the lively tunes of the Mormon past.

Impatiently, Turner turned to the big man who was guarding him. "May I ask your name?" Turner asked softly.

The big man hesitated, then said, "My name is Penrose."

"Very well, Penrose. Now I wonder if you would also be good enough to tell me why you have brought me here?"

Penrose straightened his shoulders. "To wait."

"Wait for what?"

Penrose did not respond.

"I would like very much to meet Dawson Sloat," Turner said, his words coming slow and patient, as though talking to a child. "Would you be kind enough to arrange that?"

Turner studied Penrose's face for a reaction, but there was none. "You shall wait," he repeated.

Now there was a sudden clatter of activity at the front door and the sound of approaching footsteps in the hall. A figure loomed in the doorway.

The young woman who confonted him was uncommonly tall and comely, with striking blue eyes, her blond hair center-parted and brushed back from her temples into two wings. She wore a draped dress of blue calico with ribbon-edged peplum. She stared at Turner as he rose from the sofa and Turner stepped forward, his hand extended in greeting, but the young woman did not move to accept it.

"So you are our visitor." Her eyes kept flicking back and forth, her expression a mixture of suspicion and curiousity.

"I am, indeed," Turner replied.

Her face was grave. "The Saints in this corner of the Lord's vineyard do not covet visitors." Though her words seemed harsh, there was a gentleness in her voice that assuaged their bluntness.

"I come in friendship, Sister," Turner persisted. "I wish to see Dawson."

The young woman's eyes met Turner's and held his gaze for several moments before she replied. "Of course," she said simply.

Turner breathed a sigh of relief. "And can you take me to him?"

"There is a festivity tonight," she said. "You shall be his guest."

Turner started to frame his next question but the young woman was suddenly gone, having vanished as quickly as she had appeared. Only Penrose remained with him, his dim blue eyes scrutinizing him with distrust.

"Do you have weapons?" he asked.

Turner shook his head. "No." He was glad he had not taken Hosea's advice to carry the flares and their threatening-looking launcher.

"Then you will come with me."

Penrose led the way up the darkened street, the sounds of the music and dancing growing ever louder. Turner shivered in his thin suit. The chill, clean air seemed to splinter around him, breaking to pieces at his feet.

When he was led into the big tent, the sudden bursting forth of noise and body heat had his senses reeling. He had expected a party, but had not been prepared for anything like the spectacle that lay before him now.

There were, Turner calculated quickly, at least three hundred persons crowded into the tent, caught up in the pleasure of eating, dancing and singing. The air seemed to throb with the sheer release of their animal energies. At the center of the tent stood four tall bearded men, exuberantly plunking out their melodies on their ancient, but immaculately polished instruments. The dancers were performing a lusty polka, their bodies hurtling exuberantly around the floor with a raucous abandon. They were young, most of them, attractive and healthy, faces reddened by the sun. The women wore bright calicoes and gingham and Turner noticed some young girls in ruffled pantalets, their hair tied in plaid ribbon. The men were clad in denim overalls, some in buckskins

and brightly colored shirts. A few wore cowboy hats and some of
the teenagers wore shorts and mountaineer's leggings, their an-
kles jangling with spurs. Turner's eyes fell on one handsome
young couple, their bodies whirling amid a torrid polka. In the
steamy heat, the girl's bodice had shrunk against the graceful
contours of her figure and the boy's perspiration-soaked buckskins clung like a leotard as they circled each other—two graceful
young animals in their mating dance. The young couple, like the
entire assemblage, exuded a palpable sexuality, a letting-loose of
carnal glee. Yet the faces around them reflected an almost Biblical
piety. These were God's children, Turner thought, in all their
innocent joy.

So caught up was he in the spectacle, Turner had not noticed
that the big Viking had vanished from his side. Where moments
before he was virtually a prisoner, now he was a mere invisible
onlooker whose intrusion seemed unimportant to the celebrants.
Turner's eyes searched the room for the tall, striking young
woman who had visited them before, but she was nowhere to be
seen, nor was anyone who would seem to command the special
attention of leadership. What odd games these seemingly innocent children play. Turner sensed he was being observed, his
actions carefully monitored, yet everyone now ignored him and
let him freely observe them at play.

Very well, observe them he would. He, too, could play their
patient games.

Wandering among them, Turner could see clusters of women
huddled together, laughing and gossiping. Now and then a man
would come over and ask one to dance. These were, no doubt, the
plural wives, waiting ever-patiently for their husbands' attentions, avoiding those of other men. They were strikingly good-
looking women, their faces washed clean of expectation: They
were not so much wives as vessels for procreation, Turner sensed.

Behind the women lay vast tables of food, the humid air
heavy with the aroma of pork, molasses cakes, squaw cabbage,
cornmeal and fried potatoes. The tables were decorated with
flowers, greens and pigweed. A knot of celebrants was stationed
at the table, eating and drinking. Turner helped himself to the
wassail, his taste buds pricked with the faint alcohol bite of grape
wine. The Word of Wisdom was being bent at New Nauvoo,
Turner understood—a fact which helped account for the sensual

abandon. Even as he had finished one glass, someone was refilling it, someone else handing a plate loaded down with victuals. Standing in their midst, Turner failed to notice the arrival of a newcomer, a man for whom, by dint of respect and reverence, they quickly cleared a wide path. He had a fine leonine head and long ebony hair, and his small dark eyes glowed like embers. While his chest was strong, even brawny, his legs had the wasted look of a longtime invalid. He was seated in a wheelchair. Behind him stood the tall blond woman Turner had seen before.

There was no mistaking his identity. This was Dana Sloat's secret—this formidable-looking cripple who sat assessing him with wary, intelligent eyes. He moved himself closer.

"And you are Brother Mead, of course, who has graciously descended upon us in his thundering bird to bring hosannas before the Lord on Christmas Eve." A fleeting, ironic smile played across his lips.

"Yes, I am Turner Mead, but that is not exactly why I have descended upon you."

"Ah, then you have come to read us *Doctrine and Covenants*. Verily, Brother, a Christmas oration!"

So Dawson still wished to play, Turner thought. The veiled maneuvers had concluded, but now came the word games.

"I would not presume to sermonize," Turner said. "Now that I have had the good fortune to encounter the brethren at New Nauvoo, I see they need no sermons from Salt Lake."

Dawson's face seemed almost cherubic when he smiled, but those small, smoldering eyes, positioned slightly too close together, seemed vaguely ominous. They were the eyes of a fanatic lodged incongruously in this gentle, supple face: They were the eyes of his father.

"Tonight you witness our innocent revelries," Dawson said. "We are a simple people, Brother Mead. We have gratitude for the blessings which have been poured upon us. We feel a tenderness toward the earth."

Turner noticed that the crowd around them had melted away. Though the party continued, a respectful space had been cleared so that they could have their privacy.

"Your people radiate great joy," Turner said. "That should give you satisfaction."

"No, it should give *you* satisfaction, Brother. I already know that joy, but it is you who should understand that there are still outposts of our Kingdom where the ways of Zion are practiced as our Prophet meant them to be—pure and fundamental, not vulgarized by the incursions of Gentiles. 'Doubt not but be believing, and begin as in times of old. . . .' The Book of Mormon tells us that, but those words ring hollow in our Kingdom."

"The ways and beliefs of our Fundamentalist brethren are understood by the hierarchy in Salt Lake. . . ."

"A lie, Brother!" Dawson declared, his thin voice stabbing the heavy air. "We are all children of one Father, yet we have been compelled to sever from the Church to uphold the dictates of our conscience. Our fundamentalist brothers are disfellowshiped, excommunicated, forced to scatter to the remote corners of the Kingdom which we should in all rights claim for ourselves."

"It is pointless to refight history's old controversies," Turner said, trying to assuage the sudden rage he heard in his host's voice. "When it was revealed to our great Prophet that Zion should be joined to the outside world certain compromises were mandated."

"Compromise! You cannot compromise God's teachings. Look at me, Brother Mead. I am a humble cripple but I live in God's light. I lead a loving and prosperous community. I have six lovely and fecund wives. I have sired fourteen children. And do you know why? Because I am of the royal descent of Ephraim. Because I am a Savior upon Mount Zion and my wives are Queens and Elect Ladies, whose heritage is superior to all the blood-stained nobility of the outside world. Our forebears comprise the Royalty of Heaven, dwelling in the majesty of the Celestial Kingdom. This heritage is mine without compromise. Where is there need for compromise?"

A handsome towheaded boy of seven or eight appeared bearing two mugs of wassail, which he handed shyly to Dawson and Turner. Watching Dawson sip the thick liquid, Turner saw the brooding anger in his face. "I know it is because of this . . . this apostate that you have come," Dawson said finally. "But as I sit here and regard you I ask myself, who has sent you? Has my father sent you? But then I answer, no, verily you do not resemble the gander-shanked, brush-headed pieces of meat my father would dispatch on such a mission. No, I do not believe my father sent you."

"No one sent me," Turner replied. "I come as a friend. I come out of personal concern."

Dawson guided his wheelchair still closer to him, peering up at him quizzically. "Personal concern! I did not know personal concern still reigned amid the burning evangelical fires of Salt Lake."

Turner sighed. "Let's not play games with words, Dawson. I am sure you are far more skilled than I."

Dawson did not seem to hear. "You and my father are as one. It is power that guides you, not love. Our great Prophet, Brigham Young, told us, 'All the power that wealth can bestow is a mere shadow,' but it is these shadows you chase, as does my father."

"Hiram Cobb intends you no harm. Why did you reach out to bring this man into your midst?"

Dawson sat forward in his chair, the veins in his broad neck bulging. "You speak of this Cobb as though he were a true Saint, yet he is an apostate, a doer of evil deeds. He was bent on my father's public humiliation. You must understand something, Brother Mead. I have never known love from my father, nor do I feel love toward him. The disease which crippled me in childhood rendered me an embarrassment to him—something weak and imperfect, something to be hidden from the world. Yet he has protected me. He has seen to it that I could live out my life according to the ideals which I embrace. He has seen to it that, though concealed like an animal, I could still live like a man and function like a man in God's Kingdom. And so I must protect him as he protected me. Protect him from the humiliation that Hiram Cobb sought to bring down upon him."

"Then your father knows Hiram is here? He knows your intentions?"

Dawson's face darkened. "It is *your* intentions that concern me, not my father's. You are obviously a man of lofty position—too lofty to be interested in an anonymous apostate like Hiram Cobb. Why would a man of stature secure a plane and fly all the way to New Nauvoo just to pay a visit to someone like Hiram Cobb? Why, unless he, too, wanted to wreak personal vengeance on Dana Sloat or on his crippled and demented son?"

Turner saw Dawson glowering up at him from his wheelchair, his hands whitening as he tightly clasped the sidebars. He started to rise as though in defiance of his own impotence, then sat back, his gaze shifting from Turner to the big men who now surrounded them, pressing in on them slowly, relentlessly. Watching Dawson, Turner realized this young zealot was weighing his options. Turner could easily imagine him simply dismissing his life, canceling it out, casually yet decisively, like choking off a campfire. The men surrounding them had the look of predators sensing a kill. They were awaiting the decision.

"I seek no vengeance," Turner said, struggling one last time to quell the rising tension. "I am not an ally of Hiram Cobb. I do not even agree with his beliefs. But I care for his welfare. I want to see him, to know that he is safe. I want to bring him back to Salt Lake with me in the morning. Surely these are modest aims, Dawson. They pose no threat to you."

Turner saw the crippled man shake his head slowly, then exchange knowing glances with those around them, and he knew it was all hopeless. There was no way of penetrating the layers of hatred and paranoia. He was sick of these ridiculous fanatics with their false reverence and pious rhetoric—sick of them, and scared of them, too.

"You are right, Brother Mead," Dawson said quietly. "You have gone to much trouble and expense to see your friend and I have been less than hospitable. I shall arrange for you to be taken to Hiram. I shall see that it is done."

Could it be that Hiram was really all right after all? Turner wondered. Could it possibly be? Turner saw Dawson give the signal, a quick flick of the head. He felt them close in as though a great web had descended upon him. They were merely guiding him at first, moving him across the tent, but as they moved they closed ever tighter, walking more briskly. They were not quite carrying him and yet he was moving as much from their power as from his own. They were binding his wrists—he felt that now, and also felt himself stumbling, his legs not sustaining him, yet he was moving still faster through the milling throng. Faces turned toward him as they went past; someone laughed derisively as though he were the object of some profane joke.

The frosty air hit him suddenly and they were outside, poised before a small van. Turner tried to free his hands but they'd been securely bound. They were pushing him roughly into the back seat of the van. There was a driver in front wearing a wide-rimmed hat. He sat hunched over the wheel in the darkness. The

van was moving now, picking up speed, bouncing along the rough
road. Turner's chest was heaving and his shirt was drenched in
sweat. He tugged agonizingly against the rope which bound his
wrists. His hands were growing numb.

"Where are you taking me?" Turner demanded.

"Away from this shithole—I'll tell you that." Turner heard the
words but they confounded him. The driver turned now, and
Turner saw his boyish face.

"Who are you? I know you, don't I?" Turner said.

"I'm going to get you out of here, Mr. Mead," the youth said,
his voice shrill with excitement. "I promised my mother I'd come
back and get you out and that's what I'm going to do. Hell, I owe
it to you anyway."

It was Lillian Thompson's boy! The sudden recognition stung
him alert. He remembered the boy now. As a favor to Hiram, he'd
given him a few jobs as a free-lance photographer—Hiram had
told him that no one would hire him because he'd been sent home
in disgrace as a failed missionary. And now here he was, returning
the favor!

"Why did they turn me over to you so willingly?" Turner
asked.

"They thought I was Penrose," Richard said. "It took a little,
uh, persuading to convince Penrose that I should take his place."

"Where are we headed?"

"To your plane. That's the only place we can go."

"There's no point in going to the plane. We can't get off the
ground till dawn."

"Don't worry, Mr. Mead. I've thought of everything."

Turner saw the boy's face beaming with idiot glee, like a juve-
nile delinquent off on a joyride. If Richard Thompson were indeed trying to rescue him, Turner thought, he was going about it
the same way he'd done everything else in his young life—he
was botching the job. They'd end up sitting in the futile airplane,
waiting for Dawson and his men to descend upon them once
again. And then what? Dawson would deal with them as he had
with poor Hiram. But what *had* happened to Hiram? Surely Richard would know. Turner started to frame his question as they hit
a jarring bump, his head striking the metal roof with a resounding
thud. The boy was driving at a maniacal speed down the rough

road. "Ya-hoooo!" he was shouting, waving his hat in the wind. A sick feeling lodged itself in the pit of Turner's stomach.

The plane loomed before them suddenly, crouching across the road like a great gray bird. Richard slammed on the brakes, the truck sliding through the gravel amid a cloud of flying dirt. When they'd stopped they saw Hosea before them, illuminated by the van's headlights. He was holding a rifle.

"Say something quick before he shoots," Richard told him sharply.

"It's me—Turner. We're coming out."

"Mr. Mead?" Hosea came running with a startled yelp. "What's going on?"

Richard helped Turner out of the van, freeing his wrists in the process. "We've got to get on that plane," the boy called out. "We have to be ready."

Hosea stared at him suspiciously. "Who's the hippie?"

"He's a friend," Turner said. "He's trying to help us."

"If we can't take off what's the use of getting on the plane?" Hosea said. "The van is our only hope."

"No way," Richard shouted at him, his voice a frightened whine. "They have cars faster than that old van. They'd catch up to us before we reach the highway."

Hosea raised his hands in a gesture of frustration.

"We've got to get the engines started so we can be ready," the boy repeated. "If we don't get our asses out of here we'll be boiling in tar just like that Hiram guy."

"My God. Is that what they did to Hiram?" Turner looked at Hosea, who was nodding in grim confirmation. Turner felt sickened.

"They brought the body down to the plane a few minutes ago all wrapped up in white sheets like a mummy," Hosea said. "He's quite dead, I'm afraid. What happened out there, Mr. Mead? Who did this to him?"

"Shit!" was the only word Turner could muster. It was the first time he'd ever used that word and he felt it appropriate. He thought of Hiram's voice on the telephone—always polite, always precise, always patient.

"They have enough tar left for the rest of us," Richard said. "That's why we've got to get aboard that plane."

"Can't you get this hippie fruithead to understand we can't take off on a narrow road in the middle of the night?" Hosea exploded.

"There'll be light," Richard screamed at him. "There'll be so much light you can't believe it." He bounded up the stairs into the cabin, then turned to them again. "I set a time charge under their fuel tanks. They have a big butane tank—a beauty. There's another for diesel fuel. When they go off they'll light up the sky."

Turner and Hosea stared at each other for a brief moment, then followed the boy into the cabin. Hosea sank into the pilot's seat, Turner directly behind him. "Are you absolutely positive you're telling us the truth?" Hosea said.

"It's my ass as much as yours."

"How far away are the tanks?"

"Just over that little rise up ahead."

Hosea whirled around in his seat. "My God, you'll blow us up, too."

"The tanks won't explode," Richard protested. "Just burn." He checked his watch nervously.

"He's right," Turner said. "Richard is right."

"How soon do you think the tanks will go off?" Hosea asked.

"Any moment now," Richard said. Turner saw him squirm with discomfort.

"What time did you set them for?"

The boy took a breath. "A few minutes ago."

"Shit," Turner said again.

"What do you want me to do, Mr. Mead?" Hosea said in a low rasp.

"Start the engines. We have no choice."

Cursing softly, Hosea prodded the engines to life. The noise seemed deafening after the stillness outside.

The men strapped themselves into their seats. Turner noticed Hiram's body at the rear of the cabin, looking like a pile of rags. He could feel his own nerves stretched taut.

They waited. The men kept a nervous watch on the road, alert to moving shapes. They would surely come after them soon, Turner reasoned. They would hear the engines of the plane and they would come running.

The minutes crawled like hours. The vibration from the engines sounded to Turner like an iron wheel grinding within his temple.

"Where's your big light show?" Hosea asked the boy in disgust. "I'm waiting but I'm not seeing."

Richard was perspiring heavily. "It'll come."

"You sure you rigged it right?" Hosea demanded.

"I said it will come!"

"Have you ever rigged something like this before, Richard?" Turner asked.

"No, but I know how to do it. I've watched it being done plenty of times."

"And exactly how did you know how to time those fuses?" Hosea asked.

Richard shrugged. "Look, I'm no lunatic. I saw a plane and I saw a pilot. I was going to get on this plane whether I found Mr. Mead or not."

Suddenly Hosea was out of his seat, his face livid with rage. He grasped the youth by his shirt, yanking him out of his seat as though he were a doll. "What have you done to us!" Hosea roared at him, shaking him until his head bobbed back and forth helplessly.

Turner left his seat, too, trying to restrain the big man but it was useless. Richard shrieked in pain, his face transformed suddenly into an orange mask glowing in the darkness.

Turner's eyes shot toward the windows, which were brilliantly luminescent. "Good Lord!" he said, wide-eyed.

The plane seemed to rock as the entire horizon was suddenly aglow in a lurid incandescence. There were successive shudders as the great fireball spread before them.

Richard tumbled back into his seat as Hosea released him, his eyes popping wide at the spectacle. "You see? I told you!" he shrieked at the pilot.

Yes, he had told them, Turner thought. The boy had saved them after all. He uttered to himself a quick prayer of thankfulness. Quick but heartfelt.

Moments later they started to roll.

PEEKING his head into little Dana's room, Tad realized it had been a long time since he'd tucked the children into bed. He'd all but forgotten the special sounds, smells and textures. His four-year-old son was seated stark-naked amid a small chaos of discarded clothing, toy cars and torn kites, talking to himself, as was his custom, about the day's events. Scooping him up, Tad felt his body warmth against him and smelled the musky little-boy odor, that indefinable residue of candy, dirt, baby sweat and sheer animal mischief. He gave the squirming body a quick hug, then helped him into his pajamas, feeling the skin so softly firm it seemed almost rubbery in texture. Sensing the day's end was near, Dana was suddenly a maze of flailing arms and legs, but Tad plunked him firmly into bed, planting a final kiss on his pouting cheek.

"Time for your prayers, son," Tad demanded, and the small boy responded with tentative murmurs, his eyes suddenly drowsy. "Tell me a story," Dana begged, but seconds later his eyes were tightly shut, his breath coming in tight little bursts through pouted lips.

Smiling, Tad watched him for a moment, kissed him once more, then treaded quietly from his room toward that of Emmaline who, at age seven, already seemed her mother's clone. She undressed alone, in the dark, as did her mother, draping her slight frame in a white nightgown that was all ribbon and ruffle. The moment Tad arrived she knelt in prayer, intoning the words meticulously, as though for posterity. Her small room, in contrast to Dana's, was a model of neatness and propriety, every item of clothing carefully folded, every doll or toy stowed in its assigned place. The room itself smelled faintly of soaps and perfumes, reflecting the fastidiousness of its occupant.

Having completed her prayers, Emmaline flung her arms

315

around her father and gave him a wet kiss. "I'm so glad you're home, Daddy."

"Of course I'm home," Tad protested. "I'd never miss Christmas at home."

"... I was afraid this year ..." Emmaline started to say something, but Tad grasped the little girl, holding her to him, fearing the thoughts her childlike intuition would further summon up.

"I'll always be here for you, Em. Always."

When he put her down in bed, tucking the covers, seeing her lovely reddish-blond hair against the pillow, he knew that his were not idle promises, that he would, in fact, always be here for her, tending to her myriad needs—hers and Dana's and little Heber's, too, when he was old enough to propound them. How could he ever have thought, even for a second, of leaving them? These were his children, their every word and foible comprising, in their own small way, an exalted part in his chain of being. His commitment to them was immutable; their day-to-day rituals and demands, in all their maddening repetitiveness, gave his life a lulling continuum of sound and sensation that shielded him from his own nagging urges. That was, indeed, the difference between his world and that of Pye and Gavin and the others. In their world every day had to be distinctive, every sensation, novel. Theirs was a life of sensual atrophy. They could not understand the lulling comforts of the family womb, its warmth, its sanctuary. No, it was beyond them.

He felt sorry for them. Really he did. But he knew he would always love them, and, in a sense, envy them, too, as he knew they envied him.

"No more questions tonight," Tad told Emmaline at last. "It's time for sleep."

"How early can I wake you?"

Tad smiled. "Not before seven. And no peeking at the Christmas tree in the middle of the night. Santa will get very upset."

"Awww, ..." said Emmaline, as she poked her pillow and closed her eyes.

Tad went downstairs. From the hallway he could see Nancy placing last-minute packages under the tree, checking bows and ribbons. He went to the kitchen absently, and took out the bottle of lemonade, then reconsidered. Checking Nancy once again, Tad reached for his secret vodka container, pouring himself a few swallows and downing them quickly, reacting to the freezing, syrupy fluid as it coursed down his throat.

Fortified, he went to the den to flick on the television set. He found a college basketball game and had just become involved in its action when Nancy was upon him, seating herself on the love seat. She started chattering about plans for Christmas Day, how she had reorganized their agenda so they could attend Eliza's wedding and still meet their own commitments. "I still can't comprehend why they're marrying at that mansion!" Nancy reiterated yet again, as she had several times before when Tad first broke the startling news. "A woman of her position in the Church . . ."

But Tad wasn't really listening. He had long since learned that when his wife needed to talk it was best to let her pour it all out. It was unimportant whether or not he listened; it was probably best he didn't so that he would not be tempted to take issue with any of her plans or pronouncements. The ideal circumstance for their dialogues was that he be seated, watching a basketball game or other sporting event on television, as he was presently doing, until she had simply talked herself out.

Suddenly he felt Nancy's hand in his, and, turning, saw her eyes peering earnestly at him.

"Didn't you hear what I said, darling?" she asked patiently.

"Of course I did, Nancy."

"I really mean it, Tad. I've thought it over very carefully. I want another child."

Tad felt a sudden rush of panic. "How did this come up? I mean, right out of the blue!"

"Not out of the blue, Tad. Heber is thirteen months now. It is time."

"Who decrees that it's time? Where is it so written? Did we get a reminder in the mail, like the card we get from the automobile repair shop reminding us that the Pinto needs servicing? . . ."

"Don't joke about something as serious as this, dear."

"I'm not joking. . . ."

"Is it money that's worrying you, Tad? This whole business with the Pacific merger should get you a good raise," she persisted.

So that was it! Ever since he first started talking about the merger, Nancy had probably been pondering the added income, weighing the possibilities. And there was, of course, Dana Sloat's agreement; he'd lived up to it scrupulously. Each child had one million dollars in his or her bank account, though they would not have access to it till maturity.

"It's not just money, Nancy. There are other considerations. The house is too small for another child."

"The kids can double up."

"There's the work load. The housework."

"I can cope."

"It would mean less time together. You and I talked about going to Hawaii alone this year—just the two of us. . . ."

Nancy put her finger to his lips, halting him in midsentence. She kissed him lightly on the cheek.

"I want to have another child, Tad. Tonight is Christmas Eve. I want us to make a child tonight." Her hand brushed his knee lightly, quickly stroking the inside of his thigh. It was a private signal, and he understood its meaning.

□ When Tad got out of the shower he set about his ablutions with ritualistic care. Staring at his face in the magnifying mirror, Tad saw the blond bristles that ridged his chin. He had last shaved very early that morning at Pye's. Taking out his electric razor, he ran it quickly over his face, then dabbed on some after-shave. Having completed all this, he climbed into a pair of LDS underwear—the old-fashioned kind he kept on hand for these occasions, which covered most of his arms and legs as well as the rest of his body, firmly encapsulating its wearer in the armor of virtue. He put on his bathrobe, and checked himself one last time in the mirror. Then he finished off the last swallow of vodka which he had furtively placed in the bathroom glass.

He was ready.

Tad opened the bathroom door and moved quietly down the hallway. Passing Emmaline's room, he could hear his daughter moaning softly in her sleep. Otherwise the house was still. He stopped outside the closed door of the bedroom he shared with Nancy. The mark was there—the mark he had placed on the door, as Brigham Young had done generations before to denote his evening's intentions.

He turned the knob and stepped into the room. She stood there, silhouetted in the candlelight. Standing in her flowing gown, Nancy was a vision in frills and tatted lace and flounces. Her hair was combed out in curly tendrils. As he drew closer he caught the tang of the crushed bergamot which she wore, as had her mother, and her grandmother before her.

He held her and sensed the urgency of her desire. Seated on the bed, she released the ties binding the front of his raiment. Aroused, he slowly released hers as well, caressing her breasts as her sacred garment opened slowly. They could not remove their garments, of course; such would be contrary to moral dictates. Yet, as their bodies pressed together, her ardor all but overwhelmed him. "I want a child," she whispered once more, her hands reaching out for him, her body shuddering with an ecstasy that was soaring and incorporeal, a spiritual lust.

GUSSIE Cobb looked at the clock with exasperation. It was eleven and she had not even begun her final tasks of wrapping late-arriving Christmas gifts and arranging them under the tree. She had noticed her two sons glancing with disappointment at the sparse assortment of gifts which already resided there; she knew that would turn to gleeful surprise Christmas morning when she had augmented them with the new gifts. She played this trick on them every year but they never seemed to remember.

The new gifts were modest offerings, but they had been arriving with regularity all afternoon. A car would appear, and a man or woman would stride quickly up the front walk, deposit his or her offering on the doorstep, ring the doorbell and then be off before Gussie could respond and thank them. They were subscribers, most of them—kindly, loyal people who had read their publication and felt, through it, a bonding with the Cobbs. And so on the day before Christmas they would drop off their cookies or fruitcake or other offering along with a brief note—often unsigned—of support.

The most surprising gift came from Gussie's eldest sister, Matilda, a handsome floral arrangement which had been delivered late that afternoon along with a terse note that said simply, "Love from Matty." She had not heard from Matty for three years now. They had once been quite close, even after the excommunication. Matty lived in the rural community of Delta, in southwest Utah, where her husband, Jarvis Perry, raised hay and alfalfa and was an LDS Bishop and Church stalwart. Jarvis had always looked askance at Gussie's problems with the Church, but his tolerance finally reached a breaking point when she and Hiram published an article analyzing why so many Mormon farms tended to look poverty-stricken, despite their extreme prosperity. The reason for the unpainted barns, rusting tractors and forlorn-looking animals,

320

the article suggested, was that the wily farmers wished to minimize the incomes they reported to their Bishops and hence reduce their tithes. The Cobbs' article caused a predictable stir, and
Jarvis Perry, upon hearing of this latest outburst of apostasy,
promptly served notice to his wife that their relationship with
Hiram and Gussie was to be terminated forthwith.

The breach had saddened Gussie: She loved Matty and had
enjoyed their occasional visits to the farm; she also loved watching her city-bred sons wandering wide-eyed among the fields and
farm animals. Perhaps Matty's flowers meant their link could be
restored. That would be lovely indeed.

Gussie was busily arraying the late-arriving packages under the
tree when she noticed the stern directive, Open before Christmas,
scrawled on one card. It was a crudely wrapped little package
which she tore open absently, then gaped at its contents. It was a
star! Though obviously homemade from foil and scraps of irides-
cent material, it was exquisitely formed and seemed to glow with
a special light all its own. How lovely! Gussie thought, as she
pulled her small stepladder up to the tree and fastened the star to
the top, supplanting the bedraggled angel that had resided there
for more years than she cared to remember. She was admiring her
handiwork when the jangle of the front door gave her a start.
Instinctively, she checked her watch, her hopes rising.

Hiram! It was surely Hiram!

Gussie all but leaped to the door and flung it open only to see
the diminutive figure of Cora Snow in the doorway. Her face was
ashen. Gussie backed off two steps, her lips parted, a stricken
look in her eyes. She knew instantaneously the reason for Cora's
visit. No words had to be exchanged, no platitudes of comfort or
condolence. In the last eighteen hours, she had imagined this
encounter time and again, her mind foreshadowing each movement and nuance. Now it had come at last.

DALTON Evans always treasured Temple Square at Christmas time, and tonight it seemed to project a special radiance. Buildings, trees and shrubs, encrusted by the afternoon's snowfall, now glowed pink and yellow and green and blue from the millions of tiny lights which emblazoned the entire square. Shimmering through the darkness, the old Assembly Hall beckoned like some medieval relic, while, across the square, the brightly illuminated figure of Moroni stood atop the Temple's highest peak, an abiding symbol of constancy.

Many others were in the square with him, their footsteps muffled by the fallen snow. Here and there he heard a baby's cry, but mostly the visitors were silent, as though out of reverence to the perfection that surrounded them. And it *was* perfect, Dalton Evans thought—the snow, the lights, the faint music from the Tabernacle which permeated the night. The Lord had planned that this Christmas would be perfect on Temple Square to signal his tolerance for the imperfections which lurked within. Well, Dalton Evans had come here to deal with those imperfections as best he could. He would not allow clumsiness and egotism to intrude upon God's broader vision or to obscure His grandeur.

Hearing the whine of the icy wind, he turned up the collar of his topcoat and quickened his pace. Many of his friends had fled Salt Lake for the beckoning warmth of Mexico or Hawaii, but Evans had declined. As a physician, he knew that a few days of tropical heat would enhance his own recuperative powers. The pneumonia had taken a severe toll on his physical resources. To the urgings of his wife and personal physician, his answer had been resolute: After the holidays he would go away, he had said. Christmas was meant to be spent at home. And now that his Church needed him at this moment of crisis, he was grateful that God had given him the resolve to stay close to this holy place.

Entering the Temple, Dalton Evans greeted the two guards at

322

the door and though they knew him well, showed them the required credential, his Temple Recommend. He then stepped into the elevator which descended slowly into the bowels of the Temple. When the doors opened, a long tunnel stretched out before him, looking like an endless ribbon of fluorescence. Except in inclement weather he rarely used these subterranean catacombs, which formed an invisible link between all the buildings and secret enclaves of Temple Square and were reserved for the exclusive use of its loftiest officials. Painted a bright yellow and blazingly lit, the tunnels, with their myriad surveillance devices and security checkpoints, had always struck him as eerie and forbidding. He recalled glumly how one Secret Service advance man, checking out security for an upcoming visit by the President of the United States, had informed him in awe that Temple Square was better protected than the White House. He had intended it as a compliment, but Evans did not admire his colleagues' propensity for security overkill.

Strolling along the yellow corridor, Evans approached the first of the checkpoints, manned by two uniformed guards who sprang to their feet like robots that had been electronically activated, holding themselves at rigid attention.

"Rest yourselves," he told them, "it's Christmas Eve."

"Merry Christmas to you, sir," the voices called back.

Reaching a confluence of tunnels, he paused, considering his options. It had been his intention to go directly to the office of the Prophet. Samuel Bryce was awaiting him, he knew. But standing now in the still, humid air of the catacombs, he felt a sudden languor. His energies were ebbing. It was little wonder. These past twenty-four hours there had been no time for sleep. He had spent many long hours on the telephone, laying the groundwork for the meeting that would convene at midnight—in only an hour and a half. The thought of the assemblage still awed him. It would be a historic occasion, this renewed convocation of the Council of Fifty. The very mention of its name conjured up in his mind the monolithic strength of his great Church, and the resilience of its hallowed institutions. There had been times during this past day when he'd worried whether he could bring it off—whether they would respond to the call, whether his own reserves of strength and tact were sufficient to the challenge.

But they had rallied around him, as he prayed they would.

Whenever the Church had faced times of strife, its true leaders—the members of the Fifty—had risen to the task. They had been there in Illinois to save the Kingdom from the mobs that had assassinated Joseph Smith, there in Utah when failing crops threatened to destroy Brigham Young's dream of Zion. Through the persecution, the exodus, the Great Trek, the Fifty were there, functioning always behind a curtain of secrecy, yet firm in its ultimate authority as Zion's "living constitution." Today, as in the past, few even acknowledged its existence. Many scholars of Church affairs assumed the Council had simply vanished, along with polygamy, with the advent of statehood. That was just as well, Evans felt. The Fifty functioned best this way. Its membership, representing the true wellsprings of leadership, financial and spiritual, did not need or seek recognition for their role, which had been perpetuated from one generation to the next. There had been an Alpheus Dalton Evans among the first Fifty—Joseph Smith's "select circle"—just as there was now a Dalton Alpheus Evans on the present body. Now, as then, the Fifty comprised, not the zealots and mystics, but the men of affairs, the practical men who understood the pragmatics of survival. These men had built the Kingdom and held it together amid the winds of discord. Its survival—indeed its awesome wealth and power—was their enduring triumph.

Dalton Evans' ancestors played a key part in this triumph. His great-grandfather had negotiated the contract in the name of Brigham Young for construction of the Union Pacific Railroad through Utah Territory. His great-uncle, acting on behalf of the School of the Prophets—the larger, less secretive body spawned by the Council of Fifty—saw to it that Mormons, not Gentiles, were awarded homesteads and timber rights and supervised the development of Zion's tender young economy.

And now it befell Dalton Evans to carry forth that legacy. Walking slowly through the tunnel, he understood all that his mission portended. It pained him, yet there was no escape. There were grave dangers confronting his Kingdom.

Seeking counsel with the others on the Fifty, he saw they shared his alarm. Dana Sloat's influence on the Prophet had become extreme, even insidious. His policies were rash and precipitate.

And now there were these new developments, more immediately ominous in their implications. Sloat had furtively distorted his genealogical records in an effort to conceal his ties to the darker side of the Mormon past. He had proved equally mendacious in falsifying the whereabouts and affiliations of his own son. And now the tragic events at New Nauvoo had shattered this final fabrication.

Dalton Evans had taken necessary precautions to enshroud them in secrecy—he had instructed Turner Mead to tell no one. But the facts were there nonetheless: a life had been taken; the life of a prominent apostate named Hiram Cobb. And Dana Sloat's son was inextricably linked to these events just as his forebears had been linked to Mountain Meadows.

No, there was a dark stain to this man, a stain that deepened as scrutiny grew more intense. The Fifty understood this full well. They understood the urgency of action. It was up to Dalton Evans to prepare the Prophet for the ordeal that lay ahead. It was a delicate task. Samuel Heber Bryce was a man of strong loyalties and convictions. Having Dana Sloat at his side seemed to embolden him. Indeed, Sloat was rapidly becoming more his guru than his amanuensis. Surely, the Good Lord would not look kindly on a dependency such as this—one which inevitably would intrude upon His own divine guidance. It was up to Dalton Evans to remind the Prophet of these verities, and to warn him that the Lord would reveal His displeasure. Not only the Lord, but the Fifty as well.

Having reached the end of the long corridor, he stepped into an elevator, emerging moments later at the place which had so often in the past provided him with a renewed serenity. The backstage recesses of the Tabernacle were a maze of dressing rooms and storage areas for the choir. Walking through these now empty rooms, his steps clicking against the timbered floor, he could faintly hear the voices. The concert would be ending soon. If he hurried, he could catch the final strains.

Climbing a flight of stairs, he emerged onto the balcony and looked down upon the audience, which seemed to fill every nook and crevice of the vast old building. Even the narrow balcony fringing the auditorium was packed to capacity. The choir, three hundred strong, was singing "O Come, All Ye Faithful," and their soaring voices moved him profoundly. The faces of the singers beamed with fervor as they sang. The great pipes of the organ, golden-hued in the soft light, framed them in a portrait for posterity.

His eyes suddenly moist, Dalton Evans stood transfixed by the grandeur before him. He was ready now for the Prophet.

AT two o'clock in the morning the telephone beside Dana Sloat's bed began ringing. It rang four times before Sloat, who always prided himself on being a sound sleeper, probed the darkness for the receiver.

"Who is this?"

"The front desk, sir."

Sloat checked the clock at his bedside. "Why the devil are you disturbing me?" he demanded, his words slurring together.

"They are here, sir."

"Who's here? Do you know what time it is?"

"They are on their way up, sir."

"Who is 'they'? Dammit, tell whoever it is to come back in the morning."

"Oh, no, sir." There was a note of finality in the clerk's voice that brought Sloat's senses to full alert.

"Now look here," he barked into the phone, "I'm not going to stand for this intrusion. This is the Hotel Utah, dammit— If you can't provide . . ."

"They are the captains, sir," the clerk repeated in the same benumbed tone. "The captains of the Fifty!"

It was a joke, Sloat concluded quickly. This was not the room clerk at all but some practical joker who was reciting gibberish. Sloat had just slammed the phone down when he heard the sharp knock on his door.

The captains of the Fifty awaited him now.

SHE had tried to sleep but it was fruitless, as she knew it would be. Instead, she went down to her kitchen and, not knowing what else to do, started baking Christmas cookies. It was, she knew, a mindless undertaking. She had not made Christmas cookies in years, nor had she any idea what she would do with them when they were finished. Distribute them at the wedding, perhaps—that is, if there was a wedding. With each passing hour, her apprehensions had mounted about that. Turner had left early that afternoon. Surely, if all had gone well, his plane would have returned by now, but it had become quite clear that all had not gone well. That much she admitted to herself. Somewhere, somehow, Turner's plan had faltered. He might even now be marooned in some remote encampment. He might be a prisoner. He might even be dead.

Her hands were shaking as she placed the tray of cookies into her oven—shaking so badly she repeatedly failed to slide it into the appropriate rack.

While the cookies were baking she had tried to read, but the book could not hold her attention. Ten minutes of a movie on television—a grainy old Bogart film—was all she could handle. By the time she remembered her cookies they were hopelessly charred. Furious with herself, she flung them into the garbage and grimly started mixing a new batch, then reconsidered, deciding instead to return to bed and try a romantic novel.

It was a ridiculous novel—a breathless Gothic whose erotic fantasies were thinly veiled in clumsily obvious symbolism—but she was determined to stay with it. She had to.

She was deep in a nightmare, a terrible dream where she was running endlessly through dark caves and labyrinths, when the hand on her ankle startled her awake. When she opened her eyes

328

she felt the book still in her hands and Turner was smiling down on her through weary eyes.

She sat up so swiftly that the book went flying onto the floor. She peered at him, saucer-eyed, reluctant to believe her eyes.

"It's me, Eliza. Truly it is."

She bolted into his arms. "You can't imagine how long these hours have been," she said in a near-whisper. "I've never been so scared in my life."

"I, too, my darling," he said, his voice heavy with fatigue. "I feel like a man who has just thumbed his nose at his own fate. It is not an experience I plan ever to repeat."

He held her still tighter. "Hiram is dead," Turner said softly.

"Dear God."

"If only we'd gotten there earlier—there might have been a chance."

Eliza sat before him on the bed now, clutching his hands.

"How did such a terrible thing happen, Turner? How did he die?"

Turner felt uncomfortable in her gaze. He had always told her the truth until this business had started and he promised himself he would tell her the truth someday about all that had happened this week—about Lillian Thompson and Dawson Sloat. Someday, but not now. It must remain his secret for the time being. That much he had promised Dalton Evans.

"He was with a polygamous cult," Turner said. "He was researching a story about them. They killed him."

"They are such insanely violent people . . ." Eliza's voice trailed off.

"We should visit his widow tomorrow, Eliza. We should pay our respects."

"Of course."

"After the wedding. . . ."

Eliza looked at him, brightening. "I was waiting for you to say that."

"We shall certainly not postpone our wedding! We have waited long enough."

Eliza kissed him. "You know, darling, I'd always been told that lovers were the world's most selfish people and I know now what they mean. I know I should weep for Hiram Cobb and I should feel his loss more deeply. But all I can think of is that we're together. That's all I am capable of feeling."

They held each other once again and then Turner started to say something but the words got lost in his throat. There was no need to say them, anyway. There would be lots of time.

At a few minutes before midnight, the snow was falling once again as the limousines appeared, sleek, ebony shapes darting quickly through the white mist. It had all been carefully choreographed, like some mythic ballet: Never was there more than one automobile at any given place, so that passersby would remain oblivious to the elaborate maneuver taking place around them. The limousines would stop at different corners of Temple Square, chauffeurs hopping out, holding umbrellas for their aged passengers as they strode toward the Temple. Other cars swept into the underground garage beneath the headquarters building, stopping on different floors of the multi-tiered structure. Even to the security guards, it all seemed shrouded and unobtrusive. No one would imagine that, on this frosty night, another historic ingathering was taking place—even now, as Christmas Eve was turning into Christmas Day.

The arrivals were elderly men, affluent, white-haired, patriarchal, garbed in dark suits and wearing sternly authoritative expressions. They were men who were accustomed to responsibility, the Mormon Brahmins, the wielders of power. As with Old World royalty, their whole lives had been a tacit preparation for leadership. Even as children they had been nurtured to rule: the right tutors, the right schools. They were God's favored children. Their mission was to prepare for the day, not long in the future, when the Kingdom of God would rule the world and they would be the Princes of Zion.

By midnight they had made their way briskly past the security checkpoints into the innermost precincts of the Temple. They had changed into their white Temple robes. They had held their prayer circles. The convocation could now begin.

331

GAVIN Pollard had closed his eyes but sleep would not come. He heard the rhythmic breathing across the bed. Turning, he glimpsed wisps of blond hair and the contours of her cheekbone. She was sleeping on her side, looking lovely in repose. She had been a delightful if demanding lover who had sapped his energies, and he was grateful sleep had overtaken her.

He drew himself from the bed as quietly as possible, weaving carefully toward the den. The dull throb in his temple reminded him he'd drunk too much champagne last night. An Amaretto and soda would ease the throb.

As he mixed his drink, Gavin recognized the faint aroma that clung to his skin. It was the residual scent of the girl's perfume mixed with the musky odor of lovemaking, a mixture he found at once arousing and annoying.

How appropriate, Gavin thought as he sank down on his sofa, that he would pick up a girl named Faith on Christmas Eve. He had met her at Gary Henderson's party, spotting her within moments of arriving and the scenario had unfolded with inexorable predictability. He'd introduced himself and brought her a drink. She said she was a model, which meant she worked as a secretary. She also said she was engaged to a boy back home, which meant she was hustling but being cautious about it.

Later in the evening she'd insisted that she would not go home with him, but ten minutes later her white Volkswagen convertible was right behind his Mercedes as he pulled into the driveway. Christmas Eve was a very sentimental time for her, Faith had explained as Gavin was opening the champagne; she would just have a quick drink and be on her way. Twenty minutes later she was beside him in bed, eager for his attentions.

Gavin found a zestful reassurance in these sexual rituals—the coy protestations, the modest denials, the ultimate surrender.

332

Faith had been his Christmas present to himself. He'd been spending too much time with Melody lately; her hints about becoming a live-in were growing ever more insistent. He needed a change in tempo and Faith had been a superbly exhausting change.

When the phone started ringing Gavin's instinct was to check his watch. Who would be calling at one thirty-five on Christmas morning? Clearly it was a crank call. If he wasn't afraid of awakening Faith he would let it ring.

"Sorry to disturb your Christmas. . . ."

Christ, it was Alvin Boroff. Gavin felt a flash of anger. He admired diligence, to be sure, especially in a bureau chief, but only a pain in the ass like Boroff would call from Washington at one thirty-five in the morning.

"It's an awkward time, Alvin. Let me call you tomorrow."

"I think we should talk now, Gavin. There's some weird stuff coming down."

Gavin sighed. Boroff was unrelenting all right. "How weird can it be that it can't wait till tomorrow?"

"They're stealing your goddamn company out from under you and you want to talk tomorrow! Come on, Gavin, wake up!"

Gavin hunched forward and put his drink down on the table before him. "Who's stealing the company? What the fuck are you ranting about, Alvin?"

"Give me some time to explain, that's all. . . ."

". . . Okay, explain!"

"Half an hour ago I got this call. It was from Ezra Hurlbut. Know who he is?"

"No." Goddamn Boroff always had to strut his exalted knowledge, even at a time like this.

"He's the Republican senator from Utah. He said he'd heard about our series of pieces on the political and financial activities of the Mormon Church. He said he wanted to make a deal."

"What kind of a deal? Get to the point, Alvin!"

"He said he would supply us information that would be of 'great corporate value' if we, in turn, would leave him out of the stories—just not mention him at all."

"Sounds like he's bananas. What did you tell him?"

"I told him I was in no position to make any deals until I spoke to you. But I kept him talking—kept pumping him. He sounded scared as hell, like he wanted someone to talk to. Anyway, let me give you the bottom line, Gavin. If you close the deal for those Pacific stations you're going to lose your company. That's what it comes down to. The whole thing was engineered like a charm. The deal closes and the Mormon Church assumes working control of the corporation. And do you know their first move? Your distinguished right-wing uncle, Emory Pollard, is appointed president."

Gavin's head suddenly was throbbing again. "Jesus Christ, Alvin, we already closed the deal. Is this character on the level?"

"Straight as an arrow. He knows what he's talking about, Gavin. He's the Church's chief fixer in Washington. He's the man who gets things done for the brethren."

"It still doesn't figure. Why would this Hurlbut tell us all this? He's taking a helluva risk."

"The stories pose a bigger risk. He's terrified they'll ruin his credibility in the Senate. Remember a generation ago Congress kept another Utah senator in limbo for three years, claiming he was just a tool of the hierarchy. It could happen again."

Gavin was shaking his head. "I don't know . . ."

"There's another factor, too. Hurlbut felt his power base with the brethren lay with this character Dana Sloat, the Mormon industrialist. It was Sloat who masterminded the take-over. Anyway, Sloat had promised Hurlbut he'd kill our series, but that promise ran into a snag. It seems Sloat just got bounced from his Church position in some sort of power play, so Hurlbut is scared shitless. He's sitting out there on a limb all by himself."

Gavin felt a cold anger engulf him. He was staring straight ahead, motionless. "You still there? . . ." Boroff called out nervously.

"I'm here. I was just thinking about someone else who's sitting out there on a limb. That little shit-faced buddy of mine who put me into this deal to begin with."

"Hastings?"

"Sloat's his father-in-law. Tad must have known the scenario from the start and he suckered me in."

"Sorry about that, Gavin," Boroff said. "You know, what they say about love and war applies to religion, too. What do you want me to do about the series?"

"The series?"

"The goddamn Mormon series!"

"I want it in all tomorrow's editions, just like I ordered."

"And the follow-up stories?"

"I want to run them all."

"I hear you!" Boroff's voice was suddenly exultant. "Just promise me one thing, okay?"

"What?"

"Get us out of that Pacific deal. I mean, if the Church ever takes us over they'll hoist me to the top of the Temple and dangle me from Moroni's trumpet!"

Gavin caught himself grinning despite his seething anger. "I'll find a way out, Alvin. That's my problem."

"Okay. By the way, Merry Christmas, Gavin."

"Merry fucking Christmas to you, too," Gavin replied, hanging up.

He remained seated in his den for several minutes after the phone call. Well, it had all come clear at last, as he sensed it would, but certainly not in the way he'd expected. Minafee had been right, of course. The deal smelled weird from the start. No wonder Marva and Emory had suddenly become so quietly supportive. It was all a trap, and at the center of it was his old pal Tad.

That was the part that really stung. Betrayal was such a depressing spectacle, especially betrayal by a man. Men were supposed to stick together. Gavin felt that deeply. It was part of the code.

Tad had broken that code. Gavin would have to deal with that in the appropriate way.

What a goddamn shame, Gavin thought once more, that the naked little kid on the beach in Tonga would turn out to be such a miserable prick after all this!

The Kingdom

FEELING a profound discomfort, which had been building in him all morning, Tad Hastings stepped into the rococo entry hall of the great Victorian fortress known as the McCune Mansion at five minutes before eleven on Christmas morning, Nancy at his side. There was something intrinsically disconcerting, he concluded, about marrying off one's mother, an awkwardness which was heightened by the fact that he had never met the bridegroom, though naturally knew of his reputation.

Ushered into the handsomely paneled room where the wedding was to take place, Tad could not recognize a single familiar face among the other guests. "How could Eliza marry at such a place?" Nancy whispered in confusion.

Only three hours earlier Nancy had beamed with joy as she'd unwrapped the Cartier watch Tad had given her—the watch he'd originally bought for Pye.

Taking refuge in a quiet corner, Tad scanned the faces of the arriving guests. He was truly curious to see what sort of man his mother had decided to marry. Never in his wildest dreams had he expected her to seek another husband. He felt a pang of resentment that another man would now occupy a place closer to her than he. He tried to imagine her kissing this man, making love to him—no, these actions seemed totally alien to her behavior. He had emerged from her flesh and been nurtured by her, yet knew he had no more insight into her thoughts and emotions than that of a total stranger.

Tad saw a slight, elderly man enter the room and start making his way patiently from one guest to another, hand extended. "It is an honor to meet you, Mr. Evans," Tad heard one of the others say, and then he knew, of course—he had often heard his mother talk glowingly of Dalton Evans, the retired First Counselor of the LDS Church, the man his father-in-law had succeeded.

"And you must be the son of our lovely bride," Evans said as he approached them. "You should be very proud."

"I am, sir," Tad replied, as he introduced Nancy. There was a kindliness exuded by this frail, reedlike man, which seemed to animate the room and pull together its diverse guests. Evans was introducing Nancy to Burt Hoagland, an old friend of Mead's, he said, and then others were coming over, too. Aunt Becky, Eliza's favorite sister, was at Tad's side, kissing him, and she in turn introduced a short, rotund man named Nathaniel Pomerantz, whose name Tad also recognized as a longtime friend of his mother's. He was a federal judge, the only Jewish judge in Utah's virtually all-Mormon judicial establishment. It was typical of Eliza that she would invite this flamboyant figure to her wedding.

Tad was distracted by a sudden commotion at the door as a whole cluster of guests burst into the room, chattering noisily. He was astonished to recognize the petite, if flinty, Cora Snow, followed by her twin prodigies, Jeb and Charity, the boy clad improbably in a black tuxedo, his sister in a frilly pink dress, her blond hair piled high atop her head. What in the world were the Snows doing at his mother's wedding? Tad turned in confusion to Nancy, seeing a similar question implanted on her face. But there was no mistaking Cora Snow's robust voice, booming its greetings to other guests, proudly introducing her children. The decibel level of the room was sharply heightened as new bodies kept pressing through the door. What had seemed like a somber, sparsely-attended wedding was transforming itself into a crowded and lively party. Its atmosphere, Tad sensed, was more that of a celebration than of a solemn exchange of marital vows.

"You're one of Ellis Marmer's boys, aren't you?" Cora Snow was standing in front of him, her son Jeb at her side.

"Yes, I'm Tad Hastings," he said, extending his hand.

"You should be very proud of your mother—all of us are." Cora Snow said, gripping his hand in an iron vise. "This is my son, Jeb."

Tad was grateful for Jeb's slack handshake.

"You have a real neat mother, man," Jeb offered.

Cora Snow scowled. "A neat mother is one who keeps her house clean," she corrected. "Eliza is a gracious mother."

Jeb shrugged in mild confusion. "What do I know?" he told Tad. "I never work weddings."

Tad's nervous laugh was aborted by the sudden rapt silence which gripped the room and he realized his mother had made her entrance. Tad was mesmerized. There seemed about her an almost palpable joy. She wore an ivory silk dress of great elegance, its skirt gathered slightly, with a lace bodice. The dress was an heirloom but he could not recall its lineage. All he knew was that she looked stunning in it—a woman who possessed beauty of a scale he had never before appreciated.

Next to her stood a dark-haired man with handsome, craggy features, who held his arm around Eliza's waist with an affectionate protectiveness. So this was Turner Mead! Tad had heard it said that second marriages were usually a self-mocking reenactment of the first, but Turner Mead, in caste and carriage, seemed the antithesis of Draper Hastings. Tad's father had been short, thick-necked and heavy-shouldered and had looked, Tad thought, rather like a tank. Though he had cultivated the style and civility required of high corporate position, one nonetheless saw in his demeanor the stolid, square-jawed heritage of the Mormon frontiersmen. By contrast, Turner Mead's visage was one of lean elegance, and there was a playfulness in his gaze Tad found appealing. No, Eliza was not about to marry the same man twice, whatever the apothegm.

The ceremony was beginning. Tad felt Nancy edge closer to him, felt her arm entwined in his. Aunt Becky, the matron of honor, took her position to one side, and Burt Hoagland, the best man, to the other. The room fell silent as everyone strained to hear Dalton Evans' words, which were to join Turner and Eliza. Yet as Tad listened, Evans' voice was blending with others in his mind; it was no longer Evans he was hearing but rather the words of his own Temple ceremony years earlier. He was watching his mother standing there, lovingly, at Turner Mead's side, but the image before him was that of Nancy and him, kneeling at the altar, their hands clasped in the Patriarchal grip. He remembered the sepulchral voice above them invoking the mystical words sealing them for all eternity.

"By virtue of the Holy Priesthood and the authority vested in me I pronounce you legally and lawfully husband and wife for time and 'for all eternity' and I seal upon you the blessings of the holy resurrection with power to come forth in the morning of the first resurrection clothed with glory, immortality and eternal

lives, and seal upon you the blessings of kingdoms, thrones, prin-
cipalities, powers, dominions and exaltations, with all the blessings of Abraham, Isaac and Jacob and say unto you, be fruitful
and multiply and replenish the earth, that you may have joy and
rejoicing in the day of the Lord Jesus Christ. All these blessings, together with all the blessings appertaining unto the new
and everlasting covenant, I seal upon you by virtue of the Holy
Priesthood, through your faithfulness, in the name of the Father
and of the Son and of the Holy Ghost, Amen!"

Tad remembered these sacred words pouring down upon his
kneeling body like hard rain, the immortal invocation that had
been laid upon him. And he remembered recoiling, yet struggling
desperately to conceal his panic.

"... *For all eternity!*" He had felt suddenly too young, too vulnerable, to undertake obligations of this magnitude. It was too
awesome.

How desperately he had wanted to run! Run from the Temple,
run from all the obligations and expectations that had suddenly
descended upon him.

The room around him suddenly exploded in noise. Everyone
was cheering and pumping each other's hand. Judge Pomerantz
materialized in front of him. "Mazel tov," he shouted. Nancy
cringed.

Tad looked around him. He caught sight of his mother, surrounded by well-wishers. It was now Eliza Mead. For all eternity.

UPON awakening Christmas morning, Samuel Heber Bryce put on his bathrobe and hurried to the kitchen to help himself to two sugar doughnuts, a treat which Marybeth, his stern housekeeper, would normally have denied him. Over her protestations, he had sent Marybeth home for the holidays, thus liberating himself from her dietary strictures. Seated in the kitchen with his doughnuts, reading the newspaper, Bryce savored the knowledge that his house was, for once, empty and that he had the privacy to do as he wished. Yet Marybeth's absence also rekindled the sense of loss he felt for his wife, Clorinda, whose passing, six years earlier, had left him feeling less than a complete man, as though he had lost not a wife but rather a portion of himself. When she was alive, Christmas took on the proportions more of a pageant than of a mere holiday. Their eight children, forty-five grandchildren and sixty-two great-grandchildren would descend upon their home, whose walls would all but buckle under the clamor. Christmas dinner was more akin to a banquet, with Clorinda having started her logistical preparations many weeks in advance. Bryce absolutely adored these huge if ungainly gatherings, but, as he grew older, he also found himself dreading them. The mere task of shaking that many hands, patting that many heads and summoning up that many names reduced him to panic.

This Christmas, with the help of his secretaries, he'd contacted all the adult members of the Bryce clan to inform them tactfully that they should not feel obliged to visit or call over the holidays, nor indeed to send a gift. The pressures of high office were his alibi; he'd felt a great burden had been lifted. He was, after all, an old man, who should be free to enjoy an old man's Christmas in prayer and meditation. The week's onrush of events had left him doubly grateful for this decision. His days had become pale slices wedged between the long, arduous nights. If only he could spend one or two days alone, perhaps he could again marshal his energies and address the problems which surrounded him.

The gathering of the Fifty, he felt, was a turning point. The sight of these fifty souls arrayed across the Celestial Room in their panoply of Temple robes had fortified his resolve. In their presence, he was no longer a frail old man, mired in indecision. Inspired by their prayers, he was again grateful that God had spoken to him, clarifying his vision. He had erred in entrusting such grave responsibilities to his First Counselor, Dana Sloat, but that error had been rectified. Sloat's fine, resourceful mind remained an enigma to him: It could so ably grasp the temporal problems confronting them, yet remained oblivious to the broader currents of history. The Saints were, after all, destiny's children. God had willed that the world be theirs, but the pace of history remained His pace, the rhythms, His rhythms. They were not to be challenged or tampered with. What a tragedy that all this was beyond Sloat's grasp, that his vision was obscured by the rigidities of commerce.

Samuel Bryce thought of these things as he knelt in prayer on Christmas morning, alone in the stillness of his living room. He prayed that God would continue to reveal His will to him, and guide his actions. This would be, he understood, his last Christmas on this earth, and he expressed his humble thanks that his energies felt restored, so that he could experience the radiance of the holidays.

His eyes came to rest on the photograph of his wife. How desperately he longed that Clorinda could be with him to experience this day! How keenly he missed her gaiety, her joy, even the softness of her flesh.

She was gone from him but her presence still suffused their home. He had kept the house exactly as it had been six years ago, leaving even her clothing in her closet, her linen on her bed.

He and Clorinda had moved to this modest home in the East Bench section of Salt Lake some thirty-seven years earlier when he was still a struggling young businessman, and they had never seen any reason to move. Indeed, the only outward change in their lives as a result of high office in the Church was the Cadillac limousine standing by outside, with its chauffeur-bodyguard always at the ready. But the house remained the same, just as Clorinda would have wanted.

The telephone pierced the quiet, startling Bryce out of his ruminations.

"What are you doing, Grandpa?"

Only Spud would start a conversation like that! He was delighted to hear the high, slightly hoarse little-boy voice of his favorite great-grandchild. His closeness to Spurgeon Bryce Fielding, or "Spud" as the family fondly called him, had always surprised him. As Bryce grew older, and as his position in the Church grew loftier, he could feel the gulf between himself and his progeny, could sense their awe. But the eleven-year-old Spud, who was the son of his youngest granddaughter, Amelia, had remained immune to all that. Spud still called Bryce on weekends or after school, informing him of his boyhood triumphs and defeats, and thoroughly delighting him with his dutiful reports.

"I am just sitting here by myself thinking of the past."

"By yourself, Grandpa?"

"Yes."

"Did you open your presents?"

Bryce recalled that Marybeth had arranged his gifts in two large piles under the tree in the living room: He had completely forgotten about them.

"Yes, I opened each one. I was very pleased," Bryce fibbed.

"I love the camera. Thank you, Grandpa."

The camera! He had forgotten about that, too. Three days earlier, amid all the confusion, he had asked Potter, his chauffeur, to buy the Nikon for Spud.

"I'm so glad you like it, Spud."

"Mom said I shouldn't call you today. Why is that?"

"I suppose she felt I was resting. It's been a difficult week."

"She said you're the Prophet now and I shouldn't ever bother you."

"No, I would like to hear from you just as often as always, Spud. Your calls mean a great deal to me."

"I don't think you should be all alone on Christmas, Grandpa."

"I've been rather weary. . . ."

"The sun is out and the snow has stopped. It's so pretty outside. Do you think we could take a walk?"

"A walk?"

"Are Prophets allowed to go for walks?"

He smiled; the notion had caught him by surprise. He had convinced himself that he would spend the day alone, perhaps going to the office later in the afternoon, then having a solo supper.

But the idea of seeing Spud appealed to him. How nice it would be to take a walk on Temple Square, a walk with his great-grandson. It would be refreshing, after all the meetings, the speeches, the darkened rooms, to see people strolling with their families, and to let them see him, their leader, with the boy. What a splendid idea!

"Prophets are indeed allowed to take walks," Bryce said. "I think it's the best idea I have heard all week!"

"I don't have to bring my brothers or sisters, do I?"

"No," Bryce said, "let's make this our expedition—yours and mine. Why don't you put on your parka and walk to the corner and I'll send the car to pick you up? Don't tell a soul."

"Neat," said Spurgeon Bryce Fielding.

IT seemed to Eliza to be a jovial party. Following the ceremony they had all filed into the ornate ballroom where the original guests were joined by still other well-wishers. They were a curious agglomeration and it pleased her immensely that they all seemed to be caught up in the same impromptu joy that all but overwhelmed her. Moving from one group to the next, listening to the good-natured jests, she had all she could do to keep her laughter in check, her dignity intact. If she succumbed to laughter, she sensed that she would succumb to tears, as well. What odd counterpoints—joy and sorrow. A scant fourteen hours earlier she had all but dismissed in her mind the chance of standing here as she was now doing, her new husband at her side, his hand wandering periodically into hers as they circulated through the room. That prospect had disintegrated before her eyes, as though some higher power had performed a sadistic sleight of hand. Yet now it was real once more; at least it *seemed* real. There were times during the ceremony when Eliza felt like pinching everyone to confirm their existence—it was all so improbable. Even Dalton Evans standing before them, moments earlier, bonding them in marriage, had seemed somehow chimeric, a figure in a hallucination. She wished she could interrupt him and elicit his personal reassurances that he, too, was whom he appeared to be.

Around the room, the guests were exchanging their favorite marital anecdotes. Cora Snow, having surreptitiously spiked her orange juice with champagne, reminisced about the wedding of her polygamous grandfather when she and her sisters were so incensed over his decision to take a fourth wife they sprinkled pepper into the new bride's bodice, then giggled as she sneezed uncontrollably throughout the wedding.

With the tutelage of the cherubic Judge Pomerantz, Turner and Eliza dutifully stomped on two wineglasses which had been

347

wrapped in napkins, befitting, he said, the culmination of their vows.

"There!" the judge exclaimed triumphantly. "Now you are truly a bride of Zion!"

The waiters kept circulating with platters of hors d'oeuvres and great crystal bowls filled with fresh fruit. Prodded by the guests, Charity Snow sang the "Anniversary Song," in her thin, little-girl voice, as Cora looked on proudly. Not to be outdone, her brother, Jebediah, sleepy-eyed and spacy, took out his guitar and sang:

> ". . . Some men have a dozen wives
>   and others have a score
> And the man that's got but one wife
>   Is a looking out for more. . . ."

It was an old Mormon folk song, thoroughly inappropriate for the occasion, and Eliza found it quite delightful.

Then came the toasts. Some were funny, others reverent. Dalton Evans toasted their happiness. Burt Hoagland toasted their health. Cora Snow toasted their honeymoon.

Eliza was surprised when she saw her son rise uncertainly, holding his glass before him. She thought he looked quite handsome in his dark blue suit. Nancy, Eliza noticed, glanced at him nervously.

"I would like to offer a toast," Tad began tentatively. "I must admit that I feel a bit off balance—I've never attended a wedding quite like this one. Come to think of it, I've never been to one where everyone enjoyed themselves as much." There were smiles around the room and murmurs of approval, but Tad felt Nancy tugging at his jacket, a look of panic on her face.

"Anyway, I would like to toast you, Mother," he continued, hoisting his glass of orange juice. "Seeing you here like this, I am reminded how special you are. A son has to be reminded, you know. You've always been true to yourself. That's more than can be said for most of us. I think Turner Mead is a very lucky man."

There was a brief silence in the room and then a loud clinking of glasses and a roar of approval. Eliza felt the tears flooding her eyes. She really didn't care if anyone noticed. She didn't have to care about things like that anymore. She had never been so moved by Tad or indeed by any of her children. It was as though they had both briefly, magically, climbed above the towering clutter of petty frustration and anguish that stands between parents and their children—the mutual disappointments, the abandoned expectations—and had suddenly come face-to-face, acknowledging in that briefest interlude of stunning clarity, the truth of their love. She tried to catch his eye, tried to express her gratitude if only with a fleeting glance, but it was impossible. His eyes were elsewhere; he seemed embarrassed by his outburst. The moment had passed.

After the toasts, Dalton Evans motioned Turner aside, and patted his shoulder. "Congratulations, my boy," the old man said, "you are marrying one of the great ladies of Mormondom."

Turner smiled. "I know."

"I feel like I've married off my son this morning. It's a very remarkable feeling."

"I'm grateful to you for being here. I know it has been a long night."

Dalton Evans sighed softly. "I never made it to bed last night, that is true, Turner, but I feel refreshed. I feel absolutely wonderful."

"And the Fifty, sir?. . ."

"The Council met at midnight. The Prophet told them that the Lord had revealed His wisdom. . . ."

"Then the nightmare is over."

"I have accepted the call to reassume the First Counselorship."

"That is a great relief."

"We have survived the storm, but my instinct tells me peaceful waters are still far distant. . . ."

"I understand."

Dalton Evans' eyes followed Eliza as she talked with guests across the room. "And your bride? Sloat's departure will surely change her decision to ask for her release."

Turner averted his gaze. He hated disappointing this man, whose love and loyalty had been so stalwart. "I can't speak for Eliza," he replied.

"I don't understand," Evans said. "I know it's been a bad time for her, but her faith will restore itself. The Church is the core of our being, Turner. It is a question of sacred obligation."

Turner glanced from Eliza, who was talking with guests, her

face aglow, back to Evans again. The old man nodded soberly, his face softening with compassion.

"And you, Turner? I will need you greatly in these coming months, but I sense that you, too, are gravely troubled."

Turner rubbed his palms together slowly. He wanted so desperately to serve this man, yet wondered if he could. "The commitments I made, sir. The promises of secrecy. They weigh heavily on me."

Dalton Evans pursed his lips thoughtfully. "It was a question of accommodation, Turner. Please understand that. We required Isaac Sorenson's assent to summon the Fifty and to effect Sloat's removal. Sorenson felt strongly that Sloat and his son should not be linked to Hiram's murder. It could bring great shame upon our Church."

"What exactly do the Fifty know?"

"Only what Sorenson wants them to know: that Sloat's son is a polygamist. That there were certain falsifications in Sloat's genealogical records. That he was acting precipitously in the conduct of his office. That he was jeopardizing the stability of the Mormon nation."

"So with it all Dana Sloat retains his official respectability."

"The important thing was to gain his removal, Turner."

Turner shrugged in frustration. "My problem, sir, is that I do not agree with Isaac Sorenson. And I do not want to be left alone with the terrible secret."

Evans frowned. "You haven't told Eliza about Dawson?"

"No, only Richard Thompson knows, the lad who rescued us. No one would believe anything he says, anyway. He is, after all, a felon out on bail. No, your secret is safe."

"So that leaves you and me," Evans said.

The two men stared at each other. And Dalton Evans saw a torment in his friend's eyes.

□ It was one fifteen and the party had begun to thin out when Tad saw him slip unobtrusively into the ballroom. At first he thought his eyes were playing tricks. It couldn't be Gavin Pollard—not at his mother's wedding.

Tad hurried across the room, noticing, with relief, that Nancy was caught up in conversation with Aunt Becky.

"What in the world?" was all he could manage.

"Hope you don't mind us crashing," Gavin said matter-of-factly. "We just got to town a couple of hours ago. I called your home and your little girl said we could find you here."

Tad smiled uneasily. "Listen, I'm . . . delighted to see you. It's quite a surprise."

His eyes came to rest on the willowy blonde standing at Gavin's side. She wore jeans, boots and a neon-bright green blouse that set her garishly apart from the other women in the room.

"Oh, this is Faith," Gavin offered, his manner still blasé. "Faith and I decided this morning to take a ski holiday. Spur-of-the-moment sort of thing."

"Gavin gets these impulses," Faith said with an embarrassed laugh.

Amid his mounting apprehension, Tad remembered that Gavin hated skiing. And if he were really on holiday he'd be with Melody, not this comely but decidedly cheap-looking girl.

"Well, I'm happy you're here. Would you like some food? Let me get a waiter. . . ."

"We've eaten," Gavin said in a flat voice.

"I'd offer you a drink but, you know, this is a Mormon wedding."

"We've had a drink," Gavin said.

Tad felt his eyes boring into him. "Well, uh, where will you be skiing?" The pregnant pauses were adding to his alarm.

"Skiing? Oh, I hear Park City is pretty good," Gavin said.

"I don't even know how to ski," Faith put in. "Do you think I can find an instructor up there?"

"Lots of good instructors," Tad replied.

"Anyway, since we were passing through town," Gavin said, "I thought you and I, Tad, might talk a bit about your meeting with Ellis Marmer."

"Marmer? Was I going to meet with Marmer?"

"You were planning to go to his house directly from here," Gavin said, a hard edge in his tone.

"I didn't realize that."

"You were going to discuss the cancellation of the Pacific deal, weren't you, Tad?"

Tad exhaled sharply, like a man who had just been punched in his gut. He started to say something, then fell silent.

"Tad?"

Nancy was at his side, her gaze moving from Gavin to his girl-friend. She knew something was amiss, and that this was not the time to ask. "Could you introduce me?"

"These are friends of mine," Tad said tentatively. "This is Gavin Pollard—you've heard all about him. And this is . . . uh . . ."

"Faith," the blonde said.

"Yes, Faith."

"How nice of you to come all this way for the wedding," Nancy said.

"Wouldn't miss it for the world," Gavin said.

"I've heard so much about you and I'm so proud of what you and Tad have accomplished," Nancy said. "About the deal and all."

Tad felt himself withering before them.

"Tad and I were just discussing the deal as you joined us," Gavin said. "It's a shame it didn't work out."

"Didn't work out?" Nancy squinted in puzzlement.

"It just got too complicated, didn't it, Tad? Too messy and too complicated."

Tad nodded in ageement.

"Aren't these two just terrible?" Faith said to Nancy. "Men can never leave their business problems behind them, can they?"

"I . . . don't understand," Nancy said, ignoring her.

But Tad understood. Staring at his friend, he understood that Gavin had somehow found his answers. That's the only reason he would come all the way to Salt Lake on Christmas Day. He had never really seen Gavin Pollard angry, but he was angry now, though anger seemed hardly the word for it. As Gavin and Nancy glared at each other, Tad realized his own vulnerability. Gavin knew everything there was to know about him, going back to their days on Tonga. With one short, sweet sentence about Pye, about any of it, he could blow his entire life into oblivion.

"Do you think you could introduce Faith to some of the other guests?" Tad said to his wife. "Gavin and I would like some time to talk."

"If that's what you'd like," Nancy replied, gazing at the tall blonde with obvious distaste.

They watched the two women go off, Faith moving with that hip-rolling model's walk, Nancy trudging at her side.

"All right, Gavin," Tad said when they were gone, "what's the game? What is it you want me to tell Ellis Marmer?"

"There are certain formalities. Suncorp is a publicly held company. A joint announcement must be released before the stock market opens stating that negotiations have been broken off."

Gavin, whose style of discourse was always loose and easy, was all sharp edges today, his words darting like tiny scalpels.

"And what happens if Marmer doesn't see things quite that way?"

"Your job is to see that he does. Remind him about the issue of concealment—that's the lawyer's word for it, right? When an attorney absentmindedly neglects to disclose pertinent information at the time of a transaction, that's concealment."

"I don't think that's quite what happened, Gavin. . . ."

"That's exactly what happened. Except I'd call it fraud, not concealment. I'd remind your friend Marmer about the implications of a lawsuit, not to mention action before the state bar association. Think of the publicity if a company like Suncorp filed suit against the Mormon Church on grounds of fraud!"

Gavin saw Nancy staring at them from across the room, pale with apprehension. "And don't think for a minute your father-in-law won't be involved in this lawsuit. I don't care if the brethren removed Sloat or not. He's still up to his armpits in this thing."

"What are you talking about?"

Gavin peered at him in disbelief. "You mean you don't know? No one got around to telling you?"

"Telling me what!"

Gavin shook his head in disgust. "Christ, it's really just like the Politburo, isn't it? The old farts don't even tell the next of kin. Dana Sloat got his ass kicked, Tad. He's out as First Counselor."

"I don't believe you."

Gavin took a step closer so that his face was barely two inches from Tad's. "Look, kid, I don't give a shit whether you believe me or not. You're in way over your head, do you hear me? If you want to lead some kind of double life—if you want to live one way in LA and another way up here in the clouds of Zion—that's cool with me. But you're not going to turn around and give me a royal fucking over."

"Gavin, I never meant . . ."

"Yes, you did. You meant every bit of it. You suckered me into this deal. And now you people are trying to spook me with your devious little games, like the missing article this morning. . . ."

"What missing article?"

"Sloat kept that one from you, too? I doubt it. We were going to start a series of articles on the Mormon Church—the first piece was supposed to run in this morning's paper—but guess what, Tad? It's missing! It never ran. And no one in my organization seems to be able to explain what the hell happened to it. . . ."

"Look, Gavin, I have nothing to do with any of that stuff. . . ."

Tad backed off a step, his face ashen, but Gavin closed the gap once again, one arm on each shoulder, holding him in a viselike grip. "Let me give you some advice, kid. You're going to leave this place now and I don't care whether you see Marmer or Sloat or the Prophet himself, whoever the hell that is. You're going to kill this deal, Tad. And if you don't I'm going to cut your cute little LDS balls off!"

Tad's skin was beaded with perspiration, his eyes glazed. He had the feeling everyone in the room was staring at him, that he was standing in a spotlight, his shame revealed to all. "I meant to level with you, Gavin. Really I did. As soon as I found out the facts—all of them—I was going to tell you."

Gavin released him, regarding him balefully now, like a father addressing his recalcitrant son. "Then why didn't you, kid?" he inquired softly. "Was it money? Did someone slip you a finder's fee? Did Sloat play on your religious zeal or put some kind of family pressure on you? Why?"

Tad wanted to answer but something was shutting off his words. He could hear himself gulping little wisps of air, like a fish tangled in some enormous net, floundering to free itself from a suffocating force it could neither escape nor even discern.

Gavin nodded. "I didn't think you would answer. Okay, just do what you got to do."

He saw the tears rolling down Tad's cheeks.

"You're going to do it, right, kid?"

"Yes. I'll do it."

"You know, I really believed in you. You know that, don't you? I was your friend."

Gavin turned quickly. He left the room without ever looking back.

"I have been standing here, staring at a closet full of clothing appropriate for making speeches, but nothing for going on honeymoons."

Becky looked at the empty valise, then back at her sister. "Well, Eliza, let's do the best we can. We only have an hour to get you packed."

"Hawaii!" Eliza exclaimed in exasperation. "How did I ever let Turner persuade me to go to Hawaii? I don't even own a bathing suit."

"Buy one there. Come on now—let's get started."

"Hawaii is a place for dewy-eyed teenagers!"

"All the more reason to go!" Becky replied sharply.

Eliza knew she was right, of course, but that still didn't ease her own feeling of absurdity. The notion of them checking into a hotel in Hawaii, or strolling down a moonlit beach, seemed absolutely ridiculous. When Turner had first broached the idea, on the night of his proposal, Eliza had presumed he was joking. But this morning, just before the wedding, he calmly announced he had secured the airline tickets and hotel reservation, and Eliza's heart sank. She had hoped they would spend a quiet Christmas at home together: There was so much that was in a state of flux in both their lives. So many details to attend to. Never had she contemplated a trip like this.

Part of the problem, she understood, was that she was accustomed to being in control. For as long as she could remember, her life had been totally hers to orchestrate as she saw fit. Now that had changed so swiftly it had left her feeling light-headed, like one of those heroines in romantic fantasies who are always being carried off to strange places by mysterious lovers.

It *was* a romantic fantasy, Eliza understood now—perhaps that was why Turner, in all his unpredictable wisdom, had selected

356

Hawaii to begin with. Don't fight it, Turner was saying. If you feel a bit ridiculous, so much the better.

Eliza was frantically folding things into her suitcase when she heard the phone. Becky picked it up, then said to her, "Your elegant bridegroom is on the phone."

Eliza's heart leaped. "Turner!"

"Are you packing, my darling?"

"Trying to."

"Just wanted to be sure you weren't, as they say, chickening out."

Eliza smiled. "I'd considered it after examining my wardrobe."

"Speaking for myself, Eliza, I find I have a substantial number of black suits and white shirts. I have one pair of tennis shorts but no sneakers. I have an ancient bathing suit which has a hole in an unfortunate location. . . ."

"I think we'd better go shopping together our first day in Honolulu," Eliza replied.

"Our first hour, perhaps."

"I'd better get back to my packing."

"Then see you shortly, my darling."

"Aloha," Eliza replied, hearing Turner's chuckle at the other end of the line.

Becky peeked her head in the room. "You still going, Eliza?"

Eliza smiled. "You know I am."

Becky came in and sat at the foot of the bed. "I feel like I'm seeing my sister off to camp," she said.

Eliza had been grateful, as always, to Becky for coming home with her following the wedding. It was reassuring to have her stable, sensible sister at her side. And now, as Eliza hurriedly marshaled her cosmetics and toiletries, Becky was calmly folding blouses and lingerie, even pausing to select two frilly nightgowns she felt suitable for a new bride. It was not long before the packing was completed, two valises standing strapped and zippered in the middle of the bedroom—vivid reminders to Eliza that it was all indeed reality.

Becky was about to pick up one of the suitcases to tote downstairs when she saw the bemused expression on her sister's face.

"What's in your head now, Eliza?"

"I just got one of those—what do you call them?—*déjà vus*. I was watching you and suddenly I realized we had done this before. You and I were in another house, another bedroom, but I was about to leave on my honeymoon with Draper and you were helping me pack and keeping me together. . . ."

Becky grinned. "Yes, I remember."

"You remembered all the time, didn't you?"

Becky nodded. "I wasn't going to say anything, Eliza. Some memories are best left undisturbed."

"I was skittish then, too, wasn't I?"

"Very skittish."

"And Dad was shouting from downstairs about how late I was. My goodness, it seems like only last week."

"You were supposed to have packed before the wedding but you kept putting it off."

Eliza sat down on the bed wearily. "It's so eerie to realize you've been through it all before—the same feelings, the same actions. It's as though someone were telling us we've been around too long."

"Not you, Eliza. You're just getting started. I remember someone telling me there are only two occasions in one's life when anything is possible: when you're born and when you're in love."

Eliza smiled. "Well, it's nice to leave on one's honeymoon with the knowledge that half of infinity is still within reach."

The two women grasped the suitcases and started downstairs.

DANA Sloat checked his watch impatiently. There were just a few things left to do, a few final arrangements to be made. Then he would be rid of them. He would be on his way. His Lear Jet was standing by. In just five hours he would be back on Rummers Cay, back in the warm sunshine, the clear turquoise water of the Caribbean. They would all be there for him — his lovely wives, his children with hair white as the sand. He would finally enjoy a true Christmas at their side.

What a relief it would be to escape these gray skies and gray bureaucrats—these dried-up little Churchmen living in their cold, stark homes with their arid women. It should not have surprised him that they would turn on him. What a depressing lot they were, a sad travesty on the vision of their proud forebears.

That's exactly the way the enemies of the Church would have wanted it, of course. The enemies of Joseph Smith and Brigham Young. How they had envied those virile Mormon frontiersmen with their stalwart, devoted wives! How they groveled in their sexual jealousy, shouting their pious condemnations while at the same time coveting their plural households for themselves. Those Mormon pioneers understood what a man must be willing to give in this life and what he should rightly expect in return. If he were truly a man, his God-given needs could not be satisfied by one woman alone. He could not procreate the new Kingdom through a single vessel. The good Lord had not designed woman to be man's equal, either in strength or sexual appetite. Even the Bible acknowledged this much. Thus the good Lord had revealed to his servant, Joseph Smith, that He had "justified my servants Abraham, Isaac and Jacob as also Moses, David and Solomon as . . . having many wives and concubines." And Joseph Smith had been commanded to "receive and obey these instructions . . . as a new and everlasting covenant," and obey them he did, as did his fol-

359

lowers. Little wonder their spirits had soared to such lofty dominion that they could carve an empire from the wilderness and lay the basis for the Kingdom of God on earth. Little wonder their immortal souls could leap into the great spirit world and reordain the celestial order.

These brave men would not have crumpled, as had their scions, before the tyranny of bureaucratic power, thus compromising God's holy revelation. In so doing, what a sad legacy they had spawned—a legacy of broken ideals and broken men.

Not all had been broken, of course. Throughout the Kingdom there still dwelled in many men the spirit and zeal of the founders. It even dwelled in Dawson—credit that much to him. Even though God had seen fit to leave him a cripple, Dawson, in his own clumsy, simplistic way, understood the vision. Though his body had been broken, Dawson had resisted the self-styled "revisionists" of his Church who sought to brainwash him into abandoning the ideals of old. Poor Dawson! Had It not been for that terrible disease which struck him down in childhood, who knows what heights he could have attained? He might have stood with his father, fighting their battles together, side by side.

Perhaps that was indeed why the Good Lord had seen fit to leave him a cripple. Dawson's broken body was to be an everlasting reminder of what had happened to His people, a living metaphor for the toll of Mormon compromise. No Kingdom could be built on a foundation of compromise. That's all they understood now, his brethren—their every deed reeked of compromise. Especially the dark deeds of the night before. It was a night of humiliation that would remain with him always. Its memory clung to him like an acrid odor he could not seem to banish.

It had seemed at first as though he had not yet emerged from the womb of sleep. The vast chamber to which he had been led lay bathed in darkness and was utterly still. The four men who had rushed him here, to the Temple's innermost recesses, had vanished from his side. He sensed there were others in the room, though his eyes could not delineate shapes or faces. Yet he knew they were here—spectral presences who were now to sit in judgment on him.

Sloat had felt a pervasive grogginess. They had startled him awake and hurried him through the darkened corridors and suddenly he was here, in this yawning void, the blackness weighing down upon him like an all-engulfing shroud. He was about to be plunged into some bizarre ritual—that much he knew. He had always been impatient with the mysterioso affectations of his beloved Church, but he understood their nuance. Its rituals were like quick, refracted glints of the always-looming past.

But why tonight? Why here, amid this palpable blackness?

It seemed like a vision at first, the tiniest spire of light moving slowly toward him, then halting some distance away. Sloat's eyes blurred, straining to perceive its contours.

It was the Prophet.

Swathed in white robes, he was seated now upon a purple throne fringed in gold, his figure enshrined in the slender beam of light which illuminated him alone. Though Sloat stood in darkness, he felt the Prophet's eyes upon him. Bryce was staring at him, but saying nothing.

Sloat heard a rustling. Yes, there were others in the room, many others, like a phantom council assembled in surreptitious deliberation.

"I have shed many tears, Brother Sloat." Though the Prophet spoke softly, his voice seemed to resound throughout the room like a clarion call. "I have prayed for His divine guidance in dealing with these difficult decisions. And now the Lord has spoken."

"What decisions, sir?" Sloat asked groggily. The Prophet was sitting motionless; his skin looked chalky in the beam of light. If he fell, Sloat thought, he would surely shatter like delicate ivory.

"Prepare yourself," the Prophet said. "Prepare yourself through obedience to return into the presence of our Heavenly Father in the councils of heaven."

"I'm afraid I do not understand," Sloat said, hearing the stirring of the ghostly presences surrounding them, a stifled cough, the rustling of robes.

"He had revealed His wisdom to me earlier but I had misconstrued. In my eagerness and inexperience. I had misconstrued. . . ."

"I'm afraid I am still confused, President." Sloat felt himself unraveling. Here he was, confronting his friend, his trusted ally, and yet the individual who intoned these words seemed like an alien being who now inhabited his body.

"The blame is not yours, Dana," the Prophet continued, his

brow knit in urgent contemplation. "You have tried to serve the Lord as best you can. But in your eternal family many have suffered the buffetings of Satan. The forces of the night hover like harbingers. . . ."

The Prophet knew his secrets! Sloat told himself. So did these other mysterious emanations who sat around them in this silent room. Sloat felt a spreading coldness in his limbs, as though his body awaited some renewed assurance of its prolonged existence.

"I want you to understand, Dana, that Zion is exalted above the Hills," the Prophet said, his voice almost pleading. "God looks to our Kingdom to rule the world. As His favored children, we cannot fail Him."

"I do not wish to fail Him," Sloat replied weakly.

"Those around you bear that exalted burden," the Prophet said. "They, too, cannot fail. They are the Fifty. The halcyon order who rule from Zion's Mount."

"The Fifty, sir?" Never, in his wildest imaginings, had he thought that august body would intrude itself upon his sphere of activity. Never! How could he possibly have stumbled? How could he be standing here, in the bowels of the night, his dreams and ambitions lying shattered in the darkness before him?

"I am sorry, Brother," the Prophet said, his voice wispy. "Dalton Evans has been set apart. He is First Counselor once more. It is so ordained by the Council of Fifty, which embodies His laws and holds the keys and powers thereof."

"Good God," Sloat heard himself murmur.

"Seek the solace of prayer," the Prophet said, raising his hand, his thin fingers shaking in the light. "Remember, Brother, Zion is the Garden of Peace. The Lord has spoken, Dana. He knows you understand."

Dana Sloat had said nothing. There was nothing to be said.

And he was grateful now to hear the knock at the door. That would be the hotel bellman or perhaps his driver calling for his bags. Sloat's posture stiffened when he recognized his visitor.

"An unexpected pleasure, Tad," Sloat said. The two men stood facing each other in the doorway.

"May I come in?"

"Certainly." Sloat beckoned Tad into the living room, which was dark except for the light from a single lamp. The burgundy brocade drapes were drawn against the midday brightness. "Have a seat."

"No, thank you," Tad said.

Sloat folded his lanky frame into a plush chair. "It's always nice to see you, Tad," Sloat said. "I'm afraid this morning I have a plane to catch . . ."

Tad coughed to clear his throat. "I only need a few minutes."

"I don't mean to sound inhospitable. Actually I intended to phone you and Nancy this morning. There are certain developments that I wanted to explain."

"I am aware of those developments," Tad replied sharply. "But that's not why I'm here." He turned and moved quickly to the window, pulling open the drapes abruptly, bathing the room in sunlight.

"I'd suggest again you sit down," Sloat said, squinting at his visitor, who had become a shapeless blur against the brightness.

Tad remained staring out the window, however, his back to his father-in-law. "I'm standing here because I can't even say 'good morning' to you without feeling scared, did you know that? You scare the shit out of me and when I sit across from you my words never come out right."

"Then stay where you are," Sloat said, squinting still.

"I didn't plan on coming here today," Tad said, coughing once more.

"I see." Sloat folded one leg over the other impatiently.

"But now that I'm here I'd like to tell you something," Tad said, turning to face him now. "I want to say that I would very much like to get you out of my life. Yes, that's exactly what I'd like to say."

"You're speaking impetuously, Tad. I really don't see the relevance . . ."

"The relevance?" Tad cried. "The relevance is that I am married to your daughter, lest you forgot. And if I am going to continue living with her I've got to find a way of living with myself. You're making that process very difficult, Mr. Sloat. No, I should say 'Father.' Isn't that what you once asked me to call you? Okay, Father."

"I think you would be wise," Sloat said softly, "to go home and pull yourself together."

"I feel very much 'together,' Father. I can even look you in the eye when I talk. How 'together' can I be?"

"Finish your little speech then, Tad."

"I don't have a speech. I know you always expect people to come before you with prepared speeches or, better yet, just humbly present you with their memoranda. I'm just going to stand here and say whatever comes to mind. Ever try that, Father?"

"No, I suppose not."

"Let me put your mind at ease about a few things. I'm going to stay with Nancy. I need her—I know that now. I love my children and I need them, too. I'm basically a very weak person, Father. Without certain props I would simply fall apart—my wife, my family, even my Church. There have been times when I thought I could walk away from all that, when I positively hungered to do so, but I know now how foolish I was even to think about it. I was kidding myself."

"It shows strength to need those things, not weakness, Tad."

"Then let me tell you what it is I *don't* need, Father." Tad took two strides forward, his hands poised atop the sofa. "I don't need your devious manipulations. I don't need rewards for doing your dirty work. I don't need a partnership in Ellis Marmer's law firm. I don't need Salt Lake with all its secrecy and intrigues. I don't even need your trust funds for my children—Nancy and I want to have another child, but we don't want your money. . . ."

"I don't think that's for you to decide. . . ."

"Sure it is," Tad said quickly, seating himself now on the sofa directly opposite his father-in-law, peering intently at him. "It's damned certain that I should decide. It's my child and it's my decision."

Sloat's lean face colored with anger. He rubbed his hands together, his long fingers tensely intertwined. "So your solution is to leave your law firm, your career, Salt Lake City—just leave it all. That doesn't sound very practical."

"There are law firms in Colorado. I could start over, build a new career, find new friends, put the kids in a new school. And if I get real lucky I may never have to see you again as long as I live. Do you understand?"

"Sure I understand. I understand callow immaturity, Tad. I understand childish rebellion." He got to his feet. "Now, if you're finished . . ."

Tad remained seated, facing him still. "Almost finished. There's something you're going to do for me, Father. I want you to call off that Suncorp deal—that whole shoddy arrangement. I know it was one of your schemes, but you're not going to get away with it. My friend, Gavin, won't let you, even if it means spending the rest of his life in court. . . ."

"Your friend Gavin can't do a damn thing to stop it," Sloat snapped disdainfully. "The board of directors of Suncorp met last night to elect a new president and publisher. His name is Emory Pollard. Your young friend Gavin is out of a job effective Monday."

Tad froze. "That's impossible. . . ."

"No, it's not impossible at all. You see, Tad, you and your friend Gavin are one step too late, as usual. You're both out of your league."

Sloat was walking toward the door. He saw the confusion on his son-in-law's face as he rose uncertainly to follow him. It was really hard for the boy to accept the fact that Gavin Pollard had really lost his fight. Who knew—the boy might even have promised his friend that he could reverse the situation. What foolishness!

"Did you really think," Sloat said, turning on Tad, "that you could come here and say these sorts of things to me—that you could talk to me this way merely because I am no longer First Counselor to our Prophet? Did you really think you could strike out at me now? Now that I lost my power? Let me advise you always to keep one thing in your mind, Tad—I'll never lose my power. There is nothing in the world anyone can do to weaken me. Nothing!"

For the first time he could remember, Tad saw emotion in Sloat's eyes, saw the pent-up rage and frustration. He started for the door, then paused. "I don't really give a damn whether you're weak or strong, whether you're First Counselor or even the Prophet," Tad replied. "I just want my children to be rid of people like you. That's all I want."

Sloat extended his hand stiffly. "Good-bye, Tad," he said. "Frankly, I had hoped you would turn out to be more of a man than you are."

"So had I," Tad said as he departed, leaving Sloat with his hand still extended.

THOUGH the sunlight shone brightly and unexpectedly through the hovering clouds, the narrow, gray-shingled house stood alone and forlorn, its paint peeling, its high-peaked roof in need of repair. Last night's new snow had not been shoveled from the front walk.

Having heard so much about Augusta Cobb, Eliza was nonetheless unprepared for the tall, graceful woman who opened the front door to receive them. She had expected someone slight and nervous with the intense, darting gaze she'd long observed in crusaders and fanatics. The woman who confronted her, however, seemed substantial and self-assured, her wide, fair-skinned face dominated by intelligent brown eyes and a pronounced aquiline nose. Her long brown hair was combed back from her forehead and fell loosely about her shoulders. Eliza could easily imagine this woman holding forth before a class in political science at BYU, as she had once done. What a tragedy that she had been deprived of her calling, indeed, somewhat as Eliza had now been deprived of hers.

"It's nice to meet you at last," Gussie said. "I've heard so much about you both." She took Eliza's hand and then Turner's. "I'm afraid the house is a mess with the Christmas debris."

They followed her into the cramped living room and saw the Christmas ribbons and wrappings strewn about the floor. Gussie's two boys greeted their visitors shyly. Strolling in from the kitchen, holding two glasses of white wine, was Cora Snow.

"Our paths keep crossing today," Cora said, brightening when she saw them. "Can I get you two some wine?"

"No, thank you," Eliza and Turner said together.

Cora smiled. "Well, I hope you don't mind if we indulge. Gussie and I didn't get married today, after all. We need our little nip."

"To the newlyweds," Gussie said, raising her glass.

"It was a marvelous wedding," Cora said, sipping her wine. "Everybody had a good time."

"I'm so happy for you," Gussie said. "And grateful that you would take time to come by."

"It was something we both wanted to do," Eliza said.

They all seated themselves and Gussie brought glasses of fruit juice for Eliza and Turner. "I received a most remarkable visit this morning," she said when they were all settled. "The doorbell rang and there was this gray twig of a man standing there. He introduced himself very formally. Said he was an attorney, Ellis Marmer."

Eliza frowned. "I know Marmer."

"Well, very soon after his arrival it became clear that Mr. Marmer had not come to pay his condolences. He had come to fish for information and to make a deal."

"A deal?" Turner said. "What sort of a deal?"

"If I signed a piece of paper agreeing not to attempt prosecution of the people who are responsible for killing my husband, Marmer promised to provide a generous trust fund for my sons' educations. Simple as that. A straight trade-off."

"Did he say whom he was representing?"

"He was vague. He said it would be best for all concerned—for the Church, for the Mormon people—if this tragic incident were put to rest. He was very lawyerlike, very persuasive. Even if I wanted to prosecute, I could never find a witness to Hiram's killing, he said. No one would testify. I could never get a case together."

"These cults are an outrage," Eliza said. "How can people live with that sort of savagery!"

"Marmer was very uneasy. He seemed worried that I knew more than I was letting on. That was my sense of it, anyway."

Turner crossed his legs tensely, interpolating, in his own mind, the reasons for Marmer's actions. Marmer had wanted to be certain that Augusta Cobb did not know that it was at Dawson Sloat's colony where the murder had occurred, and now he had received his assurances. As far as Augusta Cobb was concerned, Hiram had fallen victim to an anonymous band of Fundamentalists somewhere in Arizona. Turner knew differently, of course. He harbored the truth as he had promised he would. He sensed it residing somewhere in his viscera like a malignant lump, ready to fester. It was not right that he be put in this position. Not right at all.

"What did you say to the offer?" Cora asked.

Augusta Cobb sipped her wine thoughtfully. "I'm afraid I told Marmer to go to hell. I don't know if I did the right thing or not. It was something I had to do. The boys and I will manage somehow. And when it's all done we will all feel better knowing we did it ourselves, not with money that had Hiram's blood on it."

"You did the right thing," Cora said. "You should be proud of yourself."

"What's done is done. Ellis Marmer still looked very unhappy when he left. He's worried I'm going to start hiring investigators and all that. I'd like to, of course, but I also know, realistically, I'm up against a blank wall. It's all but hopeless to learn the true facts."

What an appalling shame, Eliza thought, imprisoned in her own naiveté, that Turner had not been able to learn who had perpetuated this terrible act. She felt an abiding compassion for this woman seated before her; how she wished she could have known her years earlier.

"What *are* your plans?" Eliza asked softly. "I hope you don't consider that question an intrusion. It's just that I wish there were a way we could help."

Gussie smiled wanly, taking another sip of wine. "That's such a strange word—plans. Even as children we were all told about the plans we should make for ourselves. Then we learn things don't quite happen that way—our lives unfold despite our plans, not because of them. Hiram and I didn't plan to start our magazine. We didn't plan to be apostates—hardly!"

"I know exactly what you mean," Eliza said.

"Someone offered me a teaching job last month. It's not a great job—an instructorship at a junior college in Northern California. But I'm going to take it. It will get me back to work and it will get us all out of this place. I don't want my boys growing up in an atmosphere of anger."

Eliza looked at Turner helplessly. It was so tempting to try and dissuade Augusta Cobb. "You will be missed," Eliza said. "We would all miss you terribly."

"That is very kind of you to say, but I don't think many will miss me," Gussie replied. "When it comes right down to it, I'm just a galling reminder to people of things they don't want to know. And nothing will ever change here. I once thought they would, but now I know better. It will always be the same."

"Maybe you are right," Cora said. "Maybe—but one can never be certain. There is such a wealth of goodness and humanity in our people. We all know that it's there. If only we had the leaders to tap that goodness—new leaders to challenge the hierarchy."

Gussie smiled at her friend. "This may surprise you, Cora, but Hiram would have agreed with you. Really he would. Even in the darkest times he was always optimistic."

She rose from her chair and retrieved some papers from the top of the bookcase. The pages she held looked as though they'd been knotted and thrown away, then salvaged once more. "This morning I found a letter Hiram had written. It's addressed to Samuel Bryce."

"To the Prophet?" Cora's eyebrows lifted in surprise.

"I doubt if Hiram ever intended to send it. Obviously, he threw it away, then had second thoughts. It's really quite an extraordinary letter. Let me read it to you."

Gussie held the letter before her.

"Dear President Bryce:

"You have just ascended to a lofty and noble calling. No other office in our land holds greater potential for righteous deeds.

"As you assume this high office I hope you will find time to devote your thoughts not only to the institution of the Church but also to its people. There is so much beauty in the Mormon people. A 'peculiar people,' as we once proudly termed ourselves.

"We are a people who believe in intelligence. Though ours is a young people in the total order of things, we produce more college graduates, more scientists, more men of achievement, than any other part of the world in relation to our population. Unique among the world's religions, we believe that 'The Glory of God is intelligence.'

"We believe in free agency. We are not mired, as are other peoples, in myths of predestination. We believe God wants us to make of ourselves the most that we can attain.

"We believe man is basically noble and hence our Church was conceived to be both democratic and egalitarian. We do not elevate an elite priesthood: We ourselves comprise our priest-hood.

"We believe in the just rewards of heaven, that one's eternal status is based on his total record on earth and in his preexistence.

"We believe in the family and in marriage. We believe that marriage is for all time and all eternity, not merely till death do us part.

"We believe in progress. No part of the world has grown and prospered as has Mormondom. And no part of the world has sought so altruistically to spread its progress to others.

"We believe in helping our own. Among all the world's people, none strives more diligently to aid our brothers, rather than look-ing to government for succor.

"I realize these facts are not new to you, President Bryce. Yet I ask you to contemplate them once more. I ask you to think about Mormon people, not Mormon power. I ask you to ponder our spiritual wealth, not our temporal wealth.

"I will never mail this letter, President Bryce. Thus I know you will never read it. But I hope and trust someone more eloquent and more persuasive will somehow carry its message. Faithfully yours, Hiram Cobb."

They all were silent after Gussie had finished reading. Cora's eyes had misted. Turner stared at the floor.

"That is a very moving letter," Eliza said finally. "With your permission I would like to see to it that it finds its way into the hands of the Prophet."

"I think Hiram might have liked that."

Even as she accepted the pages, Eliza felt Cora Snow's stern gaze upon her.

"Of course, we need someone to carry forth that vision," Cora said. "We all know Samuel Bryce cannot do it. That much is clear."

And of course, Eliza well understood the true thrust of Cora's remark. Amid Tuesday night's pressures and confusions, Cora's proposal that she seek public office had seemed fanciful, even bizarre, but now that it had been building in the back of her mind it didn't seem so outrageous after all. Indeed sitting here now, sharing Gussie's loss, the entire proposal suddenly was some-thing she would very much like to think about and discuss with

Turner. There would be something positively delicious about taking on Senator Ezra Hurlbut and his friends in the hierarchy.

"My opinion, Cora, is that you are correct," Eliza said. "You can never tell when someone who has played it safe over the years may suddenly decide to pick up the cudgels."

Cora smiled a triumphant smile. "I'm so glad to hear you say that, Eliza. After your honeymoon perhaps we can talk about it in greater depth."

"I would look forward to it."

Turner glanced at his bride, perplexed. There was definitely an important subtext to this exchange, he sensed, a hunch that was fortified by Eliza's look of exuberance, as though a new source of energy had suddenly opened itself to her.

This week Eliza had been like a flower opening before him, reaching out to the world in urgent new ways. It was not in what she'd said; she had, in fact, said little. But there was a new sureness about her. In the foolishness of his own egocentricity, he had presumed that his proposal of marriage had been the cause of that change, but he knew now that was not the case. The woman he had just married was seeing things she had not seen before, hearing a new voice from within.

It disturbed him, yet he knew it shouldn't. Eliza—the new Eliza—could help and understand him. The change that had overtaken her must somehow grip him as well. He could not go on with the burdens he now carried. The secrets and deceptions would poison their life together. What tormented him most of all was that he had so readily agreed to be their servant, their tool. He had rationalized it away because of his trust in Dalton Evans, but, these past few days, he had grown to suspect more and more that Evans himself was somehow a pawn being manipulated by some higher power. It was a force he could neither identify nor even envision, but it was there, hovering over them all.

He had to escape all this, that much he knew. The woman he loved had found the strength to escape. He had always known he loved her and needed her.

Now he needed her most of all.

IT came down to a question of protection, Brother Sloat. It is vital you understand that fact. You are a great resource to the Kingdom but like all resources you must be nurtured and protected. The events of the past two days must be construed in that context, Brother. In that context alone."

Isaac Sorenson was seated stiffly in the green leather chair. His compact, thick-chested body reminded Sloat somehow of a gray bullet. For several minutes Sloat had awaited him in the enormity of Sorenson's vaulted living room. His great, three-story stone house, in all its ponderous elegance, posed a marked contrast to the modest, self-effacing homes of the Prophet and other Church leaders. Only the Mormons and the Mafia, Sloat observed, sought so zealously to camouflage their considerable wealth and power behind such humble facades.

Seated opposite Sorenson now, Sloat felt an unaccustomed disquiet. He had been startled to receive the phone call from this tough, vibrant little man who served as President of the Council of the Twelve Apostles and, as such, was next in line to become Prophet. Sloat had always regarded Sorenson as an imposing personage and had understood the magnitude of his power. He was not just another of those pasty-faced, black-suited General Authorities who served as anonymous functionaries for the myriad enterprises which drew their lifeblood from their Church affiliation. No, Isaac Sorenson was his own man—a man who, like Sloat, understood the intricacies of corporate power. It had disappointed Sloat that this estimable man had maintained such a cautious distance from him, standing to one side as though measuring his dedication and assessing his performance.

What was in the old man's mind? Sloat wondered. Why had he summoned him at this late hour—now when all seemed lost, when Sloat had been preemptorily removed from office, his plans rebuffed, his hopes dashed? And all in the name of "protection"!

372

Their first several minutes together had only compounded Sloat's discomfort. Attired in a dark gray suit, Sorenson had held forth on Washington politics, conversing like a businessman who had happened to encounter a colleague at a director's meeting. But there were more serious things on his mind, that much Sloat knew. In observing those at the loftiest reaches of the Church hierarchy, he had learned that, the more important their message, the more circumlocutious their approach. Sorenson was holding true to that style.

Sorenson's gaze had fixated on an enormous painting which hung on the wall across from where he was seated. Framed in ornately carved gold, it depicted the Savior poised at the Sea of Galilee, summoning his apostles. A similar painting, Sloat knew, hung in the chamber where the Twelve Apostles regularly assembled. "I look at that painting often, Brother Sloat," Sorenson said thoughtfully. "There is an ethereal quality to that work. It is a valuable reminder to men such as you and me—men of affairs who are accustomed to determining our own destinies and those of others. It reminds us that there are forces beyond, and higher purposes to serve. However much we might aspire to shape our lives, we are ultimately at the call of the Savior and His servant, the Prophet. When we receive His summons, all else becomes trivial."

"I have sought to keep that precept uppermost in my thoughts," Sloat replied patiently. "Indeed, these past days and weeks I have been striving to carry out a lofty mandate from our Prophet. A mandate affecting the future of our people."

Sorenson nodded soberly. "I know, Brother. Those actions have not eluded my understanding, but I fear, with all respect, there are some things which might have eluded yours."

"I would beg your instruction, Brother."

"The Mormon Kingdom is not a business corporation. We are a unique and complex political organism—the most powerful functioning theocracy in the world. And within every political organism, there are diverse currents, constituencies to be served and nurtured. Our great leaders, like Brigham Young, though deeply schooled in Scripture, also read Machiavelli and Edmund Burke to understand the precepts of power. They knew how to stay in harmony with their constituencies."

"And is it your advice to me, sir, that I have lost that harmony?

That there is not sufficient support among our brethren to carry out this mandate of change?"

"I perceive widespread support," Sorenson said, his right hand gesturing expansively, "but they are a cautious lot, the brethren. They are custodians of a great trust. And though they bear that burden in the light of divine guidance, that guidance has occasionally been translated imperfectly in times gone by. There have been great triumphs in the Mormon past, but also grave mistakes."

"Mistakes? . . ."

"The gravest mistake was that of 1884. Our darkest hour."

"The decision on statehood?" Sloat peered at the old man before him, puzzled and fascinated.

"Exactly," Sorenson responded emphatically. "Statehood promised to solve all our problems. It promised security, prosperity, trade. And so our brethren decided to bite. What is your assessment of that decision, Brother Sloat?"

Sloat pondered his response. How candid should he be with this man? The silence in the vast room seemed to press down on him, broken only by the sound of Sloat's cracking knuckles.

"I will give you a businessman's assessment," Sloat replied. "I think we made a bad deal. We got something in the bargain, but we paid too high a price for it."

"I see. And how would you calculate that price?"

"We surrendered our political structure, our system of education. We ruptured the sacred bonds of church and state. We sacrificed many of our most cherished institutions, such as plural marriage. In becoming part of America, we lost our Uniqueness."

Sorenson was nodding his approval. The old man was asking the questions and apparently Sloat was giving the right answers.

"We did pay a high price, Brother, and the price keeps rising every year. Look at the appalling inequities that face us today. The people of Utah pay out in taxes vastly more than we receive in federal benefits. Billions of dollars in welfare and other federal doles are poured down the ratholes of New York or California or Pennsylvania while Utah righteously rejects one federal grant after another because we will not conform to the government's evil system of welfare."

Sorenson was growing more animated as he spoke, his cheeks

reddening with the force of his rhetoric. In the past, Sloat had observed him only at formal meetings, where his cadences were more moderate. But where was all this leading? Sloat asked himself. It seemed a strange time for political discourse.

"If our people realized how the federal government continues to loot our Kingdom of its resources, they would rise in rebellion," Sorenson continued, as he ran his hand through his fine mane of white hair. "Washington already owns two-thirds of all the land in Utah, Idaho and Nevada—land worth billions in coal, oil and grazing acreage which rightfully belongs to the Kingdom."

His eyes came to rest once again on the huge painting as he sat back in his broad leather chair. "I reflect often, Brother Sloat, on how the Savior would assess all this. I reflect upon how He would guide His children who sit and wait as the rising tides of Socialism and Communism lap at our very shores. He would not want us to sit here passively until we are engulfed by this secularist tide."

"No, he would not, sir," Sloat declared. "And that is the thinking behind the programs I have tried to put into action. . . ."

"I know," Sorenson said. "And I have been at your side. You may not have perceived my presence, but I have been there."

Sloat stared at his host skeptically.

"It is important that I clarify your perception of the sequence of developments," Sorenson said, choosing his words carefully. "When Brother Bryce received the Call, he summoned me to inform me that he would soon be in the spirit world. He confided that he was afflicted with terminal cancer. I was greatly saddened at this news. We joined together in prayerful thought. And, together, we evolved a plan."

Sloat was transfixed. "I did not know of his illness, sir."

"It was I who fostered your appointment as First Counselor. I felt it was very important that you ascend to the position under his aegis. Samuel Bryce is much beloved by the brethren. In their eyes, he is a moderate, a conciliator. Of course, you know, as do I, Brother Sloat, that our revered Prophet these recent months has had a tendency to lose focus, so to speak. He has become increasingly amenable to guidance from trusted advisers. He also has become increasingly impatient with so-called 'moderation.' "

"That is true, sir."

"So you see, if you received your Call as First Counselor under Samuel Bryce, the 'moderate,' you could continue to serve after I succeeded him as Prophet. There would be a smooth transition of ideology and power. The programs and policies you would initiate would be perceived as the 'moderate' policies of Samuel Bryce. Our timorous brethren would be assuaged, you see. In dealing with 'moderates' one must always remember there is no true core to their beliefs, so they are easier to mollify."

"But the Council of Fifty, sir . . ."

"Again, it was a question of protection. This ugly business at New Nauvoo could have been highly destructive. There are those within the hierarchy who would covet that ammunition against you, and against all of us."

"Then they know, sir? They know about my son, Dawson?"

"They know nothing. That was part of the arrangement. Within a year I will be their Prophet. All this will be forgotten and forgiven."

"I am grateful, sir."

"No, I am grateful," Sorenson said, beaming upon Sloat like a teacher gazing upon a prize protege. "I need you, Brother, make no bones about it. Zion needs you. There is much to be done."

"How can I serve?"

"For an interim period it would be best if you returned to your private business activities. You will be guided slowly but forcefully into the center of power once again. The presidency of Brigham Young University will be open next year and I think you would be ideal for that post. That will be the first step in your, shall we say, regeneration."

Sloat felt himself suddenly aglow. He was like a mountain climber who had ascended through a bank of clouds and now, from a lofty peak, could, for the first time, see the inspiring panorama that spread itself before him. The notion of the BYU presidency fascinated him, and so did the other prospects that lay beyond.

"You see, Brother Sloat, our time has come. Our time to build our Kingdom. The decision on statehood may have seemed a mistake, Brother, but it was His divine will that we suffer the agonies of statehood to strengthen us for our sacred mission. God's will was not that Zion become part of America, but that America become part of Zion. 'We are going to possess the earth,' said our great Prophet, John Taylor. 'Nations will bow to this Kingdom sooner or later and all hell cannot stop it,' Heber Kimball instructed us. It is all there, Brother Sloat—the blueprint for our destiny. And now it falls to us to seize it."

"Your words leave me speechless, sir," Sloat said with excitement. "Your vision far exceeds my own."

"At last the mood of America beckons to us," Sorenson continued, his eyes glowing with fervor. "Our lines of influence and control grow ever stronger within America's vital infrastructures of power. Even the security of the United States resides increasingly within the heart of Zion—the missiles, nuclear warheads, all of it. Our brethren in the security establishment have served us well.

"These are times of great import," Sorenson continued, his chin jutting with firm resolve. "Those of us who share this vision must work together with the unstinting zeal of the Savior's Apostles. We must cautiously lay our groundwork and then make the bold, lightning stroke. 'Thy Kingdom come, Thy will be done.' Our sacred legacy."

Even as Sloat's mind reeled, Sorenson was on his feet, guiding him to the door. They shook hands and Sloat went to his limousine for the ride to the airport. He rode in silence, his mind still struggling to assimilate the insights that had suddenly been opened to him, sifting through every word and nuance. How remarkable, Sloat thought, that this man, who only the previous evening had seemingly sanctioned his dismissal, was now presiding over his resurrection. His fortunes were being intricately guided by this sage leader who held power over them all. All these years it been he, Dana Sloat, who had always manipulated the likes of Ezra Hurlbut and Ellis Marmer and Tad Hastings— all the good soldiers who were strong on duty and weak on courage. And now Sloat knew that he, too, had been manipulated all along by someone far shrewder and more powerful than even he.

He felt humbled, yet oddly emboldened. And he sensed, deep within, a feeling of peace.

I T was a day of great splendor. Glinting off the carpet of new snow, the sunshine bathed Temple Square with an otherworldly luminescence, the mountains towering behind in a curtain of white. Strolling across the square with his great-grandson, Samuel Bryce sensed that each new step, with its changing perspectives, carried a fleeting perfection which he yearned to seize and preserve for all eternity. The small, encrusted trees stood like frozen sculpture, puncturing the sunlight with their jutting arrows of shadow. Ahead, the Temple loomed, all-protecting.

A sudden gust blew snow from its uppermost spires, the flakes shining like gems caught in a beam of light as they showered on those below.

There was a stillness in the square, though many were present, the children clad in bright-hued parkas and woolen hats, adults in holiday finery. Their voices and footsteps were hushed, as though in reverence to the spectacle surrounding them. Wisps of Christmas music hung in the air, one song interwoven with the next. Yes, time had bestowed its own poetry upon this square, Samuel Bryce thought, as he walked beside the boy.

"It's very warm," Spurgeon Bryce Fielding said, unzipping his bright yellow ski vest, "but it's also very cold. The sun feels bright as summer."

"These are God's wondrous tricks of the season," his great-grandfather said, smiling benignly. The boy's rosy cheeks dimpled when he laughed, as did his mother's. His blue eyes sparkled with delight, and they, too, reminded Bryce of his youngest granddaughter, who had now become a sober-faced matron, the mother of six children and the wife of a fast-rising insurance executive. Spud was, to be sure, a delightful boy—quick-witted, observant, impulsive. Their time spent together was always marked by sudden delights.

378

Spud stood admiring the Seagull Monument, ogling the two great birds who shone golden in the sun, their wings spread, ready to pounce on the invading locusts.

"Gulls are pretty," Spud remarked, squinting against the brightness. "Much prettier than eagles. I'm glad we have statues of gulls, not eagles."

His grandfather smiled. "It was the humble gull who saved our crops, not the proud eagle. Throughout our history, it's been the humble who have rallied to our cause, not the wealthy or the proud. Not the eagles of the world. The Kingdom of God will be built upon the toil of the humble."

Spud nodded thoughtfully, his eyes still cast upward toward the golden birds. He understands, Bryce told himself. His youthful brain is a wondrous instrument, a pantheon of new ideas and experience.

For the first time, now, Bryce noticed the clusters of people who were gathering around them. There was an old Asian man leaning on a cane, two denim-clad teenagers, a thin old woman with silver hair, a stocky young man in a farmer's woolen jacket who had a child clinging to each hand, two young Polynesians toting cameras, all of them peering in avid curiosity, their faces open, like so many windows.

Bryce surveyed those around him, surprised that he had not noticed them gathering. They were all silent, as though in reverent disbelief of the sight they were witnessing. Bryce smiled, but they seemed transfixed and did not smile back.

"Daddy . . . isn't he? . . . I've seen his picture, . . ." a child's voice said.

". . . You're the Prophet? . . ." the old Asian asked, his words uttered in quiet awe.

"He is, actually," Spud piped suddenly. He said it casually, but those around them gawked in astonishment.

Sensing the tension, Spud turned uneasily to his great-grandfather, then back to the semicircle around them. "We're just taking a walk," he said, tugging at his great-grandfather's arm to lead him away. But still others had joined the throng now, blocking their way. There was a jostling, inchoate excitement.

"Is he really alive?" another small child demanded of her mother.

"He's alive. He's my great-grandpa," Spud said defensively, hearing the nervous laugh rippling through the large crowd.

Samuel Bryce waved to them all. It was time, he knew, to talk to them.

"The Lord has blessed us with a glorious day," he said, his thin voice piercing the quiet. "I am so pleased to see you all here this morning. This place is my sanctuary. I feel a peace and inspiration within these immutable walls. I hope all of you sense God's presence here and that you will walk happily in His radiance on this fine Christmas Day."

The crowd stood motionless, hanging on every phrase. When Bryce was done a small child's voice proclaimed, "He *is* alive!" and Bryce smiled in his direction.

"*God* is alive," Samuel Bryce said, "and this is His Kingdom."

And then he clutched the hand of his great-grandson and the two of them started trudging slowly across the square, an old man with a small boy at his side.

ABOUT THE AUTHOR

Peter Bart spent fifteen years as a reporter for *The Wall Street Journal* and *The New York Times* before becoming a full-time novelist. He now makes Southern California his home.